FALLEN HERO

On a bier at the end of the room lay Luke Skywalker—like a body stretched out for a funeral.

Leia's heart thumped with dread. She wanted to turn around and leave so she wouldn't have to look at him—but Leia found her feet carrying her forward. She walked with a rapid step that became a run before she reached the end of the promenade. Han came carrying the twins, one in each arm. His eyes were red as he fought to keep tears from flowing. Leia already felt a wetness on her cheeks.

Luke lay in repose, swathed in his Jedi robe. His hair had been combed; his hands were folded across his chest. His skin looked gray and plasticlike.

"Oh, Luke," Leia whispered.

She reached out to touch him. Using her abilities with the Force, she tried to reach deeper, to brush against his life force—but she felt only a cold hole, an emptiness, as if *Luke himself* had been taken away.

Not dead.

He could not be dead. . . .

P9-BBT-643

The Jedi Academy Trilogy
Volume 3

CHAMPIONS OF THE FORCE

Kevin J. Anderson

BANTAM BOOKS

NEW YORK · TORONTO · LONDON · SYDNEY · AUCKLAND

CHAMPIONS OF THE FORCE
A Bantam Spectra Book / October 1994

ISBN 0-553-29802-X

Published simultaneously in the United States and Canada

Bantam Books are published by Bantam Books, a division of Bantam Doubleday Dell Publishing Group, Inc. Its trademark, con-
sisting of the words "Bantam Books" and the portrayal of a
rooster, is Registered in U.S. Patent and Trademark Office and
in other countries. Marca Registrada. Bantam Books, 1540 Broad-
way, New York, New York 10036.

PRINTED IN THE UNITED STATES OF AMERICA
OPM   0 9 8 7 6 5 4 3 2

Dedication

To my stepson and
"research buddy"
JONATHAN MACGREGOR COWAN,
who helped me see
"a galaxy far, far away" through
a child's sense of wonder

Acknowledgments

Much of this novel was written at the Montecito Sequoia Lodge in the redwood forests of California. Lillie Mitchell, my typist, somehow kept up with all the microcassettes I dumped on her and egged me to greater speed by asking "What happens next?" My wife, Rebecca Moesta Anderson, provided brainstorming and late-night walks to help iron out plot problems, as well as giving her personal support and love. Tom Veitch helped me work out the background of Exar Kun and the Dark Lords of the Sith, which we've written into a twelve-issue saga for Dark Horse Comics. My editor, Tom Dupree, trusted me to deliver everything on time and in good shape (and he even enjoyed the story!); his assistant, Heather McConnell, kept a million things under control at once and refrained from hanging up on me whenever I called to pester her. Lucy Wilson at Lucasfilm helped make this and all of my other *Star Wars* stories possible, and her assistant, Sue Rostoni, managed to keep the different projects from crashing headlong into each other. In our many discussions Ralph McQuarrie provided a lot more inspiration than he will admit, including designing the temple of Exar Kun and other parts of the Jedi academy. West End Games, as usual, provided an enormous amount of valuable reference material on all aspects of the *Star Wars* universe. Most of all, I owe thanks to George Lucas for creating such a wonderful universe and for letting me play in it.

1

The **Sun Crusher** plunged into the Caridan system like an assassin's knife into an unsuspecting heart.

Old beyond his years, Kyp Durron sat hunched over the controls with dark eyes blazing, intent on his new target. With the might of the superweapon—as well as powerful techniques his spectral mentor Exar Kun had taught him—Kyp would extinguish all threats against the New Republic.

Only days before, he had annihilated Admiral Daala and her two Star Destroyers in the Cauldron Nebula. On the fringes of the explosion, he had dropped off one of the Sun Crusher's coffin-sized message pods so that the galaxy would know who was responsible for the victory.

As his next target, Kyp would challenge the Imperial military training center on Carida.

The military planet was a largish world with high gravity to toughen the muscles of potential stormtroopers. Its untamed land masses provided an appropriate range of training environments: arctic wastelands, trackless rain forests, splintered mountain crags, and searing desert hardpan crawling with venomous multilegged reptiles.

Carida seemed the opposite of Kyp's peaceful homeworld of Deyer, where he and his family had lived in raft colonies on the calm terraformed lakes—but that peace had been shattered years ago when Kyp's parents had chosen to protest the destruction of Alderaan. Stormtroopers had crushed the colony, whisking Kyp and his parents to the spice mines of Kessel while conscripting his brother Zeth for the stormtrooper training center.

Now, as he orbited the military planet, Kyp's face bore the tight, hardened look of a person who has been through the raging fire of his own conscience. Shadows rimmed his eyes. He did not expect to find his brother still alive after so many years—but he intended to learn the truth.

And if Zeth was not there, Kyp had enough power to destroy the whole Caridan solar system.

A week ago he had left Luke Skywalker for dead atop the Great Temple on Yavin 4. He had stolen design parameters of the Sun Crusher from the mind of its naive creator, Qwi Xux. And he had blown up five stars to incinerate Admiral Daala and her two Star Destroyers. At the last moment Daala had tried to flee the exploding stars, but to no avail. The shock waves had been intense enough to blank the Sun Crusher's viewscreens even as fire overtook Daala's flagship, the *Gorgon*.

Since that awesome victory Kyp's obsession had gained momentum, and he had set out on a hyperspeed course toward annihilating the Empire. . . .

The Caridan defense network spotted the Sun Crusher as Kyp entered orbit. He decided to transmit his ultimatum before the Imperial forces tried anything stupid. He broadcast on a wide range of frequencies.

"Caridan military academy," he said, trying to deepen his voice. "This is the pilot of the Sun Crusher." His mind searched for the name of the ambassadorial buffoon who had caused a diplomatic incident on Coruscant by tossing his drink in Mon Mothma's face. "I wish to speak to . . . *Ambassador Furgan* to discuss the terms of your surrender."

The planet below made no response. Kyp stared at the comm system, waiting for noise to burst from the speaker.

His alarm consoles flashed as the Caridans attempted to lock on to the Sun Crusher with a tractor beam, but Kyp worked the controls with Jedi-enhanced speed, oscillating his orbit at random so they could never get a positive lock.

"I am not here to play games." Kyp's hand bunched into a fist and slammed down on the comm unit. "Carida, if you do not answer within the next fifteen seconds, I'll fire a torpedo into the heart of your sun. I think you're familiar with the capabilities of this weapon. Do you understand?"

He began counting out loud. "One . . . two . . . three . . . four . . ." He got up to eleven before a brusque voice came through the comm system.

"Intruder, we are transmitting a set of landing coordinates. Follow them precisely or you will be destroyed. Relinquish control of your ship to the stormtroopers immediately upon landing."

"You don't seem to understand what's going on here," Kyp said before he bothered to stop laughing. "Let me talk to Ambassador Furgan *now* or your planetary system is going to be the galaxy's newest bright spot. I've already blown up a nebula to wipe out a pair of Imperial battle cruisers—don't you think I'd destroy one minor star to get rid of a planet full of stormtroopers? Get Furgan, and give me a visual."

The holo panel flickered, and the wide, flat face of Furgan appeared, shoving aside the comm officer. Kyp recognized the ambassador by his heavy eyebrows and fat purplish lips.

"Why have you come here, Rebel?" Furgan said. "You are in no position to make demands."

Kyp rolled his eyes, losing patience already. "Listen to me, Furgan. I want to find out what happened to my brother, Zeth. He was conscripted on the planet Deyer about ten years ago, and he was brought here. Once you have that information, we'll discuss terms."

Furgan stared at him, knitting his heavy spiked brows. "The Empire does not negotiate with terrorists."

"You don't have any choice in the matter."

Furgan fidgeted and finally backed down. "It will take some time to access information that old. Maintain your position in orbit, and we'll check."

"You have one hour," Kyp said, then signed off.

On Carida, in the main citadel of the Imperial military training center, Ambassador Furgan looked down at his comm officer, frowning with lips the color of fresh bruises. "Check that boy's words, Lieutenant Dauren. I want to know the capabilities of that weapon."

A stormtrooper lieutenant marched in with a precise military stride that sent shivers of admiration down Furgan's spine. "Report," he said to the captain.

The helmet speaker amplified the stormtrooper's voice. "Colonel Ardax announces that his assault team is ready to depart for the planet Anoth," he said. "We have eight MT-AT vehicles loaded into the Dreadnaught *Vendetta*, along with a full compliment of troops and weaponry."

Furgan tapped his fingers on the polished console in front of him. "It seems an extravagant effort to kidnap a baby and overcome a single woman who's watching him—but this is a *Jedi* baby, and I will not underestimate the defenses the Rebels may have emplaced. Tell Colonel Ardax to prepare his team for immediate departure. I have a minor irritation that needs to be dealt with here—

and then we can go fetch a young, malleable replacement for the Emperor."

The stormtrooper saluted, whirled on one polished boot, and exited through the chamber doors.

"Ambassador," the comm officer said, scanning readouts, "we know from our spy network that the Rebels had a stolen Imperial weapon called the Sun Crusher, which can supposedly trigger the explosion of a star. And there was a mysterious multiple supernova in the Cauldron Nebula less than a week ago—just as the intruder claims."

Furgan felt a thrill of anticipation as his suspicions were confirmed. If he could get his hands on the Sun Crusher *and* the Jedi baby, he would have more power at his disposal than any of the squabbling warlords in the Core Systems! Carida could perhaps become the center of a blossoming new Empire—with Furgan at its helm as regent.

"While the Sun Crusher pilot is distracted and awaiting news of his brother," Furgan said, "we shall mount a full-fledged assault to cripple his craft. We can't let such an opportunity escape us."

Kyp stared at the Sun Crusher's chronometer, growing angrier with each ticking interval. If it weren't for the hope of learning news about Zeth, Kyp would have launched one of his four remaining resonance torpedoes into Carida's sun and backed off to watch the system explode in a white-hot supernova.

With a surge of static, the Caridan comm officer's image appeared before him, contrite and businesslike. "To the pilot of the Sun Crusher—you are Kyp Durron, brother of Zeth, whom we recruited on the colony world Deyer?" The officer spoke with a plodding voice, enunciating each word with unnecessary precision.

"I gave you that information already. What have you learned?"

The comm officer seemed to fade out of focus. "We regret that your brother did not survive initial military training. Our exercises are very strenuous, designed to discourage all but the best candidates."

Kyp's ears filled with a roar like rushing water. He had expected the news, but confirmation sent despair through him. "What . . . what were the circumstances of his death?"

"Checking," the comm officer said. Kyp waited and waited. "During a mountain survival tour he and his team were snowed in by a sudden blizzard. He appears to have frozen to death. There is some indication he made a heroic sacrifice so other members of his team could survive. I have the full details in a file. I can upload it if you like."

"Yes," Kyp said, his mouth dry. "Give me everything." He recalled an image of his brother: two boys throwing small reed boats into the water and watching them drift toward the marshes—then the look on Zeth's face after stormtroopers had crashed into their home and dragged him away.

"This will take a moment," the comm officer said.

Kyp watched the data scroll across his screens. He thought of Exar Kun, the ancient Lord of the Sith who had shown him many things that Master Skywalker refused to teach. The news of Zeth's inevitable death was like severing the remaining threads of Kyp's fragile restraint. Nothing could stop him now.

He would show murderous Carida no mercy. Kyp would remove this Imperial thorn from the New Republic's side and then move on to topple the big Imperial warlords gathering their forces near the galactic core.

He waited for Zeth's files to finish uploading into the Sun Crusher's memory. It would take a long time for him to absorb all those words, to imagine every detail of his brother's life, the life they should have had together. . . .

Emerging from the thin veil of atmosphere at the limb of the planet, a battle group of forty TIE fighters roared toward him. Another cluster of twenty came from the opposite horizon in a pincer formation. The ploy of Zeth's files had merely been a delaying tactic to keep him preoccupied as the Caridans launched an attack!

Kyp didn't know whether to be amused or outraged. A grim smile flickered across his face, then vanished.

The TIE fighters came in, firing what must have been intended as crippling laser blasts. Kyp felt the *thumps* of their impacts against the Sun Crusher, but his special quantum-layered armor could withstand even a turbolaser blast from a Star Destroyer.

One of the TIE pilots contacted Kyp. "We have you surrounded. You cannot escape."

"Sorry," Kyp said. "I'm fresh out of white flags." He used his sensors to track the lead TIE fighter from which the message had come. He targeted with his defensive lasers and let loose a volley that strafed across the ship's flat solar panel. The TIE ship broke apart in a flower of white-and-orange flame.

The other fighters retaliated from all sides. Kyp targeted with his own defensive lasers, selecting five victims. He managed to strike three.

Using the extreme mobility of the Sun Crusher, he accelerated upward just as the surviving TIE fighters sent return fire through the expanding explosions of his first round of victims. Kyp laughed out loud as two of the fighters hit each other in the cross fire.

The wall of anger rose and strengthened in him, increasing his reservoir of power. He had already given more warning than the Caridans deserved. Kyp had stated his ultimatum, and Furgan had sent out attack ships.

"That's the last mistake you'll ever make," he said.

The TIE fighters continued to fire, missing more often than not. Laser bolts *spang*ed off his armor, causing no damage. The pilots did not seem to know how to target and shoot properly. They had probably spent all their time practicing in simulation chambers, without ever fighting an actual space battle. Kyp relied instead on the Force.

He shot back, obliterating another ship, but decided that further fighting was not worth his time. He had a bigger target. Two fast TIE interceptors streaked after him as he pulled out of planetary orbit and set a course for the star at the heart of the system.

The only damage they could possibly do to the Sun Crusher would be to take out its tiny laser turrets. Daala's forces had once succeeded in disabling the Sun Crusher's external weaponry, but New Republic engineers had repaired it.

Another breached TIE fighter spurted flash-frozen atmosphere as it exploded. Kyp darted through the debris, straight toward the sun. The surviving Imperials charged after him, still firing. He paid them no heed.

Over and over in his mind he rolled images of Zeth, imagining his brother frozen and hopeless in a training exercise for an army he had never wanted to join. The only way for Kyp to cauterize that memory was to purge the entire planet with fire, a fire only the Sun Crusher could unleash.

He activated the firing systems for his resonance torpedoes. The high-energy projectile would be pumped out in an oval-shaped plasma discharge from the toroidal generator at the bottom of the Sun Crusher.

Last time Kyp had fired the torpedoes into supergiant stars in a nebula. Carida's sun was an unremarkable yellow sun, but even so, the Sun Crusher could ignite a chain reaction within the core. . . .

As Kyp swooped in toward the blazing ball of yellow fire, flickering prominences reached out of the star's chromosphere. Boiling convection cells lifted hot knots of gas to the surface, where they cooled and sank back into the churning depths. Dark sunspots stood out like blemishes. He sighted on one of the black spots as if it were a bull's-eye.

Kyp primed the resonance torpedo and spared a moment to glance back. His TIE pursuers had split off, unwilling to come so close to the glaring sun.

Fail-safe warning systems flashed in front of Kyp, but he disregarded them. When the control system winked green, he depressed the firing buttons and shot a sizzling green-blue ellipsoid deep into Carida's sun. Its targeting mechanisms would find the core and set up an irrevocable instability.

Kyp leaned back in the comfortable pilot's seat with a sigh of relief and determination. He had passed the point of no return.

He should have felt elated, knowing it was only a matter of time before the military academy was finally extinguished. But that knowledge could not wash away the grief he felt for the loss of his brother.

Alarms screamed through the citadel of the military training center. Stormtroopers ran along flagstoned halls, taking emergency positions at strategic points as they had been drilled; but they didn't quite know what to do.

Ambassador Furgan's face held a comical expression of shock. His bulging eyes looked as if they might pop out of their sockets. His lips scraped together as he fought for words. "But how could all of our TIE fighters miss?"

"They didn't miss, sir," Comm Officer Dauren said. "The Sun Crusher seems to have impenetrable armor, better than any shielding we've ever encountered.

"Kyp Durron has reached our sun. Although our readings are scrambled from coronal discharges, it appears that he has launched some sort of high-energy projectile." The comm officer swallowed. "I think we know what that means, sir."

"If the danger is real," Furgan said.

"Sir—" Dauren wrestled with rising agitation, "we have to assume it's real. The New Republic was pointedly uneasy about being in possession of such a weapon. The stars in the Cauldron Nebula did explode."

Kyp Durron's voice broke over the intercoms. "Carida, I warned you—but you chose to trick me instead. Now accept what you've brought upon yourselves. According to my calculations, it'll take two hours before the core of your sun reaches a critical configuration." He paused for a beat. "You have that amount of time to evacuate your planet."

Furgan slammed his fist down on the table.

"Sir," Dauren said, "what are we going to do? Should I organize an evacuation?"

Furgan leaned over to flick a switch, toggling to the hangar bay in the lower staging area of the citadel. "Colonel Ardax, muster your forces immediately. Get them aboard the Dreadnaught *Vendetta*. We will launch our Anoth assault team within the hour, and I will accompany them."

"Yes, sir," the reply came.

Furgan turned to his comm officer. "Are you certain that boy's brother is dead? Nothing we can use for leverage?"

Dauren blinked. "I don't know, sir. You told me to delay him, so I made up a story and sent a fake file. Do you want me to check?"

"Of course I want you to check!" Furgan bellowed. "If we can use the brother as a hostage, perhaps we can force that boy to neutralize the effects of this Sun Crusher weapon."

"I'll get on it immediately, sir," Dauren said, and hammered his fingertips on the datapads.

Six of Furgan's training commanders, summoned by the

wailing alarms, marched into the control center and saluted briskly. Standing shorter than his commanders, Furgan clasped his hands behind his back, pushing his chest out as he addressed them.

"Take an inventory of all functional ships on Carida. Everything. We need to download the data cores from our computers and take as many personnel as possible. I doubt we'll be able to evacuate them all; therefore, choices will be made on the basis of rank."

"Are we just going to abandon Carida without a fight?" one of the generals said.

Furgan screamed at him, "The sun is going to blow up, General! How do you propose to fight that?"

"Evacuation on the basis of rank?" Dauren said in a small voice, looking up from his panel. "But I'm only a lieutenant, sir."

Furgan scowled down at the man hunched over his control panels. "Then that gives you all the more incentive to find that kid's brother and force him to rescind that torpedo!"

Through half-polarized viewports Kyp watched the surviving TIE fighters pull away and swoop back toward Carida. He smiled with satisfaction. It would be good to watch the Caridans' panicked scramble as they tried to grab everything of value on an entire planet.

Over the next twenty minutes he watched streams of ships launch away from the main training citadel: small fighters, large personnel transports, StarWorker space barges, and one deadly looking Dreadnaught battleship.

Kyp was annoyed at himself for allowing the Imperials to haul so much weaponry away. He was sure it would eventually be used against the New Republic; but at the moment Kyp took his pleasure from eradicating the solar system.

"You can't escape," he whispered. "A few might get away, but you can't all escape." He glanced at his chronometer. Now that instabilities had begun pulsing out of the star, he could get a more accurate determination of how long it would take for the sun to explode. The Caridans had twenty-seven minutes before the first shockwave struck.

The flow of ships had petered out, and only a few scrap-heap vessels struggled out of the gravity well. Carida did not appear to be well supplied with vessels; most of their prime equipment must already have been commandeered by Grand Admiral Thrawn or some other Imperial warlord.

The holopanel flickered, and the image of the comm officer appeared. "Pilot of the Sun Crusher! This is Lieutenant Dauren calling Kyp Durron—this is an emergency, an urgent message!"

Kyp could well imagine that anyone still on Carida might have an urgent message! He took his time answering just to make the comm officer squirm. "Yes, what is it?"

"Kyp Durron, we have located your brother Zeth."

Kyp felt as if someone had thrust a lightsaber through his heart. "What? You said he was dead."

"We checked thoroughly and found him in our files after all. He is stationed here in the citadel, and he has not managed to find transport off Carida! I've summoned him to my comm station. He'll be here in a moment."

"How can that be!" Kyp demanded. "You said he died in training! I have the files you sent me."

"Falsified information," Lieutenant Dauren said bluntly.

Kyp squeezed his eyes shut as hot tears sprang to fill his vision: sudden overwhelming joy at knowing Zeth was still alive, anger at having committed the most fundamental mistake of all—*believing* what the Imperials told him.

He snapped a glance at the chronometer. Twenty-one minutes until the explosion. Kyp wrenched at the Sun

Crusher's controls and shot back toward the planet like a laser blast. He doubted he had enough time to rescue his brother, but he had to try.

He stared at the time display ticking away. His vision burned, and he felt a jolt go through him every time a number ticked down.

It took five minutes to get back to Carida. He orbited around the massive planet in a tight arc, crossing over the line from night into day. He set course for the small cluster of fortresses and buildings that made up the Imperial training center.

Lieutenant Dauren appeared again in the small holographic field, dragging a white-armored stormtrooper into view. "Kyp Durron! Please respond."

"I'm here," Kyp said. "I'm coming to get you."

The comm officer turned to the stormtrooper. "Twenty-one twelve, remove your helmet."

Hesitantly, as if he had not done so in a long time, the stormtrooper tugged off his helmet. He stood blinking in the unfiltered light as if he rarely looked at the world through his own eyes. Kyp saw a heartrending image that reminded him of the face he saw when he looked in a reflection plate.

"State your name," Dauren said.

The stormtrooper blinked in confusion. Kyp wondered if he was drugged. "Twenty-one twelve," he said.

"Not your service number, your *name*!"

The young man paused for a long time, as if pawing through rusty, unused memories until he came out with a word that sounded more like a question than an answer.

"Zeth? Zeth Dur . . . Durron."

Kyp didn't need to hear him speak his name, though. He remembered the tanned, wiry boy who swam in the lakes of Deyer, who could catch fish with a small hand net.

"Zeth," he whispered. "I'm coming."

The comm officer waved his hands. "You can't make it

in time," he said. "You must stop the Sun Crusher torpedo. Reverse the chain reaction. That's our only hope."

"I can't stop it!" Kyp answered. "Nothing can stop it."

Dauren screamed, "If you don't, we're all going to die!"

"Then you're going to die," Kyp said. "You all deserve it. Except for Zeth. I'm going to come for him."

He plowed like thunder through the high atmosphere of Carida. Heated air pearled off the sides of the superweapon as a shock front pushed a shield in front of him. Sonic booms rippled behind him.

The planet surface approached with gut-wrenching speed. Kyp soared over a cracked, blasted wasteland with craggy red rocks and fractured canyons. Out in the flat desert he saw geometric shapes, tracks of precise roads laid down by the Imperial corps of engineers.

The Sun Crusher shot like a meteor over a cluster of bunkers and metallic huts. Isolated stormtroopers marched about in drills, unaware that their sun was about to explode.

On the chronometer seven minutes remained.

Kyp called up a targeting screen and found the primary citadel. The air tugged at his ship, buffeting him with heavy winds, but Kyp did not care. Flames from the ignited atmosphere flickered off the quantum armor.

"Give me your specific location," Kyp said.

The comm officer had begun sobbing.

"I know you're in the main citadel building!" Kyp cried. "Where exactly?"

"In the upper levels of the southernmost turret," Zeth answered precisely, responding in a military manner, slipping back into stormtrooper training.

Kyp saw the jagged spires of the military academy rising from a cluttered plateau. Kyp's scanners projected an enlarged image of the citadel, pinpointing the turret Zeth had mentioned.

Five minutes remained.

"Zeth, get ready, I'm coming in."

"To rescue us both!" Dauren said.

Kyp felt a twinge inside. He wanted to leave the comm officer who had lied to him, who had made him despair and forced him into the decision to destroy Carida. He wanted to let the lieutenant die in a burst of incinerating solar flame—but that man could help him, for now.

"Get yourselves into an open area. I'm going to be there in less than a minute. You can't get up to the roof in time, so I'm going to blast it off."

Dauren nodded. Zeth finally overcame his own confusion and said, "Kyp? My brother? Kyp, is that you?"

The Sun Crusher streaked over the jagged minarets and pinnacles of the Caridan citadel. A mammoth wall surrounded the entire fortress. Out in the courtyard hundreds of low-ranking refugees scrambled about in tiny fliers aiming up into the skies, though with no hyperdrive capability they could never outrun the fury of the supernova.

Kyp decelerated abruptly until he hovered over the fortress. Suddenly the Sun Crusher lurched from side to side as automatic perimeter lasers targeted him and fired.

"Shut down your defenses!" he screamed at the comm officer. He wasted time targeting and firing at the perimeter lasers. Two of the weapon emplacements blew up in roiling smoke, but the third, a blaster cannon, scored a direct hit against the Sun Crusher.

The superweapon spun end over end, out of control until it smashed into one of the tall turret walls. Kyp managed to get control again and raised the vehicle up. No time to vent his anger. No time to do anything but get to the tower.

Kyp watched the chronometer click down from four minutes to three.

"Take shelter!" he said. "I'm going to blast open the roof."

He targeted with one of his weapons and fired—but he received an ERROR message. The laser turret had been damaged by his collision with the tower. Kyp swore and spun the ship around so he could target with a different laser.

After a short controlled burst, the roof of the tower melted inward. Chunks of synrock and metal reinforcement girders sprayed into the air. Kyp flicked on his tractor beam to yank the debris away before it could collapse into the lower floors.

He brought the Sun Crusher over the smoking crater that had been the rooftop. He pointed his scanners down and saw two people scramble out from under the desks where they had taken shelter.

Two minutes.

Kyp hovered over them. If he lowered his ship, they could reach the ladder to the hatch, where they could climb into the shielded Sun Crusher. He already had an escape route programmed in.

As Kyp dropped toward them, Lieutenant Dauren stood up and battered Zeth on the back of the skull with a broken plasteel shard. Zeth fell to his knees, shaking his head and pulling out his blaster in reflex. The comm officer ran to the Sun Crusher's ladder, but Kyp—furious at seeing what Dauren had done—raised the ship out of the man's reach.

Scrambling, waving his arms, the comm officer jumped up to reach the rungs of the ladder, but he missed and slapped his hands across the hull instead. The quantum armor was still smoking hot from Kyp's fiery plunge through the atmosphere. Dauren screamed as it burned his hands.

Falling back to the ground, Dauren turned just in time to see Zeth point the blaster at him. With precise stormtrooper training Zeth targeted and fired. The comm officer flew backward, his chest a black hole. He collapsed among the debris.

One minute.

Kyp maneuvered the Sun Crusher back into position, lowered the ladder; but Zeth collapsed to his knees; blood streamed down the back of his head, streaking the white stormtrooper armor. Zeth could not move. He had been too badly injured by the comm officer.

Thinking rapidly, Kyp locked on to his brother's limp form with the tractor beam, yanking him up off the floor and drawing him toward the Sun Crusher. This would be it. Kyp left the controls and scrambled to the hatch. He would have to open the hatch, climb down the ladder, and haul his brother up inside. He reached for the locking mechanism that would open the Sun Crusher—

And then Carida's sun exploded.

The shock wave roared through the atmosphere, bringing instant incinerating fire. The entire citadel turned into a storm of flames.

The Sun Crusher tumbled end over end, and Kyp flew against the far wall of the cockpit, his face plastered against one of the external viewscreens. He saw the faint afterimage of Zeth's body disintegrating into a fading silhouette as the stellar energy ripped across Carida.

Kyp hauled himself into the pilot seat. In shock, he used his Jedi instincts to punch the sublight engines. The first wave from the supernova had been the prompt radiation, high-energy particles shot out with the explosion of the star. A minute or so later the heavier radiation would come.

As rippling waves from the second hurricane of energy struck Carida and cracked the planet open, the Sun Crusher accelerated far beyond its red lines along the preprogrammed escape route.

Kyp felt gravity stretching his face into a grimace. His eyelids squeezed closed, and anguished tears flowed backward across his temples with the pull of acceleration.

The Sun Crusher blasted out of the atmosphere and entered hyperspace. As starlines formed around him and the supernova made one last grab with hands of flame, Kyp let out a long anguished cry of despair at what he had done.

His scream vanished with him into hyperspace.

L eia Organa Solo emerged from
the *Millennium Falcon* on Yavin 4, ducking her head as
she walked down the landing ramp. She looked toward the
towering edifice of the Great Massassi Temple.

It was a cool morning on the jungle moon, and mist rose
from the ground, clinging to the low treetops and brushing
against the stone ziggurat like a thin white shroud. *A
funeral shroud*, she thought. For Luke.

It had been a week since the trainees at the Jedi academy had found Luke Skywalker's motionless body atop
the temple. They had brought him inside, done their best
to care for him—but they did not know what to do. The
best New Republic medics had found no physical damage. They agreed that Luke still lived, but he lay in
complete stasis. He responded to none of their tests or
probes.

Leia had little hope of doing anything herself, but she
could at least be with her brother.

The twins came clomping down the *Falcon*'s ramp, seeing who could make the loudest banging noises with their

small boots. Han stood between Jacen and Jaina, holding their hands. "Be quiet, you two," he said.

"Are we going to see Uncle Luke?" Jaina asked.

"Yes," Han answered, "but he's sick. He won't be able to talk to you."

"Is he dead?" Jacen asked.

"No!" Leia answered sharply. "Come on. Let's get into the temple." The twins scampered ahead down the ramp.

The sharp jungle smells brought warm and fresh memories to Leia as she walked across the clearing. Fallen trees, decaying leaves, and flowers mixed into a potent brew of scents. She had proposed the empty ruins as a site for Luke's academy, but Leia had never managed to visit—and now she had come only to see her brother lying in state.

"I'm not looking forward to this," Han mumbled. "Not at all." Leia reached over to squeeze his hand; he gripped hers, holding tighter and longer than she expected him to.

Robed figures emerged from the temple, drifting out of the early-morning shadows. She quickly counted a dozen. In the lead she recognized the rusty-orange face of a Calamarian female, Cilghal. Leia herself had seen Jedi potential in the fishlike woman and had urged her to join Luke's academy. Cilghal had managed to use her proven ambassadorial skills to hold the twelve students together in the terrible days following the fall of their Jedi Master.

Leia recognized other candidates gliding across the dew-damp ground: Streen, an older man with wild hair tucked haphazardly beneath a Jedi hood; he had been a gas prospector on Bespin, a hermit hiding from the voices he heard in his head. She saw tall Kirana Ti, one of the witches of Dathomir whom Leia and Han had encountered during their whirlwind courtship. Kirana Ti stepped forward, flashing a bright smile at the twins; she had a daughter of her own, only a year or so older than the twins, who remained in the care of others back on her homeworld.

Leia also identified Tionne, with long silvery hair that flowed down the back of her robe. Tionne was a student of Jedi history who wanted desperately to be a Jedi herself.

Then came hard-bitten Kam Solusar, a once-corrupted Jedi whom Luke had dragged back to the light side. And Dorsk 81, a streamlined, slick-skinned alien who had been cloned generation after generation, because his society believed they had already developed the perfect civilization.

Leia didn't recognize the other handful of Jedi candidates, but she knew Luke had been diligent in his Jedi search. The call still rang out across the galaxy, inviting those with the potential to become new Jedi Knights.

Even though their teacher now lay in a coma.

Cilghal raised a flippered hand. "We are glad you could come, Leia."

"Ambassador Cilghal," she said. "My brother—has there been any change?" They walked heavily back toward the oppressive temple. Leia believed she already knew the answer.

"No." Cilghal shook her squarish head. "But perhaps your presence will do something that ours cannot."

Sensing the solemn mood, the twins refrained from giggling and exploring the musty, stone-walled rooms. As the party entered the gloomy ground-level hangar bay, Cilghal led Leia, Han, and the twins to a turbolift.

"Come on, Jacen and Jaina," Han said, grabbing their hands again. "Maybe you can help Uncle Luke get better."

"What can we do?" Jaina asked, her liquid-brown eyes wide and hopeful.

"I don't know yet, honey," he said. "If you come up with any ideas, let me know."

The turbolift doors flowed shut, and the platform rose to the top levels of the temple. The twins clung to each other in sudden uneasiness. They had not recovered from their fear of turbolifts since the last time they had ridden one all the way down to the decaying bottom levels of Imperial City. But the ride was over in a moment, and they stepped out into the grand audience chamber of the Great Temple. Skylights spilled sunlight on a broad, polished-stone promenade that led to a raised stage.

Leia remembered standing on that stage years before, after the Death Star had been destroyed, presenting medals to Han, Chewbacca, Luke, and the other heroes of the battle of Yavin. Now, though, her breath caught in her throat. Han groaned beside her, a deep, grieving tone that she had never heard him make before.

On a bier at the end of the room lay Luke—like a body stretched out for a funeral in an echoing, empty chamber.

Her heart thumped with dread. She wanted to turn around so she wouldn't have to look at him—but Leia's feet compelled her forward. She walked with a rapid step that became a run before she reached the end of the promenade. Han followed, carrying the twins, one in each arm. His eyes were red as he fought to keep tears from flowing. Leia already felt a wetness on her cheeks.

Luke lay in repose, swathed in his Jedi robe. His hair had been combed; his hands were folded across his chest. His skin looked gray and plasticlike.

"Oh, Luke," she whispered.

"Too bad you can't just thaw him out," Han said, "like you rescued me from Jabba's Palace."

Leia reached out to touch Luke. Using her own abilities with the Force, she tried to reach deeper, to brush against his spirit—but she felt only a cold hole, an emptiness as if *Luke himself* had been taken away. Not dead. She had always felt she would somehow know if her brother died.

"Is he sleeping?" Jacen said.

"Yes . . . in a way," she answered, not knowing what else to say.

"When will he wake up?" Jaina asked.

"We don't know," she said. "We don't know how to wake him up."

"Maybe if I give him a kiss." Jaina clambered up to smack the motionless lips of her uncle. For an absurd moment Leia held her breath, thinking that the child's magic just might work. But Luke did not stir.

"He's cold," Jaina mumbled. The little girl's shoulders slumped with disappointment when her uncle failed to wake.

Han squeezed Leia's waist so hard that it hurt, but she didn't want her husband to stop holding her.

"He's been unchanged for days," Cilghal said behind them. "We brought his lightsaber with him. We found it beside his body on the rooftop."

Cilghal hesitated, then moved to stare down at Luke. "Master Skywalker told me I have an innate talent for healing with the Force. He had just begun to show me how to develop my skills—but I've tried all I know. He is not sick. There's nothing physically wrong with him. He seems frozen in a moment of time, as if his soul has left and his body is waiting for him to come back."

"Or," Leia said, "waiting for us to find a way to help him return."

"I don't know how," Cilghal said in a thin, husky voice. "None of us knows—yet. But perhaps working together we can figure it out."

"Do you have any inkling about what really happened?" Leia asked. "Have you found any clues?"

She could sense the sudden spike of Han's turmoil. Cilghal looked away with her big Calamarian eyes, but Han answered with grim certainty. "It was Kyp. Kyp did this."

"What?" Leia said, whirling to stare at him.

Han answered in a tumble of words. "The last time I saw Luke, he told me he was afraid for Kyp." Han swallowed hard. "He said that Kyp had started dabbling in the dark side. The kid stole Mara Jade's ship and took off somewhere. I think Kyp came back here and challenged Luke."

"But why?" Leia asked. "What for?"

Cilghal nodded, as if her head were too heavy for her. "We did find the stolen ship in front of the temple. It is still here, so we don't know how he flew away again . . . unless he fled into the jungles."

"Is that likely?" Leia asked.

Cilghal shook her head. "We Jedi trainees have pooled our talents and searched. We do not detect his presence on Yavin 4. He must have left on another ship somehow."

"But where would he get another ship?" Leia asked, but suddenly she remembered astonished New Republic astronomers reporting the impossible news that an entire group of stars in the Cauldron Nebula had gone supernova at the same time.

She whispered, "Could Kyp have resurrected the Sun Crusher from the core of Yavin?"

Han blinked. "How could he possibly do that?"

Cilghal hung her head gravely. "If Kyp Durron has managed that, then his power is far greater even than we feared. No wonder he was able to defeat Master Skywalker."

Han shuddered, as if afraid to accept what he knew was true. Leia could sense his emotions like a maelstrom within him. "If Kyp is on the loose with the Sun Crusher," he said, "then I'll have to go and stop him."

Leia snapped around to look at him, thinking how Han always leaped headfirst into challenges. "Are you getting delusions of grandeur again? Why does it have to be you?"

"I'm the only one he might listen to," he said. He looked aside, staring down at Luke's cadaverous face. She saw his lips trembling.

"Look, if Kyp doesn't listen to me, then he won't listen to anyone—and he'll be lost forever. If his power is as great as Cilghal thinks, that kid is not an enemy the New Republic can afford to have." He gave one of his lopsided grins. "Besides, I taught him everything he knows about flying that ship. He couldn't possibly do anything to me."

It was a somber dinner with the Jedi trainees.

Han used the *Falcon*'s food synthesizers to create a repast of heavy Corellian food. Leia picked at some spiced, fried strips of a woolamander that Kirana Ti had hunted in the jungle. The twins stuffed themselves with messy fruits and berries. Dorsk 81 devoured a bland and unappealing-looking meal of heavily processed food cubes.

Conversation was minimal, little more than forced pleasantries. They all feared to discuss what really preoccupied them—until Kam Solusar said in a hard-edged voice, "We hoped you would bring us news, Minister Organa Solo. Give us some guidance as to what we should do here. We are Jedi students with no Master. We've learned a little, but not enough to continue training on our own."

Tionne broke in. "I'm not sure we should try to learn things we don't understand. Look what happened to Gantoris! He was consumed by some evil thing he inadvertently found. And what about Kyp Durron? What if we get lured to the dark side without knowing it?"

Old Streen stood up and shook his head. "No, no. *He's* here! Don't you hear the voices?" When everyone turned to look at him, Streen sat down and hunched his shoulders, as if trying to hide under the Jedi robe. He snuffled and cleared his throat before continuing. "I can hear him. He's whispering to me now. He talks to me always. I can't get away from him."

Leia felt a rush of hope. "Luke? You can hear Luke talking to you?"

"No!" Streen whirled at her. "The Dark Man. A dark man, a shadow. He talked to Gantoris. He talked to Kyp Durron. You shine the light, but the shadow always stays, whispering, talking." Streen placed his hands against his ears and pressed his temples.

"This is too dangerous," Kirana Ti said, knitting her eyebrows. "On Dathomir I've seen what happens when a large group falls to the dark side. The evil witches on my planet made things terrible for centuries—and the galaxy was saved only because they had no spaceflight. If the witches had managed to spread their dark workings from star system to star system . . ."

"Yes, we should all stop our Jedi exercises," Dorsk 81 said, blinking his large yellow eyes. "This was a bad idea. We shouldn't have even tried."

Leia slapped both her hands hard on the table. "Stop this talk!" she said. "Luke would be ashamed to hear his students saying such things. With attitudes like that, you'll never become Jedi Knights."

She fumed. "Yes, there is a risk. There will always be risks. You've seen what happens to someone who isn't careful—but that simply means you must *be careful*. Don't be seduced by the dark side. Learn from the sacrifice that Gantoris made. Learn from how Kyp Durron was tempted. Learn from the sacrifices your Master made in an attempt to protect you all."

She stood and looked at each one of them. Some flinched. Some met her gaze.

"You are the new generation of Jedi Knights," she continued. "That is a great burden, but you must bear it, because the New Republic needs you. The old Jedi protected the Republic for a thousand generations. How can you give up after the first challenge?

"*You* have to be the champions of the Force, with or without your Jedi Master. Learn as Luke learned: step by step. You must work together, discover the things you don't know, fight what has to be fought. But the one thing you can't do is give up!"

"She is right," Cilghal said in her maddeningly calm voice. "If we surrender, the New Republic will have one less weapon against evil in the galaxy. Even if some of us fail, the rest of us must succeed."

"Do or do not," Kirana Ti said, and Tionne finished the phrase that Master Skywalker had drilled into them. "There is no try."

Her heart pounding, her stomach watery, Leia slowly sat down. The twins stared at their mother in amazement, and Han gripped her hand in admiration. She breathed deeply, began to let herself relax—

When suddenly a strangling outcry of death shattered her soul. It sounded like an avalanche within the Force, an outcry of thousands upon thousands of lives wiped out in an instant. Around the table the other Jedi candidates, all those sensitive to the Force, clutched at their chests or their ears.

Streen let out a long wail. "It's too many, too many!"

Leia's blood burned through her veins. Painful claws skittered down her spine, plucking her nerves and sending jolts through her body. Both of the Jedi twins were crying.

Baffled, Han grabbed Leia's shoulders and shook her. "What is it, Leia? What happened?" He apparently had felt nothing. "What?"

She gasped. "It was . . . a great disturbance . . . in the Force. Something terrible just happened."

With a cold wash of dread Leia thought of young Kyp Durron, turned to the dark side and now armed with the Sun Crusher.

"Something terrible," she said again, but she could not answer Han's other questions.

3

The Force moved through all things, weaving the universe into an invisible tapestry that tied the smallest living creature to the largest star cluster. Synergy made the total far greater than the sum of its parts.

And when one of those threads was torn, ripples spread through the entire web. Actions and reactions . . . great shock waves that affected all who could hear.

The destruction of Carida screamed through the Force, building power as it reflected off other sensitive minds. It rose to a tumult that struck—

And woke.

Sensory perceptions rushed back to Luke Skywalker like a storm, freeing him from the smothering nothingness that had trapped and frozen him. His final shout still echoed in his ears, but now he felt strangely numb.

The last thing he remembered was the serpent-shaped tendrils of black Force wrapping around him. Rising from the summons of Exar Kun and Luke's misguided student

Kyp Durron, the serpents of Sith power had sunk their fangs into him. Luke had been unable to resist their combined might. He had tried to use his lightsaber, but even that had failed.

Luke had fallen into a bottomless pit deeper than any of the black holes in the Maw cluster. He did not know how long he had been powerless. He remembered only an emptiness, a coldness . . . until *something* had jarred him loose.

Now, as the sudden clamor of sensory impressions filled him, it took him some time to sort out and make sense of what he could see: the walls of the grand audience chamber, the lozenge-shaped stones, the translucent tiles set out in hypnotic patterns, the long promenade and the empty benches spread like frozen waves on the floor, where once the entire Rebel Alliance had celebrated their victory over the first Death Star.

Luke's head buzzed, and he felt giddy. He wondered why he should feel so insubstantial, until he looked down—and saw his own body still lying prone and motionless below him, eyes closed, face expressionless.

Astonishment and disbelief blurred Luke's vision, but he forced himself to focus again on his own features. He saw the faded scars from when the wampa ice creature had attacked him on Hoth. His body was still draped with the brown Jedi robe, his hands crossed lightly on his chest. The lightsaber lay at his hip, a cylinder of silent plasteel, crystals, and electronic components.

"What's going on?" Luke said out loud. "Hello?"

He heard the words thrum through his head like vibrating transmissions, but they made no sound at all in the air.

Finally Luke looked at *himself*—the part of himself that was aware—and saw an insubstantial image, like a ghost reflection of his body, as if he had reconstructed a hologram using his impression of what he looked like.

His spectral arms and legs appeared to be garbed in a flowing Jedi robe, but the colors were washed-out and weak. Everything was sketched with a lambent blue glow that sparkled as he moved.

With a rush of awe and astonishment Luke suddenly *knew* what had happened. Several times he had encountered wavering spirits of Obi-Wan Kenobi and Yoda, and his own father, Anakin Skywalker.

Was he dead, then? It sounded ludicrous because he didn't *feel* dead—but he had no point of comparison. He recalled how Obi-Wan's and Yoda's and Anakin's bodies had all vanished upon their deaths: Obi-Wan and Yoda leaving only crumpled robes, Anakin Skywalker leaving only the empty body armor of Darth Vader.

Why, then, had his own body remained intact, stretched out on the raised platform? Could it be because he was not yet entirely a Jedi Master, completely given over to the Force—or could it be that he was not truly dead?

Luke heard a whirring as the turbolift rose to the top chamber. The sound seemed eerie and unnatural, as if he were using senses other than his ears to hear.

The turbolift doors slid open. Artoo-Detoo extended his front wheeled foot and rolled out, moving slowly, almost respectfully, along the polished stone promenade. The droid proceeded toward the raised platform.

Luke's shimmering image stood in front of his body where it lay in state, and he watched with joy as the little astromech droid came to him.

"Artoo, am I glad to see you!" he said. He expected the droid to bleep with wild excitement. But Artoo gave no indication that he heard or detected Luke.

"Artoo?"

Artoo-Detoo trundled up the ramp to Luke's shrouded body. The droid hooted, a low, mournful sound that expressed deep grief—if droids could feel such emotions. It tore Luke apart to see his mechanical friend looking at the body; his optical receptor winked from red to blue and back again.

Luke realized that the droid was taking readings, checking on his body's condition. He wondered if Artoo would detect anything different, now that Luke's spirit had been set free; but the droid gave no sign.

Luke attempted to move over to Artoo, to touch the polished barrel-shaped body. It took him a moment to figure out how to move his ghostly "legs." His image skimmed across the floor with a dizzying fluidity. But when he stroked Artoo, his hand passed directly through.

He felt no contact with the plasteel of the droid's body, no sensation of the floor against his ethereal feet. Luke tried walking completely through the droid, hoping somehow to scramble Artoo's sensors, but Artoo continued to take readings, unperturbed.

The droid gave another sad hoot as if in farewell, then spun around and whirred slowly back toward the turbolift.

Luke called out. "Wait, Artoo!" But he held little hope the droid would hear.

A quick idea came to him: rather than using his illusory hands, he reached out with the Force. He thought of how he and Gantoris had used little nudges from the Force to rattle metal antennas in the airborne ruins of Tibannopolis on Bespin.

Luke reached out invisibly to tap Artoo's shell, hoping to make a loud *spang* that would at least let the droid know something was amiss. He pushed and thumped with all his intangible might, and succeeded only in what he thought was a barely audible bump against the droid's metal casing.

Artoo paused, but while Luke gathered strength to make another Force assault, the droid dismissed the unexplained sound and entered the turbolift. Inside the turbolift, Artoo turned his optical sensor once more toward the body of his master, made a low, sliding whistle, and then the doors whisked closed. Luke heard the humming of the platform as it dropped back down to the lower levels of the Great Temple.

Luke stood in the echoing grand audience chamber all alone—awake again, but insubstantial and apparently powerless. He would have to find some other way to solve his predicament.

He looked out through the temple skylights into the blackness of the jungle moon's deep night, and he wondered what he could do to save himself.

4

With a Wookiee bellow of impatience, Chewbacca urged the last members of the Special Forces team onto the remaining troop transport. The other transports had been shuttling up and down from Coruscant orbit all day, carrying weapons, equipment, and personnel to the strike force already assembled in space.

The heavily armed battle group consisted of one escort frigate and four Corellian corvettes—enough firepower to occupy the secret Imperial think tank, Maw Installation, and to overcome any resistance from the weapons scientists stranded there.

The last three stragglers hustled up the ramp, clad in light armor and securing tight packs onto their shoulders. Chewbacca watched the soldiers strap into their seats before he punched the ALL CLEAR button to raise the boarding ramp.

"Your impatience is not helping, Chewbacca," See-Threepio said. "The tension level is already substantial, and you're simply making things worse. I have a bad feeling about this mission already."

Chewbacca growled at him, disregarding his comment. Impatient, he picked up the droid and dropped him with a metallic clatter into the only remaining spare seat—which was, unfortunately, next to Chewbacca's own.

"Indeed!" Threepio said as he dutifully hooked himself in. "I'm doing my best. This isn't my area of expertise, you know."

Chewbacca settled into a seat that had never been designed to accommodate a creature of his massive proportions. He bent his hairy knees nearly to chest level. He wished he could be with Han in the *Millennium Falcon*, but Han and Leia had gone to see Luke Skywalker, and Chewbacca felt his stronger duty was to go rescue the Wookiee prisoners left inside Maw Installation.

The rest of the assault team shifted in their seats, looking around, double-checking their mental lists of equipment and procedures. Page's Commandos, a crack assault troop, would be handling most of the front-line mission, with plenty of New Republic firepower to back them up. The Special Operations Commander, General Crix Madine, had given the Special Forces thorough briefings on strategy for the planned occupation. The soldiers were fully trained and competent.

Chewbacca just wished the pilot would hurry up and take off. He blew out a long sigh through his rubbery lips, thinking uneasily of Han. He had waited a long time for an opportunity to rescue the tortured Wookiee slaves, though.

When he, Han, and young Kyp Durron had been captured by Admiral Daala at Maw Installation, Chewbacca had been forced to work with captive Wookiees aboard the Star Destroyers and down in the Installation itself. The Wookiees had been imprisoned for more than ten years, working at hard labor, and the resistance had gone out of them. The thought of their ruined lives made Chewbacca's blood boil.

Not long ago, with Threepio's dubious abilities as translator, Chewbacca had addressed the New Republic Council. He urged them to occupy the Installation and rescue the Wookiee prisoners, as well as to keep the new weapon designs from falling into Imperial hands. Seeing Mon Mothma's support, the Council had agreed.

With a mechanical whir and a thump of metal against metal, the landing struts of the transport drew up inside the hull. With a lurch the transport rose on its repulsorlifts, then headed off the landing platform, rising into the sky as the metropolis of Imperial City glittered below.

Threepio began talking to himself. Chewbacca marveled at how sophisticated the droid's electronic brain must be to consistently find so many things to complain about.

"I simply don't understand why Mistress Leia ordered me to go with you. I am always happy to serve in any capacity, naturally, but I could have assisted greatly in watching the children while she visited Master Luke on Yavin 4. I've been doing a good job of taking care of the twins, haven't I?"

Chewbacca grunted. Threepio continued. "True, we misplaced them at the Holographic Zoo for Extinct Animals, but that was only one time, and it all turned out right in the end." He swiveled his golden head.

As the acceleration increased, Chewbacca closed his eyes and growled at him to be quiet. Threepio ignored him. "It would have been nice to see Artoo-Detoo again at Master Luke's Jedi academy. I haven't spoken to my counterpart in a long time."

Threepio did not slow down as he changed subjects. "I really don't know what use I'm expected to be on this military mission. I've never been very skilled at combat. I don't like combat. I don't like excitement in any form, though I seem to have encountered enough of it."

Inertia pushed Chewbacca back against his uncomfortably small seat as the transport accelerated toward the congregation of battleships in orbit around Coruscant.

Threepio continued, and continued. "Of course I understand that I am technically supposed to help sift through the data in the Maw Installation computers, and I suppose I could be of some use translating the languages of alien scientists—but certainly there must be some other droid better qualified for that type of work? Isn't General Antilles taking along an entire team of slicer droids to get encrypted information? Page's Commandos are experts in this sort of thing. Why do I have to go along and do all the hard work? It seems unfair to me."

Chewbacca barked a sharp command. Threepio turned to him with his yellow optical sensors glowing in indignation. "I will *not* be quiet, Chewbacca. Why should I listen to you after you put my head on backward in Cloud City?

"If you yourself had spoken up during the preparations for putting this team together, you could have convinced them to let me stay with Mistress Leia. But you thought I might be an asset to this mission, and now you're just going to have to listen to me."

With a sigh of annoyance Chewbacca reached over and hit the power switch on the back of Threepio's neck. The droid fell silent, his words slurring to a stop as he slumped forward.

On the troop transport Page's Commandos—noted for their intense training, cold efficiency, and utter professionalism—took a moment to applaud Chewbacca's action.

On the command bridge of the escort frigate *Yavaris*, General Wedge Antilles looked across space. Sunlight reflected off the metal hulls of his fleet. He had asked

for command of this mission because he wanted to return
to where Qwi Xux had spent so much of her life—to where
the secrets of her lost memory might lie hidden.

The *Yavaris* was a powerful ship, despite its fragile
appearance caused by the thin spine that separated its
two primary components. At the frigate's aft end a boxy
construction contained sublight and hyperdrive engines
and the power reactors that drove not only the engines but
also twelve turbolaser batteries and twelve laser cannons.
On the other end of the connecting rod, separated from the
engines, was the much larger command section, hanging
down in an angular structure that contained the command
bridge, crew quarters, scanners, and cargo bays that carried two full X-wing fighter squadrons for the assault.

The escort frigate held a crew of about nine hundred
seasoned soldiers, while the rest of his fleet—four Corellian
corvettes—carried one hundred on each vessel.

Wedge brushed his dark hair away from his forehead
and set his square jaw. The last of the troop transports
had docked on the frigate, bringing the remainder of the
handpicked raiders.

Han Solo had reported that Maw Installation was no
longer protected by Admiral Daala's Star Destroyers, which
had been lured out of the black hole cluster to wreak havoc
across the galaxy. The precious weapons information and
scientists inside the Installation were undefended. Probably. Wedge was prepared for surprises, especially from
a congregation of Imperial weapons designers.

On the command bridge of the *Yavaris*, Wedge toggled
on the intercom. "Prepare to depart," he said. The four
corvettes folded around the escort frigate in a diamond
formation. Ahead, Wedge saw throbbing blue-white light
as banks of heavy engines pulsed to life.

The corvettes' huge engines were twice as large as the
living compartments and the hammerhead-shaped control
section. Princess Leia had been riding a corvette when

Vader's Star Destroyer had captured her, demanding that she return the stolen Death Star plans, so long ago.

He watched the light-embroidered nightside of Coruscant veer away from the fleet as they angled up out of orbit, past metallic docking stations and heavy parabolic mirrors that directed magnified sunlight to warm the higher frozen latitudes.

He wished Qwi had stayed with him to watch the departure, but she was down in their quarters reviewing information tapes, studying . . . studying. Since her memory would not come back of its own accord, Qwi intended to fill the gaps with the missing information as quickly as possible.

She also had a deep revulsion toward watching a planet from orbit. It had taken Wedge much quiet encouraging before she finally told him that the sight reminded her of her youth, when she had been held hostage aboard an orbital training sphere under the harsh tutelage of Moff Tarkin. Qwi had been forced to watch as Victory-class Star Destroyers obliterated the honeycomb settlements of her people whenever students failed their examinations.

Thinking of the terrible things the Empire had done to the delicate and lovely Qwi made Wedge clench his teeth. He turned to the bridge crew. "Ready for hyperspace?"

"Course set, sir," the navigation officer answered.

Wedge vowed to do what he could to fill Qwi's life with joy . . . once they had conquered Maw Installation.

"Move out," he said.

Inside windowless quarters in the protected lower decks of the *Yavaris,* Qwi Xux stared into the tutorial screen and blinked her indigo eyes. She skimmed file after file, absorbing the information as enthusiastically as a Tatooine desert sponge grabbed droplets of moisture.

A small portrait holo of Wedge sat inside a cube atop her worktable. She glanced at it frequently, reminding herself what he looked like, who he was, how much he meant to her. None of her memories were certain after Kyp Durron's assault on her mind.

She had initially forgotten Wedge himself, forgotten the times they had spent together. He had desperately told her everything, showed her pictures, taken her out to the same places that the two of them had visited on the planet Ithor. He had reminded her of the reconstruction site of the Cathedral of Winds they had visited on Vortex.

Some of these things caused elusive images to flicker in the back of her mind, enough that she knew they had been there once . . . but she could not grasp them anymore.

Other things Wedge told her exploded back into her thoughts with full clarity, enough to bring stinging tears. Whenever that happened, Wedge was there to hold her in his arms and comfort her.

"No matter how long it takes," he had said, "I'll help you to remember. And if we can't find all of your past again . . . then I'll help you make new memories to fill those spaces." He brushed her hand, and she nodded.

Qwi reviewed the tapes of her speech before the New Republic Council, where she had insisted that they dispose of the Sun Crusher and stop trying to analyze it. The Council members had grudgingly agreed to mothball the project by plunging it into the core of a gas-giant planet. But now it appeared that this had not been sufficient to keep the superweapon away from an anger and determination as powerful as Kyp Durron's.

As she reviewed the holotaped speech she had given, she heard the words in her own voice, but did not remember speaking them. She placed the memories in her mind, but they were external views of herself as seen and recorded by others. She heaved a deep breath and scrolled to the next data file. A cumbersome method, but it would have to do.

Much of her basic scientific knowledge remained intact, but certain things were completely gone: insights she had gained, new weapons designs and new ideas she had developed. It seemed that when Kyp had rummaged around in her brain, yanking out anything that had to do with the Sun Crusher, he had erased whatever he found questionable.

Now Qwi had to rebuild what she could. It didn't bother her that knowledge of the Sun Crusher had been obliterated. She had previously vowed to tell no one how the weapon worked—and now telling would be impossible, even if she wanted to. Some inventions were better erased. . . .

The Maw assault fleet had been under way for almost a full day, heading toward the Kessel system. Qwi had been studying much of the time, sparing only a moment to talk to Wedge when he came to visit after completing his duties on the command bridge. When he brought her food, they ate together, making small talk, spending their time looking into each other's eyes.

As she sat at the data terminal, Wedge would come and stroke her narrow shoulders, massaging until her tense muscles turned buttery and warm. "You're working too hard, Qwi," he had said more than once.

"I have to," she answered him.

She recalled her youth, when she had studied desperately, cramming knowledge of physics and engineering and weaponry into her pliable young brain for Moff Tarkin. She alone had survived the rigorous training. Kyp's heavy-handed scouring of her mind had left her with those painful childhood memories—memories she would just as soon forget.

There were some things she could not recapture from data tapes or tutorial programs. She had to go back inside Maw Installation, into the laboratories where she had spent so many years. Only then could she determine which memories would come back and how much of her past she would have to sacrifice forever.

The intercom rang out, and Wedge's voice flooded into their quarters. "Qwi, would you come up to the bridge, please? There's something I'd like you to see."

She acknowledged, smiling at the sound of his voice. She took a turbolift up to the frigate's command towers and stepped out onto the bustling bridge. Wedge turned to greet her—but her indigo eyes were drawn to the broad viewport at the front of the *Yavaris.*

She had seen the Maw cluster before, but her mouth still dropped open in awe. The incredible maelstrom of ionized gases and superheated debris screamed past the edges of the bottomless black holes in a great whirlpool of color.

"We came out of hyperspace near the Kessel system," Wedge said, "and we're lining up our vector to go in. I thought you might want to watch."

She swallowed a lump in her throat and stepped forward to take his hand. The black holes formed a maze of gravity wells and dead-end hyperspace paths; only a few dangerously "safe" courses made passage possible through the tangled labyrinth.

"We downloaded the course from the Sun Crusher," Wedge said. "I hope nothing's changed, or we'll all have a big surprise when we try to make it through."

Qwi nodded. "It should be safe," she said. "I double-checked the route."

Wedge looked at her warmly, as if her verification gave him more confidence than all the computer simulations.

The black hole cluster was an impossible astronomical oddity; for thousands of years astrophysicists had attempted to determine its origin—whether some freak galactic combination had led to the birth of the black holes, or whether some impossibly ancient and powerful alien race had assembled the cluster for its own purposes.

The Maw sent out deadly radiation and was even now drawing the Kessel system to its eventual doom. For the present, though, the Empire had found a stable island within the cluster and had built its secret laboratory there.

"Let's go then," Qwi said, looking out at the brilliant gases flaring in incredible slow motion. She had much to learn—and a score to settle. "I'm ready."

The ships of the Maw assault fleet spread apart, arrowing one by one into the heart of the black hole cluster.

5

One wing of the rebuilt Imperial Palace had been converted into a crèche for the water-loving Calamarian people, humid quarters for those brought by Admiral Ackbar and trained as his specialized starship mechanics.

The crèche had been built of smooth plasteel and hard metal fashioned to look like a reef within the towering palace. Some of the round portholes looked out upon the glittering skyline of Imperial City, while others gazed in on an enclosed water tank that circulated around the rooms like a trapped river.

A loud venting of mist from the humidity generators startled Terpfen out of nervous contemplation. He looked around his quarters wildly, swiveling his circular eyes, but he saw nothing in the shadows, only a jewel-blue light shining through the water windows. He watched as a gray-green glurpfish oozed its way along the channel, filtering microorganisms from the brine. No sound intruded other than the steam generators and bubbling aerators in the wall tanks.

Terpfen had heard nothing in his mind, felt no compulsion from his Imperial masters on Carida for more than a day, and he didn't know whether to be frightened . . . or hopeful. Furgan usually taunted and jabbed him regularly, just to remind him of his constant presence. Now Terpfen felt alone.

Rumors flew around the Imperial Palace. Distress signals had been detected from Carida, and then all contact had broken off. New Republic scouts had been dispatched to inspect the area. If Carida had somehow been destroyed, then perhaps the Imperial hold on his brain had been severed. Terpfen could finally be free!

He had been taken prisoner during the vicious Imperial occupation of the water world Calamari. Like many of his people, Terpfen had been dragged to a labor camp and forced to work at the starship-construction facilities.

But Terpfen had been damned to undergo a special kind of training. Taken off to the Imperial military planet of Carida, he had suffered weeks of torture and conditioning as xenosurgeons removed portions of his brain and replaced them with vat-grown organic circuits that allowed Furgan to use Terpfen as a perfectly disguised puppet.

The poorly stitched scars on his swollen head had served as badges of his ordeal once he was released. Many Calamarians had also been severely tortured during the occupation, and no one suspected Terpfen of treachery.

For years he had tried to resist his Imperial masters; but half of his brain was not his own, and the Imperial controllers could manipulate him at will.

He had sabotaged Admiral Ackbar's expanded B-wing fighter so that it crashed on Vortex, destroying the precious Cathedral of Winds and disgracing Ackbar. Terpfen had planted a tracer on another B-wing, which had allowed him to obtain the location of the secret planet Anoth, where baby Anakin Solo lived in isolation, protected from prying eyes and minds. Terpfen had passed that crucial information to a greedy Ambassador Furgan—even now the Caridans must be mounting an attack to kidnap the third Jedi child.

Terpfen stood before the aquarium window in his dim quarters, watching the glurpfish sluggishly go about its business. An aquatic predator swooped toward it, flailing spear-tipped fins and jagged jaws. The predator would fall upon the glurpfish . . . just as the Imperial forces would fall upon the helpless child and his lone protector, Winter, who had once been Leia's close companion and confidant.

"No!" Terpfen smashed his flipper hands against the thick glass. The vibrations startled the fanged predator, and it shot away in search of other prey. The protoplasmic glurpfish, unaware of what had just happened, continued on its way, sifting the water for microscopic food.

Perhaps his Caridan masters had only been distracted temporarily by other things . . . but if Terpfen hoped to accomplish anything, he had to make his move now. He swore that it didn't matter what damage it did to his own brain.

Ackbar himself remained in self-imposed exile on Calamari, working with his people to repair the floating cities that had been devastated in Admiral Daala's recent attack. Ackbar claimed to have no further interest in New Republic politics.

Since an assault was to be launched against young Anakin, Terpfen would go directly to Leia Organa Solo. She could mobilize New Republic forces and thwart the Imperials. But she and Han Solo had just departed for the jungle moon of Yavin. . . .

Terpfen would have to go there, commandeer a ship, and meet her face-to-face. He would confess everything and put himself at her mercy. She might execute him on the spot, as would be her right. But even that would be a just punishment for the damage he had already done.

His mind made up—at least for as long as it remained *his* mind—Terpfen took a last look around his quarters. Turning from the aquarium windows that reminded him of the homeworld he had left behind, he took a last glance at the faceted skyline with its kilometer-high skyscrapers, winking landing lights, gleaming shuttles rising toward the aurora that blanketed the night.

Terpfen doubted he would ever see Coruscant again.

He didn't have time for a ruse.

Using his own security access codes, Terpfen entered the starfighter servicing bay and walked briskly, confidently. His body odor was laced with tension, but if he moved fast enough, no one would notice until it was too late.

The large launch doors had been sealed for the night. Two Calamarian starship mechanics stood around one of the B-wing fighters. A group of chattering Ugnaughts worked under the hyperdrive motors of a pair of X-wing fighters that had been jacked together to exchange navicomputer information.

Terpfen walked toward the B-wing. One of the Calamarians saluted him as he approached. The other lowered herself out of the pilot compartment, slinging down a webbed sack of tools. From his own terminal Terpfen had already checked the status of this fighter, knew it was ready to launch. He didn't have to ask the question, but it distracted them.

"Repairs completed as planned?"

"Yes, sir," the male Calamarian said. "What are you doing up so late?"

"Just attending to some personal business," he said, and reached into a pocket of his flightsuit. He whipped out a blaster pistol set to STUN. He fired in a sweeping arc, catching both Calamarians with blue ripples. The male slumped to the ground without a sound. The female dangled on the rung, unconscious as she thumped against the side of the B-wing; finally her elbow went slack, and she dropped to the hard floor in a tumble.

Over by the X-wings the Ugnaughts stopped chattering and stood up in amazement; then they began squealing. Three ran to the comm alarm next to the controls of the launch doors.

Terpfen took aim and squeezed the firing button again, cutting the Ugnaughts down. The others raised their stubby hands in surrender; but Terpfen could not risk taking captives, so he stunned them as well.

Moving purposefully, he hurried across the slick-plated floor to the controls of the launch door. From the enameled badge on his left breast, he withdrew a disguised slicer chip the Imperials had provided months ago, in case he should need to make a quick escape. Now, though, Terpfen used the Imperial technology for the benefit of the New Republic.

Terpfen jammed the small wafer into the input slot and punched three buttons in succession. The electronics hummed, scanning the information in the chip. The slicer chip convinced the controls that Terpfen had the appropriate override codes, that he had authorization from both Admiral Ackbar and Mon Mothma.

With a groan and a thud, the heavy launch doors split apart. The night winds whistled outside the hangar bay, gusting into the chamber and bringing the chill air.

Terpfen strode to the repaired B-wing, slid his broad hands under the arms of the fallen male Calamarian, and dragged him across the slick floor. He dumped the mechanic beside the slumped bodies of the stunned Ugnaughts.

When Terpfen moved the female mechanic, she moaned softly. Her arm hung at an awkward angle, broken in the fall. Terpfen hesitated a moment in guilty misery, but the accidental injury couldn't be helped. A few hours in a bacta tank would patch her up just fine.

By then Terpfen would be on his way to Yavin 4.

He clambered into the pilot seat of the B-wing and powered up the controls. All the lights winked green. He sealed the hatch. With the speed of the B-wing's engines, he could make it to the Yavin system in record time. He had to.

Terpfen raised the awkward-looking craft on its repulsorlifts and maneuvered toward the open launch doors.

Screeching alarms penetrated the enclosed cockpit, vibrating from the servicing bay. Terpfen twisted his head to see what had gone wrong—and spotted another Ugnaught, one who had apparently been hiding inside the cockpit of an X-wing. The lone Ugnaught had squirmed out in a panic and scurried over to the alarm panel.

Terpfen cursed under his breath and knew that he had to hurry. He had hoped not to fight his way out.

He punched the maneuvering jets and shot out of the wide mouth of the launching bay. His stolen B-wing streaked away from the immense towers of Coruscant and headed out on a high-energy straight-line path to orbit.

He couldn't waste time fooling the New Republic security monitors. Terpfen would appear to be an Imperial saboteur stealing a starfighter. If they captured him, they would interrogate him until it was too late to help young Anakin Solo. Terpfen had done many terrible things against his will, but now that he was free from Imperial control, any failure would be his own fault. He could blame no one else.

It surprised and dismayed him how rapidly the Coruscant security forces scrambled to intercept him. Four X-wings soared by at low altitude and vectored in on his single fighter.

Terpfen's comm buzzed. One of the pursuing pilots said, "B-wing, you have made an unauthorized departure from the palace. Return immediately, or you will be fired upon."

Terpfen merely increased power to the shields surrounding his ship. The B-wing was one of Ackbar's prize contributions to the Rebellion, and it was far superior to the old-model X-wings. Terpfen could outrun them, and his shields could probably survive several direct hits—but he didn't know if he could withstand the combined firepower of four X-wings.

"B-wing fighter, this is your last chance," the X-wing pilot said, and fired a low-energy bolt that spattered against Terpfen's shields. The warning shot nudged the B-wing, but caused no damage.

Terpfen punched the throttle, kicking in the afterburners that launched him toward the aurora and a low planetary orbit that his onboard navigational systems marked with heavy red danger lines.

A year before, the battle to regain Coruscant and overthrow the warring Imperial factions had been won only at the cost of incredible destruction. Many ruined battleships remained in low orbit, collected there in a great garbage pile. Crews had been dismantling them for months, repairing those that could be salvaged, sending others down to burn up as they made their spectacular descent through the atmosphere. Such work, though, had low priority during the crisis phase of the formation of the New Republic. A large junkyard of debris still orbited in well-marked lanes.

Terpfen, however, had previously scanned the placement of the twisted hulks and made his own personal orbital chart. He had found a dangerous path through the maze, so narrow he would have to fly with no margin for error—but it seemed his best chance. He was certain the alarm had sounded across Coruscant's full security systems, and before long squadrons of fighters would come screaming in to converge on him.

Terpfen didn't want to fight. He didn't want to cause more death and damage. He wanted to escape as quickly and as painlessly as possible.

As he left the blanket of atmosphere behind him, the X-wings followed in his wake, firing in earnest now. Terpfen refused to shoot back, although if he crippled one or more of the starfighters, he would have an easier time escaping. But he did not want the death of an innocent pilot on his conscience. He had too many deaths to deal with already.

In the blackness of space he flitted past glimmering shards of metal, reactor pods, and hull plates from blasted freighters. He skimmed up and over a tangled cluster of girders and a largely intact planar solar array from a destroyed TIE fighter.

Up ahead the breached hull of a capital ship—a Loronar Strike Cruiser—hung as little more than a framework of structural beams and split plating after its hyperdrive engines had blown up during a direct hit.

Terpfen streaked toward the hulk, knowing that the blast cavity in its middle was wide enough for a B-wing to pass directly through. He had already studied the path, and he hoped the risk would cause his pursuers to pull back and give him just enough time to launch into hyperspace.

Without slowing Terpfen shot through a gaping opening in the Strike Cruiser's hull. Two X-wings peeled off, another managed to follow directly in his wake. The fourth shifted a micron too far and clipped its wings against a ragged strut. The X-wing spun and slammed into the wreckage; its fuel cylinders detonated.

Terpfen felt claws of dismay sink into his heart. He had never meant for anyone to die.

The last X-wing hung hotly behind him, firing repeatedly in outrage at the death of his partner.

Terpfen checked his shields and saw that they had begun to fail under the pummeling. He did not blame the other pilot for his anger, but neither could he surrender now. He studied his control panels. The navicomputer had plotted the best course to the Yavin system.

Before his shields could buckle, Terpfen took a short course directly out of the orbital debris field. The X-wing came at him again with all weapons blazing. Upon reaching open space Terpfen punched the hyperdrive engines.

In an instant the B-wing shot forward, impossibly out of the reach of the other fighter. With white starlines that looked like spears to impale him, Terpfen vanished into hyperspace with a silent bang.

6

Standing in front of the *Millennium Falcon,* Han Solo held Leia in a long embrace. The oppressive humidity of the jungle moon clung to them like wet rags against their skin. Han hugged Leia again, smelling her scent. The corners of his lips drifted upward in a wistful smile. He could feel her trembling against him—or perhaps it was his own hands.

"I really do have to go, Leia," he said. "I've got to find Kyp. Maybe I can stop him from blowing up more star systems and killing more people."

"I know," she said. "I just wish we could arrange to have our adventures *together* a little more often!"

Han tried unsuccessfully to give her his famous no-care grin. "I'll work on it," he said; then he kissed her long and hard. "Next time we'll manage."

He bent down to gather the twins in his arms. Jacen and Jaina clearly wanted to go back inside and play in the temples.

The children had found a small group of furry woolamanders nesting in an unused wing of the Great Temple, and Jacen claimed in his broken sentences that he knew how to talk to the creatures. Han wondered just what the hairy and noisy arboreal animals were saying back to the boy.

He backed toward the boarding ramp. "You know I need you to stay here in safety with the kids," he said to Leia. "And with Luke."

She nodded. They had been through this all before. "I can take care of myself. Now, get going. If you can do anything to stop Kyp, you shouldn't be wasting time here."

He kissed her again, waved goodbye to the twins, and vanished into the ship.

In a rotating cocktail lounge high up in Imperial City, Lando Calrissian yanked the fruit stick out of his drink before it could take root at the bottom of the glass. He sipped the fizzy concoction and smiled across the table at Mara Jade.

"Sure I can't get you another drink?" he asked. She looked absolutely beautiful with her exotic hair, high cheekbones, generous lips, and eyes the color of expensive gemstones. She hadn't touched her first drink yet, but he made certain he still shone with confidence.

"No thanks, Calrissian. We've got business to discuss."

The windows of the observation lounge showed the glittering former Imperial Palace and crystallike spires and skyscrapers that extended to the fringes of the atmosphere. Hover barges drifted above the buildings, flashing announcements in numerous languages, ferrying tourists out to watch the sunset and the brightening aurora. A pair of mismatched moons hung in the sky, shining down on the bustling city.

Musical notes drifted into the air from a complex multilayered bank of keyboards in the middle of which sat a purplish-black, tentacled creature. With a flurry of cilia, the creature played a staggering number of keys at a time. Instead of eyes on its lumpy head, it was studded with tympanic membranes of varying sizes so it could hear music over an incredible range. Its tentacles flailed, striking upper keys, drawing out lower resonances, playing tunes both too high and too low for the human ear.

Lando took another sip and leaned back in his chair with a sigh and a soft smile. He had draped his slick burgundy cape over the back of his chair. Mara Jade wore only a tight-fitting jumpsuit; her curves looked like hazardous paths through a complicated planetary system.

Lando looked across at her. "So you think the Smugglers' Alliance would be interested in an arrangement for distribution of glitterstim spice from Kessel?"

Mara nodded. "I think I can guarantee that. Moruth Doole let the spice mines fall into a shambles. Black-market smuggling from the Imperial Correction Facility has made the entire planet a pain in the soft parts for any self-respecting runner trying to earn a living. It took powerful crime lords like Jabba with enough strong-arm just to make it worthwhile."

"I'll make it worthwhile," Lando said, folding his hands together on the tabletop. "I received a million-credit reward from the Duchess of Dargul, and I can invest it to bring the systems up to a more sophisticated level."

"What exactly are your plans?" Mara asked, leaning closer to him.

Lando responded by leaning over the table himself, bringing his large brown eyes close to hers. His pulse raced. She frowned and sat up straight again, still waiting for him to answer.

Rebuffed, Lando looked for words. "Uh, I don't have any great fondness for the prison where Doole centered his operations, but I think I can use that as a starting point. Dismantle most of the old correction facility, but use the buildings for a new base.

"And I don't plan to use slave labor, either. I figure we can get worker droids. On Nkllon I got familiar with some sophisticated mining systems, and if I use supercooled devices, the infrared signatures won't attract those energy spiders that caused so much trouble before."

"Droids can't handle everything," Mara said. "You're going to need some people down there. Who will you get to run a miserable operation like that?"

"Miserable to humans maybe," Lando said, locking his hands behind his back and sitting straight, "but not to some other species. In particular, I've got in mind an old friend of mine, Nien Nunb, who was my copilot on the *Falcon* during the Battle of Endor. He's a Sullustan, a little creature who grew up living in tunnels and warrens on a tough volcanic world. He'd consider the spice mines a luxury resort!" Lando shrugged at Mara's skeptical look. "Hey, I've worked with him before and I trust him."

"Sounds like you've got most of the answers, Calrissian," Mara said. "But so far it's all just talk. When are you planning to go to Kessel and get to work?"

"Well, I lost my ship there. I've got to get back to Kessel to pick up the *Lady Luck* and start my operations." He raised his eyebrows. "Say, you wouldn't be willing to give me a lift to the system, would you?"

"No." Mara Jade stood up. "I would not."

"All right, then. Will you meet me on Kessel in one standard week? By then I should have a good feel for how things are going to go. We can lay down the foundation for a long and lasting relationship." He smiled at her again.

"*Business* relationship," she said, but not quite as sharply as she might have.

"You sure you won't have dinner with me?" he asked.

"I've already eaten a ration bar," she said, and turned to leave. "One standard week. I'll see you on Kessel." She turned and left.

Lando blew her a kiss, but she didn't see him . . . which was probably a good thing.

At the keyboards the tentacled musician played a mournful tune of unreciprocated emotional resonances.

In the stuffy Council chambers Han Solo swallowed a lump in his throat before he addressed the gathered senators and generals and Mon Mothma herself.

"I don't often talk to this"—he tried to think of the appropriate flowery language Leia would use in front of politicians—"this, um, august assemblage, but I need some information fast."

Mon Mothma sat up weakly. Nearby a medical droid tended the silent monitoring and life-support systems attached to the Chief of State's body. Her skin looked grayish, as if it had already died and was waiting to fall off her bones. As she declined, she had given up all pretense of hiding her failing health.

According to Leia, Mon Mothma had only a few weeks to live with her strange, debilitating disease. Seeing the woman now, though, Han wouldn't have laid odds she would survive even that long.

"What exactly," Mon Mothma began—then paused to heave a deep breath—"do you need to know, General Solo?"

Han swallowed again. He couldn't hide the truth, though he hated to admit it. "Kyp Durron was my friend, but he went wrong somehow. He attacked Luke Skywalker. He took the Sun Crusher and blew up the Cauldron Nebula to destroy Admiral Daala's fleet. Leia and all the Jedi trainees on Yavin just experienced what they called 'a great disturbance in the Force,' and she's convinced that Kyp might have done something else."

General Rieekan spoke in his gruff voice, looking at Han with weary eyes. Rieekan had been the commander of Echo Base on Hoth, and he had seen many hard times. "Our scouts have just come back, General Solo. Your friend *did* use the Sun Crusher again. He destroyed the Caridan star system, site of the Imperial military academy."

Han felt his throat go dry, though the news was no great surprise, considering how much Kyp hated the Empire.

"This slaughter must stop. It goes beyond even the Emperor's atrocities," the aging tactician, General Jan Dodonna, said. "The New Republic does not employ such barbarous tactics."

"Well, *he* does!" interrupted Garm Bel-Iblis. "And he has obliterated two crucial Imperial targets. While we may not agree with Durron's methods, his success rate is nothing short of astonishing."

Mon Mothma interrupted, somehow finding the energy to speak a harsh sentence. "I will not allow this young man to be portrayed . . . as a war hero." She paused for a deep breath and raised her clenched hand to signal that she had not yet finished. "His personal crusade must stop. General Solo, can you halt Kyp Durron?"

"I've got to find him first! Give me the reconnaissance information your scouts gathered from the Cauldron Nebula and Carida. Maybe I can track him down. If I could just talk to him face-to-face, I'm sure I could make the kid see reason."

"General Solo, you will have access to everything you desire," Mon Mothma said, spreading her palms on the synthetic stone surface in front of her, as if to support herself. "Do you require . . . a military escort?"

"No," he said, "that might scare him off. I'll take the *Falcon* and go myself. If I'm lucky, maybe I can bring the Sun Crusher back, too." Han gazed slowly around the Council chamber. "And this time let's make sure we destroy it completely."

Packing the *Falcon*, Han had almost finished his last-minute emergency preparations when he heard a voice behind him. "Han, old buddy! Need some help?"

He glanced over his shoulder to see Lando Calrissian striding toward him across the hangar bay, ducking under the flat aerofoil of an X-wing starfighter.

"Just leaving, Lando," he said. "Don't know how long I'll be gone."

"I heard," Lando said. "Hey, why not let me come along? You'll need a copilot, with Chewbacca gone on the Maw mission."

Han hesitated. "I'm doing this by myself. I can't ask anyone else to go with me."

"Han, you're crazy to fly the *Falcon* alone. You don't know what sort of hostile situations you're going to get into. Who'll be at the controls if you need to go up into the gun well?" Lando flashed his most winning smile. "You've got to admit, I'm the obvious choice."

Han sighed. "Chewbacca would be my first choice—I miss that fuzzball, you know? At least he doesn't try to gamble the *Falcon* away from me."

"Awww, we don't do that anymore, Han," Lando said. "We promised, remember?"

"How could I forget?" Han groaned. Lando had beaten him in their last round of sabacc, claiming ownership of the *Falcon*—and then he had given the ship back to Han, just to impress Mara Jade. "But what's your take on this, you old pirate?" Han said, raising his eyebrows. "Why do you want to come along so bad?"

Lando shuffled his feet on the polished floor of the landing bay. At the other end of the chamber a sublight engine started up, blatted, then coughed as a team of mechanics scrambled over the fuselage of a dismantled A-wing.

"To be honest . . . I need to get to Kessel within a week."

"But I'm not going anywhere near Kessel," Han said.

"You don't know *where* you're going yet. You're looking for Kyp."

"Point taken. What's at Kessel?" Han asked. "I didn't think you'd want to go back there soon, after what happened last time. I sure don't."

"Mara Jade's going to meet me there in a week. We're partners in a new spice-mining operation." He beamed, tossing his burgundy cape over his shoulder.

Han tried to cover his skeptical smile. "And does Mara herself know about this partnership, or are you just talking big?"

Lando looked hurt. "Of course she knows . . . sort of. Besides, if you get me to Kessel, maybe I can find the *Lady Luck* again, and I can stop hitching rides with people. This is getting old."

"That's for sure," Han said. "All right, if we go near Kessel, I'll take you there—but my priority is tracking Kyp."

"Of course, Han. That's understood," Lando said, then mumbled under his breath, "just as long as I get to Kessel within a week."

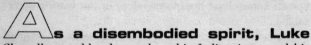

7

As a disembodied spirit, Luke
Skywalker could only watch as his Jedi trainees and his
sister Leia filed into the grand audience chamber. Artoo-
Detoo trundled ahead, like an escort, silently coasting to
a stop before the platform on which he lay.

The other Jedi trainees stood in a row in front of the
motionless form. They stared respectfully at his motionless body as if they were attendees at a funeral. Luke
could sense emotion pouring from them: grief, confusion,
dismay, and deep anxiety.

"Leia," he called in his echoing otherworldly voice.
"Leia!" he screamed as loud as he could, trying to break
through the other-dimensional walls that restrained him.

Leia flinched, but didn't seem to hear. She reached
forward to grip the arm of his cold body. He heard her
whisper, "I don't know if you can hear me, Luke, but I
know you're not dead. I can sense you're still here. We'll
find a way to help you. We'll keep trying."

She squeezed his limp hand and turned away quickly.

She blinked to cast away the tears welling up within her eyes.

"Leia . . . ," he sighed. He watched as the other Jedi candidates followed her back to the turbolift. Once again he found himself all alone with his paralyzed body, staring at the echoing walls of the Massassi temple.

"All right," he said, looking for another solution. If Artoo couldn't hear him, and if Leia or the other Jedi trainees could not identify his presence, then perhaps Luke could communicate with someone on his own plane of existence—another glistening Jedi spirit he had spoken to many times before.

"Ben!" Luke called. "Obi-Wan Kenobi, can you hear me?"

His voice hummed through the ether. With all the emotional firepower he could dredge from the bottom of his soul, Luke shouted into the silence. "Ben!"

Growing more concerned at hearing no answer, he called for others. "Yoda! Father—Anakin Skywalker!"

He waited, but there was no response.

. . . Until he sensed a *coldness* ripple through the air like an icicle slowly melting. Words trembled from the walls. "They can't hear you, Skywalker—but I can."

Luke spun around and saw a crack form in the stone walls. It grew darker as a tarlike silhouette oozed out and congealed into the shape of a cowled man whose features were distinct now that Luke could see him in the spirit plane. The stranger had long black hair, shadowed skin, and the tattoo of a black sun emblazoned on his forehead. His eyes were like chips of obsidian and just as sharp. His mouth bore a cruel scowl, the expression of one who has been betrayed and has had much time to think bitter thoughts.

"Exar Kun," Luke said, and the dark spirit understood him perfectly well.

"Do you enjoy having your spirit trapped away from

your body, Skywalker?" Kun said in a mocking voice. "I have had four thousand years to get accustomed to it. The first century or two are the worst."

Luke glared at him. "You corrupted my students, Exar Kun. You caused the death of Gantoris. You turned Kyp Durron against me."

Kun laughed. "Perhaps it was your own failings as a teacher. Or their own delusions."

"What makes you think I'll stay like this for thousands of years?" Luke said.

"You will have no choice," Kun answered, "once I have destroyed your physical body. Trapping my own spirit inside these temples was the only way I could survive when the final holocaust came. The allied Jedi Knights devastated the surface of Yavin 4. They killed off the few Massassi people I had kept alive, and they destroyed my own body in the inferno.

"My spirit was forced to wait and wait and *wait* until finally you brought your Jedi students here, students who could hear my voice once they learned how to listen."

An echo of fear rang through Luke's mind, but he forced himself to sound calm and brave. "You can't harm my body, Kun. You can't touch anything physical. I've tried it myself."

"Ah, but I know other ways to fight," Kun's spirit said. "And I have had endless millennia to practice. Rest assured, Skywalker, I will destroy you."

As if finished with his taunting, Kun sank like smoke through the cracks in the polished flagstones, descending to the heart of the Great Temple. In his wake he left Luke alone but more determined than ever to break free from his ethereal prison.

He would find a way. A Jedi could always find a way.

When the twins suddenly started crying on their cots beside her, Leia woke up with a feeling of dread.

"It's Uncle Luke!" Jaina said.

"He's gonna be hurt," Jacen said.

Leia bolted upright and felt a series of whistling, tingling vibrations through her body, unlike anything she had ever encountered before. She sensed more than heard the howling wind, a gathering storm trapped inside the temple—centered in the grand audience chamber where Luke lay.

She threw on a white robe, cinched it around her waist, and dashed into the hall. Several other Jedi trainees emerged from their quarters, also sensing an indefinable dread.

The twins jumped out of their beds, and Leia called back to them, "You two stay here." She doubted they would. "Artoo, watch over them!" she shouted to the droid, who was buzzing in confusion down the corridors, lights flashing.

"Come to the grand audience chamber," Leia cried to the Jedi trainees. "Hurry!"

Artoo spun around in the hall and returned to the children's quarters; the droid's confused bleeps and warbles followed Leia down the hall. She rode the turbolift to the top. When it stopped and opened its doors, storm winds howled around the vast, open chamber. Leia stumbled out into a cyclone.

Cold rivers of air gushed through the horizontal skylights high in the walls. Ice crystals sparkled as the temperature plummeted. Wind drawn in from every direction struck the center of the room and spun around, corkscrewing, picking up speed in an irresistible force.

Streen!

The old Bespin hermit stood on the outskirts of the storm with his brown Jedi robe flapping around him. His wild gray hair writhed around his head as if charged with static. His lips mumbled something incomprehensible, and his eyes remained closed as if he were having a nightmare.

Leia knew that even powerful Jedi could not manipulate large-scale phenomena like the weather; but they could move objects, and she realized that was what Streen did now. Not changing the weather, but simply moving the air, drawing it in from all directions, creating a self-contained but destructive tornado that struck toward Luke's body.

"No!" she shouted into the starving wind. "Streen!"

The cyclone struck Luke, buffeted his body, and lifted it into the air. Leia ran toward her paralyzed brother, feet barely touching the ground as the powerful winds knocked her sideways. The storm wrenched her off balance, and she found herself thrown through the air, flying like an insect toward the stone walls. She spun around and reached out, calming herself enough to use her own abilities with the Force, to nudge her body away. Instead of being crushed against the stone blocks, she slid softly to the floor.

Luke's body continued rising, tugged upward by the hurricane. His Jedi robe wound around him as the winds spun him like a corpse launched out of a star-freighter air lock into the grave of space.

Streen didn't seem aware of what he was doing.

Leia staggered to her feet again and jumped. This time she rode the circling air currents, flying around the fringe of the cyclone toward her helpless brother. She reached out to grab the tail of his robe, felt her fingers clutch rough fabric, and then burn as the robe was snatched away from her. She fell back to the floor.

Luke had been drawn up into the tornado's mouth, rising toward the skylights.

"Luke!" she cried. "Please help me." She had no idea if he could hear her, or if he could do anything. Gathering strength in her leg muscles, she leaped into the air again. It might be possible to use her Jedi skills of levitation for a brief moment; Luke had done it several times, although she herself had never mastered the skill. Now, though, it mattered more than it ever had before.

As Leia sprang upward, the wind caught her. She rose high enough to grab Luke's body. She wrapped her arms around his waist, twisted her legs around his ankles, holding him, hoping her weight would drag him down.

But as they started to drop, the winds picked up in intensity, howling and roaring. Leia's skin went numb from the blinding wintry cold. They shot toward the roof of the grand audience chamber, toward the widest skylight, where jagged icicles hung like javelins.

Leia suddenly knew what Streen intended to do to them, whether consciously or unconsciously. They would be sucked out of the Great Temple, tossed high into the sky, and then allowed to crash thousands of feet to the spear-pointed branches of the jungle canopy.

The turbolift door opened. Kirana Ti charged out, followed by Tionne and Kam Solusar.

"Stop Streen!" Leia shouted.

Kirana Ti reacted instantly. She wore thin but supple red armor from the scaled hides of reptiles from Dathomir. She had been a warrior on her own world, fighting with untrained and unhoned skill in the Force, but she had also fought in physical combat as well.

Kirana Ti launched herself forward on long, muscular legs, ducking her head as she charged into the cyclonic wind that surrounded Streen. The old hermit stood entranced, spinning slowly around with his arms dangling at his sides and his fingertips spread apart, as if trying to catch something.

Kirana Ti staggered as she hit the wind, but she wrenched her head aside, spread her legs, and dug the toes of her bare feet against the stone floor for traction. She shoved forward into the wind and finally shattered through into the dead zone of the storm. She tackled Streen to the flagstoned floor and locked his arms behind his back.

Streen cried out, then blinked his eyes open. He looked

wildly around in confusion. Instantly the wind stopped blowing. The air fell still.

High up at the ceiling of the grand audience chamber Leia and Luke plunged toward the unforgiving flagstones below. Luke fell like a doll, and Leia tried to remember how to use her levitation skills, but her mind went blank with panic.

Tionne and Kam Solusar raced forward, stretching out their arms, using what they had been taught. Less than a meter above the crushing stones, Leia found herself slowed, pausing in the air beside Luke's body. They drifted gently to the floor. Leia cradled Luke against her, but her brother did not respond.

Streen sat up, and Kam Solusar ran over to help Kirana Ti hold him. The old hermit began to weep. Kam Solusar gnashed his teeth and looked as if he wanted to kill the old hermit then and there, but Kirana Ti stopped him.

"Don't hurt him," she said. "He doesn't know what he was doing."

"A nightmare," Streen said, "the Dark Man talking to me. Whispering to me. He never lets go. I was fighting him in my dream." Streen looked around for sympathy or encouragement.

"I was going to kill him and save us all, but you woke me." At last Streen realized where he was. He looked around the grand audience chamber until his gaze fell upon Leia holding Luke.

"He tricked you, Streen," Kirana Ti said in a hard voice. "You weren't fighting the Dark Man. He was manipulating you. You were his tool. If we hadn't stopped you, you would have destroyed Master Skywalker."

Streen began sobbing.

On the raised platform Tionne helped Leia lift Luke back onto the stone table. "He doesn't seem injured," Leia said.

"By sheer luck," Tionne said. She wondered aloud,

"Did the ancient Jedi Knights have to deal with challenges like this?"

"If they did," Leia said, "I hope you manage to find the old stories. We need to learn what those Jedi did to defeat their enemies."

Streen stood, shaking himself free of the gripping hands of Kirana Ti and Kam Solusar. The old man's face was filled with outrage. "We must destroy the Dark Man," Streen said, "before he kills all of us."

Leia felt a grip of unbearable cold in her heart, knowing that Streen was right.

8

Being Chief Administrator of Maw Installation was a great enough burden under normal circumstances, but Tol Sivron had never counted on doing it without Imperial assistance. Standing inside the empty conference room, Sivron stroked his sensitive Twi'lek head-tails and stared out the viewport into the empty space around the secret facility.

He had never liked Admiral Daala and her overbearing manner. In the years they had been stranded in the Maw, Sivron had never felt as though she understood his mission to create new weapons of mass destruction for Grand Moff Tarkin—to whom they both owed enormous favors.

Daala's four Star Destroyers had been assigned to protect Sivron and the precious weapons scientists, but Daala had refused to accept her subordinate position in the scheme of things. She had let a few Rebel prisoners steal the Sun Crusher and kidnap one of Sivron's best weapons designers, Qwi Xux. Then Daala had abandoned her post to chase after the spies, leaving him alone and unprotected!

Sivron paced the conference room, puffed with pride and saddled with disappointment. He shook his head, and his two wormlike head appendages slid across his tunic with a tingle of sensory perceptions. He gripped one of the head-tails and wrapped it heavily around his shoulders.

The handful of stormtroopers Daala had left behind served little purpose. Tol Sivron had compiled a full tally of the soldiers: 123. He'd filled out official reports, gathered their service records, compiled information that might someday be useful. It wasn't clear to him exactly *how* this information would be useful, but Sivron had based his career on compiling reports and gathering information. Someone, somewhere, would find it worthwhile.

The stormtroopers obeyed his orders—that was what stormtroopers *did,* after all—but he was no military commander. He didn't know how to deploy the soldiers if Maw Installation was ever attacked by Rebel invaders.

During the last month he had kept the Maw scientists working harder to come up with better prototypes and functional defenses, writing contingency plans and emergency procedures, outlining scenarios and prescribed responses to every situation. *Being prepared is our best weapon,* he thought. Tol Sivron would never stop being prepared.

He had requested frequent progress reports from his researchers, insisting that he be kept completely up-to-date. The storage room adjacent to his office was piled high with hardcopy documents and demonstration models of various concepts. He didn't have time to review them all, of course, but it comforted him just to know they were there.

He heard footsteps approach and saw his four primary division leaders escorted to the morning briefing by their designated stormtrooper bodyguards.

Tol Sivron did not turn to greet them, staring with a thrill of pride at the huge spherical skeleton of the

Death Star prototype rising over the cluster of rocks like a framework moon. The Death Star was the Installation's greatest success. Grand Moff Tarkin had taken one look at the prototype and given him a medal on the spot, along with Bevel Lemelisk, its main designer, and Qwi Xux, his primary assistant.

The four division leaders took their seats around the briefing table, each bringing a hot beverage, each munching on a reconstituted morning pastry. Each carried a hard-copy printout of the morning's agenda.

Sivron decided he would keep the meeting brief and to the point—no longer than two, possibly three, hours. They didn't have much to discuss anyway. As the Death Star orbited out of sight overhead, he turned to face his four top managers.

Doxin was a man wider than he was tall, complete-ly bald except for very dark, very narrow eyebrows that looked like thin wires burned into his forehead. His lips were thick enough that he could have balanced a stylus on them when he smiled. Doxin was in charge of high-energy concepts and implementations.

Next to him sat Golanda. Tall and hawkish with an angular face, pointed chin, and aquiline nose that gave her face the general shape of a Star Destroyer, she was about as beautiful as a gundark. Golanda led the artillery innovations and tactical-deployments section. In ten years she had not stopped complaining about how foolish it was to do artillery research in the middle of a black hole cluster where the fluctuating gravity ruined her calculations and made every test a pointless exercise.

The third division leader, Yemm, was a demonic-looking Devaronian who excelled in saying the right thing at the right time. He supervised documentation and legal counsel.

Last of all, seated at the far corner of the table, was Wermyn, a tall, one-armed brute. His skin had a purplish-green cast that left his origin in question. Wermyn was in charge of plant operations and keeping Maw Installation up and running.

"Good morning, everyone," Tol Sivron said, seating himself at the head of the table and tapping his needle claws on the tabletop. "I see you've all brought your agendas with you. Excellent." He scowled at the four stormtroopers standing outside the door. "Captain, please step outside and close the door. This is a private, high-level meeting."

The stormtrooper made no answer as he ushered his companions outside and sealed the door with a hiss of compressed gases.

"There," Tol Sivron said, shuffling papers in front of him. "I'd like you each to report on recent activities in your division. After we've discussed the possible implications of anything new, we can then brainstorm strategies. I take it our revised Emergency Plans have been distributed to all members of this facility?" Sivron looked at Yemm, the paperwork person.

The Devaronian smiled pleasantly and nodded. The horns on his head bobbed up and down. "Yes, Director. Everyone has received a copy of the full three-hundred-sixty-five-page hard-copy document with instructions to read it diligently."

"Good," Sivron said, checking off the first item on his agenda. "We'll leave time at the end of the meeting for new business, but I'd like to move right along. I still have a lot of reports to review. Wermyn, would you like to begin?"

The one-armed plant operations division leader rumbled through a detailed report on their supplies, their power consumption rates, the expected duration of fuel cells in the power reactor. Wermyn's only concern was that they were running low on spare parts, and he doubted they would ever receive another shipment from the outside.

Tol Sivron duly noted that fact in his log pad.

Next, Doxin slurped his hot beverage and gave a report of a new weapon his scientists had been testing. "It's a metal-crystal phase shifter," Doxin said. "MCPS for short."

"Hmmmm," Tol Sivron said, tapping his chin with a long claw. "We'll have to think of a catchier name before we present it to the Imperials."

"It's just a working acronym," Doxin said, embarrassed. "We've constructed a functioning model, though our results have been inconsistent. The tests have given us reason to hope for a successful larger-scale implementation."

"And what exactly does it do?" Tol Sivron asked.

Doxin scowled at him. "Director, I've filed several reports over the past seven weeks. Haven't you read them?"

Sivron flinched his head-tails instinctively. "I'm a busy man, and I can't recall everything I read," he said. "Especially about a project with such an uninspired name. Refresh my memory, please."

Doxin grew animated as he spoke. "The MCPS field alters the crystalline structure of metals—e.g., those in starship hulls. The MCPS can penetrate conventional shielding and turn hull plates into powder. The actual physics is more complicated, of course; this is just an executive summary."

"Yes, yes," Tol Sivron said. "That sounds very good. What were these problems you encountered?"

"Well, the MCPS worked effectively over only about one percent of the surface area on our test plate."

"So it might not be terribly useful?" Tol Sivron said.

Doxin rubbed his fingers across the polished table surface, making a squeaking sound. "Not exactly true, Director. The one percent effectiveness was distributed over a wide area, leaving pinhole failures over the entire surface. Such a loss of integrity would be enough to destroy any ship."

Sivron grinned. "Ah, very good! Continue your studies and continue filing those excellent reports."

Golanda, the hatchet-faced woman in charge of artillery deployment and tactical innovations, talked about cluster-resonance shells based in part upon preliminary theoretical work for the Sun Crusher.

Yemm interrupted Golanda's summary by standing up and crying out. Sivron frowned at him. "It's not time for new business, Yemm."

"But, Director!" Yemm said, gesturing madly toward the viewport. The other division leaders stood in an uproar.

Tol Sivron finally whirled to see silhouettes against the gaseous backdrop of the Maw. His Twi'lek head-tails uncurled and stood out straight behind him.

A fleet of Rebel warships appeared inside the Maw. The invasion force he had dreaded for so long had finally arrived.

With two Corellian corvettes at point and two at his flanks, General Wedge Antilles brought the escort frigate *Yavaris* toward the mismatched cluster of rocks that formed Maw Installation.

Qwi Xux stood pale blue and beautiful at the observation station beside him, looking tense yet eager to ransack her old quarters for clues to her lost memories.

"Maw Installation," Wedge said into the comm channel. "This is General Antilles, Commander of the New Republic occupation fleet. Please respond to discuss terms of your surrender."

He felt arrogant as he said it, but he knew they had no way of fighting off his fleet. Hidden in the midst of the black holes, without Admiral Daala's Star Destroyers to defend it, the Installation depended on inaccessibility rather than firepower for protection.

As his ships approached the cluster of rocks, Wedge

received no response. But when the open metal framework of the Death Star prototype orbited up from behind the planetoids, he felt a stab of terror.

"Shields up!" he said instinctively.

But the Death Star did not fire, gracefully orbiting back out of view again.

As Wedge brought his fleet in closer, a tracery of laser fire shot toward them from small buildings and habitation modules on the misshapen asteroids. Only a few of the beams managed to strike, reflecting harmlessly off the ships' shields.

"All right," Wedge said. "Two corvettes. Surgical strikes only. We want to remove those defenses, but don't damage the Installation itself." He shot a glance at Qwi. "That place holds too much important data to risk losing it."

Wedge watched the enormous banks of engines behind the foremost two corvettes as they rained destructive blasts upon the asteroids. Bright-red spears lanced down to pulverize the rocks.

"This is too easy," Wedge said.

A desperate signal came from one of the corvette captains. His image flickered as he beamed a transmission on the emergency channel. "Something's happening to our hull! Shields aren't effective. Some new kind of weapon. Hull walls are weakening. Can't pinpoint where—"

The transmission cut off as the corvette became a ball of fire and shrapnel.

"Back off!" Wedge shouted into the open channel, but the second corvette plunged forward, choosing instead to use his full complement of dual turbolaser cannons as well as a pair of proton torpedoes that had been specially installed for the occupation mission. "Captain Ortola! Back off!"

The captain of the second corvette blasted the nearest planetoid. Proton torpedoes sizzled with uncontained

energy. Turbolaser blasts ignited volatile gases and flam-
mables, reducing the small planetoid to incandescent dust.

"That won't be a problem anymore, sir," Captain Ortola
said. "You may deploy the strike forces at your leisure."

Howling warnings shrieked through the Maw Installation's intercom so monotonously that Tol Sivron found it
difficult to plan his speech.

"Your attention, please," he said into the intercom.
"Remember to follow your emergency procedures."

Outside, stormtroopers hustled up and down the white-
tiled corridors. The stormtrooper captain was yelling and
directing his troops to set up defensive positions at vital
intersections. No one bothered to refer to the carefully
written and tested contingency scenarios Tol Sivron and
his managers had spent so much time developing.

Gritting his pointed teeth in annoyance, Sivron raised
his voice into the intercom. "If you need another copy
of your emergency procedures, or if you have difficulty finding one, contact your respective division leader
immediately. We will see to it that you receive one."

Hanging above Maw Installation, the Rebel ships looked
like nightmarish constructions, brushing aside the Installation's defensive lasers as if they were mere insect bites.

Doxin sat by an interlaboratory communication station
and cheered as he saw one of the Rebel corvettes crumble,
disintegrating into a cloud of pulverized metal plate and
escaping fuel and coolant gases.

"It worked!" Doxin said. "The MCPS worked!" He
tapped the receiving jack in his ear, listened, and frowned
with his enormous lips. When Doxin wrinkled the brow on
his bald head, the ridges rippled all the way up to his
crown like rugged-terrain treads.

"Unfortunately, we won't get a second shot, Director.
The MCPS seems to have malfunctioned," Doxin said.

"But I do believe the original success against an actual target has proved the system worthy of additional development."

"Indeed," Tol Sivron agreed, looking admiringly at the expanding cloud of debris from the corvette. "We must have a follow-up meeting."

"The system is presently off-line," Doxin said.

The second Rebel corvette came in with all weapons blazing, and the asteroid housing the offices and labs of the high-energy concepts incinerated under the barrage.

"It appears to be unquestionably out of commission," Sivron said.

Doxin was deeply disappointed. "Now we'll never conduct a post-shot analysis," he said with a sigh. "It's going to be hard to compile a full report without actual data."

A loud *whump* reverberated through the facility. Tol Sivron peered out into the hall as his division leaders crowded to get a view. White-and-gray smoke curled down the corridors, clogging the ventilation systems.

The screens on the computer monitors inside the conference room went blank. As Sivron stood up to demand an explanation, the lights in all the offices winked out, replaced by a pale-green glow of emergency systems.

The stormtrooper captain rushed up with a clatter of boots on the tiled floor.

"Captain, what's going on?" Tol Sivron said. "Report."

"We have just successfully destroyed the main computer core, sir," he said.

"You did *what*?" Sivron asked.

The captain continued in his staccato voice. "We need your personal codes to access the backup files, Director. We will irradiate them to erase the classified information."

"Is that in the emergency procedures?" Tol Sivron looked from right to left for an answer from his division leaders. He picked up the hardcopy of the Emergency

Procedures manual. "Captain, which page did you find that on?"

"Sir, we cannot allow our vital data to fall into Rebel hands. The computer backups must be destroyed before the invaders take possession of this facility."

"I'm not sure we addressed that contingency when we wrote the manual," Golanda said with a shrug, flipping pages as well.

"Perhaps we'll have to put that in an addendum?" Yemm suggested.

Standing, Wermyn shuffled through the papers with his one meaty hand. "Director, I see here in Section 5.4, 'In the Event of Rebel Invasion,' Paragraph (C). If such an invasion appears likely to succeed in gaining possession of the Installation, I am to lead my team in a mission to the power-reactor asteroid and destroy the cooling towers so that the system will go supercritical and wipe out both this base and the invaders as well."

"Good, good!" Tol Sivron said, finding the right page and verifying the words for himself. "Get to it."

Wermyn stood up. His swarthy greenish-purple skin flushed darker. "All these procedures have been approved, Director, but I don't quite follow our next step. How is my team going to get to safety? In fact, how are any of us going to get to safety once I've set up the chain reaction?"

A stormtrooper's voice cut through the alarm chatter on the intercom. "Rebel troops have entered the base! Rebel troops have entered the—" The words ended in a squawk of dead static.

"Sound the evacuation order," Sivron said, beleaguered. He stared out the sweeping viewing window with his close-set, beady eyes. Rebel battleships pummeled the Installation. Then a glinting metal framework rose into view, an armillary sphere the size of a small moon.

"Just go and take care of the reactors, Wermyn," Tol

Sivron said. "We'll fall back and evacuate to the Death Star prototype. We can swing by and pick you up, then make our escape. We'll abandon the Rebels to their deaths and take our precious knowledge back to the Empire."

Three transports bearing New Republic strike teams landed on the Installation's central asteroid, blasting through the closed bay doors with their forward laser cannons. As the transports opened egress doors like mechanical wings, the teams flooded out of the passenger compartments and fanned into defensive phalanxes. Crouched low, heads ducked behind blaster-resistant armor, they held high-energy rifles in front of them.

Chewbacca let out a Wookiee bellow as he thumped down the ramp, holding his bowcaster in front of him. He squeezed a hairy paw around the stock and pointed the crossbow-shaped weapon. His fur bristled. He smelled smoke, oil, and coolant fumes. Chewbacca scooped the air with his hairy paw, gesturing for the elite team of Page's Commandos to follow.

Blaster shots rang out as four stormtroopers fired from ambush. A member of one of the other strike teams went down, then forty blaster bolts converged on the Imperial soldiers.

Chewbacca remembered being a prisoner in the Maw Installation, when he had been forced to perform maintenance on Admiral Daala's ships. He had been tempted to sabotage one of their gamma-class assault shuttles, but knew that it would only get him killed while causing no irreparable harm to the Imperial forces.

Now, though, Chewbacca kept thinking of the other Wookiee slaves. He remembered their bowed heads and patchy fur, their gaunt frames. The fire in their eyes had gone out after years of hard and hopeless labor.

With a barely contained snarl he also remembered the sadistic lump of a man who served as the Wookiee "Keeper," watching over the slave detail no matter where they were assigned. His blazing eyes, broken-glass voice, and deadly force whip had kept the Wookiees in line through intimidation.

Alarms shrieked through the intercoms, pumping Chewbacca's adrenaline and anger. He growled for the teams to hurry. He thought about See-Threepio still onboard the flagship *Yavaris* and was glad the protocol droid would not be in all the cross fire now. Chewbacca didn't want to have to put Threepio back together all over again.

He approached a vast rock-walled workroom, where he remembered performing endless hours of heavy labor. The doors stood sealed by heavy blast shields with rivets the size of Chewbacca's knuckles.

He hammered on the metal door with his flat palm. Behind him Page's Commandos rummaged in their packs. Two members rushed forward with thermal detonators in each hand. They placed the detonators at critical junctures on the blast door and flicked the timer switches. Amber lights winked on and off, counting down.

"Back away!" one yelled.

Chewbacca loped after the team as they ran around the corner just in time to hear a muffled explosion. An instant later a much louder sound reverberated as the heavy blast door clanged to the floor.

"Move out," the strike-team leader said.

Chewbacca charged forward through the smoke as he pushed into the sealed bay. He heard thin hissing sounds, like lightning strikes mixed with outraged bellows of pain. The captive Wookiees were in such a frenzied state that they had forgotten their own language.

As the smoke cleared, Chewbacca was disappointed to find the battle already over—but he was elated that the Wookiees had finally taken a stand upon hearing the alarms and sensing that the tide of their misery had turned.

Nine Wookiees had converged on the Keeper, who now stood backed against a half-disassembled *Lambda*-class Imperial shuttle. The Keeper was barrel-shaped with oily skin enhanced by a sheen of terrified sweat. His lips pulled back in a snarl of defiance, and he kept lashing out with serpent strikes of his force whip. The Wookiees growled, trying to come close enough to rip him apart with their claws.

Chewbacca let out his own roar of challenge. Some of the Wookiees glanced up at the rescue force, but other hairy giants were so transfixed by their chance to get the Keeper that they paid no heed.

"Drop your weapon," the commando-team leader said to the Keeper. All of the blaster rifles were directed toward him. It amused Chewbacca to see the cruel man glance at the New Republic force with an expression of relief.

The Wookiees continued to snarl. They looked worse now than they had appeared only months earlier. No doubt without the protection of Admiral Daala's fleet, the Keeper had forced the slaves to work even harder to arrange other defenses for Maw Installation.

"Drop your weapon, I said!" the strike-team commander insisted.

The Keeper flicked his force whip once more, driving the Wookiee mob back. Chewbacca saw the three largest males in front, their fur streaked and patchy, burned from lashes of the whip and shiny with waxlike welts from old scars. The oldest gray-furred Wookiee, whom Chewbacca remembered as Nawruun, crouched by the edge of the shuttle, hiding under the sharp panels of the ship's upfolded wings. The old Wookiee's bones seemed twisted and crushed from years of labor, but the anger in his eyes was brighter than a star.

The Keeper raised his force whip, stared at the Wookiees, then at Page's Commandos. The human team leader fired a warning shot, which *spang*ed off the chamber walls. The Keeper raised his other hand in surrender, then let the handle of his force whip fall to the ground. It clinked on the smooth deck plates.

"All right, now, back away," the team leader said.

Chewbacca offered his own words in the Wookiee language. The astonished prisoners stood tense for a moment. The Keeper looked ready to collapse in terror, when suddenly old Nawruun dived to the floor, lunging with a hairy paw to snatch the handle of the whip. He fumbled the activation switches.

The Keeper shrieked and backed against the wall, looking for someplace to hide. Chewbacca yowled for the Wookiees to stop, but they didn't hear him as they all surged forward, claws extended, ready to shred the Keeper into bloody pieces.

Nawruun sprang upon the man's barrellike form. Though he was misshapen and old, the hunched Wookiee gripped the force whip like a club and tackled the Keeper to the floor. The burly man screamed and flailed.

The other Wookiees fell upon him. Nawruun jammed the handle of the force whip into the Keeper's face and switched on the weapon at full power.

The lance of lashing energy drilled into the Keeper's head, skirling fireworks inside his brainpan. Sparks came out of his eye sockets, until the Keeper's skull shattered, showering the hysterical Wookiee prisoners with gore.

Silence thundered down upon the chamber.

Chewbacca walked carefully forward as the surviving Wookiees withered. Without any stamina or fury, they backed away from the corpse of their tormentor. Old Nawruun stood again and stared blankly down at the force whip in his hand. He let it drop.

It struck the floor with a hollow sound, and Nawruun

crumpled beside it. His body shuddered, and he made hollow sounds as he wept.

Tol Sivron tried to find a comfortable place to sit back and relax in the pilot compartment of the Death Star, but the prototype had not been designed for niceties.

Racks of equipment stood surrounded by bare wires and clumsy welds. Girders and reinforced framework blocked his view of most of the embattled Installation, but he could see that the Rebel forces had overrun the facility.

At the outer perimeter of the clustered planetoids, the tangled cooling towers and radiation vanes of the power reactor suddenly glowed bright and began to collapse.

Wermyn's gruff voice came over the radio. "Director Sivron, our explosives have destroyed the coolant systems. The power reactor will soon go supercritical. I don't think the attackers can stop it. Maw Installation is doomed."

"Very well, Wermyn," Sivron said, dismayed at the loss of capital equipment—but what could he do, after all? His Imperial guardians had deserted him. He and his division leaders had done quite a creditable job of putting up a fight. Without any military help they couldn't be expected to succeed against a well-armed strike force, could they? Besides, they were following established procedure. No one could fault them for that.

Sivron looked at the stormtrooper captain and at the other three division leaders. The rest of the Maw scientists and stormtrooper contingents had taken refuge inside the prototype's supply and control rooms.

"I have not had a chance to read the complete technical readouts of this battle-station prototype." Tol Sivron looked around. "Does anyone know how to fly this vessel?"

Golanda looked at Doxin, who in turn looked at Yemm. The stormtrooper captain said, "I have had some experience flying attack vehicles, sir. Perhaps I can interpret the controls."

"Good, Captain," Tol Sivron said. "Ummm . . ." He stood up from his command chair. "Do you need to sit here?"

"No need, sir. I can handle it from the pilot station." The captain went over to a bolted-together row of controls.

"They must have detected Wermyn's explosions," Doxin said, watching the Rebel attack ships clustered around the reactor planetoid. Two more shuttles descended as teams were deployed down to the power station. The combined Rebel firepower would block all rescue attempts.

"Now, how are we supposed to get Wermyn?" Sivron said.

Yemm began to flip through the Emergency Procedures manual again. "I don't think we addressed that contingency either."

Tol Sivron's head-tails thrashed in extreme annoyance. "That's not very good, is it?" He scowled, trying to figure out how he could adapt on the spot. Twi'leks were good at adapting. Sivron had managed to adapt when he left his home planet of Ryloth; he had adapted when Moff Tarkin had assigned him as director of the think tank. Now he would adapt his plans again to make the best of a situation that was growing worse by the minute.

"All right, so there's no time to rescue Wermyn. Change of plans. Our duty is to the Empire. We must take this Death Star prototype and make a rapid retreat."

Wermyn himself had seen the Rebel strike teams coming down to retake the reactor planetoid, and he contacted Tol Sivron again with a more frantic tenor in his voice. "Director, what can I do to assist you? How are you planning to rescue us?"

Tol Sivron opened the channel and said in his gravest, most sincere voice, "Wermyn, I just want you to know how much I admire and respect you for your years of service. I regret that your retirement cannot be as long and as happy as I had hoped it would be. Once again, accept my appreciation. Thank you."

He signed off, then turned to the stormtrooper captain. "We need to get out of here now."

When the heaviest fighting began to die away, Qwi Xux shuttled down to the Installation with Wedge Antilles. Qwi saw the planetoids growing larger as they approached. She had spent most of her life down there, but she remembered little of it.

Other than the destruction of the first corvette, the New Republic fleet had suffered minimal losses. The Maw scientists had put up even less resistance than Wedge had feared. Qwi looked forward now to going through her old labs, eager to find her own files in hopes of answering some of her questions . . . but afraid to learn the answers.

Wedge reached over to hold her hand. "It'll be fine. You'll be a great help. Wait and see."

She looked longingly at him with her large eyes. "I'll do my best." But something caught her attention, and she pointed quickly. "Look, Wedge! We've got to stop it."

The Death Star prototype rose away from Maw Installation under its own power, glistening in the reflected light of the gas cloud.

"According to my own records, Maw Installation had a fully functional prototype," Qwi said. "If they take that Death Star into New Republic space—"

Before she could complete her sentence, the gigantic sphere of the Death Star shot away toward the edge of the black hole cluster and vanished into the masking clouds of superhot gas.

9

Terpfen stood in the looming
shadow of the Great Temple as Yavin's early daylight increased, warming the jungles until mists rose in the air.

Paralyzed with fear in front of the towering, ancient
ziggurat, Terpfen swiveled his circular eyes to look back
to the landing area where his stolen B-wing fighter rested,
humming and ticking as it cooled among the cropped
weeds. He saw discolored smears on its hull from where
the pursuing X-wing fighters on Coruscant had scored
direct hits.

Looking up, he spotted several of the Jedi candidates,
tiny figures atop the temple. As the jungle moon orbited
around the gas giant, the configuration of the system set
up an unusual phenomenon that had filled the Rebels with
wonder when they first established the small moon as a
secret base.

Bright sunlight streaming through the upper layers of
the Yavin primary refracted in many different colors, then
struck the moon's atmosphere, filtered through the rising

mists to let loose a shower of rainbows that lasted only minutes with each dawn. The Jedi trainees, gathered to watch the rainbow storm high above, had seen his ship land. They were coming.

In a slick fighter jumpsuit that bore no insignia, Terpfen felt his heart pounding, his mind whirling. Confessing his traitorous acts frightened him the most—but Terpfen had to face it. He tried to rehearse his words, but decided that it would not help. There was no good way to share the terrible news.

He felt dizzy, ready to faint, and grasped the cool, moss-covered blocks of the temple with one flippered hand. He feared that Carida had somehow found him again, that Furgan was sinking his clutches into the organic components that had been substituted for parts of Terpfen's brain.

No! It was *his* mind now! He had not felt the tug from his Imperial controllers for over a day now. He'd forgotten what it was like to think his own thoughts, and he had tested the new freedom with growing wonder. He fantasized about overthrowing the Empire, about throttling bug-eyed Ambassador Furgan.

And during these thoughts no shadowy presence squashed his mind. He felt so . . . free!

He realized the faintness was just his numbing fright. The feeling passed, and Terpfen stood straight again as he heard footsteps approach.

The first to emerge into the bright daylight was Minister of State Leia Organa Solo herself. She must have run to the turbolift, expecting that the B-wing fighter carried some emergency message from Coruscant. Her hair looked mussed and windblown, and shadows haunted her eyes. Her face wore a concerned frown, as if something else already troubled her.

Terpfen felt the cold despair increase within him. She

would be even more agonized after he told her that the Imperials knew the location of her son Anakin.

Leia stopped and looked gravely at him, sizing him up. Her brows drew together in thought, and then she said his name. "I know you. Terpfen, right? Why have you come here?"

Terpfen knew that his battered bulbous head and the lumpy mappings of scars made him recognizable even to humans. Behind Leia came several Jedi students Terpfen did not recognize, until he saw Ambassador Cilghal. The female Calamarian's large round eyes seemed to bore into his soul.

"Minister Organa Solo . . . ," Terpfen said in a quavering voice. Then he collapsed to his knees, partly in abject misery and partly because his legs refused to support him any longer. "Your son Anakin is in grave danger!"

He hung his scarred head. Before she could fire off laser-sharp questions, Terpfen confessed everything.

Leia stared down at Terpfen's scarred head and felt as if she were being strangled. Luke and Ackbar's intricate security and secrecy about Anoth had been breached! The Empire knew where to find her baby son.

Leia understood little about the defenses on the sheltered, hellish world. Now her servant and friend Winter was the only protection baby Anakin had.

"Please, Minister Organa Solo—we must go to Anoth at once," Terpfen said. "We must send them a message, evacuate your child before an Imperial strike squad can reach him. While I was under Furgan's influence, I transmitted Anoth's coordinates to Carida, but I did not keep a copy of them. I destroyed that information. You must take us there yourself. I will do whatever I can to help, but we must move quickly."

Leia made ready to leap into action, ready to do anything necessary to save her son. But a paralyzing realization brought her up short. "I can't contact Anoth. Even *I* don't know where the planet is!"

Terpfen stared at her, but she couldn't read expressions on his angular, aquatic face. She continued. "It was kept secret from me, too. The only ones who knew were Winter—and she's *on* Anoth—and Ackbar, who is now hiding on Calamari, and Luke, who's in a coma. I don't know how to get there!"

She steadied herself, trying to recall how fast-thinking she had been in her younger days. On the first Death Star she had taken charge during Han and Luke's ill-planned rescue. She had known what to do then. She had acted quickly and without hesitation.

But now she had three children to care for, and her new priorities seemed to scramble her single-mindedness. Han had already departed to search for Kyp Durron and the Sun Crusher. She'd been left here with the twins, supposedly to keep them safe. She couldn't just leave now.

Ambassador Cilghal seemed to sense her thoughts. "You must go, Leia. Go save your son. Your twin children will be safe here. The Jedi students will protect them."

As if suddenly freed of something she hadn't known was binding her, Leia felt plans plunge into her conscious mind. Relaxing, she became cool and decisive. "All right, Terpfen, you're coming with me. We'll go to Calamari as fast as we can. We'll find Ackbar, and he can take us to Winter and Anakin." She looked at the traitor with a complex mixture of anger and hope, pity and sorrow.

He turned away. "No. What if the Imperials activate me again? What if I am forced to commit some new sabotage?"

"I'll keep my eyes peeled," she said in a hard voice. "But I want you to come see Ackbar." She thought of the Calamarian admiral's misery, how he had gone to hide in the wilderness of his planet so others would not have to look at his shame. "You're going to explain to him that he wasn't at fault in the Vortex crash."

Terpfen worked his way back to his feet. He wobbled on his feet, but finally stood firm. "Minister Organa Solo," he said. His voice sounded as if he had swallowed something unpleasant. "I—I am sorry."

She shot a look at him, but she felt adrenaline pumping through her, a need to be on the move, to do anything possible. Hesitation could mean the loss of everything.

"Apologize when this is all over," she said. "Right now I need your help."

10

The *Millennium Falcon* emerged from hyperspace near the coordinates of the destroyed Caridan star system.

Han Solo polarized the segmented viewport to look out at the rubble that had recently been a group of planets and a burning sun; now he saw only a slash of still-glowing gases, a sea of radiation from the supernova. The sheer destruction was on a scale greater even than when he had emerged from hyperspace to find Alderaan reduced to broken debris—back before he had even met Leia, before he had thrown his lot in with the Rebellion, and before he had believed in the Force.

Carida's exploded star had spewed stellar material in a thick band around the ecliptic, vast curtains of roiling gases that glowed and crackled with intense energy across the spectrum. A shock wave plowed through space, where it would dissipate over thousands of years.

Under his high-resolution scanners Han spotted a few twisted cinders, burned-out lumps of worlds that had been the outer planets in the system. Now they shone like embers in a dying fire.

Lando Calrissian sat beside him, his mouth open in amazement. "Boy, that kid sure knows how to cause damage."

Han nodded. His throat felt dry and raw. It felt strange not to have Chewbacca in the copilot's seat. He hoped his Wookiee friend was having an easier time on his mission than Han was.

The *Falcon*'s sensor banks barely coped with the overloading energies that pulsed through the wreckage of the Caridan system. X rays and gamma rays hammered against his shields. But Han saw no sign of Kyp.

"Han, what do you think you'll find with all this static? If you're real sharp and real lucky, you might detect an ion trace from the Sun Crusher's sublight engines, but in the middle of a supernova you'll never pick up the track. Odds are—"

Han cut him off with a raised hand. "Never quote me the odds. You know better than that."

Lando grinned. "Yeah, I know, I know. So what are we going to do? What was the point of coming to this system?"

Han pressed his lips together, searching for an answer. It had felt right to come to Carida to pick up Kyp's trail. "I want to see what he saw," he said, "think like he might have been thinking. What was going through his mind?"

"You know him better than I do, buddy. If he ignited the Cauldron Nebula to wipe out Admiral Daala, and now he blew up the Imperial military training center, where would he go next? Think for yourself. What would be your next target?"

Han stared out at the inferno of what had been Carida's sun. "If my goal was to strike out at the Empire, causing as much damage as possible . . . I would head for . . ." He turned sharply and looked at Lando.

Lando's deep-brown eyes flew open. "That's too dangerous. He wouldn't go there!"

Han said, "I don't think dangerous has anything to do with it."

"Let me guess. Next, you'll say that we're going to follow him to the Core Systems."

"You got it, old buddy." Han set the coordinates in the navicomputer, and he heard Lando mumble to himself.

"Now I'll never get to Kessel on time."

The glowing gases of Carida's exploded star funneled around them as space elongated. The *Falcon* shot into hyperspace, heading far behind enemy lines and deep into the heart of the remaining forces of the Empire.

Near the bright heart of the galaxy, where stars lay close together in uncharted configurations, the resurrected Emperor had gathered his defenses to make a last stand. But since Palpatine's destruction, the Imperial warlords had fought each other for control. With no military genius like Grand Admiral Thrawn to unify the remnants, the Imperial war machine had withdrawn into the protected Core Systems. The warlords had left the victorious New Republic to lick its wounds while they vied for supremacy in their own corner of the galaxy.

But when one military leader managed to come out on top, the forces would strike against the New Republic. Unless Kyp Durron destroyed them first.

Han and Lando found an exploded red-dwarf star on the fringes of the Core. The small, dim sun had been unremarkable, and according to the *Falcon*'s planetary atlas, had no habitable worlds. However, scouts had determined that the red-dwarf system sheltered a starship-construction yard, weapons depot, and storage for archives shielded in thick vaults deep within several lifeless, rocky planets.

Han looked out the viewport and saw that the small star

had exploded in a less-spectacular fashion than Carida's sun, a fizzle without enough mass to generate a significant chain reaction. But the shock fronts had still pulverized and incinerated the closely orbiting planets.

"He's done it again," Han said. "You can't miss a trail like the one Kyp is leaving."

Lando squinted at the scanners. "I'm tracking eleven Victory-class Star Destroyers heading out of the system."

"That's just great," Han said. He had enough to worry about with Kyp and the Sun Crusher; he didn't want to tangle with an Imperial fleet at the same time. "Have they picked us up yet?"

"Don't think so. There's still a lot of radiation and interference from that explosion. Looks to me like they just packed up and ran."

Han felt hope blossom in him. "You think this happened recently? Kyp just triggered the star explosion?"

"Could be."

"All right. Then you'd better scan for—"

"Already got him, Han. The Sun Crusher is sitting high above the ecliptic like he's just . . . watching."

"Plot a course," Han said, sitting up straight. "We're going after him. Full speed."

He punched the thrusters, and the *Falcon*'s bank of sublight engines blazed white. The acceleration shoved Han and Lando back into their seats as the ship made a graceful loop, heading above the orbital plane and approaching the blip on their sensors. As the *Falcon* closed the gap, though, the Sun Crusher began to flit away.

"He's spotted us. After him!" Han said. "If he jumps to lightspeed, we've lost him."

The *Falcon* shot forward. Han sighted on a bright speck moving across their path against the starfield.

"Want me to power up the lasers, Han?" Lando asked. "We're not going to shoot him, are we? What if he doesn't stop?"

"Wouldn't do any good to shoot him—not with that quantum armor of his." Han opened a comm channel. "Kyp, it's me, Han Solo. Kid, we've got to talk to you."

In answer the Sun Crusher winked as it changed course and increased speed.

"Punch it," Han said. "Let's go."

"We're already pushing the red lines," Lando said.

"She'll hold together," Han answered, then bent to the comm system again. "Hey, Kyp, listen to me."

The Sun Crusher arced around and began to grow larger in the viewport.

"Ah . . . Han?" Lando said. "He's coming right at us."

Han felt exhilarated, glad that Kyp was turning around to talk with them.

"I think he's going to ram us," Lando said.

Han blinked in disbelief. He bent over the transmitter. "Kyp, don't do this. Kyp! It's me, Han."

The Sun Crusher hurtled past them, swerving at the last moment to fire a burst of lasers from the defensive weapons mounted on its hull. Han heard the blasts thump against the *Falcon*, but they caused no damage.

"Must have been a warning," Lando said.

"Yeah, some warning," Han answered. "Kyp, why don't—"

The young man's brittle voice finally came at them. "Han, leave me alone. Go away. I've got work to do."

"Ummm, Kyp—that's what I'd like to talk with you about," Han said, suddenly at a loss for words.

The Sun Crusher hurtled toward them as if for another strafing run. As the small craft rushed past, Han worked the controls and yanked out with the *Millennium Falcon*'s tractor beam, latching on to the small superweapon. "Hey, I caught him!" Han said in surprise.

The momentum of the Sun Crusher was enough to jerk the *Falcon* around, but the tractor beams held. Han pumped up the power, increasing his invisible grip. Finally both ships came to a relative dead standstill high above the orbital plane of the exploded red-dwarf star.

"All right, Han," Kyp said. "If this is the way you want it . . . I can't let you stop me." The comm system fell silent.

"I don't like the sound of that," Lando said.

Kyp's voice returned. "One of these resonance torpedoes is enough to make a whole star blow up. I'm sure it'll make short work of a piece of junk like the *Falcon*."

Han looked out at the crystalline shape of the Sun Crusher. The toroidal projector glowed a crackling blue and green, powering up to launch one of its projectiles at point-blank range.

"I've got a bad feeling about this," Han said.

11

The midmorning light shone through open skylights into the temple's grand audience chamber. Golden sunbeams dappled the polished flagstones, reflecting onto the rough-hewn walls.

From the raised platform behind his motionless body, the spirit of Luke Skywalker watched as Cilghal led the young twins on another visit. Cilghal held the twins' hands, gliding forward with fluid steps. This morning she wore her bluish ambassadorial garment instead of her drab Jedi robe. Behind the Calamarian ambassador came a guilt-ridden Streen beside muscular and supple Kirana Ti.

Artoo-Detoo hovered close to Luke's body, like a sentry rolling back and forth. The astromech droid had taken it upon himself to guard the Jedi Master after the devastating storm. Luke found the little droid's loyalty deeply touching, though not surprising.

Han and Leia's twin children stared wide-eyed at Luke, and his spirit watched them back longingly. Unable to communicate, he felt trapped. What would Obi-Wan have done in such a situation? He believed the Force would give him an answer, if he knew where to look.

"You see, children? Your Uncle Luke is safe. We rescued him last night. Your mother helped. We all helped. We're still trying to find some way to wake him up."

"I am awake!" Luke shouted into the empty spirit plane. "I've got to find a way to communicate that to you."

The twins stared at the motionless body. "He is awake," Jacen said. "He's right there." The little boy tilted his dark eyes up to gaze directly at Luke's spirit.

With a jolt Luke stared back at Jacen. "You can see me, Jacen? Can you understand me?"

Both Jaina and Jacen nodded their heads.

Cilghal wrapped her hands around their shoulders and steered them away. "Of course he is, children."

Thrilled and suddenly hopeful, Luke started to drift after them, but Streen came to the platform and threw himself to his knees, looking so stricken that waves of confusion rippled from him like a physical blow to Luke.

"Master Skywalker, I am deeply sorry!" Streen said. "I listened to the wrong voices in my head. The Dark Man tricked me. He will never do that again." Streen looked up, his eyes unfocused, flicking from side to side. He seemed to stare at Luke as well.

"Can you see me too, Streen? Can you hear me?" Luke thought fast, wondering if his abilities had changed.

"The Dark Man came to me," Streen said. "But I sense you're here too, Master Skywalker. I will never doubt you."

Kirana Ti squeezed Streen's shoulder. Luke's mind raced. Exar Kun could communicate with the others, if only in subtle ways—and now Luke knew that was possible for him too. He could already speak to the twins. Elation swept over him.

He began to make plans as the other Jedi candidates filed out of the echoing room. Now he was confident he could save himself, perhaps with the help of his Jedi students, his new generation of Jedi Knights.

From the stone walls behind him an otherworldly voice said, "How touching. Your clumsy students still imagine they can save you—but I know more than they do. My training wasn't limited by cowardice, as yours was."

Exar Kun stood black and wavering. "Gantoris was mine, and he is destroyed. Kyp Durron remains under my tutelage. Streen is already mine. The others will also begin to hear my voice." He raised his spectral arms. "It is all falling into place.

"I shall resurrect the Brotherhood of the Sith, and with your Jedi trainees I shall form the core of an invincible Force-wielding army."

Luke rounded on him, still not knowing how to fight this intangible enemy. Exar Kun laughed, as if an idea had just occurred to him. "I came to you first in a dream disguised as your fallen father, Skywalker . . . perhaps I should appear to them in your own form. They will certainly follow the teachings of the Sith if the words come from your mouth."

"No!" Luke said. With his astral body he leaped to tackle the shimmering silhouette of the Sith lord. But though his sparkling body passed smoothly through the shadow, Exar Kun did seem to discorporate momentarily.

Luke felt a spear of ice plunge through his core as he touched Kun, but he stood firm while the Dark Lord reeled against the stone wall, seeping back into the cracks to escape.

"I've already been tempered by the dark side," Luke said. "I came out stronger. You are weak because you know *only* the evil teachings. Your understanding is no greater than that of my apprentices."

Before he vanished, Exar Kun called back, "We shall see who is stronger."

• • •

The sun had set behind the giant ball of Yavin. With the onset of the moon's half night, the sky was lit only by an orangish glow reflected from the gas giant, giving the jungle a ruddy appearance.

Colonies of jabbering woolamanders settled down in the high branches for the night. In the underbrush, predators and prey moved through dances of survival. Sapphire-blue piranha beetles buzzed low over the sluggish rivers in search of victims. Other insects hummed their mating songs.

Far deeper in the jungle, though, night creatures rose out of shadowy caves and flapped their jagged wings. Hissing and mindless, they followed a burning compulsion that drove them toward the Great Temple. . . .

The creatures' wings made sounds like wet cloth striking stone as they flapped against downdrafts in the rapidly cooling air. Purplish veins pulsed as their black hearts beat swiftly, giving them energy for the long flight.

Two heads spread out on long, sinuous necks from each muscular torso. A wicked tail dangled behind each creature, ending in a hooked stinger that glistened with crystals of poison. Iridescent scales glittered in the coppery dusk light, as if illuminated by stoked embers. Yellow reptilian eyes widened their pupil slits, seeking their target.

Alchemical monsters created long ago during the dominion of Exar Kun on Yavin 4, these creatures had lived for generations in the black and dripping grottoes of distant mountains. Now three of them had awakened, called to destroy the body of Luke Skywalker.

The flying creatures struck the open skylights at the apex of the ziggurat. With metallic claws they scrabbled on the weathered stones that framed narrow windows. Each creature's double heads bobbed up and down, hissing and snapping in anticipation.

Folding their batlike wings against them, they squirmed through the skylights into the open chamber. Moving together, the creatures descended toward Luke's helpless body, long talons extended. . . .

Luke's image shimmered but cast no light in the dim chambers where the twins lay sleeping. The door was open. Cilghal sat up studying in her own room across the corridor, but she could not yet hear Luke's voice. The boy Jacen could—and Luke had no time.

"Jacen," he said with his muffled inside-the-head voice. The boy stirred. Beside him Jaina sighed and rolled over in her sleep. "Jacen!" Luke said again. "Jaina, I need your help. Only you can help me."

The boy woke up, blinking his dark eyes. He scanned the room, yawned, then fixed his eyes upon Luke's image. "Uncle Luke?" he said. "Help? Okay."

"Wake your sister and follow me. Tell her to raise the alarm and bring all the other Jedi. But you have to help me now! Maybe you can hold them off long enough."

Jacen didn't ask questions. By the time he shook his sister, she had already started to awaken. She too saw Luke, and the boy needed only a few words to explain the situation.

Jacen trotted down the hall on his little legs. Luke drifted in front of him, urging Jacen faster, faster, toward the turbolift.

Jaina ran into Cilghal's quarters and screamed, "Help, help!" at the top of her lungs. "Uncle Luke needs help." The Jedi trainees surged out of their quarters.

Suddenly alarms rang out. Luke realized that Artoo, still standing sentry duty in the grand audience chamber, must have triggered them. He didn't know, though, what the astromech droid could do against the monstrous winged creatures summoned by Exar Kun.

Jacen hesitated inside the turbolift while Luke showed which button to push. "Hurry, Jacen!" Luke said. The turbolift shot upward and spilled them into the vast, dim chamber.

Down at the end of the promenade, Artoo hummed back and forth, whistling and warbling shrilly. His arc-welding arm extended, flashing blue sparks, but the reptilian creatures flapped into the air, circling around the sluggish droid as if they considered Artoo to be no threat.

Two of the creatures flapped up from the raised platform upon hearing the turbolift doors open. They honked and hissed, spitting at the very small boy who emerged alone to challenge them.

Artoo squealed, as if thankful for any sort of help. The alarms continued to hammer through the temple.

The third creature perched at the edge of the long stone table on which Luke's body lay. Its two heads bobbed forward to let out a dual squeal of annoyance. One of the heads snapped down to tear a mouthful of cloth from Luke's robe. The other head curled back scaled lips and flashed a jagged row of fangs.

"They're angry," Jacen said as if he had some kind of empathy with the creatures. "They're . . . wrong."

"Chase them away from my body, Jacen," Luke said, eyeing the poisonous stingers on their tails, the vicious teeth, the sharp claws. . . . "Go help Artoo. The others will be here in just a few seconds."

Without fear Jacen shrieked like a wild warrior as he ran toward the monsters on his stubby legs. He flailed his arms, yelling.

Two of the creatures squawked and swooped into the air, then flapped their leathery wings to dive at him. Artoo whistled a warning.

Jacen ducked at the last moment. The creatures dragged their hooked metallic claws on the flagstone floor, sending up showers of sparks. The boy didn't slow. He ran toward the last of the reptilian creatures, who stared hungrily down at Luke's soft, closed eyelids.

Jacen reached the raised platform. The third creature rose into the air, thrashing with its scorpion tail and snapping with both heads full of clacking fangs.

Unable to fight for himself, Luke paralleled the boy as Jacen struggled up onto the raised platform. Grim and determined, the boy stood guard by his uncle's motionless form. Artoo came up beside Jacen, his welding arm still crackling.

Then Luke saw what to do—if it was possible, if he could manage to use his skills in such a way. Next to his robed body lay a black cylinder studded with power buttons.

"Jacen," Luke said, "take my lightsaber."

The three flying creatures circled the chamber, croaking at each other as if receiving instructions from the Exar Kun.

Without hesitation the boy picked up the lightsaber handle. It was as long as his small forearm.

"Don't know how," Jacen said to Luke.

"I'll show you," Luke said. "Let me guide you . . . let me *fight* with you."

Talons extended, the three flying creatures plunged toward the boy, squealing with bloodlust in their eyes.

Jacen held the smooth handle in front of him and pushed the activation button. With a loud *snap-hiss* the lightsaber's deadly shaft blazed in the dimness. The little boy planted his feet apart, raised the glowing blade, and prepared to defend the Jedi Master, Luke Skywalker.

Cilghal scooped Jaina up in her arms and ran down the halls as Dorsk 81 and Tionne joined her at the turbolift.

They rose to the highest level, ready to battle for their Master, as they had done against the unleashed storm. But even Cilghal's greatest fears did not prepare her for the astonishing sight that greeted her as she entered the grand audience chamber.

Little Jacen held a lightsaber in his hand with all the grace and confidence of a master swordsman. The trio of flying creatures came at him, jabbing with their dripping stingers, snapping with long teeth, reaching with hooked claws. But Jacen pirouetted with the energy blade, wielding the lightsaber as if it were an extension of his arm. The blade crackled and hummed through the air.

Artoo-Detoo, agitated, buzzed back and forth, doing his best to keep the creatures from coming too close to Master Skywalker's body. Jacen continued to fight.

One of the lizard creatures darted in with gnashing fangs, but Jacen deftly cleaved off a head with one smooth stroke. He left only a smoking neck stump as the other head of the two-headed monster writhed and flailed and spat. The creature crashed to the floor and flopped its leathery wings against the flagstones.

The remaining two monsters struck with their scorpion stingers. The little boy swung the lightsaber, neatly slicing off one pointed stinger, then rolled out of the way as gouts of black poison spurted from the amputated end. The evil liquid burned on the ancient Massassi stones like acid, boiling with greasy gray-and-purple smoke.

Maddened with pain, the injured thing flapped in the air until it grappled against its companion, rending with claws and snapping with two heads full of tearing teeth. It struck with the useless stump of its stinger, but the stronger creature stabbed with its own stinger—leaving a burning hole in the torso of its attacker, a hole that continued to burn and sizzle as the poison ate deeper and deeper.

The stronger flying lizard latched its jaws on to the

scaly throat of the other. When its victim had ceased its struggles, the survivor released its claws, flapping higher as the dead carcass fell with a thud onto the floor. Artoo came forward to zap the limp creature, making certain it was dead.

Cilghal, Tionne, and Dorsk 81 froze on the threshold of the turbolift, watching the impossible tableau. "We've got to help him!" Dorsk 81 said.

"How?" Tionne asked. "We have no weapons."

Cilghal assessed the furious battle. "Perhaps Jacen doesn't need our help."

Jaina snatched her hand free from Cilghal's grip and scrambled down the promenade even as the others hesitated for a fraction of a second. Cilghal ran after her.

The last of the reptiles shrieked through double throats, infuriated by the attack of its companion. It dived down in an unstoppable plunge. Jacen stepped back to meet it, holding the lightsaber poised at his shoulder, waiting for the right moment.

Coolly, as the creature came in with dripping fangs and outstretched claws, Jacen swung in a clean arc with grace and skill, perfectly in command of his reflexes. The glowing blade struck and severed both throats in one sizzling flash. The carcass of the creature, reflexively convulsing its wings, crashed into Jacen and drove him to the floor.

Artoo rolled forward to help, bleeping.

"He is all right," Jaina called, finally reaching the raised platform. "Jacen!"

"Jaina!" Cilghal shouted, catching up with her.

The tip of the lightsaber appeared, smoking and blazing through the carcass as Jacen cut his way free of the stiff wings. Cilghal assisted him.

In surprise Jaina looked up to see the first fallen creature lurch back up, clinging to life with its remaining head, still desperate to kill Luke. With one stump of its severed neck still oozing dark blood, it clutched the edge of the stone table and hauled itself up, snapping its scorpion tail in convulsive twitches and preparing to sting. Its wings flapped, helping it balance on the table where it could rip apart Luke's body.

In one last moment of defiance, pushed on by the evil spirit controlling it, the wounded creature struck toward Luke's unprotected throat.

But Jaina arrived first. The little girl jumped up and grabbed its wings, yanking backward with all her weight. Writhing and snapping, the creature tried to bite down on the hands holding its leathery wings.

A mere second behind Jaina, Cilghal wrapped her powerful Calamarian hands around the creature's long serpentine throat even as Jaina continued to yank backward at its wings. Cilghal let out a high grunt as she wrung its neck, crushing a succession of vertebrae as if they were dry twigs.

The thing slumped down across the table, finally dead.

Jaina panted and slid into a squat. Jacen climbed to his feet and looked around as if confused. He blinked his eyes sleepily, then, with a deft movement of one small finger, deactivated the lightsaber. The humming sound of the blade vanished into the sudden silence of the chamber.

The turbolift opened, and the remaining Jedi trainees rushed out, drawing up short as they saw the carnage.

Tionne reached the raised platform. Her silvery hair flowed behind her like a comet's tail. She bent over Luke's body and, with an expression of disgust, gripped the still-oozing reptilian carcass of the last slain creature and flung it away from the Jedi Master.

Cilghal rushed to Jacen just as he calmly replaced the lightsaber beside Luke's motionless form. She grabbed him, hugged him, and then stared in awe at the little boy. Only moments ago this not-quite-three-year-old child had fought like a legendary lightsaber duelist.

Dorsk 81 and the other Jedi trainees came forward. "He

fought as well as a Master!" Dorsk 81 said. "It reminded me of the duel between Gantoris and Master Skywalker."

"Uncle Luke was with me," Jacen said. "He showed me. He's here."

Cilghal blinked her large round eyes.

"What do you mean?" Tionne asked.

"Can you see him now?" Dorsk 81 said.

"Yes, he's right there," Jaina pointed to thin air. "He says he's proud of us." She giggled. Jacen giggled too, but he looked exhausted, covered with dark ichor. He slumped down on Cilghal's lap.

The Jedi trainees looked at each other, then gazed at the open air above Luke's prone body. Artoo whistled in confusion.

"What else does he say?" Cilghal said.

Jacen and Jaina both sat still for a moment, as if listening. "Exar Kun. He's making the trouble," Jacen said.

Jaina finished, "Stop Exar Kun. Then Uncle Luke can come back."

12

L eia sat next to Terpfen in uneasy silence during the entire journey from Yavin 4 to the ocean world of Calamari. Terpfen said virtually nothing, crouched over the controls as if unable to bear the weight on his shoulders.

The small ship descended through the cloud-swirled atmosphere of the sapphire world toward one of the wrecked floating cities where Ackbar had been overseeing heroic salvage operations. As the ship streaked toward the sunlit water, Leia saw golden trails reflected off the choppy waves.

She felt an eerie sense of déjà vu, thinking of when she and Cilghal had come to this planet in search of Ackbar in his exile. She felt this time she was coming full circle, riding with the unwilling Calamarian traitor to redeem Ackbar . . . but more important, to enlist the admiral's assistance in a rescue operation to save her son.

"Reef Home salvage team, this is—" Terpfen hesitated. "This is Minister of State Leia Organa Solo's ship. We must speak with Ackbar. Do you have a place for us to land?"

After only a moment Ackbar's own voice responded. "Leia coming to see me? She's certainly welcome here." Then Ackbar added, "Terpfen, is that you?"

"Yes, Admiral."

"I thought I recognized your voice. I would delight in seeing both of you."

"I'm not so sure, sir," Terpfen said.

"What do you mean? Is something wrong?" Ackbar replied.

The Calamarian hung his scarred head, wrestling with his answer. Leia leaned over to the microphone. "It's best if we explain face-to-face, Ackbar," she said in a soft but firm voice. It still felt awkward not to address him by his rank.

Terpfen nodded a painful thanks to Leia. He brought the ship down in a steep dive toward the ocean surface, then pulled up with room to spare and cruised over the wavetops until they approached a cluster of floating vessels and a turmoil in the slate-gray water.

Organic-looking barges with articulated crane apparatus extended down into the water. Bloated, inflated ships like enormous bellows blazed exhaust fire as their engines drove fans to pump air into the submerged hulk of Reef Home, one of the majestic Calamarian floating cities that had been sunk in Admiral Daala's recent attack.

Leia had been on Calamari trying to convince Ackbar to reclaim his rank when Daala's Star Destroyers had struck. Squads of TIE bombers had managed to sink Reef Home and damage several other cities. But Ackbar had come out of his seclusion and rallied the Calamarian forces to victory.

Now Leia watched the white froth as the hulk of the city heaved itself to the surface. Bubbles simmered around the lumpy dome of Reef Home. Figures clambered over the exposed metal, attaching grappler cables from the towering cranes on the surrounding barge ships. The bellows pumps continued to gush air into Reef Home's sealed compartments, forcing out the water that had flooded deck after deck.

In the water, groups of dark figures—tentacle-faced Quarren—worked at the edge of the derelict city, prying open wave doors, patching breaches in the hull, and scavenging the ocean floor to find lost possessions.

As Terpfen brought the ship to land on the wet expanse of the main crane barge, the domed city shouldered its way higher above the choppy ocean.

Leia emerged from the small ship and stopped to catch her balance on the gently swaying deck. Cool salt spray struck her, making her gasp at the cutting wind and the iodine tang of drifting seaweed. One of the figures in the water used a jetpack to scoot away from the salvaged city, climbing a long ladder up the side of the crane barge.

Leia recognized Ackbar as he scrambled with enthusiasm onto the barge deck and stood dripping before them. He peeled off a thin translucent membrane from his face and took a deep breath of fresh air.

"Leia, I greet you," he said, raising a flipper hand. "We're making great progress in resurrecting Reef Home City. Our crews should have it refitted and ready for habitation within a few months.

"And Terpfen!" he said with heartbreaking joy as he strode to embrace his former chief starship mechanic. Terpfen stood stiffly, unable to speak a word.

Leia's immediate need was too great for pleasantries. "Ackbar," she said, "the Imperials have learned the location of Anoth. Winter and baby Anakin are in grave danger at this very moment. You must take us to them right away. You're the only one who knows the location."

Ackbar stood in shock, and Terpfen broke away from his embrace. "I have betrayed us, Admiral," he said. "I have betrayed us all."

Working hard to appear useful and important, Ambassador Furgan stood on the control deck of the Dreadnaught *Vendetta*. As they came out of hyperspace and approached the planet Anoth, he stepped forward. "Shields up," he said.

"Already done, sir," Colonel Ardax answered from the command station. Ardax wore a crisp olive-gray Imperial-navy uniform with his cap firmly planted on his short-trimmed hair. He drew in a deep breath to broaden his shoulders.

Throughout the journey to Anoth the colonel had annoyed Furgan by making decisions for himself without asking for input. Ardax was altogether too independent for Furgan's tastes. True, Furgan was merely the administrative head of the Caridan military academy—*former* military academy, now that the Rebel terrorist Kyp Durron had destroyed it—but he was still the most important person on this entire ship; his opinion should be valued.

He still thought of the roaring explosion of Carida's star, the echoed screams of those low-ranking individuals and all the valuable equipment he had left behind. Furgan's glorious dreams of resurrecting the Empire had dwindled to a point—but it was a laser-bright point. If he could just get his hands on the Jedi baby, there would be hope for the galaxy once more.

The *Vendetta* passed through a broken belt of asteroids scattered along Anoth's orbit. The planet itself had shattered into three components: two large chunks in contact, scraping and creating static discharges so that titanic lightning bolts blasted between them; farther out circled a smaller, misshapen rock that held a breathable atmosphere in its lowlands. In a century or two the three chunks would pulverize each other to space dust, but at the moment Anoth was a hidden and protected haven.

Until now.

"Looks like a rather ... rugged place to raise an infant," Colonel Ardax said.

"It'll toughen him up," Furgan said, "an appropriate beginning to the rigorous training he will undergo if he is to be our new Emperor."

"Ambassador Furgan," Ardax asked, raising his eyebrows, "do you have any indication of exactly where we should look for this alleged stronghold?"

Furgan thrust out his purplish lower lip. The spy Terpfen had provided the planet's coordinates, nothing more. "You can't expect me to do your entire job for you, Colonel," he snapped. "Use the Dreadnaught's scanners."

"Yes, sir." The colonel gestured toward the technicians at the analysis and sensor panels.

"We'll find it, sir," a wide-eyed corporal said, staring at a screen that showed a simplified computer diagram of the Anoth system's three components. "There's not much down there, so it shouldn't be hard to pick them out."

Furgan stumped to the turbolift at the rear of the control deck. "Colonel, I'm going down to inspect the MT-AT vehicles. I trust you can handle everything here without me?"

"Yes, sir," Ardax said, a bit too emphatically.

As the turbolift swallowed him, Furgan thought he heard a muttered comment from the Dreadnaught captain, but the words were cut off by the closing metal doors. . . .

Down in the *Vendetta*'s hangar bay and staging area Furgan stepped into a flurry of stormtrooper activity. White-armored troopers jogged in tight formation across the metal-plated floor, carrying weapons, stashing siege gear and power packs inside the cargo holds of the MT-ATs.

On Carida, Furgan had followed the design and development of the new Mountain Terrain Assault Transports, and he relished the opportunity to see them used in actual combat. He would follow in the rear of the assault, letting fully trained troopers face the initial hazards, though there was little to worry about—a woman and a child hiding on a rock? How much resistance could they offer?

Furgan ran his stubby fingers across the polished knee joint of one of the MT-AT walkers. Designed for ground assaults on remote mountain citadels, the MT-ATs' articulated joints and sophisticated claw footpads could scale even vertical surfaces of rock. On each joint were mounted supercharged lasers that could penetrate a half-meter-thick blast door. Two small blaster cannons hung on either side of the low-slung pilot's compartment to shoot down harrying fighter ships out of the sky.

Furgan stared at the beautiful construction, smooth lines, and glossy armor, marveling at the MT-AT's incredible capabilities. "Splendid machine," he said.

The stormtroopers paid no attention to him as they finished their preparations.

Colonel Ardax's voice came over the intercom. "Your attention, please! After some difficulty with electrical discharges and ionization interference in this system, we have pinpointed the secret base. Prepare to deploy the strike force immediately. Let's make this a clean and quick kill. That is all." Ardax signed off.

"You heard the colonel," Furgan said as the stormtrooper teams began to clamber aboard their MT-AT vehicles. They would be dropped from orbit on a thunderous plunge through the atmosphere, encased in a thermal-resistant cocoon that would detach upon striking the surface.

One trooper scrambled alone into his cockpit, hauling extra weapons, interrogation devices, and intelligence-gathering equipment.

"You!" Furgan said. "Stow all that in the cargo compartment. I am riding with you."

The stormtrooper looked at him in silence for a moment, his polished eye visor staring blankly.

"Do you have a problem with that order, sergeant?" Furgan asked.

"No, sir," the voice crackled through the helmet speaker. The stormtrooper methodically removed the equipment and stowed it in the undercompartment.

Furgan heaved himself into the second seat and strapped in. He pulled two sets of the crash webbing around his body to make sure he landed without injury. He didn't want to limp in triumph into the defeated Rebel stronghold. He waited impatiently as the rest of the stormtroopers completed preparations, slipped aboard their assault transports, and locked themselves down.

When the launching bay dropped out from beneath his feet like a trapdoor, Furgan grabbed the arms of his chair and cried out. The transports plunged like heavy projectiles into the waiting atmosphere. Even in its thick cocoon the MT-AT jounced and rocked as if it were being struck by cannon blasts. He tried unsuccessfully to stop his yell of panic.

Beside him the stormtrooper pilot said nothing.

Inside the stronghold on Anoth, Leia's personal servant Winter glanced at the chronometer and at the giggling dark-haired baby. It was time to put young Anakin to bed.

Though the triple planet Anoth had its own unusual cycle of days, nights, and twilights, Winter insisted on keeping their chronometers set to Coruscant standard time. Outside, the thin skies rarely brightened to more than a dark purple with flashes of searing yellow as electrical discharges blasted across space.

The planetoid was a stormy world, its surface covered with stone pinnacles like mammoth cathedrals reaching up to the limits of Anoth's low gravity. Riddled with caves from thousands of geological inclusions that had weathered and volatilized away during centuries of planetary stresses, the rock spires provided a sheltered hiding place.

Winter picked up the baby in her arms and bounced him against her hip as she went deeper into the facility. Anakin's shielded bedroom was brightly lit and decorated with soothing pastel colors. Tinkling music filled the air, a cheerful melody mixed with quiet wind and rushing water.

A boxy rectangular GNK power droid waddled from station to station in the room, charging the batteries of Anakin's self-aware toys. "Thank you," Winter said out of habit, though the droid had only minimal interactive programming. The power droid burbled a response and shuffled out in a slow walk on accordioned legs.

"Good evening, Master Anakin," said the caregiver droid in Anakin's chambers. An enhanced protocol model, the TDL droid was programmed to perform a majority of the functions required to care for a young child. TDL models had been marketed across the galaxy as nanny droids for busy politicians, space military personnel, and even smugglers who had children but too little time to spend with them.

The TDL droid had a silvery surface with all corners and sharp edges smoothed for comfort. Because nannies and mothers were expected to need more than the usual set of hands, TDL nanny droids had four fully functional arms, all of which were covered with warm synthetic flesh—as was the torso—to provide a more nurturing experience for a baby held in robot arms.

Anakin cooed with pleasure to see the droid, said a word resembling its name. Winter patted the baby on the back, saying good night.

"Do you have a preference from the large selection of lullabies and bedtime music I have available, Mistress Winter?" the droid said.

"Make a random selection," Winter answered. "I want to get back to the operations room. Something . . . doesn't feel right tonight."

"Very well, Mistress Winter," the nanny droid said, cradling Anakin in her arms. "Wave good night." She plucked up Anakin's pudgy hand and puppeted a wave.

Winter made it to the door of the operations room just before the intruder alarms went off. She rushed into the control center, scanning the big screens that showed outside images of the stark landscape.

Sonic booms thundered through the thin air, as large objects streamed down in a tight cluster. Winter saw the last of a group of projectiles impact at the base of the nearest spire of rock.

Winter activated the automated defense systems. She closed the massive shield doors that covered the entrance to the hangar grotto. Through the rock she could feel the heavy vibration as the metal doors slammed together.

She saw movement below, just out of range of the cameras. Then a long metal leg bent up on a huge articulated joint; a foot spiked with claws smashed into the rockface, creating traction with explosive bolts. Then the huge machine levered itself out of view around an outcropping.

Winter enhanced the audio pickup, listening to the groaning sounds of straining machinery, pulleys and grinding engines, the clank of treads.

Working rapidly, she switched to another set of image enhancers mounted on a distant pinnacle. The picture that appeared made her gasp in amazement and fear— an extreme reaction, considering her usual unemotional and inflectionless manner.

The smoldering hulks of protective reentry pods lay strewn about the landscape. The metal shells had cracked open like black vermin eggs and unleashed mechanical monstrosities—eight-legged, arachnidlike machines.

Each of the heavily jointed legs moved along different axes as the clawed feet helped the ellipsoid body scuttle over rugged terrain, finding footholds in the rock and scaling the sheer peak in which Winter and Anakin hid.

Eight Imperial Spider Walkers swarmed up the stone pinnacle, firing bright-green blasts against the thick walls of the stronghold, searching for a way in.

13

The Jedi trainees gathered in the dusty, abandoned war room of the Great Temple. They had chosen it as the most fitting place to plan their battle against Exar Kun.

On the third level of the ancient ziggurat the war room had once been used by the Rebel Alliance as a control center for their secret base. Here the tactical genius General Jan Dodonna had planned the strike against the first Death Star.

Cilghal and the others had cleared away much of the debris that had collected in the decade since the Rebels had left the base behind. Multicolored lights flickered on the control panels of the few functional sensor networks; grime-caked viewing plates and cracked transparisteel screens made the signals refract and glitter. Atop a tactical map the tiny hash-mark footprints of a skittering reptile were overlaid with the larger clawed prints of some predator that had chased after it.

Sealed behind the protection of thick stone walls, the war room allowed no outside illumination. Newly restored glowpanels in the corners made the place shine brightly, but also enhanced the shadows.

Cilghal looked at the group of Jedi trainees. A dozen of the best . . . but now they were gripped with fear and indecision, unprepared for the trial forced upon them.

Some—such as Kirana Ti, Kam Solusar, and, surprisingly, Streen—reacted with outrage to the long-dead Lord of the Sith. Others, particularly Dorsk 81, were filled with an unreasoning fear, afraid to challenge the dark power that had been sufficient to warp other students and defeat Master Skywalker. Cilghal herself did not look forward to the fight, but she vowed to do everything she could against their unwanted enemy.

"What if Exar Kun can hear our plans?" Dorsk 81 said, his large eyes shining in the harsh lights. "Even here he might be spying on us!" His voice rose, and his yellow-olive skin mottled with panic.

"The Dark Man can be everywhere," Streen said, leaning across the cluttered table. His frizzy gray hair still looked windblown. He fidgeted as he glanced around the room, as if afraid someone were watching.

"There's no other place we can go," Cilghal said. "If Exar Kun can find us here, he can find us wherever we go. We must operate on the assumption that we can still fight him." She gazed at the candidates. She had taken great pains to develop her oratory skills as ambassador for Calamari. She had used her voice and her wits to great success in the past, and now she took advantage of her gift. "We have enough real problems to confront—there's no need to manufacture worse ones from our imagination."

The others murmured in agreement.

"Tionne," Cilghal said, "much of our plan depends on your knowledge of ancient Jedi lore. Tell us what you know about Exar Kun."

Tionne sat up in a battered and uncomfortable chair beside one of the dilapidated tactical stations. Across her lap lay the double-boxed musical instrument on which she played old ballads to anyone who would listen.

Tionne had only a small amount of Jedi potential. Master Skywalker had made that clear to her, but she would not be swayed from her resolve to become one of the new Jedi Knights. She had become enamored of Jedi legends, traveling from system to system, digging through ancient writings and folktales, compiling tales of the Jedi from thousands of years before the Dark Times.

The Jedi Holocron had been a treasure trove, and Tionne had spent much of her time studying it, replaying forgotten legends, clarifying details. But the Holocron was destroyed when Master Skywalker had asked the simulated gatekeeper, the ancient Jedi Master Vodo-Siosk Baas, to tell of his student Exar Kun, who had rebuilt the Brotherhood of the Sith. . . .

Tionne flicked molten-silver hair over her shoulders and looked at the other trainees with her eerie mother-of-pearl eyes. Her lips were thin and pale, bloodless with tension.

"It's very difficult to find verifiable legends from the Great Sith War. That was four thousand years ago, and it was incredibly devastating—but apparently the old Jedi Knights were ashamed of how they had failed to protect the galaxy. Many of the records were distorted or destroyed, but I think I've pieced together enough." She swallowed, then continued.

"Kun seems to have built his primary stronghold on this jungle moon. He enslaved the Massassi race to build all these temples as focal points for his power."

She looked around, sizing up the Jedi trainees. "In fact, this gathering reminds me of the Great Council on the planet Deneba, when most of the old Jedi Knights met to discuss the dark tide rising through the galaxy. Master Vodo-Siosk Baas—who had trained Exar Kun—became a martyr when he tried to turn his student back to the light side. When Master Vodo did not succeed, the other Jedi banded together in a massive strike force such as had never before been gathered.

"Though Kun had enormous power, it seems that the key"—Tionne tapped the side of her instrument with a glistening fingernail—"the *key* was that the other Jedi combined their might. They fought together as a unit where all the pieces fit together, as components in a much larger machine powered by the Force.

"I've found only sketchy information, but it seems that in the final battle the unified Jedi wiped out most of the jungles on Yavin 4, laying waste to everything in their efforts to destroy Exar Kun. Kun drained dry the life force of all his Massassi slaves in one last gambit. The ancient Jedi succeeded in destroying much of what he had built and obliterated Kun's body, but he somehow managed to preserve his spirit within the temples. For all these years."

"Then we must finish the job," Kirana Ti said, standing up. She wore her reptilian body armor all the time now, unencumbered by a Jedi robe because she did not know when she might need to fight at a moment's notice.

"I agree," Kam Solusar said. His gaunt face held the expression of a man who had long ago forgotten how to smile.

"But how?" Streen said. "Thousands of Jedi could not obliterate the Dark Man. We are only twelve."

"Yes," Kirana Ti said, "but this time Exar Kun doesn't have a race of enslaved people to draw upon. He has no resources but himself. Besides, Kun has already been defeated once—and he knows it."

"And," Cilghal interjected, gesturing around the table, "all of us have trained together from the beginning. Master Skywalker made us to be a team. Leia called us champions of the Force—and that is what we must be."

• • •

Standing at the pinnacle of the Great Temple, Luke Skywalker's shimmering form could not feel the cool twilight breeze as the lumbering orange hulk of the gas giant cast fading light across the jungles. Luke watched a flock of batlike creatures take to the air and swarm across the treetops in search of night insects.

He remembered his nightmare when Exar Kun, disguised as Anakin Skywalker, had urged Luke to dabble in the dark side. Against the backdrop of history Luke had seen the labors of the broken Massassi erecting mammoth temples, working until crushed by sheer labor. Luke had cast off that nightmare, but he had not interpreted its warning soon enough.

Now he turned to see the hooded form of Kun standing black against the jungle landscape, but the sight no longer had the power to make him afraid. "You're growing bolder, Exar Kun, to keep showing yourself to me—especially when your attempts to destroy my body continue to fail."

In the aftermath of the reptilian creatures' attack, Luke had watched Cilghal tend his body's minor wounds, cleaning them and binding them with the meticulous care and empathy he had sensed from her first days at the Jedi academy. Cilghal was a born Jedi healer.

She had spoken aloud to Luke's spirit, though she couldn't see him. "We will do whatever we can, Master Skywalker. Please keep faith in us."

Luke had indeed maintained his faith. He felt it throbbing within him as he confronted Exar Kun atop the temple, where the Sith Lord and Kyp Durron had defeated Luke once before.

"I have been toying with you." Kun waved his silhouette hand. "Nothing will affect my plans. Some of your students are already mine. The others will soon follow."

"I don't think so," Luke said with fresh certainty. "I have instructed them well. You might show them easy ways to glory, but your tricks carry a high price. I have taught them diligence, confidence in their own worth and abilities. What you offer, Exar Kun, is mere parlor magic. I have given them the true strength and meaning of the Force."

"Do you think I don't know of the laughable plans they make against me?" Kun said. The spirit of the Dark Lord seemed to be growing more full of bluster and threats. Perhaps his confidence was shaken.

"It doesn't matter," Luke answered. "They will defeat you anyway. Your imagined power is your weakness, Exar Kun."

"And your faith in your friends is yours!" Kun snapped back.

Luke laughed, feeling his strength and determination increase. "I've heard talk like that before. It was proved wrong then, and it will be proved wrong now."

The black outline of Exar Kun rippled in an unseen breeze. As the shadow vanished, Kun's last words were, "We shall see!"

14

Standoff.

Han Solo felt cold sweat spring from his forehead as he looked out from the cockpit of the *Millennium Falcon*. In front of him the Sun Crusher powered up its supernova torpedo launcher.

Han pounded his fist on the console. "Hold it, kid!" he shouted. "Just hold it. I thought you were my friend."

"If you were my friend," Kyp's voice croaked through the speaker, "you wouldn't try to stop me. You know what the Empire did to my life, to my family. The Empire lied to me one last time—and now even my brother is dead."

At the copilot's station Lando scrambled at the controls. His big eyes flicked back and forth, and he turned to Han, waving frantically for him to shut off the voice pickup.

"Han," he whispered, "remember when you and Kyp took the Sun Crusher away from Maw Installation? And Luke and I were there waiting to intercept you?"

Han nodded, not sure what Lando was getting at. "Sure."

"Back then we linked the ships together because the *Falcon*'s navicomputer wouldn't work." He raised his eyebrows and spoke very slowly. "Listen . . . we've still got the Sun Crusher's control codes in here."

Suddenly Han understood. "Can you do anything with that? You're not even familiar with the Sun Crusher's systems."

"Don't have much choice, do we, buddy?"

"All right," Han said in a needlessly low voice, because the voice pickup was switched off. "I'll keep him talking—you work to deactivate the Sun Crusher." Lando, with a skeptical but determined frown, continued his programming.

Han toggled on the comm system again. "Kyp, don't you remember when we went turbo-skiing at the poles of Coruscant? You led me down one of the dangerous paths, but I went after you because I thought you were going to fall on your face. Don't you remember that?"

Kyp didn't answer, but Han knew he had struck home.

"Kid, who got you out of the spice mines of Kessel?" he said. "Who broke you out of the detention cell on the *Gorgon*? Who was with you during the escape from the Maw? Who promised to do everything he could to make your life worth living again after your years of misery?"

Kyp answered in a halting voice. "It didn't work."

"But why not, kid? What went wrong? What happened on Yavin 4? I know you and Luke didn't get along—"

"It had nothing to do with Luke Skywalker," Kyp snapped so defensively that Han knew it wasn't true. "There in the temples I learned things Master Skywalker would never teach. I learned how to be strong. I learned how to fight the Empire, to turn my own anger into a weapon."

"Look, kid," Han said, "I don't claim to understand anything about the Force. In fact I once said it was a hokey religion full of mumbo jumbo. But I do know that what you're saying sounds dangerously close to the dark side."

After a deep pause Kyp said haltingly, "Han ... I—"

"Got it!" Lando whispered.

Han nodded, and Lando punched in the control sequence.

A rapid succession of lights twinkled on the control panel as the override command was transmitted across the narrow bridge of space. In the black gulf lit only by a backwash of dull light from the exploded red-dwarf star, the Sun Crusher suddenly went dark: the lights in its cockpit, the aiming beacons on its laser cannons, and the blaze of plasma at the end of its toroidal torpedo generator.

"Yes!" Lando shouted. Han gave a whoop of triumph, and the two of them reached out to slap their hands together.

"Let me talk to him," Han said. "Does he still have power to his comm system?"

"Channel open," Lando said. "But I don't think he's very happy—"

"You tricked me!" Kyp's voice screamed through the speaker panel. "You claimed to be my friend—and now you've betrayed me. It's just like Exar Kun said. Friends betray you. A Jedi has no time for friendship. You should all die."

Astonishingly, the power in the Sun Crusher surged back to life again, despite Lando's overrides. The lights came on in a blaze.

"It's not my fault!" Lando squawked, scrambling to reroute the command. "I didn't know he could bypass it so fast!"

"Kyp can do things with the Force that you and I can't understand," Han said.

The energy torpedo launcher fired up with a flare of intense plasma, brighter than before, ready to launch at the *Falcon*.

And this time Kyp did not hesitate.

15

Streen dozed cross-legged on the cold flagstone floor before Master Skywalker. He folded his arms over his knees, comfortable in the many-pocketed jumpsuit he had brought with him from his lonely days as a gas prospector on Bespin. He could no longer smell the bitter sulfurous taint of rich plumes of deep-layer gases.

Now Streen had a greater mission—to guard Master Skywalker.

Low-slanted light from outside elongated the shadows in the grand audience chamber. Twelve candles, one placed by each of the Jedi trainees, flickered around Luke's body, shedding a faint but protective glow into the motionless air. The small bright points glittered as the darkness gathered all around.

Streen muttered to himself. No, he would not listen to the Dark Man's words. No, he would not serve Exar Kun's purposes. No, he would not do anything to harm Master Skywalker. No!

In his lap, cool and hard against his callused hands, he held the handle of Luke's lightsaber.

This time he could fight it. This time the Dark Man would not win. Some of the other Jedi trainees had expressed grave misgivings about letting Streen near Master Skywalker, especially armed with a lightsaber. But Streen had begged for his chance at restitution, and Kirana Ti had spoken on his behalf.

The others would watch over him. Master Skywalker would be in danger, but they had to take the risk.

Streen let the fuzzy caress of sleep work its way into his mind. His grizzled head nodded to his chest. Whispering voices sounded like breezes in his mind, forming gentle words, soothing phrases . . . cold promises.

The words demanded that he wake up, but Streen resisted them, not knowing if they were evil suggestions or the insistences of his companions. When Streen felt he had waited long enough, he allowed himself to snap awake.

The voices fell silent as he blinked his eyes. Another voice, external this time, replaced the silence. "Wake up, my student. The winds are blowing."

Streen focused on the black form of Exar Kun in the center of the throne room. In the flickering candlelight and dim rays from the dying day, Streen could see chiseled features on the onyx silhouette, more detailed than he had ever seen before on the shadow of the Dark Man.

Exar Kun turned a well-defined face toward him, completely ebony as if molded from lava stone: high cheekbones, haughty eyes, a thin, angry mouth. Long black hair like carbon wires swept across his shoulder, gathered in a thick ponytail. Padded armor covered his body, and the pulsing tattoo of a black sun burned from his forehead.

Streen climbed slowly to his feet. He felt calm and strong, angry at how the Dark Man had set a sharp hook in his own weakness and had dragged him along. "I won't do your bidding, Dark Man," he said.

Exar Kun laughed. "And how do you propose to resist? You are already mine."

"If you believe that," Streen said, and took a deep breath, strengthening his voice, "then you have made your first mistake." He brought up the handle of Luke's lightsaber, igniting it with a loud *snap-hiss*.

Exar Kun's shadow flinched backward, much to Streen's surprise and satisfaction.

"Good," Kun said with false bravado, "now take the weapon and cleave Skywalker in two. Let us be done with this."

Streen took one step toward Exar Kun, holding the green lightsaber before him. "This blade is meant for you, Dark Man."

"If you think that weapon will have any effect on me," Kun said, "perhaps you should ask your friend Gantoris— or have you forgotten what happened to *him* when he defied me?"

A vision flashed through Streen's mind: Gantoris's crisped corpse incinerated from the inside out, his body turned to ash from the incredible fires of the dark side. Kun must have intended for that memory to drive Streen to despair; Gantoris had been his friend; he and Gantoris were the first two trainees Master Skywalker had found on his Jedi search.

But rather than causing panic or dismay, the memory increased Streen's determination. He strode forward, staring down the shadowy man. "You are not wanted here, Exar Kun," he said. To his continued surprise the shadow of the ancient Sith Lord drifted back from him, down the promenade.

"I can find other tools, Streen, if you prove difficult. I will show you no mercy when I have gained control once more. My Sith brothers will use the power stored within this network of temples. If you defy me, I can find new ways of inflicting pain far beyond the capabilities of your imagination—and you will endure all of them!"

Kun's shadow drifted farther away . . . and a tall figure emerged from the left stone stairwell into the grand audience chamber: Kirana Ti clad in her polished reptilian armor, her muscles rippling in the pale candlelight, her curves making her look supple yet deadly.

"Are you running away, Exar Kun?" Kirana Ti said. "Frightened off so easily?"

Streen held his position, still gripping the lightsaber.

"Another foolhardy student," Kun said, whirling to face her. "I would have come to you in time. The witches of Dathomir would be fine additions to a new Sith Brotherhood."

"You'll never get a chance to ask them, Exar Kun. You are trapped here. You won't leave this chamber." She pressed forward to intimidate him by her very closeness.

Kun's shadow distorted, but he held his ground. "You cannot threaten me." Kun loomed over her.

Streen felt a stab of cold fear at the movement, but Kirana Ti ducked swiftly, fluidly, into a fighting stance. She reached to her waist and snatched one of the tools hanging there.

A loud crackle seared the air, and she stood holding another ignited lightsaber. A long amethyst-and-white blade extended from the handle, humming like an angry insect. She thrashed the lightsaber from side to side.

"Where did you get that weapon?" Kun demanded.

"It belonged to Gantoris," she said. "He once tried to fight you and failed." She slashed with the lightsaber, and Kun flinched back toward Streen. "But I will succeed."

Kirana Ti stalked toward the platform where Luke's body lay, where Streen stood on guard with the other lightsaber. Kun was trapped between them.

Another Jedi trainee emerged from the right-side stair-well—grim and wiry Kam Solusar. "And if she fails," he said, "*I* will pick up the lightsaber and fight you." He marched forward, closing the distance to join her.

Then Tionne came from the opposite stairwell, throwing her challenge at Exar Kun as she walked up to the platform. "And I will fight you as well."

Cilghal stepped in with Jacen and Jaina, each holding one of her hands. "And we will fight you. We will all fight you, Exar Kun."

The remaining Jedi trainees flooded into the chamber, converging in a group that surrounded the Dark Lord of the Sith.

Kun raised his opaque arms in a sudden brisk gesture. With a flicker of wind the twelve candles around Master Skywalker's body snuffed out, plunging the room into deep shadow.

"We're not afraid of the darkness," Tionne said in a firm voice. "We can make our own light."

As his eyes adjusted, Streen saw that all twelve of the Jedi candidates were limned with the faintest sheen of an iridescent blue glow that grew brighter as the new Jedi converged around Exar Kun.

"Even joined together, you are too weak to fight me!" the shadowy man said.

Streen felt his throat constrict, his windpipe close. He choked, unable to breathe. The black silhouette turned, staring at those who resisted him. The Jedi trainees grasped their throats, straining to breathe, their faces darkening with the effort.

Kun's shadow expanded, growing darker and more powerful. He towered over Streen. "Streen, take your lightsaber and finish these weaklings. Then I will allow you to live."

Streen heard the blood sing in his ears as his body strained for oxygen. The rushing sound reminded him of blowing wind, gale-force storms. Wind. Air. He grasped the wind with his Jedi powers, moving the air itself and making it flow into his lungs, past Kun's invisible stranglehold.

Cool, sweet oxygen filled him, and Streen exhaled and inhaled again. Reaching out with his power, he did the same for all the other Jedi students, nudging air into their lungs—helping them breathe, helping them grow stronger.

"We are more powerful than you," Dorsk 81 said, gasping, in a tone that mixed challenge with amazement.

"How you must hate me," Exar Kun said. Desperation tinged the edges of his voice. "I can feel your anger."

Cilghal used the silken ambassadorial voice she had worked so hard to develop. "There is no anger," she said. "We don't hate you, Exar Kun. You are an object lesson for us. You have taught us much about what it is to be a true Jedi. By observing you we see that the dark side has little strength of its own. You have no power that we do not have. You merely used our own weaknesses against us."

"We have seen enough of you," Kam Solusar said grimly from the edge of the circle, "and it's time for you to be vanquished."

The Jedi trainees stepped closer together, cinching the circle around the trapped shadowy form. Streen held his lightsaber high, while across the circle Kirana Ti raised hers to a striking position. The nebulous glow around the new Jedi Knights grew brighter, a luminous fog that joined them in an unbroken ring, a solid band of light forged by the power of the Force within them.

"I know your flaws," Kun said stridently. "You all have weaknesses. You—" The shadow lunged toward the streamlined form of Dorsk 81. The cloned Jedi candidate flinched, but the other trainees gave him strength.

"You: Dorsk 81, a failure!" He sneered. "Eighty generations of your genetic structure were perfect, identical— but you were an anomaly. You were an outcast. A flaw."

But the olive-skinned alien would not back down. "Our differences make us strong," he said. "I've learned that."

"And you"—Exar Kun whirled to Tionne—"you have no Jedi powers. You are laughable. You can only sing songs about great deeds, while others go out and actually do them."

Tionne smiled at him. Her mother-of-pearl eyes glittered in the dim light. "Someday the songs will tell of our great victory over Exar Kun—and I will sing them."

The glow continued to brighten as the synergy between the trainees grew more powerful, weaving threads to reinforce their weak spots, to emphasize their strengths.

Streen wasn't sure exactly when another image joined the Jedi candidates. He saw a new form without a physical body—short and hunched, with withered hands held in front of it. A misshapen funnel face, whiskered with tentacles, stared with small eyes hooded by a shelf of brow. Streen recognized the ancient Jedi Master Vodo-Siosk Baas, who had spoken to them from the Holocron.

Kun's image also saw the ancient Jedi Master, and his expression froze in a sculpted grimace of astonishment.

"Together Jedi can overcome their weaknesses," Master Vodo said in a bubbly, congested voice. "Exar Kun, my student—you are defeated at last."

"No!" the shadow screamed in a night-rending voice as the silhouette fought to discover a part of the circle he could breach.

"Yes," came another voice, a strong voice. Opposite Master Vodo glimmered the faint, washed-out form of a young man in Jedi robes. Master Skywalker.

"The way to extinguish a shadow," Cilghal said in her calm and confident voice, "is to increase the light."

Kirana Ti stepped forward with the lightsaber that had been built by Gantoris. Streen met her with Luke Skywalker's lightsaber. The two stared into each other's eyes, nodded, and then struck with the brilliant luminous blades.

Their beams crossed in the middle of Exar Kun's shadowy body—pure light intersecting pure light with an explosion of lightning. The flash of dazzling white seemed as bright as an exploding sun.

Darkness flooded out of the shade of Exar Kun. The blackness shattered, and fragments flew around the circle, seeking a weak heart in which to hide.

Streen and Kirana Ti kept their lightsabers crossed, the energy sizzling and searing.

With the Force, Streen touched the winds again. The air inside the grand audience chamber swirled with increasing coriolis force to form a whirlwind. The cyclone grew tighter in an invisible knot around the shredded shadow, trapping it and carrying it up toward the rooftop and out, flinging it into the vast emptiness.

Exar Kun vanished with only a brief, curtailed scream.

The Jedi Knights stood joined together for a final moment, relishing the shared Force. Then, in exhaustion and relief and triumph, they separated from each other. The unearthly glow dissipated around them.

The image of the alien Master Vodo-Siosk Baas stared toward the ceiling, as if to catch a last glimpse of his conquered student, and then he too disappeared.

With a wheezing cough as he expelled long-trapped air from his lungs and drew in a fresh breath, Master Skywalker groaned and sat up on the stone platform.

"You've—done it!" Luke said, gaining strength with each lungful of cool, clean air. The new Jedi Knights surged toward him. "You have broken the bonds."

With squeals of delight Jacen and Jaina ran to their Uncle Luke. He pulled them into his arms. They giggled and hugged him back.

Luke Skywalker smiled out at his students, his face glowing with pride for the group of Jedi Knights he had trained.

"Together," he said, "you make a formidable team indeed! Perhaps we need no longer fear the darkness."

16

In the Sun Crusher's pilot seat Kyp
Durron crouched over the controls. He stared at the *Millennium Falcon* as if it were a demon ready to spring
at him. His fingernails scratched down the metallic surface of the navigation panels like claws trying to dig
into flesh.

His mind had been swimming with the bittersweet
memories of happy times with Han, how the two of them
had careened over the ice fields in a frantic turbo-ski run,
how they had made friends in the blackness of the spice
mines, how Han had pretended not to be all choked up
when Kyp left for the Jedi academy. Part of him was
appalled at the idea of threatening Han Solo's life, that
he would want to destroy the *Millennium Falcon*.

It had seemed an easy threat, the obvious thing to do.
But it came from a dark shadow in the back of his mind.
The whispering voice chewed at his thoughts, haunted
him constantly. It was the voice he had heard during
his training on Yavin 4 in the deepest night and in the
echoing obsidian pyramid far out in the jungles, and on

top of the great ziggurat from which Kyp had summoned the Sun Crusher out of the core of Yavin.

Troubled by that voice, Kyp had stolen a ship and fled to the forest moon of Endor to meditate beside the ashes of Darth Vader's funeral pyre. He had thought to go far enough away to escape Kun's influence, but he no longer thought that was possible.

Kyp had traveled to the Core Systems, but still he felt the chains binding him to the Dark Lord, the malevolent obligations required by the Sith teachings. If he tried to resist and think for himself, the angry tauntings returned with full force, the snapped words, the coercions, the veiled threats.

But Han Solo's words tugged at him too—weapons of a different sort that made his heart grow warm, melting the ice of anger. Right now Exar Kun's voice seemed distracted and distant, as if preoccupied with another challenge.

As Kyp listened to Han's words, he realized that his friend, knowing little about Jedi teachings, had put his finger on the truth. He *was* following the dark side. Kyp's weak justifications crumbled around him in a storm of excuses built on a fragile foundation of revenge.

"Han . . . I—"

But just as he had been about to speak warmly to Han, to open up and ask his friend to come talk with him— suddenly his controls went dead. An override signal from the *Falcon*'s computer had shut down the Sun Crusher's weapons systems, its navigation controls, its life support.

The black net of anger fell over him, smothering his kind intentions. In outrage Kyp found the power to send a burst of controlling thought through the integrated circuits in the Sun Crusher's computer. He flushed the alien programming, wiping pathways clean and rebuilding them in an instant. He remapped the functions with a sudden mental pinpoint that made the Sun Crusher whole again. The systems hummed as they returned to life, charging up.

Exar Kun had also been betrayed by his supposed partner, the warlord Ulic Qel-Droma. Now Han had betrayed Kyp. Master Skywalker had also betrayed him by failing to teach the appropriate lessons . . . appropriate defenses against Exar Kun. In his head the voice of the Sith Lord shouted for him to kill Han Solo, to destroy the enemy. To let his anger flow through and be strong.

It overwhelmed Kyp. He squeezed his dark eyes shut, unable to watch as his hands gripped the control levers for launching the torpedo. He primed the system. The screens blinked with warning signals, which he disregarded.

He needed to destroy something. He needed to kill those who had betrayed him. His fists gripped the firing handles. His thumbs rested on the launch buttons, squeezing, ready—

Squeezing—

And then the haunting voice of Exar Kun rose to a wail in his mind, an utterly forlorn scream as if he were being torn out of this universe and exiled to another place entirely, where he could torment Kyp Durron no more.

Kyp snapped backward in his control seat as if an invisible tow cable had been severed. His arms and head dangled like a puppet with suddenly snipped strings. The cool wind of freedom whistled through his mind and body. He blinked his eyes and shuddered with revulsion at what he had been about to do.

The *Millennium Falcon* still gripped the Sun Crusher in its tractor beam. As Kyp saw the battered old ship, Han Solo's prize possession, he felt a tidal wave of despair.

Kyp reached out to the energy torpedo controls and vehemently canceled the firing sequence. The plasma generator flickered and faded as the energy died away.

Without the presence of Exar Kun inside him, Kyp felt isolated, suddenly in free fall—but independent.

He opened the communication channel but couldn't form words for a few moments. His throat was dry. It felt as if he hadn't had anything to eat or drink in four thousand years.

"Han," he croaked, and said louder, "Han, this is Kyp! I . . ." He paused, not knowing what next to say—what else he *could* say.

He hung his head and finally finished, "I surrender."

17

he Twi'lek Tol Sivron still felt
jangled from his horrendous passage through the Maw,
escaping from the Rebel invasion force and riding the
gravity between black holes.

His long head-tails tingled with a rush of impressions,
delighted to see that the information he had long ago stolen
from Daala's secret files—the list of tortuous safe routes
through the black hole cluster—had been accurate. If the
course map had been the least bit imprecise, he and his
retreating crew would not be alive now.

The Death Star prototype lurched under full power as it
emerged safely from the cluster, but just as it sped away
from the sinuous, brilliant gases, the propulsion systems
fizzled and went off-line.

Sparks showered from panels as the stormtrooper captain shut down the engine power and rerouted systems.
Yemm attempted to use a manual fire-extinguishing apparatus to squelch flames licking out of a nearby console,
but he succeeded only in short-circuiting the intercom
systems.

Golanda and Doxin flipped furiously through repair manuals and design specifications.

"Director," the stormtrooper captain said, "we have successfully broken free from the Maw, though the strain has caused a good deal of damage."

Doxin looked up, scowling. "I remind you that this was a nonhardened prototype, never meant to be actually deployed."

"Yes, sir," the stormtrooper said in an inflectionless voice. "As I was about to say, I believe the damage can be repaired in only a few days. It is a simple matter of bypassing circuits and reinitializing computer systems. I believe after this shakedown the prototype will be in much better shape for combat."

Tol Sivron rubbed his hands together and smiled. "Good, good." He leaned back in the pilot's chair. "That will give us time to select a suitable target for our first attack."

Golanda called up a navigational chart, displayed across the viewscreen. "Director, the Kessel system is very close, as you know. Perhaps we should—"

"Let's get the propulsion units up and running again before we plan too far ahead," Doxin interrupted. "Our ultimate strategy may depend on our capabilities."

Yemm tore the cover off the communications panel and squinted down into the morass of blackened wires, sniffing the burned insulation.

Golanda kept studying her station, calling up readings from the prototype's exterior sensors. "Director, I've found something puzzling. Looking at the gas turbulence that surrounds the black hole cluster, it appears that another very large ship has recently entered the Maw, only moments ago. It seems to have followed one of the other paths Admiral Daala designated as a safe route through to the Installation." She looked at him, and Tol Sivron flinched away from her unpleasant face. "We just missed them."

Sivron didn't know what she was talking about, nor why it should concern him. All of these frantic problems were like stinging insects buzzing around his head, and he swatted at them.

"We can't do anything about that now," he said. "It's probably another Rebel ship coming to mop up the invasion of our facility." He sighed. "We'll get back at them, as soon as we get the Death Star up and running again."

He leaned back in his pilot's chair and closed his beady eyes, longing for just a moment's peace. He wished he had never left his home planet of Ryloth, where the Twi'lek people lived deep within mountain catacombs in the habitable band of twilight that separated the baking heat of day from the frigid cold of endless night.

Tol Sivron thought of more peaceful days, breathing the stale air through gaps in his pointed teeth. The heat storms on Ryloth brought sufficient warmth into the twilight zone to make the planet habitable, though desolate.

The Twi'leks built their society around the governorship of a five-member "head-clan" who led the community in all matters until such time as one of them died. At this point the Twi'leks cast out the remaining members of the head-clan to the blasted wasteland—and presumably to their deaths—while they selected a fresh group of rulers.

Tol Sivron had been a member of the head-clan, pampered and spoiled by the benefits of power. The entire clan was young and vigorous, and Sivron had expected to reap the benefits of his position for many years—spacious quarters, Twi'lek dancing women renowned throughout the galaxy, delicacies of raw meat that he could tear with his pointed teeth and savor the spicy liquid flavors. . . .

But the good life had lasted barely a standard year. One of his idiot companions had lost his balance on a scaffolding while inspecting a deep-grotto construction project and had fallen to impale himself upon a ten-thousand-year-old stalagmite.

According to their custom, the Twi'lek people had exiled Tol Sivron and the other three members of the head-clan into the blasted deserts of the dayside to face the heat storms and the scouring wind.

They had resigned themselves to death, but Tol Sivron had convinced the other three that if they worked together, they could survive, perhaps eke out an existence in an uninhabited cave farther down the spine of mountains.

The others had agreed, clinging to any hope; and then, as they slept that night, Tol Sivron had killed them all, taking their meager possessions to increase his own chances of survival. Covering himself with thick layers of garments stripped from the dead bodies of his companions, he had trudged across the fiery landscape, not knowing what he was searching for. . . .

Tol Sivron had thought the glittering ships were mere mirages until he stumbled into the encampment. It was a rugged training base and refueling station for the Imperial navy, frequented by smugglers but supported by the Empire.

Tol Sivron had met a man named Tarkin there, an ambitious young commander who already had several ships and who intended to make the small outpost on Ryloth a strategically important refueling station in the Outer Rim.

Over the years, Tol Sivron had worked for Tarkin, proving himself to be an unparalleled manager, a skillful arranger of the complex business that Tarkin—then *Moff* Tarkin, then *Grand* Moff Tarkin—had under way.

Sivron's career had culminated in his directorship of Maw Installation—which he had now fled in the face of a Rebel invasion. If Tarkin was still alive, the embarrassing retreat would no doubt figure negatively in Tol Sivron's next performance appraisal.

He had to do something to make up for it, posthaste.

"Director," Yemm said, interrupting his thoughts. "I think the comm system is functioning again. It will be ready to use as soon as I log the modifications into its maintenance record."

Sivron sat up. "At least something works around here."

Yemm entered numbers into one of the computer stations and nodded his horned head at Tol Sivron. "Ready, Director."

"Turn it on," he said. "Let me speak to the crew." His last words echoed through the speakers, startling him. He cleared his throat and leaned closer to the voice pickup on the pilot's chair.

"Attention, everyone! Hurry with those repairs," he snapped into the intercom. His voice sounded like the commands of a deity as he spoke through all levels. "I want to destroy something as soon as possible." He switched off.

The stormtrooper captain turned to him. "We will do our best, sir. I should have final repair estimates within a few hours."

"Good, good." He stared across the open emptiness of space, looking at all the possible starpoint targets.

Tol Sivron had in his possession one of the most devastating weapons in the galaxy. But it remained untested. For now.

18

The second timed detonation occurred just as Wedge Antilles and his assault squad charged into the Maw Installation's power-reactor complex. Shaped charges planted by a sabotage crew exploded at the base of the reactor's cooling towers, shutting down the enormous generator that powered the facilities, the laboratories, the mainframe computers, and life-support systems.

Wearing mottled brown-and-gray body armor, Wedge had led his assault team across the connector-tube catwalks to the power asteroid. But just as the squad entered, gouts of gray smoke spurted through the tunnels, carrying dust and debris along with a hot wind.

Wedge shook his head to clear his ringing ears. He climbed to his knees and then to his feet again. "I need an assessment of the damages," he shouted. "Quick!"

Three of the leading soldiers raced down the hall only to encounter a group of Maw Installation personnel fleeing the wreckage. The saboteurs were led by a one-armed brute of a man with purplish-green skin and a sour expression.

Wedge's team snapped up their weapons, training the barrels of their blaster rifles on the saboteurs, who halted with a clatter like machine components locking into place. The one-armed man skidded to a stop and looked around wildly. The rest of his crew glared at the New Republic soldiers.

"Drop your weapons!" Wedge said.

The large brute raised his single hand, palm outward, to show that he carried no weapons. Wedge was surprised to see that the others were also unarmed.

"It's too late to stop anything," the one-armed man said. "I am Wermyn, Division Leader for Plant Operations. Accept my surrender. My team and I would appreciate it if you'd get us off this rock before the whole thing explodes."

Wedge pointed to four of his soldiers. "Use binders, see that the prisoners are secured. We've got to get that power reactor functioning again, or we'll have to evacuate."

The Maw saboteurs did not resist as the squad took them into custody, though Wedge's men looked confused about how to apply binders to Wermyn's single arm.

Wedge and the technicians proceeded cautiously into the reactor housing. The heat struck him like a sandwhirl during the hot season on Tatooine. The air smelled thick with acrid lubricants, molten metal, and charred high-energy explosive.

Red warning lights flooded the chamber, reflecting from whistling jets of steam like droplets of flying blood. Laboring pumps and engines thudded with a pounding beat that made Wedge's skull ache. A large reactor component had been slagged, left with ragged, dripping edges.

He squinted as the techs ran forward, yanking handheld detectors from their belts to study radiation leaks. One trotted up to Wedge. "Both the primary and the backup cooling pumps have been destroyed. Our friend Wermyn was right. He has initiated a meltdown, and there's nothing we can do to stop it. We can't fix this equipment."

"Can we shut down the reactor?" Wedge said.

"It's been locked on, and the controls are destroyed," the tech answered. "I suppose there's a chance we could reroute and rig up temporary systems in an hour or two, but if we shut the reactor down, we also terminate power and life support to the Installation."

Wedge looked around the wreckage as his stomach sank. With his boot he kicked a broken piece of plasteel shielding. It clattered hollowly across the floor until the throbbing engines swallowed the sound.

"I didn't lead this strike force just to let all the scientists and the Death Star get away while the whole Installation is destroyed under my feet." He drew a deep breath and tapped his fingers together in an attempt to concentrate, as Qwi often did, though he wasn't sure it worked.

Then he yanked the comm link from his hip and gripped it, toggling on the frequency for the flagship *Yavaris*. "Captain," he said, "get me some engineering experts right away. We need to rig up emergency cooling pumps for the main power reactor.

"I know we don't have much equipment, but our hyperdrive cooling systems shouldn't be too dissimilar to what this reactor uses. Take one of the corvettes off line and remove the engine pumps. We've got to get something working down here to hold us until we can remove everything of value."

The two technicians looked up at Wedge and smiled. "That just might work, sir."

Wedge ushered them back to where the prisoners were held, vowing not to let the Imperials win so easily.

Qwi Xux felt like a stranger in her own house. She walked timidly into the room she had identified as her former laboratory, expecting something to jump out at her, memories to come flooding back.

The illumination came on, shedding a cold white glow on the design apparatus, her computer terminals, her furniture. This place had been her home, the center of her life for more than a decade. But it looked like a foreign land to her now. She stared in amazement and sighed.

See-Threepio whirred as he followed her into the room. "I still don't know why I'm here, Dr. Xux. I can assist you in assimilating the leftover data, but I'm a protocol droid, not a slicer. Perhaps you should have brought my counterpart Artoo-Detoo? He's much better at this sort of thing than I am. He is a fine model, but a bit too headstrong for a droid, if you catch my meaning."

Qwi ignored him as she stepped farther into the room, walking on tiptoes. Her skin felt cold and clammy. The air smelled stale, empty. She trembled as she ran her fingers along the cool synthetic stone of the thick support pillars. She caught a flash of distant memory—a ragged Han Solo tied to this pillar, barely able to hold his head upright after the "deep interrogation" Admiral Daala had performed on him. . . .

Qwi went over to the lab table, picked up her spectral-analysis sensors, materials-properties analyzers, stress and strain simulators, and a holographic 3-D design projector that glittered darkly under the bright lights.

"My, this appears to be a completely adequate workspace, Dr. Xux," Threepio said. "Spacious and clean. I'm sure you accomplished a great deal here. Believe me, I've seen far more cluttered research areas in facilities on Coruscant."

"Threepio, why don't you take an inventory of the equipment you see," Qwi told him, just to keep the droid quiet so she could think. "Pay particular attention to any demonstration models you find. Those could be significant."

Qwi discovered a small musical keypad lying half-hidden in a pile of printouts and handwritten notes. Beside the keypad stood the milky eye of a powerless computer terminal.

She switched the terminal on, but the screen demanded her password before it would allow her access to her own files. So much for that.

Qwi picked up the musical keypad and cradled it. The instrument felt familiar and yet alien. She touched a few of the keys and listened to the soft, high notes that issued from it. She remembered standing in the shattered debris of the Cathedral of Winds, picking up a fragment of one of the windpipes and blowing a slow, mournful melody through it. The winged Vors had snatched the flute from her, insisting that there be no more music until the cathedral itself was rebuilt. . . .

But this keypad held her own music. Qwi vaguely recalled using it, but she couldn't quite picture for what. A flickering image came to mind, like a slick, wet fruit that slipped from her fingers every time she tried to grasp it—*setting the keypad down, suspecting she might never come back.* . . . She winced, drew a breath, and tapped her fingers together, trying to think.

Han Solo! Yes, she had left everything untouched as she attempted to rescue Han and escape with the Sun Crusher.

She let her long blue fingers dance across the musical keys. Her mind remembered no particular sequence, but her body knew. Her hands moved by habit, tapping out a quick loop of melody. She smiled—it seemed so familiar to her.

When she finished the sequence of notes, her computer screen winked, PASSWORD ACCEPTED. She blinked her indigo eyes, astonished at what she had done.

ERROR, the computer printed. MAIN DATABASE UNAVAILABLE . . . SEARCHING FOR BACKUPS. FILES DAMAGED.

Qwi suspected Tol Sivron might have destroyed the computer core before fleeing in the Death Star prototype. But she must have left *something* stored within the temporary memory of her own terminal.

RECOVERED FILES FOLLOW, the screen said.

Qwi looked through a window into her own journals, her personal notes. Her heart pounded as she scanned words she herself had typed—but it was *not* herself. It was another Qwi Xux, a Qwi from the past who had been brainwashed by Imperials, a Qwi who had been twisted as a child and forced to perform to the utter limits of her mental abilities.

Taking shallow breaths, she read her daily accounts with growing uneasiness: the experiments she had performed, simulations she had run on the computer, meetings she had attended, endless progress reports she had filed for Director Sivron. Though she remembered none of it, it appalled her to realize that she had done nothing but work. Her only joy had come from completed experiments—her only moments of excitement, when tests proved her designs to be reliable.

"Was this all my life was?" Qwi asked. She scrolled down, scanning day after identical day. "How . . . empty!" she muttered.

"Excuse me?" Threepio said. "Did you ask for assistance?"

"Oh, Threepio." She shook her head and found tears stinging her eyes.

She heard footsteps in the outer corridor and turned as Wedge entered the lab. His face was smudged with grime, his uniform rumpled. He looked sweaty and exhausted, but she rushed to him and hugged him. He squeezed her shoulders, then ran his fingers through her feathery pearlescent hair.

"Is it bad?" he said. "Sorry I couldn't be here when you first entered the lab. I had an emergency."

Qwi shook her head. "No, I had to face this myself anyway."

"Find anything useful?" He stepped away from her, becoming the general again. "We need to know how many scientists were at the Installation. Most got away on the Death Star, but any information you have . . ."

Qwi stiffened and looked back at her computer terminal. "I'm not sure I can help you." Her voice carried a desolate, lost quality. "I've been looking over my daily life. It doesn't look like I *knew* any of the other scientists. I . . . I had no friends here." She looked at him, widening her depthless eyes.

"More than ten years of my life, and I knew no one. I worked. I thought I was dedicated. Defeating universal challenges meant a great deal to me—but I didn't even know what it was for. All I cared about was finding the next solution. How could I have been so naive?"

Wedge gave her an encouraging hug. He felt so warm and comforting against her. "That's all over, Qwi. It'll never happen to you again. You've been let out of a cage, and I'm here to help show you the rest of the universe— if you'll come along with me."

"Yes, Wedge." She looked up at him with a faint smile. "Of course I'll come with you."

Wedge's comm link beeped at him from his waist, and he pulled it out with a sigh. "Yes, what is it?" he said.

"General Antilles, we've brought down some temporary equipment to the reactor facility. We modified the critical components taken from one of the corvettes, as you suggested. We've managed to emplace them, and the systems are marginally functional. The core temperature levels of the reactor have begun dropping, and we expect them to go below the red lines within the next several hours."

"Good. Do we have a time limit here, then?" Wedge said.

"Well . . . ," the technician's voice answered, "the reactors are still shaky, but they're stable for now."

"Good work," Wedge said. "Pass along my commendations to your people."

"Yes, sir."

Wedge switched off and smiled at Qwi. "See, everything's working out after all," he said. She nodded, raising her face to look through the long, narrow window at the top of the wall. Pools of hot gas drifted around the Maw's black holes.

They seemed safe here, walled off from the conflicts of the galaxy. Qwi had fought her greatest personal battles, and now she could allow herself to relax just a little.

But before she could turn away, she saw a shadow appear in the multicolored nebula—a huge triangular shape, like a spear point plunging through the gases and emerging into the safe gravitational island.

Qwi stiffened, biting back an outcry of panic.

Wedge let go of her and whirled, looking up.

"Oh, dear!" Threepio said.

Battered and blackened, an Imperial Star Destroyer came through the Maw with its weapons already powering up. Its once-white hull was blistered and streaked with burn marks; its shielding plates damaged by an inferno of destruction.

Admiral Daala's flagship, the *Gorgon,* had returned to Maw Installation.

19

The Imperial Spider Walkers as-
cended the steep, pitted stone pinnacle. Their long
metal legs bent at odd angles as their claws hauled
them toward the heavy blast doors protecting Winter and
baby Anakin.

Winter stood in the operations room, her jaw clenched,
her eyes narrowed, as she viewed the progress of the
assault transports. They had reached her first line of
defenses.

When establishing the Anoth hiding place, Admiral
Ackbar and Luke Skywalker had been unwilling to rely
entirely on secrecy. They had tried to plan for every possible attack scenario. Winter had hoped she would never
need to test those contingency plans, but now she had to
fight for the child's life—and her own.

Winter looked down at her status panels: the Foreign
Intruder Defense Organism was primed and ready for automatic strike. She anticipated that FIDO could take out at
least two of the Spider Walkers. She watched, gripping
the edge of the consoles to steady herself.

Scuttling up the rock wall with insectile legs, the Spider Walkers reached a line of caves, small openings to a labyrinth of dead ends and grottoes within the stone.

Winter tensed as the first two MT-ATs passed, unsuspecting, over the black openings. The uppermost assault walker paused and fired a preemptive strike against the blast doors above with two forward lasers. A muffled thump and clang reverberated through the sealed installation.

As the second Spider Walker also prepared to fire, masses of whiplike tentacles lashed out of the hidden caves, long ropes each ending in a razor-sharp pincer claw. The tentacles took the Spider Walkers completely by surprise.

Two of FIDO's writhing arms locked around the first walker and ripped it from the cliff face. Before the machine could use its pneumatic claws to grasp the rock again, FIDO tossed the Spider Walker over the edge.

The MT-AT tumbled in a long clatter of wildly gesticulating legs. On its way down the Walker clipped another of the assault transports; the two plummeted together and exploded in a fiery crash on the jagged ground below.

The second Spider Walker fired with its laser cannon into the dark caves. One of FIDO's tentacles, black and smoking, withdrew like a flicked whip, vanishing deep into the tunnels; but other tentacles emerged from different openings to wrap around the Walker in a stranglehold. In desperation the turbolaser fired again, dislodging chunks of rock. FIDO squeezed, bending the articulated legs until their hinges groaned and thick rivets popped out.

Sensor-tipped tentacles comprehended what the cockpit of the MT-AT was for. FIDO's heavy plasteel claws smashed through the armored canopy, tearing open the roof and plucking out two stormtroopers to toss them over the precipice like gnawed bones discarded after a feast. Unmanned, the walker skidded down the cliff face as the remaining five assault transports scuttled out of the way.

Winter clenched her fist and slowed her shallow breathing. She tried to calm herself. The defending semiorganic droid had succeeded in removing three of the attacking machines, but the remaining five would almost certainly destroy FIDO.

Ackbar had proposed modeling a guardian droid after the dreaded sea monster from Calamari, the krakana. Calamarian scientists had designed a resilient, partially sentient machine that mimicked many of the krakana's most fearsome traits. Its tentacles were threaded with durasteel cables, its pincers plated with razor-edged alloys. FIDO's existence centered on protecting the base. The droid tentacles writhed out from the cavern, searching for more prey.

Three of the remaining assault walkers hauled themselves up on either side of the catacomb openings to fire repeatedly into the caves. Unexpectedly, from an apparently empty side hole, another trio of tentacles grabbed one of the Spider Walkers, dragging it toward the central cluster of cave openings.

Winter marveled at the tactic. Not only was FIDO destroying another one of the vehicles, it was also using the MT-AT as a shield. But the other Walkers did not stop shooting. Stormtroopers considered each other expendable for the sake of a mission.

The occupants of the captured Spider Walker continued to fire. FIDO dragged the MT-AT closer, crushing it against the rock like a thick-skinned jewel fruit. At close range the stormtrooper pilot powered up his low-slung, high-power blaster cannons and fired a combined blast into the caves. The enormous explosion ripped out a vast chunk of the catacombed understructure. Flames and dust, broken rocks and volatile gases, sprayed in a plume that rose into the violet skies of Anoth. The backwash vaporized FIDO's body core and, simultaneously, detonated the captured Spider Walker.

Inside the operations room FIDO's diagnostic panel went blank. Winter rubbed her fingertips along the smooth surface of the screen. The first line of defense had taken out half the assault transports. "Good job, FIDO," she whispered. "Thank you."

The multilegged assault transports began pounding against the blast doors. The thumps of turbolaser impacts and the screeching resistance of heavy metal filled the air.

Winter knew what she had to do. She toggled on the other automatic defense systems before fleeing the operations room. With silent footsteps she hurried down to the grotto, where Admiral Ackbar had recently come to visit her in his personal B-wing. Winter wished the Calamarian admiral could be at her side right now. She knew she could always count on him, but right now she had to act for herself and young Anakin.

She ruthlessly clamped down on her personal fears and forced herself to do what had to be done. No time for panic. She ran along the tunnels, leaving the metal hatches open for escape once the stormtroopers saw her. When she emerged into the landing grotto, the repeated thudding explosions from outside nearly deafened her.

The blast doors buckled inward, dented and glowing cherry-red as continued laser fire melted away the outer armor, chewing into the super-dense metal core. The doors bent as she watched; a split appeared in the middle.

Articulated claws pushed through the opening. Laser strikes continued around the attachment bolts until the left-side door twisted. The other door hung askew in its track.

Whistling wind shrieked into the landing grotto as Winter stood ready to face the assault.

With a whir of straining engines, the Spider Walkers clambered into the chamber, bristling with weapons and manned by crack stormtroopers.

• • •

The Dreadnaught *Vendetta* maintained its position in orbit. Colonel Ardax touched his fingertips to the voice pickup in his ear, listening to the report from the assault team on the planetoid below.

"We have succeeded in breaching the blast doors, Colonel," the stormtrooper commander said into the radio. "Losses have been heavy. Rebel defenses are stronger than anticipated. We are proceeding with caution, but we expect to have the Jedi child in hand shortly."

"Keep me updated," Ardax said. "Report to me when the mission is completed, and we will arrange for pickup." He paused. "Was Ambassador Furgan one of the casualties?"

"No, sir," the stormtrooper said. "He was in the rearmost assault transport and faced no direct danger."

Colonel Ardax signed off. "A pity."

Ardax was looking out at the three locked planetoids when sudden alarms rang through the *Vendetta*'s control deck. "What's that?"

A lieutenant looked up from his sensor station, his face ashen. "Sir, a Rebel battleship has just come out of hyperspace! It outguns us by a substantial margin."

"Prepare to take evasive action," Colonel Ardax said. "It appears that we've been betrayed." He drew a cold breath through gritted teeth. Furgan must have somehow given away their plans to Rebel spies.

The wide communications screen sizzled with gray static that resolved into the image of a fish-headed Calamarian. "This is Ackbar, in command of the star cruiser *Galactic Voyager*. Surrender and prepare to be boarded. Any New Republic hostages you have taken must be returned unharmed."

"Reply, Colonel?" the communications officer said.

"Our silence is enough of an answer," Ardax said. "Right now our primary objective is to survive. The surface team is forfeit. Set course to fly between the two close components of Anoth. The electrical discharges will mask us from their sensors, and from that point we can escape into hyperspace. Shields at maximum."

"Yes, sir," the tactical officer said. The navigator set a course.

"Full speed ahead when ready," Colonel Ardax said. He paced on the control deck.

With a lurch the *Vendetta* accelerated toward the broken planet. The Rebel battleship fired at them. The Dreadnaught rattled and shook as heavy explosions struck its shields.

"They outgun us, sir, but they are aiming to disable, not to destroy."

Colonel Ardax raised his eyebrows. "Ah, of course— they think we've got the child already! Let's not convince them otherwise."

The *Vendetta* sped into the grinding jaws of the broken world.

Leia squeezed until her nails bit into the smooth fabric of Ackbar's command chair on the *Galactic Voyager*. The battered old Dreadnaught wheeled in its orbit and set a new course. "They're calling your bluff, Admiral," she said.

"They are not responding," Ackbar agreed.

"They won't respond," Terpfen said, sullen at an auxiliary station. "They will run. If they already have the baby, there is nothing to keep them here. They won't risk a fight against a superior battleship."

Leia swallowed, knowing Terpfen was right. She wished Han could be beside her right now.

"Then we must not let them get away," Ackbar said. He had stuck close to Terpfen's side throughout the journey. During the mustering of the rescue force, Ackbar had snatched the most loyal members of his salvage crew on Reef Home City; he had gathered others from the starship construction yards in orbit. In all that time he had not once mentioned Terpfen's treachery.

Ackbar and Terpfen were having some kind of silent conflict, a wrestling of wills. Ackbar claimed he understood how the other had been manipulated. He himself had been a prisoner of the Empire, but instead of being programmed as a spy and saboteur, he had served as an unwilling liaison to Moff Tarkin. Though those times had been oppressive, Ackbar had managed to turn his close association with the cruel strategist into an advantage during Admiral Daala's attack on Calamari. Now, he claimed, it was time for Terpfen to use his misery against the Imperials as well.

As Leia watched from the bridge of the *Galactic Voyager*, the blunt-ended Dreadnaught ignited its sublight engines. She closed her eyes, gripped the back of Ackbar's chair, and sent out a tendril of thought with her mind to seek the presence of baby Anakin, hoping to find him or comfort him.

She sensed her baby across the vast distance of space, but could not pinpoint his location, feeling only his presence in the Force. She could make no direct contact, could not see him. Anakin could still be on Anoth, or he could be a prisoner aboard the Dreadnaught.

"Crippling strikes only. Fire all forward weapons," Ackbar said in a maddeningly calm voice. "Cause only enough damage to prevent them from entering hyperspace."

High-powered energy beams splashed against the *Vendetta*'s heavy shields. Residual radiation glowed from the hits, showing minor damage to the Imperial ship's hull. But the Dreadnaught continued to accelerate.

"He's going between two of the planetoids," Leia said. Terpfen leaned forward with interest, swiveling his round eyes as he concentrated. "He's trying to use the static discharges as camouflage," he said. "With so much ionization scramble we'll lose him on our sensors. Then he can escape on any heading before we find him again."

Leia breathed deeply to subdue her anxiety. They were so close—why else would the Dreadnaught run, unless they already had Anakin on board? Again she tried to sense where the baby was.

The two atmosphere-swathed fragments of Anoth's primary body loomed ahead of the Dreadnaught, with only a tight channel between the lumps. Fingernails of lightning skittered from one atmosphere to the other as the orbiting shards built up an incredible electrostatic charge.

"Increase speed," Ackbar said. "Stop them before we lose them in the static."

The Dreadnaught captain still refused to respond.

"Fire again," Ackbar said. "Increase power."

Turbolasers struck the starboard side of the *Vendetta*, shoving it visibly to one side with the momentum of the blasts. Its shields buckled; parts of the Dreadnaught's sublight engines were crippled. But the captain continued his flight. The blue-white exhaust glow increased as the engines powered up, readying for a jump into hyperspace.

"No!" Leia cried. "Don't let them take Anakin away!" Before she could finish her sentence, the Dreadnaught passed into the narrow passage between the split planet.

A blinding blue tracery of static blanketed the outer shields of the *Vendetta*, like a half-formed cocoon. The glow of an ionization cone spread out in front of it as it plowed through the thickening atmosphere into spectacular storms.

Leia squeezed her eyes shut, concentrating, concentrating. If she could establish a link between Anakin's mind and hers, she had some minuscule chance of tracking him once the Dreadnaught vanished into hyperspace.

She sensed the people onboard the Imperial battleship—but she felt no glimmer of her own son, nor of her longtime companion Winter. Leia reached out wider with her searching thoughts as the *Vendetta* plowed through the thin bottleneck of atmosphere.

The giant armored ship was like a metal probe between a pair of fully charged batteries. The Dreadnaught became a short circuit across the two supercharged atmospheres.

A colossal lightning bolt blasted through the atmosphere and linked across the warship like a chain of fire. A river of raw power slammed into the *Vendetta* from both sides, obliterating it in a hurricane of searing electricity, leaving only a burned afterimage on the screen.

Ackbar gasped audibly and hung his head. Terpfen slumped in his chair, but Leia observed the destruction with only part of her mind. She cast across space—until at last she found the bright point that was her youngest son, Anakin.

Terpfen stood up as if already bound in thick chains. "Minister Organa Solo, I submit myself to—"

Leia shook her head. "No punishment, Terpfen. Anakin is still alive. He's on the planet. But right now he's in terrible danger. We have to hurry."

20

Winter crouched by the metal hatch outside the landing grotto. She held a blaster pistol in one hand, knowing her white hair and light robes would make her easily visible even in the dimness.

Four huge mechanical assault transports picked their way over the wreckage of the left blast door and halted with hissing engines in the middle of the grotto. Transparisteel canopies flipped up with a high-pitched whir to disgorge stormtroopers.

Flicking her eyes from side to side, Winter took a quick inventory. Each of the four Spider Walkers carried two troopers—eight targets. She steadied her blaster and aimed at the nearest white-armored soldier.

Winter fired off three shots in quick succession. She couldn't tell how many actually hit the trooper, but he flew backward with his armor blasted to pieces. Other soldiers boiled out of the transports, firing in her direction.

Winter hunched down, but could not get another shot in. The last Spider Walker opened up to reveal one stormtrooper and a squat man with huge eyebrows and thick lips.

The other troopers had pinpointed Winter's position next to the door and hammered repeated blasts at her. She backed toward the open hatch.

Winter had two choices: she could either run back and stay with Anakin to defend him with her life—or she could lure the seven remaining invaders away from the baby and do her best to dispose of them.

Winter squeezed the firing button of her blaster without aiming. Bright streaks ricocheted around the grotto. The squat man ducked under the low-slung cockpit of a Spider Walker. "Go get her!" he yelled.

One of the stormtroopers, still in the cockpit of an MT-AT, brought laser cannons to bear and shot at the wall beside her head, leaving a smoking crater.

The squat man screamed from his hiding place under the MT-AT, "Don't kill her. Use stun until you have the child. You"—he gestured to the trooper who had emerged from the Spider Walker with him—"come with me, we'll . . . provide reconnaissance. The rest of you—capture that woman!"

Exactly as Winter had hoped. She fled down the corridor, knowing that most of the assault team would follow her. She sped along the sloping tunnels, ducking low through jagged archways, slamming heavy air-lock doors behind her as she passed into a deeper level of the installation.

The stormtroopers followed, making short work of the thick hatches by using focused thermal detonators that blasted the metal doors out of their seams.

Winter led them through the labyrinth of passages, farther and farther away from baby Anakin. The stormtroopers would be completely disoriented by now.

The troopers fired whenever they got a clear shot, but Winter managed to avoid being blasted to pieces. She heaved a sigh of relief—the only emotional release she allowed herself—when she finally succeeded in leading the troopers into the subterranean generator room and computer core.

The chamber itself was a dim morass of tangled equipment, cooling ducts, metal pipes, and throbbing life-support systems. The computer core glowed with oblong green lights that flickered in a waterfall pattern. The computers themselves, incorporated into the pumping stations and generator housing, formed a surrealistic cluster of twisted metal and plastic and a confusion of transparisteel diagnostic screens, input/output terminals— more equipment than anyone could possibly fathom a purpose for.

Winter knew the equipment was just stage dressing to hide the real purpose of the chamber.

The troopers hesitated at the threshold, as if suspecting a trap within the shadows. Winter pointed her blaster and fired seven rapid shots at them. The stormtroopers dived for cover and then, when Winter did not fire again, charged into the dim room after her.

Winter did not try to hide. She ran to the glowing pillar of the computer core and then into shadows on the other side of the chamber, surrounded by conduits and tubes and flashing lights that served no purpose. The stormtroopers moved toward her, still shooting.

Winter fired several more times, just to provoke them, and to make sure they remained within the chamber. One of her shots ricocheted off a gleaming surface and flew into the side of a stormtrooper, melting the white armor from his right arm.

Winter appeared to be cornered at the far side of the room as the troopers advanced toward her—five of them, one hanging back with an injured arm.

The Imperial soldiers got halfway across the space before the walls begin to writhe and move.

Jointed pipelines and conduits, bulky control decks, and spherical readout panels shifted, clicking together into specific components. Winter heard pieces locking into place, metal against metal, connections linking up.

The machine-filled walls suddenly became a squad of burly assassin droids assembled out of disguised components. The droids activated their weapons, forming a shooting gallery whose only purpose was to destroy stormtroopers.

Winter had no need to issue commands. The assassin droids knew exactly what they were supposed to do. They had been programmed to ignore her and the Jedi children, but they knew their targets well.

From all sides the assassin droids opened fire on the five pursuers. The cross fire of deadly beams cut down the white-armored Imperials in less than two seconds, leaving only piles of smoldering wreckage, fused and melted armor, and useless weapons in dead hands. None of the stormtroopers had an opportunity to fire a single shot.

One of the troopers groaned once, hissed in pain, then fell into the silence of death. The shadows cast a blanket over the carnage.

Heaving a sigh of relief, Winter stepped over the bodies, which were still sizzling from the massacre. She looked down at the expressionless black visors of the Imperial enemy. "Never underestimate your opponent," she said.

Ambassador Furgan crouched low as the stormtrooper sprinted ahead of him down the lumpy rock corridors.

Furgan had no combat training and no experience, but he did his best to imitate his companion's fluid movements. He held his blaster rifle in hand, glancing down repeatedly to make sure the weapon was powered up.

The tunnels were dim and shadowy, lit by white glowtubes mounted along the ceilings. The stormtrooper pressed his armor back against the wall and held his weapon around a corner to see if he drew any fire; then he jogged down to the next intersection of tunnels.

They passed door after door, unsealing each room, ready to snatch the helpless child and run back to their MT-ATs. Furgan and the trooper found storage compartments filled with crates of supplies and equipment, the dining room, empty sleeping quarters—but no child.

Far beneath them Furgan heard the patter and distant echo of blaster fire. He glared back toward the sounds. "I told them not to shoot her down. Why didn't they listen to me?" He turned to the stormtrooper. "Now we'll have to find the child all by ourselves."

"Yes, sir," the stormtrooper said, without expression.

The next metal door was locked and sealed. No one responded when the stormtrooper hammered with his white gauntlet. He withdrew a pack of tools from his utility belt, removed a high-powered cutting laser, and slashed open the door's control panel. Moving with nimble fingers despite the thick gloves, he rewired the sparking controls.

The door ground open, exposing the pastel colors of a room filled with toys, a plush bed . . . and a four-armed nanny droid backed into a protective position in the corner to shelter a small child.

"Ah, here we are at last," Furgan said. He stepped inside looking around for booby traps. The trooper flanked him, maintaining his defensive position, blaster rifle in hand. Furgan saw no other defenses, just the TDL droid.

"Please leave," the nanny droid said in a sweet, grand-motherly voice. "You are disturbing the baby."

Furgan let loose with a full-throated laugh. "The only defense they managed was *one nanny droid*?" He chuckled again. "We sent an entire assault team to take a baby away from a nanny droid?"

The TDL droid stood in front of the baby, who sat very still on the floor. The droid used her lower set of arms to unfold a blaster-proof metal apron from the base of her torso to shield the baby from stray laser fire.

"You may not have this child," the droid said. "I must warn you that my programming is to protect him at all costs."

"How touching. Well, I'm going to take that child—at all costs," Furgan said, nodding with a triumphant smile to the stormtrooper. "Go get the baby."

The stormtrooper took one step forward. The droid held out all four hands in an imperative gesture to stop. "I'm sorry, but I cannot allow that," the nanny droid said calmly. "Close your eyes, baby Anakin."

"What are you waiting for?" Furgan snapped at the trooper. "It's only a nanny droid."

With a whir and a click all four of the droid's hands detached and dropped to the floor, exposing the blaster barrels hidden in each of her wrists. "I am an *enhanced* nanny droid," she said with prim emphasis, "and you will not harm this child." She let loose with all four barrels, firing gouts of deadly energy.

The four beams struck the approaching stormtrooper before he could swing up his blaster rifle. He was hurled back against the wall, shards of white armor flying away from smoking black wounds.

Furgan yelled in astonishment and terror. He swung up his blaster rifle and depressed the firing button long before he took time to aim. A flurry of incandescent bolts sprayed across the room, reflecting from the pastel walls, bouncing off the corners.

Furgan ducked, but continued to fire. The nanny droid centered all four blaster arms on him—but Furgan raked his stream of blaster bolts across her rounded head and soft, flesh-encased torso, succeeding more through luck than skill. Sparks flew and molten metal showered in all directions.

Beneath the blaster-proof apron, the baby began to wail.

Bruise-colored lips curved upward in a smile, Furgan stepped over the debris of the nanny droid and the dead stormtrooper to retrieve the child. He reached down to grab one of little Anakin's arms and yanked him into the air by the cloth of his pajamas. Furgan wasn't quite sure how to hold a baby, especially one that continued to squirm as this one did.

"Come with me, little one," he said. "You are about to begin a whole new life of galactic importance."

21

Han Solo longed to get closer to Kyp Durron in the Council chambers on Coruscant, wanting to comfort his young friend—but the armed New Republic guards surrounding Kyp made it impossible for anyone to approach.

Kyp moved slowly, as if walking barefoot across shattered glass. His eyes were dull. His face was seamed with new lines, as if the dark spirit of Exar Kun had shed his four thousand years of existence onto Kyp's shoulders.

The Sun Crusher had once again been impounded by New Republic security, and Mon Mothma had declared the entire area off limits. There would be no further research into the workings of the superweapon. Kyp's chaotic vengeance had demonstrated how horrible the Sun Crusher truly was.

Inside the Council chambers the air smelled thick and oppressive from too much tension and too little ventilation. The stone added a musty old smell to the room. The place made Han uneasy and claustrophobic.

The Council members wore their formal uniforms like armor, frowning like ancient sentinels, passing judgment. Some looked as if they hadn't had any rest. Han felt deeply troubled to be facing them without Leia. She had departed from Yavin 4 with Terpfen, supposedly to go see Ackbar, but he had not been able to learn what had happened to her. Leia certainly knew how to take care of herself, though, and he did not dare leave Kyp alone with the predators here.

Mon Mothma, flanked by her ever-present medical droids, seemed only partially aware of what was going on. None of the other Council members had suggested removing her from office while she was still willing to attend meetings, though Mon Mothma contributed little. Han was stunned by how much the Chief of State had worsened in just the last few days.

One of the functionaries beside the sculpted door arch tapped on a long chime, sending a pure tone into the air to call the attendees to order.

Han didn't know much about the protocol of government, but he didn't plan to stand by and do nothing while Kyp was trounced by bureaucratic bigwigs. Before one of the members could speak, Han stepped forward. "Hey! Could you let me put in a word for my friend, Kyp Durron?"

Aging General Jan Dodonna hauled himself to his feet. Ancient and weathered, like a piece of gnarled driftwood, the bearded general still seemed filled with energy. His eyes flashed at Han. "The prisoner may speak for himself, General Solo. He has certainly shown no reluctance to *act* for himself. Let him answer our questions now."

Chastised, Han stepped back and looked at the floor, tracing patterns made by cracks in the inset flagstones. Since Dodonna had the lectern, he leaned forward to look down at Kyp. The young man lifted his tousled head and blinked sheepishly at the old tactician.

"Kyp Durron," Dodonna said, "you stole the Sun Crusher. You attacked and temporarily incapacitated the Jedi Master Luke Skywalker. You blew up the Cauldron Nebula and obliterated two other inhabited star systems. I will not debate the tactical significance of your actions—but we cannot tolerate juggernauts who make up their own orders and cause wholesale destruction on a whim!"

The other Council members agreed. General Rieekan's deep, thick voice reverberated through the chamber. "This Council had already decided that the Sun Crusher would never be used. We disposed of it in a safe and protected place, but you *knowingly* thwarted our wishes."

The other members fell quiet after Rieekan's words. They seemed eager to add their own condemnations, but realized there would be little point in it.

After a moment of silence Kyp spoke. His voice sounded impossibly thin and small, reminding Han and everyone else there just how young this boy was. "I have no excuse for my actions. I'll accept the consequences."

"Even if your actions demand the death penalty?" the obese Senator Hrekin Thorm asked. "Such destruction as you have caused can warrant nothing less than execution."

"Wait a minute!" Han said. The Council members glared at him, but he ignored their silent rebukes. "I know, I know—but listen to me for a minute. Kyp wasn't himself. He was possessed by the evil spirit of a Sith Lord who has since been defeated. And he did do some good. He destroyed Daala's fleet. How many lives did he save by doing that? We are at war, after all."

Mon Mothma's words wheezed from her cracked lips. Her voice came out in a ragged whisper. The rest of the chamber fell into a deep hush as she began to talk. "Kyp Durron," she said, "you have the blood of millions, perhaps billions, on your hands. We are a governing body here, not a judicial council. We have no right to decide your fate. You—" She gasped as if using most of her energy just to fill her lungs. "You must be judged by the Jedi Master. We are not qualified to judge your crimes."

She raised one of her hands to gesture toward Han. "Take him to Yavin. Let Master Skywalker decide his fate."

22

Leia, Ackbar, and Terpfen joined the rescue party from the *Galactic Voyager*, swooping through the violet skies of Anoth. Ackbar took the lead in his own B-wing. His weapons systems were powered up and ready to attack any ground assault team the Dreadnaught had deployed.

The starfighters soared over the fanged landscape toward the stone turret that Ackbar and Luke had chosen for the base. Leia saw signs of damage that made her blood run cold, smoke and debris from an attack. "We're too late," she whispered.

Part of the spire had been blasted away, and soot splattered the eroded surface. Below, she saw the still-smoldering remains of several horrific mechanical spiders.

Ackbar's voice came over the ship-to-ship intercom. "Winter must be putting up a good fight. Our emplaced defensive systems are functioning as planned."

Leia swallowed to clear her dry throat. "Let's just hope that's good enough, Admiral."

The fighters targeted in on where the blast doors had been melted aside. One of the heavy metal shields still hung in place in its tracks. The rescue ships maneuvered around the four Walkers that cluttered the floor of the landing bay. Ackbar, Leia, and Terpfen sprang out of their cockpits as other Calamarian fighters joined them.

"Terpfen, go with Minister Leia and half the fighters directly to the nursery. See if the baby is still there. I will take the other troops down into the lower levels to find Winter. I think I know what her strategy would have been."

Leia, not bothering to argue, yanked out her own blaster pistol. With a hardened expression she took the lead, running to see that her child was safe.

The team swarmed down the maze of convoluted tunnels toward the nursery. Leia glanced around her as she jogged but saw no signs of blaster fire on the walls. Weapons rattled against body armor as the Calamarians ran to keep pace with her.

As they rounded the last corner toward Anakin's room, Leia swerved to keep from tripping over the slow-moving power droid who plodded along on its rounds, unconcerned with the turmoil. Leia paid the walking battery no further heed when she saw the door to the nursery yawning open.

"Oh, no," she said, lurching to a cautious stop just as Ambassador Furgan backed out, clutching a squalling Anakin to his broad chest.

Both Leia and Furgan froze for a moment, staring at each other. Furgan's eyebrows jerked up in a muscular twitch like birds about to leap into flight.

The Calamarian rescuers leveled their weapons at Furgan. He held the baby in front of him like a shield.

"Give Anakin back to me," Leia said, her voice dripping with greater threat than an entire fleet of Star Destroyers could convey.

"I'm afraid not," Furgan said, and wrapped a broad hand around Anakin's fragile neck. His wild eyes flicked from side to side. "Point your guns away from me, or I'll snap his neck! I've gone through all this to get the Jedi baby, and I'm not going to give him up. He's my hostage, and the only way he stays alive is for you to let me go."

He edged along the tunnel. His back scraped against the rough, lumpy wall. Furgan locked his eyes on the weapons pointed at him, but he held the baby out, squeezing the boy's throat. "Even if you stun me, I can still crush his windpipe. Drop your weapons!"

"Back off," Leia ordered, taking a step backward.

The Calamarian defenders stepped to the side, clearing a path for Furgan—all except for Terpfen. He stood holding his hands in front of him like sharp claws.

Furgan saw the swollen, sagging Calamarian head, the tracery of blunt scars—and suddenly recognized him. "So, my little fish, you betrayed me after all. I didn't think you had the strength of will."

"I found the strength," Terpfen said. He stepped toward Furgan. Anakin continued to squirm in the ambassador's arms.

"Stop!" Furgan said. "You have enough on your conscience, little fish. You wouldn't want to add the death of this baby to it."

Terpfen made a low gurgling noise that was some kind of Calamarian snarl. Furgan kept his wild gaze fixed on all those cornering him as he slid backward toward the Spider Walkers and his only escape.

In his grasp baby Anakin's deep-brown eyes flashed, as if he were deep in thought.

Suddenly Furgan cried out as he stumbled against the squarish, waddling power droid that had silently crept up behind him. The power droid gave out a small jolt of electricity, shocking Furgan.

The ambassador tripped and fell, still holding the child. The power droid shuffled out of the way with a squeal of something like terror.

As the Calamarian defenders snatched up their weapons again, Terpfen lunged forward to grab the baby out of Furgan's hands.

The other Calamarians fired at Furgan, but the squat man rolled across the floor, got to his knees, and launched himself around the corner, moving far faster than Leia would ever have thought possible.

"After him!" Terpfen cried. He passed baby Anakin to Leia and dashed off in pursuit of Furgan.

As hot tears flowed from her eyes, Leia hugged her youngest son, trying to find words that would console him—but nothing came to mind, so she just made cooing noises. She sank to the floor, rocking him back and forth.

Ackbar's broad feet slapped on the stone floor as he ran deeper into the catacombs. His lungs burned in the dry air, but still he insisted on more speed. He pulled ahead of the others. So far Winter had followed exactly the guidelines he had established for defense of the base.

He knew from the wreckage outside that the Foreign Intruder Defense Organism had done its job, eliminating half the Spider Walkers before they could breach the blast doors—but it had not been enough. Winter would have proceeded down to trigger the camouflaged assassin droids.

The other team members clattered behind him. He could smell dust and engine oil in the dry air, and also a sharp, damp smell like copper and smoke—blood.

The robed form of Winter sprang around the corner, holding a blaster in front of her, ready to fire. But she froze. For just an instant a smile of delight crossed her face. "Ackbar! I knew you would come."

Ackbar strode toward her, resting his hand on her arm. "I arrived as fast as I could. You are safe?"

"For the moment," she said. "The defenses have eliminated all but two of the intruders, according to my inventory."

"Are you certain?" he said.

"I never forget anything," Winter said, and Ackbar knew it was true.

"Leia and the rest of my team should be getting Anakin now," he said, then continued softly, "We split up so that I could determine if you required assistance."

She nodded. The expression on her face softened. "I will not feel comfortable until I see the baby safe."

"Let's go," Ackbar said, still out of breath. Together they began the long run uphill.

Terpfen raced feverishly up sloping corridors. His feet were raw, bleeding from running on the textured floor, but still he ran. He didn't care if this race killed him. He had to get to Furgan before the ambassador escaped.

Furgan had jerked his controls and made Terpfen reveal damning secrets of the New Republic, forced him to sabotage Ackbar's B-wing so that it had crashed into the Cathedral of Winds, made him betray the location of the Jedi baby.

Terpfen would pay his personal debt in any way he could—but Furgan would also have to pay the price.

With determination coursing through his veins, Terpfen passed the other Calamarian pursuers. Through the dimness he could hear Furgan scurrying forward like a krabbex.

"Follow!" Terpfen wheezed as he shot past the others.

Terpfen leaped over fallen hunks of metal shrapnel, blasted doors that the invading stormtroopers had blown away. He emerged into the landing grotto to find Furgan already scrambling into one of the unoccupied MT-ATs.

"You can't escape, Furgan!" Terpfen shouted. He paused to catch his breath against the melted but now cooled hatch.

Furgan slung one leg over the edge of the Spider Walker and settled himself into its cockpit. His face wrinkled as if someone had scrunched it up from the inside.

"We already destroyed your Dreadnaught in orbit," Terpfen said. Finding energy deep within him, he staggered toward the walker. He heard the other troops catching up.

Furgan looked amazed at the news, but then his face smoothed again with disbelief. "I know better than to trust you, little fish. Your whole life is a lie."

Furgan closed the transparisteel canopy. The engines hummed to life. One of the outer blast doors had been completely torn away; the other hung half-open. Wind sighed through the opening. In the clotted purple sky the two larger components of Anoth rode overhead like stone clouds exchanging lightning across the silence of space.

Terpfen snarled and ran to another Spider Walker. He was a chief starship mechanic. He had helped the Imperials work on their combat vehicles and their Star Destroyers. He could run any equipment—probably better than Furgan himself.

In his panic Furgan had trouble making all eight of the Walker's legs move in sequence to make progress across the grotto floor, but he finally plowed ahead, swiveling the laser cannons on the joints of the articulated legs to blast one of the B-wing fighters that stood in the way.

Terpfen powered up his Spider Walker and slammed down the canopy. The machine had crude controls and sluggish response, nothing at all like the streamlined controls used on Mon Calamari Star Cruisers.

Furgan's vehicle approached the large opening at the cliff's edge, and Terpfen knew from the design of the MT-AT that it could climb straight down the rockface. He didn't quite know how Furgan would escape once he got to the bottom; he doubted the ambassador had thought that far ahead.

Terpfen found the fire controls and shot his lasers three times, taking out one joint of the other Walker's legs. The lower portion of the metal limb sheared off and fell to the grotto floor with a clang.

Off balance, Furgan's Walker scuttled in a drunkard's circle until he managed to compensate for the lost limb. Once again he made for the exit.

Terpfen saw the powerful blaster cannons slung beneath his cockpit—if he fired both of them in the enclosed grotto, it would obliterate Furgan's assault transport . . . but the explosion would also destroy him and his own Walker, and probably most of the B-wings as well.

Then Terpfen saw other rescuers streaming into the grotto. Admiral Ackbar himself came from a different entrance and stood with his own team next to a white-clad woman whom he recognized as Leia's companion Winter.

He could never fire the blaster cannons now. But he vowed not to let Furgan escape. Working the controls, Terpfen lunged the eight-legged vehicle forward in pursuit just as Furgan's machine tottered on the edge.

Ackbar arrived in time to see the beginning of the battle between the two Spider Walkers. Terpfen's lasers blasted out, striking the ambassador's MT-AT. Furgan didn't seem to have a plan, intending only to get away. Terpfen's Walker scuttled forward. Its clawed footpads struck sparks from the landing-bay floor.

Terpfen blasted again and again with his lasers. Furgan fired back, but his shot missed, scoring sharp flakes of rock from the grotto wall.

Terpfen's MT-AT charged ahead, raising its two front clawed legs, and grabbed the metal limbs of Furgan's transport, raising it partway off the floor. Furgan's vehicle reached out with its own legs to grasp the edge of the cave opening, trying to haul itself forward and away.

Terpfen fired directly at the transparisteel canopy of the cockpit, but the laser shots could not pass through the shielded surface. His Spider Walker grappled with Furgan's vehicle, four mechanical legs planted firmly on the stone floor, four legs *pushing* with all his engine's capacity.

A large chunk of rock shattered at the claw grip. With a horrible sound of rending, tearing metal, Furgan's walker finally broke free of the grotto opening.

Terpfen's MT-AT pushed forward and forward. Inside the cockpit of the ambassador's vehicle, Furgan frantically grabbed the controls but did not seem to know which to use.

Terpfen continued his relentless blasting with the lasers. He shoved Furgan's walker completely through where the blast door had been blown away and held out the thrashing MT-AT over open space.

Terpfen released his grip.

Ambassador Furgan's multilegged vehicle flailed as it dropped through the air on a long plunge toward the jagged landscape far below. Before the assault vehicle could actually strike the ground, Terpfen fired both of his powerful blaster cannons. The beams blew up Furgan's MT-AT with a blinding flash just above the spiked rocks.

And then, inexplicably, Terpfen's walker continued its own forward motion, moving mechanical legs to drive him over the edge in a suicidal plunge.

Ackbar instantly knew what Terpfen intended. Not wasting time with a shout that would not be heard, he lunged for the blast-door controls.

Just as the thrashing metal legs vanished over the lip of the cliff, Ackbar punched the buttons, hoping that the skewed half of the door still functioned just enough. The heavy metal plate crashed down on top of the last footpad of Terpfen's Spider Walker, pinning it to the cliff and preventing it from falling.

"Help him!" Ackbar cried.

The other Calamarians scrambled forward, accompanied by the admiral himself. Secured with a tow cable from one of the B-wings, they lowered themselves over the cliff to open the canopy of Terpfen's walker. Inside they found him shuddering and nearly unconscious with shock. The team rigged a sling and hauled him to the safety of the grotto.

Ackbar bent over him, looking stern. He called Terpfen's name until the scarred Calamarian finally stirred. "You should have let me die," he said. "My death should have been my punishment."

"No, Terpfen," Ackbar said, "we cannot choose our own punishment. There is still much you can contribute to the New Republic, still a great many things to do before you will be allowed to give up."

Ackbar straightened, realizing that those words could just as well apply to himself, after he had run away to hide on the planet Calamari.

"Your punishment, Terpfen," he said, "will be to live."

23

The *Falcon* cruised over the lush treetops of Yavin 4, and Han Solo set the ship down in front of the Great Temple. He bounced down the landing ramp.

Leia and the twins practically tackled him as they rushed to greet him. "Daddy, Daddy!" Jacen and Jaina cried in peculiarly overlapping voices. Leia, back from Anoth, cradling the one-year-old against her chest, squeezed Han and gave him a long kiss as Anakin played with her hair. The twins jumped up and down against Han's legs, demanding the attention that was their due.

"Hello there, little guy!" Han grinned down at Anakin; then he looked deep into Leia's eyes. "Are you all right? You've got a lot of details to tell me. That message you sent wasn't very explicit."

"Yeah," she said. "You'll get the whole story, when we have some quiet time, just the two of us. I'm glad all of our children are home to stay, though. We'll protect them ourselves from now on."

"Sounds like a great idea to me," Han said, then chuckled and shook his head. "Say, weren't you telling *me* that I shouldn't go off and have adventures by myself?"

Han stepped away from the *Falcon* as he saw Luke Skywalker striding toward him across the flattened landing grid. Artoo-Detoo puttered along next to him as if reluctant ever to leave his master's side again.

"Luke!" Han cried. He ran to give Luke an enthusiastic hug. "Great to see you up and around again. About time you quit napping."

Luke clapped him on the back and smiled with dark-ringed eyes that shone with an inner brightness stronger than ever before. As he conquered each seemingly insurmountable obstacle, Luke's Jedi powers grew greater and greater—but, like Obi-Wan Kenobi and Yoda, a Jedi Master learned to use his powers even less, relying on wits instead of showmanship.

In the dense jungle surrounding the Massassi temple a squawking racket boiled up as a gang of woolamanders startled a pair of feathered flying creatures; the woolamanders hurled rotten fruit as the flying creatures flapped into the air, shrieking down at their tormentors.

Han glanced toward the disturbance, but Luke's gaze remained fixed on the *Falcon*, as if held by a powerful magnet. Han turned to look—and stopped.

Kyp Durron, still wrapped in the slick black cape that Han himself had given him, descended the boarding ramp. His eyes locked on Luke's, and the two Jedi stared at each other as if psychically linked.

Han stepped away from Luke, and the Jedi teacher silently walked across the weed-strewn landing grid. Kyp reached the end of the ramp, planted his feet on the soil of Yavin 4 again, and stood looking penitent.

Han could tell from Kyp's rigid posture and his set jaw that the young man was terrified at having to face his Jedi Master. Han felt cold, not wanting to be trapped between two people he counted among his dearest friends.

Leia took the children off to one side, watching the encounter warily. Concern furrowed her brow as she flicked her gaze from her brother to Kyp and back again.

Luke walked toward his student slowly, as if gliding over the ground. "I knew you would come back, Kyp."

Han watched him, and it seemed that Luke had no anger in his bearing, no fury or need for vengeance.

"Exar Kun is destroyed?" Kyp asked hoarsely, but he knew the answer already.

"Exar Kun will have no influence on your future training, Kyp. The question is, what will *you* do with your abilities?"

Kyp blinked his eyes in shock. "You—you would let me continue my training?"

Luke's expression softened further. "I had to witness the death of my first teacher. I also had to confront Darth Vader, my own father. I have done other difficult tasks.

"I did not plan these things, but each time I passed through the fire of an ordeal such as those, I emerged a more powerful Jedi. You, Kyp, have been thrown into the flames. I must determine whether you have been consumed—or tempered into a great Jedi. Can you forsake the dark side?"

"I . . ." Kyp stumbled over his words. "I will try."

"No!" Luke shouted with the first glimmering of anger that Han had heard in his voice. "There is no *try*. You must *believe* you will do it, or you will fail."

The jungle fell silent. Kyp hung his head, and his nostrils flared as he took a deep breath. The young man's dark eyes glittered as he looked back up into Luke's face.

"I want to be a Jedi," he said.

24

Lando Calrissian felt as if the million-credit reward was burning a hole in his account. He needed to invest it soon.

It was a new feeling for him to have such a large sum of money and nothing practical to do with it. He had won control of Bespin's Tibanna gas mines in a sabacc game, and he had served for years as Baron Administrator of Cloud City. He had run metal-mining operations on the superhot planet Nkllon, and now with his huge reward from the blob races on Umgul, Lando saw no reason why he could not make a successful operation out of the spice mines of Kessel.

"I really appreciate your taking me, Han," Lando said. He reached over to slap his friend's shoulder in the cockpit of the *Millennium Falcon*. He knew that Han was not terribly pleased to leave Leia and his children again so soon, even if only for a day to drop him off at Kessel. He suspected, too, that Han was also worried about Chewbacca and the Maw occupation force, who had sent no word since advancing into the black hole cluster.

Since the Maw lay near Kessel, Han probably hoped to learn some news.

"It'll be worth it, if only to keep you from begging for rides all the time," Han said, looking in the opposite direction. He glanced out the front viewport. "I still think you're crazy to want to go to Kessel—even crazier to want to stay there."

Ahead, the small planet orbited near its faint sun. The misshapen lump of Kessel had too little gravity to hold its own atmosphere, and so the gases streamed into space like a tenuous mane flowing out from its barren rocky outline. A large moon, on which the alien prison lord Moruth Doole had stationed his garrison of pirates, climbed over the limb of Kessel, emerging from the wispy corona of escaping air.

"Last time I came here with Chewie," Han said, shaking his head, "we got shot down. I promised myself I'd never come back—and now it's only been a couple of months, and here I am again."

"That's just because you're a good friend, Han. I really appreciate it. Mara Jade wouldn't want me to be late."

Han smirked. "If she remembers to show up, you mean."

Lando laced his fingers behind his neck, staring at the rising moon as the *Falcon* arrowed in to a close orbit. "She'll be there," Lando said. "I'll bet she's been counting down the days."

"Wish I had Chewie back as a copilot," Han muttered, rolling his eyes. "At least he didn't say such hokey things."

At the mention of Chewbacca, both men subconsciously looked toward the glowing tapestry of ragged gases surrounding the Maw cluster. Somewhere inside, Chewbacca and the rest of the strike force should be mopping up their efforts to retake the Maw Installation. The black holes made communication impossible, so they had no way of knowing what had happened during the occupation.

"I hope he's all right, Han," Lando said quietly.

Han leaned forward to finger the controls on the comm unit. He hesitated, and his face sagged for an instant; he flicked on the transmitter, then cleared his throat, businesslike again. "This is Han Solo on the *Millennium Falcon,* approaching Kessel."

Lando watched Han's left hand drift to the hyperspace controls. A new course had already been programmed into the navicomputer. Han was ready to dash away at a moment's notice if anything suspicious happened.

"We're looking for Mara Jade, a representative of the Smugglers' Alliance," Han continued. "We, uh, request permission to land on the garrison moon. Please acknowledge before we come any closer." Han's face was lined with concern.

"Don't be so nervous, Han," Lando said. "Things have changed on Kessel. You'll see."

Han's voice took on a defensive tone. "I just don't want to take any chances after what's already happened."

Before Lando could respond, Mara Jade's crisp, businesslike voice came over the speaker. Lando felt his heart warm at hearing her subtle tones. He imagined her soft lips moving, forming the words.

"You're half a day late, Solo," she said.

"Well, Lando here wanted to make himself look presentable," Han said, grinning, "and you know how much time that could take."

Mara gave a short, sharp laugh, and Lando glared at Han. "Come on in, then," she said. "I've brought a defensive fleet from the Smugglers' Alliance. The garrison moon is secure. We'll discuss our business there. I have an escort coming for you—something I think Calrissian will appreciate."

Lando smiled broadly. "She's planned some kind of surprise for me! Probably a token of her affection."

"Oh, brother." Han rolled his eyes again.

Han checked the coordinates on his navigation console and vectored in toward the large station on Kessel's moon.

Disguised as potential investors in the spice-mining operations, Lando Calrissian and Luke Skywalker had been shuttled up to this moon by froglike Moruth Doole. Doole had done his best to show off the spice-mining operations in hopes that Lando would sink his blob-won credits into the facility.

With a shudder Lando remembered how all the ships in the hangar bay had launched after them when he and Luke had stolen Han's repaired *Falcon*. The Kessel pirate fleet had run headlong into Admiral Daala's Star Destroyers, as they charged out of the Maw cluster after Han Solo. The two fleets had crashed into each other, inflicting horrendous damage, but Han, Luke, and Lando had fled into hyperspace before seeing the outcome of the battle. . . .

Now a single small ship appeared over the misty horizon of Kessel. "This is Jade. I'm your escort. Follow me."

The space yacht approached, then spun about to dart toward the moon. Han increased the *Falcon*'s speed.

Lando sat up sharply, his eyes blinking in astonishment. "Hey, that's my ship!" he cried. "That's the *Lady Luck*. That's—"

"Well," Han said, "at least that saves us the trouble of looking for it."

Lando grabbed the comm unit. "Mara, you found my ship! I can't thank you enough." He lowered his voice. "If there's anything I can do to repay you, anything in your wildest dreams . . ."

"Keep talking like that, Calrissian, and I might just send this ship on autopilot into the sun."

Lando leaned back in the seat with a sigh and a smile. He flashed a glance at Han. "She's such a kidder."

The space yacht *Lady Luck* looked sleek and angular with propulsion pods slung below. Her hull gleamed, none the worse for wear, somehow unscathed from the devastating battles on Kessel.

Lando fidgeted, anxious to see Mara again, anxious to sit back in the plush cushions of his own pilot chair, to luxuriate in the smell and feel of his own ship.

They entered the cave mouth of the moon garrison, flying past the thick blast doors into the garish light of a large landing bay. The atmosphere-containment fields closed behind them and repressurized the habitable area. The *Falcon* coasted in on its repulsorlifts and landed in a broad polished area beside the *Lady Luck*.

Mara Jade swung out, clad in a tight metallic jumpsuit with a helmet tucked under her right elbow. As she tossed her head to loosen her dark, reddish-brown hair, she narrowed her eyes. Lando stared with a warm-cold shudder at the energy and intelligence that radiated from this woman. He marveled at her generous curves, her tough exterior.

"Hey, Mara," Han said, "where did you find Lando's ship? We thought we were going to have to spend days combing the surface for it."

"Right where Lando claims he landed it. Seems nobody had time to strip her down and remove the identification markings."

Lando glanced around the garrison bay, but all the ships looked unfamiliar, custom designs—not the barely moving scrap heaps that had made up Doole's fleet. These were emblazoned with markings unique to each vessel, though each carried a crosshatched design on the wing.

Mara noticed his inspection. "That's our new insignia for the Smugglers' Alliance," she said. "Not too obvious, but enough for us."

"What happened to all of Doole's ships?" Lando sniffed the enclosed dry air, smelling the powdered rock and spilled hyperdrive fuel that made the air sour and unpleasant.

"Ninety percent of Doole's ships were obliterated in their tangle with Daala's Star Destroyers. Most of the surviving pilots took their ships and fled into hyperspace. No one knows where they are now—and frankly, I don't really care.

"When a few New Republic relief ships came in, they evacuated most of the inhabitants, the prisoners in the Imperial Correction Facility, a few holdouts in the city of Kessendra. Nobody *wants* to make a life on Kessel if they have another option."

"So what you're saying," Lando said, letting his hopes rise, "is that Kessel is deserted, ready for the taking?"

"Yes," Mara said. "I've talked over your proposal with some members of our Alliance, and it sounds good to us. Not only have you proved your ability in your other ventures, but you've also got strong connections with the New Republic, which will allow efficient distribution channels for glitterstim. You've even got enough money to invest in the new infrastructure." She shrugged. "Sounds like a good deal all around."

Lando beamed. "I knew you'd realize that being partners with me is a very good deal."

Mara turned abruptly and continued with her discussion, ignoring his insinuation. "But we need to move right away. We've heard talk of other, less-scrupulous crime lords arranging to take over the mines. The spice tunnels are empty, ripe for the plucking. Frankly, we'd rather deal with *you*, Calrissian, than someone who's going to bring in his own teams and cut the Smugglers' Alliance out of the entire operation. That's why we brought our forces here to hold it, just in case some Hutt crime lord gets any ideas."

"Makes sense to me," Han said.

Lando rubbed his hands together, looking at the other ships in the bay. Various smugglers moved around, humans and aliens, burly-looking men and women, people he wouldn't want to meet alone in the dim lower levels of Coruscant. "Should we go down and have a look at the real estate?"

"Fine." Mara snapped to attention. "Let's go ahead and take your ship, Calrissian. You pilot her."

Lando reveled in the feel of his controls again, running his hands along the soft, polished seats. This was his own space yacht, specially built to his personal design. Now he was riding in the cockpit with a beautiful, intelligent woman, heading down to a planet where he intended to make a fortune. He didn't think the day could possibly get better.

He was right.

When they soared low over the parched and blasted surface of Kessel, they cruised past one of the major atmosphere factories, which had once spewed manufactured air to replenish the constant loss from the low gravity.

But the tall stack stood half-collapsed. Black blaster scorches mottled its pale exterior. The baked, dry ground—already lifeless except for a few tufts of extremely hardy vegetation—had been torn up by TIE bombers and space-based turbolaser strikes.

"Over half of the atmosphere factories are out of commission," Mara explained. "Admiral Daala did a lot of damage. Seems she thought this was a Rebel base, so she struck at anything that showed up on her targeting screens."

Lando had a sinking feeling deep in his chest. "This is going to take more work than I had anticipated," he said. But he consoled himself by calculating the unclaimed wealth within the tunnels below and thinking of how he could get teams of droids, Sullustans, and other races to work for shares in the profits. It might take a little longer to earn back his investment, but the demand for pure

glitterstim was so high that he could raise his prices—
at least until he turned a profit.

"I'm heading toward the prison," Lando said. "That
fortress should have withstood the attack from space. I
think I'll use that as my base of operations. It'll take
some conversion, but we should be able to adapt it into
the control center for our new manufacturing complex."

The speed of the *Lady Luck* rapidly ate the kilometers
across the empty landscape until a towering trapezoid
stood like a great monument on the barren surface.

The old Imperial prison was made of synthetic rock,
flat, unappealing tan veined with other colors. An outcropping of crystal windows jutted from the slanted smooth
front. Tubed elevator shafts rode along the angled corners.
The place was streaked with burn marks, but appeared
undamaged.

Lando heaved a sigh of relief. "At least the building looks intact," he said. "Something's going right for
a change. This'll be a great place to start." He smiled at
Mara. "You and I should christen our new headquarters!"

Mara Jade frowned and kept looking out the front
viewport. "Ah . . . there is one problem, Calrissian."

Lando and Han turned to look at her. The prison loomed
higher as the *Lady Luck* continued to approach.

Mara continued. "Well, you see, Moruth Doole has
holed himself up inside the prison building. He's scared
to death, doesn't know what to do. All of his cohorts have
fled or been killed, and now he's using the sophisticated
prison-defense systems to keep everyone else out."

The fortress looked impenetrable, a huge hulking mass
of stone armor. Lando had no desire whatsoever to see
Moruth Doole again, and neither, he knew, did Han.

"I wish you had mentioned that detail a little sooner,"
Lando said with a grimace as he brought the *Lady Luck*
in for a landing.

25

Inside the rigid cleanness of the medical chambers in the old Imperial Palace, Terpfen stood silent and patient. He waited and watched the massaging bubbles in the bacta tank working on Mon Mothma's ailing body.

The medical chambers glowed with sterile whiteness. The tiles on the floor and walls had been acid scoured; utensils and surgical equipment gleamed silver and chrome. Wall monitors blinked with a steady, throbbing rhythm, proclaiming the declining state of Mon Mothma's health.

Outside the chamber doors two New Republic guards stood watch, making certain no one could intrude.

Sound-absorption panels in the ceiling deadened the mechanical whispers in the large chamber. Two bullet-headed medical droids hovered on either side of the tank, tending Mon Mothma and paying no attention to Terpfen.

Beside him Ackbar stood tall and strong. "She'll be finished soon," he said. Terpfen nodded, not eager to speak to Mon Mothma—but resigned to the necessity of it.

In these chambers the Emperor had himself undergone rigorous treatments as dark-side workings rotted his physical body. Perhaps the same facilities could remove the scourge within Mon Mothma's body. Terpfen had little hope of that, though, now that he knew what had caused it. . . .

Mon Mothma blinked her greenish-blue eyes through the murk of the tank solution. Terpfen couldn't tell if she could focus on them standing outside, or if she merely sensed their presence. She moved her head, and the thick air hose drifted with her. Bubbles pummeled her body, forcing invigorating solutions through her pores.

Mon Mothma released her grip on the stabilizers within the tank and floated up. The droids assisted her in getting out. She stood sagging, dripping as her lightweight robes dribbled solution into drainage grates on the floor. Even the thin wet robes seemed as heavy as a leaden shroud to her. Her auburn hair clung like a skullcap. Her eyes were sunken, her face chiseled with deep canyons of pain and weakness.

She filled her lungs and exhaled, resting the flat of her hand against the medical droid's green shoulders. She raised her head with obvious effort and acknowledged her visitors.

"The treatments give me strength for only about an hour. Their effectiveness decreases every day," she said. "Soon it will be useless, I'm afraid, and I will no longer be able to perform my functions as Chief of State. The only question is whether I resign before the Council removes me. . . ." She turned to Terpfen. "Don't worry, I know why you are here."

Terpfen blinked his glassy eyes. "I don't believe—"

She raised a hand to cut off his objections. "Ackbar has spoken to me at great length. He has considered your case thoroughly, and I agree with his conclusions. You were not acting of your own free will, but were merely a victim. You have redeemed yourself. The New Republic can't afford to throw away defenders who are willing to continue the fight. I have already issued a full pardon for you."

She wavered, on the verge of slumping backward. The two medical droids moved to help her to a chair. "I wanted to make sure that got done before . . ."

Ackbar made a grumbling noise as he cleared his throat. "I am also here to tell you, Mon Mothma, that I have decided to stay. I will request that my rank be reinstated, now that it is clear the crash on Vortex was not solely due to my error, as I had originally thought. The people of Calamari are resilient, and they are strong—but if the New Republic is not also strong, my work at home will be fruitless, because we will face a galaxy full of shadows and fear."

Mon Mothma smiled at Ackbar, a sincere expression of relief. "Ackbar, knowing that you will be here makes me feel stronger than any of these treatments ever did." Then she showed a deeper misery and let her chin sink into her hands, a moment of weakness she would never have displayed in front of the Council. "Why did this disease have to strike me now? I'm mortal just like everyone else . . . but why *now*?"

Terpfen walked across the slippery floor, feeling the cold, polished surface on the soles of his broad feet. He bowed his scar-traced head. At the doorway the two New Republic guards stiffened at seeing the known traitor so close to their Chief of State, but Mon Mothma showed no alarm. Terpfen looked down at her.

"That is what I have come to discuss with you, Mon Mothma. I must tell you what has happened to you."

Mon Mothma blinked, waiting for him to continue.

Terpfen searched for the right words. His mind seemed so empty now that the implanted biological circuits had been neutralized. He had hated the insistent compulsions from Carida, but now he was left alone with his own thoughts—no one else inside his skull to taunt him, or to guide him.

"You are suffering from no disease, Mon Mothma. You have been poisoned."

She jerked in sudden shock but did not interrupt him.

"It is a slow, debilitating poison targeted specifically to your genetic structure."

"But how was I exposed to this poison?" She looked hard at him, not accusing, but insisting on answers. "Did you do it, Terpfen? Was this another of your programmed actions?"

"No!" He reeled backward. "I have done many things—but this is not one of them. You were poisoned by Ambassador Furgan himself, as dozens of people watched. During the diplomatic reception at the Skydome Botanical Gardens. Furgan carried his own refreshment because he claimed you might try to poison *him*. He had two flasks, one on each side of his hip. In one flask he carried his true beverage, in the other he carried a poison specifically developed for you. He pretended to propose a toast and then tossed a glassful of the poison into your face. It seeped into your pores and has been multiplying and attacking your cells ever since."

Both Ackbar and Mon Mothma stared at him in astonishment.

"Of course!" she said. "But it's been months. Why did they choose such a slow-acting . . ."

Terpfen closed his eyes, and the words came to him as if he were reciting a script. "They wanted a long, debilitating decline for you because of the damage it would do to the New Republic's morale. If you were simply killed, you could become a martyr. Your death might have galvanized support from otherwise neutral systems. But with a slow, progressive weakening, it could be seen as the decay of the Rebellion."

"I see," Mon Mothma said.

"Very shrewd," Ackbar said. "But what are we to do with this information? What else do you know of the poison, Terpfen? How can we treat it?"

Terpfen heard the silence in his head like a scream. "This is not a true poison. It is a self-replicating swarm of nano-destroyers: microscopic, artificially created viruses dismantling Mon Mothma's cells one nucleus at a time. They will not stop until her life ceases."

"Then what do we do?" Ackbar persisted.

Finally the helplessness and all the pain within Terpfen built until it spilled out of him like a star finally reaching its flash point.

"We can do nothing!" he shouted. "Even knowing about this poison does not help us, because there is no cure!"

26

The battered Star Destroyer
Gorgon barely survived its passage through the gravitational
whirlpool into the Maw cluster.

Admiral Daala strapped herself to a command chair
on the bridge as the Star Destroyer was buffeted by tidal
forces that would rip the ship apart if their trajectory
deviated from its charted path. Daala had ordered her
crew to stand down and take refuge in protective areas,
to buckle themselves into their stations and prepare for a
rough ride. Of the very few known paths inside the Maw
cluster, she had chosen the shortest, the "back door," but
still her ship was in no shape to withstand the enormous
stresses for long.

Many of the *Gorgon*'s stabilizers had blown in their
narrow escape from the multiple supernova explosion in
the Cauldron Nebula. Shields had failed at the end—
but they had held long enough. The *Gorgon*'s once-ivory
metallic hull was now streaked and scarred. Outer layers of armor had boiled away, but Daala had taken a
gamble.

She had been lucky fleeing from the exploding suns, while only seconds behind her the *Basilisk* had vaporized in flame, disintegrated by the outrushing supernova shock wave. But Daala had ordered the *Gorgon* to plunge blindly into hyperspace mere moments before the explosive front had reached her rear thrusters. The desperate leap knocked them headlong on a reckless course through the hazards of the universe. The *Gorgon* would have been obliterated if they had stumbled onto an interdimensional path that passed through the core of a star or planet. But through some miracle of fate that had not happened.

The *Gorgon* had emerged in an uninhabited void in the Outer Rim. Their shields had failed, life-support systems partly burned out, and the hull had been breached in several areas that let the atmosphere squeal into the vacuum of space until those compartments were sealed off.

Collectively gasping from their narrow escape, Daala's crew had set about effecting repairs. It took her navigators a day just to determine their galactic position because they had gone so far afield. Armored spacetroopers in totally contained environment suits walked over the external skeleton of the *Gorgon*, removing ruined components, patching weak spots in the hull, rigging replacements from their meager inventory of spare parts.

The Star Destroyer had drifted in the uninhabited space between stars. One of the engines was permanently damaged, and three of the aft turbolaser batteries were dead. But Daala had let none of her crew rest until the *Gorgon* was functional again. They had a mission to complete. She did not allow herself the luxury of rest, either, tirelessly marching down corridors, inspecting repairs, making personnel assignments, prioritizing maintenance tasks.

Daala had done well for more than ten years, drilling her stormtroopers and her space navy personnel. They were used to grueling labor, and they performed admirably now that they were faced with a true crisis.

Grand Moff Tarkin had given her command of four Star Destroyers to protect Maw Installation. But her first ship, the *Hydra,* had been lost even before she could bring her fleet out of the Maw cluster. The *Manticore* had been destroyed behind the moon of Calamari, unable to run when some Calamarian tactical genius had second-guessed Daala's strategy. Her third ship, the *Basilisk,* already injured in the battle against smuggler forces at Kessel, had not been able to flee the supernova explosions fast enough.

Daala had been helpless to stop the attrition of her forces. She had planned a fabulous and devastating attack on the Rebel capital world of Coruscant, but before she could strike, Kyp Durron had used the Sun Crusher against her.

During the long days of repairs Daala had come to terms with her failure. She had misplaced her priorities. Her only reason for existence should have been to protect Maw Installation, not to wage a private war against the Rebellion. Once the Rebels knew of the Installation, they would no doubt attempt to steal its secrets. Her priority now was to fulfill the mission that Tarkin had given her.

The *Gorgon* was wounded, unable to proceed at full thrust; but still Daala approached the Maw with all possible speed. She would return to the Installation and protect what remained of it, to the best of her ability. There would be no such thing as surrender. She had a job to do, a duty she had sworn to her superior officer Tarkin.

Now Admiral Daala clung to her command chair and kept her eyes open against the blazing swirls from the inferno of trapped gases. The *Gorgon* plunged through the barrier of black holes and followed a convoluted path. Daala felt her insides tugged as she passed gravity wells so deep they could crush an entire planet to the size of an atom.

The windowports dimmed, but still Daala did not close her emerald eyes. Presumably only she knew the detailed route, but young Kyp Durron had found his way, and she assumed that other Jedi Knights could perform the same feat.

Daala heard a system squeal with automatic alarms as some critical component failed. Sparks shot out of one of the sensor stations, and a lieutenant strained against the pull of acceleration to bypass the systems.

In his seat Commander Kratas spoke through clenched teeth. "Almost there," he said, his voice barely audible above the racket.

A series of automatic warning signals echoed through the bridge—and suddenly the colors washed away from the front viewport like a blindfold being ripped from her eyes. The Star Destroyer had stumbled into the shielded calm at the center of the cluster.

She recognized the isolated clump of interconnected planetoids gathered in a loose configuration. Glittering lights showed that the facility still functioned. In a rapid assessment she saw that the framework of the Death Star prototype was gone—and in its place she saw a Rebel frigate and three Corellian corvettes.

"Admiral!" Kratas said.

"I see, Commander," she answered in a clipped voice.

She unbuckled her restraints and stood up, automatically smoothing down the olive-gray uniform that clung to her trim body. Sweat prickled like tiny insect stings on her skin as she stepped onto the command platform and walked closer to the viewport as if responding to a summons.

Her gloved hands gripped the bridge railing as if to strangle something. Black leather squeaked against enameled metal. The Rebels had come, just as she had feared—and Daala had arrived too late to stop the invasion!

Her lips grew white as she pressed them together. She believed the *Gorgon* had survived for a purpose. And now, as she returned to Maw Installation, it seemed as if the spirit of Grand Moff Tarkin were looking over her shoulder, guiding her. She knew what she was destined to do. She could not fail a second time.

"Commander, power up all functional weapons systems," Daala said. "Shields up. Approach the Installation."

She looked back at large-browed, weak-chinned Commander Kratas, who snapped to attention.

"It appears we have some work to do," Daala said.

27

Kyp Durron ducked under a thorny vine as a flock of scarlet insect-birds thrummed into the air. Acrid stinging thistles brushed against his arm, his face. Overhead, the interlocked branches rustled as arboreal creatures fled from the noise. Sweat dripped from Kyp's dark hair, and the oppressive air felt like a moist blanket, smothering him.

He did his best to keep up with Master Skywalker, who flowed through the jungle thickets, finding secret paths that allowed him to pass unhindered. Kyp had once used dark tricks to dodge spiny debris and find the easiest routes through the underbrush; now, though, even the thought of such techniques made him shudder with revulsion.

Once, when he had gone on a jungle sojourn with Dorsk 81, Kyp had brashly used a Sith technique to generate an unappetizing aura around himself, driving away gnats and bloodsucking pests. Now, though, Kyp tolerated the misery as Master Skywalker led him far from the Great Temple.

They had left the other Jedi trainees to continue their independent studies. Master Skywalker was proud of them. He said that the trainees were reaching the limits of the techniques he himself could teach them. The new Jedi Knights would grow in their own directions, discover their own greatest strengths.

But since the time he had come within a razor's edge of blasting Han Solo with the Sun Crusher, Kyp had been reluctant to use his power, afraid of what it might drive him to do. . . .

Master Skywalker took Kyp alone out into the jungles, leaving the great pyramid behind as Artoo-Detoo wobbled and jittered, bleeping with displeasure at being left behind.

Kyp wasn't sure what the Jedi teacher wanted from him. Master Skywalker said little as they trudged for hour after hour through the dripping rain forest and the oppressive humidity, the insect-laden air, the claw-thorns of brambles.

Kyp was intimidated to be alone with the man he had defeated through Exar Kun's evil powers. Master Skywalker had insisted that Kyp arm himself—that he wear the lightsaber built by Gantoris. Did Luke intend to challenge Kyp to a duel—a duel to the death this time?

If so, then Kyp vowed not to fight. He had allowed his anger to cause too much destruction already. It was only by a miracle that Master Skywalker had survived the onslaught of Sith treachery.

Kyp had recognized the dark side when Exar Kun whispered in his ear, but he had been too overconfident, thinking he could resist where even Anakin Skywalker failed. But the dark side had swallowed him whole—and now Kyp questioned all of his abilities and wished he could just be free of his Jedi talent so he need not fear what he might do with it.

At the edge of a clearing, with tall grasses stroking against each other, Master Skywalker came to a halt. Kyp stopped beside him to see two ferocious-looking predators, iridescent in scales of pale purple and mottled green for camouflage in the thick vegetation. They looked like hunting cats crossbred with large reptiles: their shoulders were square, their forearms as powerful as heavy pistons. They had three eyes across their boxy faces, yellow and slitted, unblinking as they stared at the intruders.

Master Skywalker gazed back at them in silence. The breeze stopped. The predators growled, opening their mouths to expose scimitar fangs, and let out a purring howl before they melted back into the jungle.

"Let's continue," Master Skywalker said, and walked across the clearing.

"But where are we going?" Kyp asked.

"You'll see soon enough."

Unable to bear his feelings of isolation and loneliness, Kyp tried to keep the Jedi teacher talking. "Master Skywalker, what if I fail to distinguish between the dark side and the light side? I'm afraid that any power I use now might also lead me down the path of destruction."

A feathery-winged moth flitted in front of them, seeking nectar from the bright flowers that blossomed among the creeping vines. Kyp watched the moth's flight until suddenly, from four different directions, sapphire-winged piranha beetles zoomed in to strike, ripping the moth's wings to shreds. The moth fluttered and struggled, but the piranha beetles devoured it before it could even fall to the ground. The beetles buzzed so close to Kyp's face that he could see their saw-toothed mandibles ready to tear flesh to shreds; but the beetles ratcheted away to seek other prey.

"The dark side is easier, faster, more seductive," Luke said. "But you can identify it by your own emotions. If you use it for enlightenment to help others, it may be from the light side. But if you use it for your own advancement, out of anger or revenge, then the power is tainted. Don't use it. You will know when you are calm, passive."

Kyp listened and knew that he had done everything wrong. Exar Kun had given him false information. The Jedi Master turned to him; his face looked haggard with the weight on his shoulders. "Do you understand?" Master Skywalker asked.

"Yes," Kyp answered.

"Good." Master Skywalker parted the branches on the other side of the clearing to expose a sight that made Kyp stop cold in his tracks. They had come from a different direction, but Kyp could never forget the site itself. Fragments of burning ice trickled down his spine.

"I feel cold," he said. "I don't want to go back there."

They stepped out to where the vegetation dropped off at the edge of a glassy-smooth lake, a circular reflecting pond where the water looked clear and colorless and reflected the cloudless skies above like a pool of quicksilver.

In the center of the pond sat an island of volcanic rock on which perched a sharply angled split pyramid made of obsidian. Two halves of the steep pyramid had been spread apart to bracket the polished black statue, a towering colossus of a man with flowing hair, bulky uniform, and a long black cape. Kyp knew the image all too well.

Exar Kun in life.

Inside that temple Kyp had received his initiation into the Sith teachings, while Dorsk 81 had lain in an unnatural coma against the wall. The spirit of Exar Kun had meant to destroy the cloned Jedi student on a whim, as a gesture of power, but Kyp had stopped him, insisting instead that the Sith Lord teach him everything. He had seen things that still left yammering nightmares in the depths of his mind.

"The dark side is strong in that place," Kyp said. "I can't go in there."

Master Skywalker said, "In your fear lies caution, and in that caution lies wisdom and strength." He squatted on a comfortable rock at the edge of the crystalline lake. He shaded his eyes against the light reflecting from the surface of the pool.

"I will wait here," Master Skywalker said, "but you must go inside."

Kyp swallowed, terror and revulsion rising within him. This black temple symbolized everything that had rotted his core, everything that had led him astray, all the mistakes he had made. The dark lies and goading of Exar Kun had caused Kyp to kill his own brother, to threaten the life of his friend Han Solo, to strike down his Jedi teacher.

Another shiver passed through him. Perhaps this was his punishment.

"What will I find in there?" Kyp asked.

"Ask no more questions," Master Skywalker said. "I can give you no answers. You must choose whether to carry your weapon with you." He nodded toward the lightsaber handle clipped to Kyp's waist. "You will have only what you bring with you."

Kyp touched the ridged handle of the lightsaber, afraid to turn it on. Did Master Skywalker want him to leave it behind or take it? Kyp hesitated. Better to have the weapon and not use it, he decided, than to need it and be without.

Trembling, Kyp went to the water's edge. He looked down and observed the tall columns of stone that stopped just beneath the surface of the water, providing submerged stepping stones.

Tentatively, he set one foot on the first stone. The water rippled around his foot. He drew a deep breath, raised his head high, and fought back the echoing voices in his head. He had to face this, whatever it was. He did not look back at Master Skywalker.

He crossed the water and climbed onto the lichen-encrusted lava rocks of the island, walking the narrow path that led to the triangular entrance of the temple.

Beneath the towering statue of Exar Kun, the black opening glittered with implanted Corusca gems. Incised runes and hieroglyphics broke the polished brightness of the obsidian. Kyp stared at the writings, finding that he could summon some of their meaning back to him; but he shook his head to clear the words from his thoughts.

The temple seemed to breathe a cool air current that seeped in and out of the enclosed space. Kyp did not know what he would find inside. His body stiffened with anticipation. He looked around, refusing to call out. Kyp took one step into the doorway and looked up at the dour chiseled face of the long-dead Sith Lord. Then he entered the temple chamber.

The walls glittered with an inner light that had been trapped within the volcanic glass. Tracings of frost spiraled in a frozen dance up and down the walls. In the far corner a cistern dripped, filled with chilled water.

He waited.

Suddenly Kyp's stomach wrenched. His skin crawled. He blinked as his vision blurred. The air around him grew grainy as if the light itself had splintered inside the temple.

He tried to turn, but found himself moving sluggishly as if the air resisted him, solidifying around him. Everything flickered.

Kyp staggered deeper into the temple, trying to move quickly, but his body would not respond with its customary speed.

A shadow rose from the black wall, an ominous form, human-shaped. It gained power, growing as Kyp fed it with his fear. The figure rose higher, oozing out of the cracks, out of a blackness from beyond time, a featureless silhouette that nevertheless seemed familiar to Kyp.

"You're dead," Kyp said, attempting to sound angry and defiant, but his voice was uncertain.

"Yes," the oddly familiar voice spoke from within the shadows. "But still I live within you. Only you, Kyp, can make my memory strong."

"No, I'll destroy you," Kyp said. In his hand he felt the black power crackling, the ebony lightning he had used to strike Master Skywalker: the power of fanged serpents, the dark teachings of the Sith. How ironic it would be to use Exar Kun's own power against him! The energy grew stronger, begging to be unleashed, demanding that he give himself over to it so he could eradicate the black shadow for all time.

But Kyp forced himself to stop. He felt his heart pounding, his blood singing in his ears, his anger taking control—and he knew that was wrong. He took deep breaths. He calmed himself. This was not the way.

The black Sith power faded from his fingertips. The shadow waited; but still Kyp forced his power back, smothered his anger. Anger was exactly what Exar Kun would want. Kyp could not give in to it now.

Instead he reached for the lightsaber at his hip, pulled it free, and flicked on the power button. The violet-white blade shone in an arc of cleansing electricity, purest light.

The shadow hovered, as if waiting to do battle with him, waiting for Kyp to make the first move. It lifted its nebulous arms, blacker than anything Kyp had seen before. Kyp raised Gantoris's lightsaber to strike, proud of what he was about to do. He would use a Jedi weapon instead—a weapon of light to strike the darkness.

He made ready to swing. The shadow hung poised, as if stunned—and Kyp halted again.

He could not strike out, not even with a lightsaber. If he attacked Exar Kun, he would still succumb to the temptation and ease of violence, regardless of the weapon he chose.

The lightsaber handle felt cold in his grip, but Kyp switched the power off and clipped the handle to his belt. He stood alone, face-to-face with the shadow that now seemed his own size, merely the black outline of a human wearing a shroud.

"I will not fight you," Kyp said.

"I am glad," said the voice, which became clearer now, more maddeningly familiar. Not Exar Kun at all. It never had been.

The shadowy arms reached up to pull back the cowl, exposing a luminous face that clearly belonged to Kyp's brother, Zeth.

"I am dead," the image of Zeth said, "but only you can keep my memory strong. Thank you for freeing me, brother."

The image of Zeth embraced Kyp with a brief, tingling rustle of warmth that melted the ice in Kyp's spine. Then the spirit vanished, and Kyp found himself alone again in a musty, empty temple that no longer held any power over him.

Kyp stepped into the warm sunlight again, free of the shadows. On the opposite shore he saw Master Skywalker stand up and look at him. Luke's face wore a broad grin, and he opened his arms in a celebratory gesture.

"Come back and join us, Kyp," Master Skywalker called. His voice echoed across the flat surface of the still water. "Welcome home, Jedi Knight."

28

The immense barricade doors of the Imperial Correction Facility did not budge, nor did they open when Han knocked. Naturally.

He stood with Lando and Mara Jade outside on the scoured landscape of Kessel, dressed in an insulated jumpsuit taken from the *Lady Luck*'s stores. Mara leaned closer to Han, her shout muffled through the breath mask covering her mouth.

"We could bring down a full-scale assault team from the moon," she said. "We have enough firepower."

"No!" Lando shouted. His dark eyes shone with excitement and anxiety. "There must be a way to get in without damaging my facility!"

The cold, dry wind stung Han's eyes, and he turned his head to protect them from the breeze. He remembered gasping for air when Skynxnex, Moruth Doole's henchman, had dragged him and Chewbacca into the spice mines without giving them breathing apparatus. Right now Han wanted nothing more than to kick the toadlike Doole out of the prison so that his frog eyes could blink and his fat lips pump together as he tried to fill his lungs.

Doole, an administrator of the Correction Facility, had dealt in black-market glitterstim, making deals with Han and other smugglers to deliver the precious cargo to gangsters such as Jabba the Hutt. But Doole had a habit of delivering his partners into Imperial hands whenever it proved convenient. Doole had ratted on Han long ago, forcing him to dump his cargo—which had made Jabba very angry. . . .

Han did not want to be back on Kessel. He wanted to be back home with his wife and children. He wanted to have his companion Chewbacca back. He wanted to take a nice, relaxing vacation. For once.

"I've got a better idea," Mara said, interrupting Han's thoughts. She craned her neck to look up at the murky sky. "Up on the garrison moon I brought along Ghent, our slicer. You might remember him. He used to be one of Talon Karrde's top aides. He can crack into anything."

Han remembered the brash young slicer: an enthusiastic kid who knew electronics and computer systems intimately, but didn't know when to keep his mouth shut. Han shrugged. They didn't need social skills now; they needed someone who could crack through the defenses.

"Okay, bring him down along with the *Falcon*," Han said. "I've got a few gadgets inside my ship that might help us out, too. The sooner we can get in, the sooner I can get going."

Lando agreed. "Yes, any way to enter without doing too much damage . . ."

Mara pursed her lips. "I'm also going to bring in a team of fighters. I've got four Mistryl guards and a handful of other smugglers who are getting fidgety with our new alliance. Some of them have been complaining that it's been too long since they had a good, satisfying fistfight."

An hour later, cold and uncomfortable even in the insu-

lated suit, Han sat on the *Lady Luck*'s thruster pod. He saw
the faltering plumes from two distant atmosphere-factory
stacks, but the rest of the world stood lifeless. He knew
from experience, though, that deep within the spice mines
lurked hideous energy spiders, waiting to strike any creature they found.

Han heard a sonic boom reverberate through the thin
atmosphere, a high-pitched sound mixed with the thunder
of sublight engines. He scanned the sky until he saw the
pronged disk of the *Millennium Falcon*.

The ship landed in a powdery white clearing beside the
Lady Luck. The ramp slid out, and five smugglers emerged:
two tall, well-muscled women—Mistryl guards—a hairy,
tusk-faced Whiphid, and a reptilian Trandoshan; each
wore a uniform with the crosshatched insignia of the new
Smugglers' Alliance. The smugglers bristled with weapons;
their bulging belts contained enough recharge packs for an
entire assault.

Last down the ramp, still fumbling to adjust a breath
mask over his face, came Ghent the slicer, with tousled
hair and rapidly blinking, alert eyes. He nodded cursorily
at Mara, then fixed his entire attention on the barricade
gates. Slung over his shoulder was a satchel crammed with
tools, diagnostic apparatus, splitters, rerouting circuits,
and security-cracking equipment. "Should be a piece of
cake," Ghent said.

Mara Jade and Lando sat next to Han and watched
Ghent fall to work with total concentration, not the least
distracted by the miserable environment of Kessel.

Han said, "I certainly never dreamed I'd be trying so
hard to break *into* the Kessel prison."

Cowering behind a locked door in the lower levels of
the Imperial Correction Facility, Moruth Doole longed for
the good old days. Compared to the constant paranoia he

had endured for the past several months, even life under the Imperial yoke had been paradise.

After he had taken over the prison years ago, Doole had moved into the warden's office, where he could spend much time staring out at the landscape, observing the desolate purity of the alkali wastelands. He had fed upon tender flying insects. Whenever the whim struck him, he had mated with one of his captive female Rybets in his personal harem.

Now, though, since Daala's attack, he had moved into one of the high-security prison cells for protection. He had tried to make preparations, establish defenses, because he knew someone was going to come after him, sooner or later.

The cell walls were thick and blast proof. The lights shone down, burning shapes into his blurry vision. He tapped the mechanical eye that helped him to focus. The device had broken during the space battle around Kessel. Doole had tinkered with the mechanical components, putting its gears and lenses back together; it no longer worked quite properly, though, and his vision winked out from time to time.

Doole paced the cold stone floor of his cell. Everything had fallen apart. The planet Kessel had been abandoned, leaving only smoking rubble on the surface and destroyed hulks of ships strewn across the system all the way to the black hole cluster. Doole couldn't even get a ship of his own to escape. He didn't *want* to stay here—but what choice did he have?

Even the blind larvae—the large-eyed creatures whom Doole had locked inside pitch-black rooms to process the mind-enhancing spice, glitterstim—were growing restless. He had cared for them, given them food (a meager amount, to keep their growth down, but enough for survival), but now they had begun to struggle.

Doole snorted, making a squeaking sound with his

bloated lips. The larvae were his own ungrateful children, immature Rybets who had not yet undergone their final metamorphosis. Blind and wormlike, almost as large as Doole himself, the larvae were perfect workers to wrap the spice fibers in opaque sheaths, since even brief exposure to light would spoil the product. His children could work in the blackness, and be happy. And what sort of gratitude did they show him?

A few larvae had gotten loose, fleeing blindly through the winding prison passages, hiding in shadowy cells, waiting in darkened wings to ambush Doole if he came looking for them. But he was not going to look. He had more important things to do.

To make things worse, one of the largest male larvae had freed all of Doole's specially picked females! The females had fled into the labyrinth of the prison, so that during this time of greatest terror, Doole couldn't even relieve his tension with an occasional visit to the harem.

He had no choice but to remain locked inside his office cell, pace the floor, and be alternately bored out of his mind and scared out of his wits. When he did make his way to the storerooms, he emerged heavily armed, waddled quickly down the corridors, and came back with as much food as he could carry.

He had an escape tunnel, of course. He had blasted a channel into the spice mines directly under the prison. Doole could lose himself for a long time in that network, but he still couldn't get off-planet. And lately the tunnels had become a far more dangerous place.

After Daala's attack most of the spice miners had fled. Without guards and construction and loud machinery, the spiders had surged upward to lay down their glitterstim webs along the walls. Looking with specially adapted kinetic energy detectors, Doole had spotted swarms of the monsters in the deepest shafts, migrating closer to the surface.

In despair Doole sat on his bunk and smelled the dank

air of the dungeon. At another time he might have found it comforting and cool, but now he just rested his sucker-tipped fingers against damp jowls and stared at the monitors.

He was astonished to see a ship land outside. And even though all humans generally looked alike to him, Doole was certain he recognized one of the three intruders pummeling his armored door: Han Solo, the man he hated most in the entire universe, the man who had caused all this misery!

At the ominous prison gates Han watched as Ghent the slicer worked diligently on the problem. He jacked in all manner of equipment, components stolen out of other systems, barely functional combinations that somehow found loopholes around defense systems.

Ghent raised a triumphant fist into the grainy sunlight. The reinforced latticework of the defensive portcullis rode up on invisible tracks. With a hollow clunking sound the shipping and receiving gates split apart, squealing and creaking as they lumbered into the thick walls. A gust of higher-pressure air bled out of the prison.

The four large smugglers shouldered their weapons and plodded forward, crouched over and ready to fight. The two Mistryl guards took the lead, sliding along the walls. The burly Whiphid and scaly Trandoshan strode brashly down the middle of the hall.

No attack came from the dark passageway. "Let's go find Moruth Doole," Han said.

None of his options looked good, but Doole had to make choices. He had watched Han Solo and his group of commandos force their way in—and Kessel was supposed to be the toughest prison in the galaxy. Hah!

Doole didn't know how to use the built-in defense systems, the external laser cannons, the disintegrator fields. He was helpless without his right-hand man, Skynxnex, but the scarecrowish fool had gotten himself killed chasing Solo through the spice tunnels, devoured by one of those energy spiders.

As a desperate measure Doole had come to the conclusion that he must trust his own children, the blind larvae he kept in blackness since the moment they writhed out of the gelatinous egg mass in the harem wing's breeding pools.

Doole rushed down the corridors, gathering weapons from the prison's armory. He carried two satchels of blaster pistols over his shoulder as he opened the protective vaults. Suddenly exposed to the light, the larvae reared back like caterpillars, blind eyes bulging as they attempted to sense the identity of the intruder.

"It's only me, only me," Doole said. Bright light stabbed at them, illuminating their pale skin. Damp vestigial hands reached up, small fingers and arms short and weak, not completely formed. Wormlike tendrils quivered below their mouths as the larvae made soft burbling noises.

Doole herded the oldest and strongest of the larvae along ramps to the lower levels. He would station them as guardians inside his cell. Being blind, they probably couldn't hit anything with the blasters, but he hoped they would at least fire with enthusiasm once he gave them the orders. Given enough cross fire, Doole could hide behind a blast-proof screen and hope the firefight would kill Solo's team.

As Doole ushered them toward his cell, he smelled the musky wetness of their fear and uncertainty. The immature Rybets did not like change, preferring a rigid daily routine until eventually they molted and became adults, gaining intelligence and self-awareness.

Distracted by trying to think of what other defenses he

might bring to bear, he was startled by a high-pitched scream echoing from three of the nearby chambers. Several of the freed female Rybets sprang out, wailing and throwing sharp objects at them.

Doole ducked as broken shards of transparisteel, sharpened knives, and heavy paperweights flew at him. Doole tried to grab a blaster from one of the two satchels on his back, but a drinking mug struck him on the soft side of his head. He dropped one of the satchels and ran wildly down the corridor, waving his sucker-tipped hands.

Most of the larvae followed him, but a few split off to stay with their mothers. Doole ran, wanting only to get back to the safety of his cell. Finally slamming the thick door behind him, he emptied his remaining satchel and placed fully charged blasters in the hands of six potential defenders.

"Just point it toward whatever noise you hear," he said. "When they break in, it's up to you to shoot. This is the firing button."

The smooth-skinned creatures shivered and ran their sensitive mouth tendrils over the barrels of the weapons.

"You point it, and it makes a blast." Doole repositioned the pistols in their vestigial hands, pointing them toward the door.

Without warning the vision in his mechanical eye flickered again, and Doole couldn't see a thing. He moaned in terror. The escape tunnel was sounding better and better.

With a growing dread in the pit of his stomach, Han Solo hurried down the prison corridors. The entire place was full of cold shadows, echoing with emptiness.

Over the comm link Mara Jade said, "We've found him, Solo. He's barricaded in one of the dungeons. We tapped into the surveillance cameras. He's got some creatures standing with him, and they appear to be armed."

"On my way," Han said.

When he reached the lower corridors, Han saw heavy barricades thrown in place across a sealed door. Mara watched the operation as the two female Mistryl guards placed concussion detonators around the door seal.

Lando paced nervously. "Don't do any more damage than you have to," he said. "I've got enough repairs to make here on Kessel as it is."

The two women ignored him as they sprinted out of the way. They ducked their heads and covered their ears as a rapid *thud thud thud* echoed from the concussion detonators.

They heard a volley of sudden blaster fire from inside the sealed chamber, a high-pitched shriek of energetic beams striking and ricocheting off the walls.

"No, no! Not yet!" came a howling voice that Han recognized as Moruth Doole's.

With a final *thump* the last concussion detonator blew the bottom off the door. The hairy Whiphid rushed forward to elbow the heavy plates aside.

"Look out," Mara called.

The Whiphid ducked and rolled as the soft larvae flailed, pointing their blasters and firing in every direction. Their huge glassy eyes spun around without seeing anything.

"Get them!" Doole yelled. The larvae whirled at the sound of his voice and fired their blasters toward Doole himself. But he had already ducked behind a thick piece of wall plating. "Not at me!"

Hissing, the reptilian Trandoshan shot inside, cutting down two of the blind larvae. He lumbered into the chamber, but before the other smugglers could rush in, another explosion came from the ceiling. Han, Mara, and the Mistryl guards used the distraction to muscle their way forward, ducking down and firing again. Han took out another of the larvae just as the ceiling collapsed in flaming chunks.

Wailing for revenge, swarms of female Rybets dropped through the ceiling into Doole's private cell. Each bore a blaster of her own and fired repeatedly at the metal shield Doole hid behind until its center glowed a cherry-red.

The blind larvae targeted on the new noise—but then as if suddenly they understood, as if they could communicate with their own mothers, the larvae turned and directed their fire toward Doole as well.

"Stop, stop!" Doole cried.

Han crept in beside Lando, not wanting to draw fire in the midst of this civil war. Doole yelped and dropped the superheated protective shield. His mechanical eye popped off and broke into a thousand bouncing and rattling components on the floor. His long squishy fingers punched a hidden control button, and a trapdoor opened beneath him. With a mindless squeal Doole leaped through an access hatch into an escape tunnel, down into the cold black mines.

"Hurry, before he gets away!" Lando said. "I don't want him running around in my spice mines."

The surviving larvae flowed forward as if they wanted to plunge into the tunnels after Moruth Doole, either to follow him or to chase him. But the amphibious females grasped the larvae and held them back with gentle cooing sounds. Their wide eyes looked on the invading smugglers with apprehension.

Han rushed toward the trapdoor and dropped to his knees, pushing his face into the darkness. He heard Doole's splatting footsteps diminishing as he ran on webbed feet deeper into the catacombs.

The larvae shot several blaster bolts into the passages after him. Long spears of heat bounced along the tunnel walls, knocking boulders loose. The light sparked a scintillating glare of activated glitterstim.

Then Han heard a new sound that turned his blood cold. A faint but chilling noise, hundreds of sharp legs like ice picks scrambling down the tunnel. Han could still hear Doole's footsteps getting fainter and fainter as he fled. Han heard the *tik tik tik* of multilegged creatures, attracted by the heat of a living body . . . and Doole's gasping, ragged breath as the Rybet searched blindly for a way out.

Han heard many more sets of pointed legs scrabbling, like a stampede from converging tunnels as the energy spiders found nourishment after the long silence in the spice mines. Han's skin crawled.

At the tail end of a high-pitched and gut-wrenching scream, Doole's footsteps suddenly stopped. The scream cut off abruptly, as did the sound of running ice-pick feet. The instant silence seemed even more horrible than the scream, and Han quickly pulled up the trapdoor and secured it before the energy spiders could seek other prey.

He sat back, heart pounding. The smugglers looked grimly satisfied at the battle they had won. The Whiphid leaned against a wall with arms crossed. "A good hunt," he growled.

The Trandoshan glanced from side to side, as if seeking something to eat.

The female Rybets hauled away the blasted larvae, tending the injured, mourning over the dead.

Han sighed as Lando sank down next to him. "Well, Lando," he said, "now you can start remodeling."

Han, Lando, and Mara rode back up to the garrison moon in the *Falcon*. Mara and Lando spoke more easily to each other, now that Lando wasn't pushing so hard to get the slightest word or smile from her. Mara had even stopped avoiding Lando's gaze or raising her chin whenever he spoke. She spent most of her time reassuring him that the *Lady Luck* would be just fine behind the security fields of the reoccupied prison. Lando didn't seem to believe her entirely, but he did not want to disagree with Mara Jade.

"We've got a lot of paperwork to do," Mara said. "I have all the standard contracts and agreements up at the moonbase. We can take care of the formalities between us, but there are still a lot of forms to digitize and sign, a lot of records to cross-reference."

"Whatever you say," Lando said. "I want this to be a long and happy partnership. You and I need to figure out how we can best implement production on Kessel. It's in the best interests of both of us to get the glitterstim flowing soon, especially since I'm going to have to sink so much of an investment into the mining work again."

Han listened to them talk but devoted most of his thoughts to his family. "I just want to go home. No more side trips."

The *Falcon* sped away from the wispy corona of escaping air toward the large moon. Once leaving the turbulent atmosphere of Kessel, they coasted smoothly in the vacuum of space as if on glass.

Suddenly an alert flashed on their communications panel from the moonbase. "Warning! We've detected a large vessel approaching Kessel—and I mean *large*."

Han reacted instantly. "Lando, check the scanners."

Lando stared at the copilot station and sat up quickly, his eyes as big as viewports. "Not just large," he said.

Han could see the globe-shaped object through the viewport. Spherical, but skeletal, crossbraced and arched with giant girders. The size of a miniature moon.

"It's the Death Star."

The repairs took longer than expected, much to Tol Sivron's frustration, but the prototype was finally ready to approach, and attack, the nearest planetary system.

Sivron shifted in his seat, pleased to observe the

stormtrooper captain giving all the right orders. Delegating responsibility was the first lesson of management. He liked sitting in the pilot's chair while others did the work.

Squat, bald Doxin leaned forward from one of the other chairs. "The target is coming into view, Director Sivron."

"Good," Sivron said, looking at the streaked atmosphere fuzzing around the planet and its close-orbiting moon.

"There seems to be significant ship activity in the area," Yemm, the Devaronian, said. "I'm tracking and documenting it for posterity. We'll want a careful record in case we need to file a report on the performance of this prototype."

"It's a Rebel base," Tol Sivron said. "No doubt about it. Look at those ships. Look at its position. This must be where our prisoner Han Solo came from."

"How can you be sure?" said Golanda.

Sivron shrugged. "We need to test this Death Star, right? We've got a handy target right here—so it might as well be a Rebel base."

The stormtrooper captain sat at the tactical station. "We're picking up numerous alarms from the moonbase. It appears to be some sort of military installation."

A flurry of ships departed from a large opening in the moon, spewing a random collection of well-armed and fast cruisers around Kessel.

"They can't get away from us," Tol Sivron said. "Target the planet. You may fire when ready." He smiled, and his pointed teeth formed a serrated edge against his lips. "I've got a good feeling about this."

Doxin grinned in breathless delight. "I never thought I'd get a chance to see this weapon in action."

"It's never been calibrated, you know," Golanda said with a sour expression.

"It's a planet-destroying superlaser," Doxin shot back. "We can turn that whole world into rubble. How well does it need to be calibrated?"

"Targeting now," the stormtrooper captain said.

In shielded firing chambers below, lit only by flickering blazes of colored light from complex control panels, other stormtroopers functioned as Death Star gunners, after having been told to scour the instruction manuals.

"What's taking so long?" Tol Sivron fidgeted against the uncomfortable fabric of the command seat.

Suddenly the white-noise background hum of the operating systems dropped an octave. The lights dimmed on the panels as the prototype consumed an incredible amount of energy.

Out the front viewport, past main support struts that arched like giant steel rainbows over their heads, smaller superlaser beams fired out of the Death Star's focusing eye, phasing together at the intersection point. The green beam gained in power and lanced out in an immense blast, greater in diameter than a starship.

Its target erupted in a blaze of smoke, fire, and incandescent rubble.

Tol Sivron applauded.

Yemm took careful notes.

Doxin let out a cry of triumph and amazement.

"You missed," Golanda said.

Tol Sivron blinked his small dark eyes. "What?"

"You hit the moon, not the planet."

He saw she was right. The moon that had served as a garrison for the fighter ships had exploded into fragmented rubble that was raining down in spectacular meteor showers on the planet Kessel.

The fighter ships that had evacuated from the moonbase swarmed about in a flurry, like fire-mantids disturbed from their nests during mating season.

Tol Sivron coiled and uncoiled his naked head-tails, feeling tingles along his nerve endings. He leaned back in the chair and waved a clawed hand in dismissal.

"That can be corrected. The target was irrelevant.

At least now we know the prototype is fully functional." He nodded approvingly. "Just as all the progress reports said."

Sivron took a deep breath, feeling the thrill build within him. "Now we can put this weapon to use."

Leia was amazed that Mon Moth-
ma still clung to life. Anxiously, she stood over the death-
bed of the Chief of State, looking at the kaleidoscope of
medical apparatus and life-support systems that refused
to let Mon Mothma die.

The auburn-haired woman had once been such a fiery
rival of Leia's father on the Senate floor; now she could
no longer stand on her feet. Her skin was gray and translucent, thin as crumpled parchment on a framework of
bones. Her eyelids struggled open as if they were heavy
blast doors. Her eyes took a long time to focus on her
visitor.

Leia swallowed, feeling hot lead in her stomach. She
reached out with trembling fingers to touch Mon Mothma's
arm, afraid that the slightest pressure could cause bruises.

"Leia . . . ," Mon Mothma whispered, "you came."

"I came because you asked me to," Leia said.

Han had dropped her and the children off on Coruscant,
grumbling about having to go away again with Lando, but
promising to return in only a few days. She would believe

that when it happened. In the meantime Leia was shocked to see the accelerating decline of Mon Mothma's condition.

"Your children . . . are safe now?"

"Yes. Winter is staying here to protect them. I won't let them be taken from me again."

Leia would be even busier than before; she would see less of Han, less of her children. Momentarily she envied the peaceful life of a lower functionary who could leave work at the end of the day and go home, letting unfinished tasks wait for tomorrow. But she had been born a Jedi and raised by Senator Bail Organa. Her life had been focused toward a greater destiny, and she could not shirk either her public or her private burden.

Leia took a deep breath, tasting the nauseating chemicals that clung to the air, the disinfectants, the medicines, the ozone smell of atmospheric sterilizers.

She felt so helpless. Her excitement at defeating the Imperial strike force and rescuing her son seemed trivial in the face of Mon Mothma's battle against the slow-acting poison. Leia took little consolation in knowing that Ambassador Furgan was no longer alive to gloat.

"I . . . ," Mon Mothma spoke ponderously, "have tendered my resignation to the Council. I will no longer serve as Chief of State."

Leia realized that empty encouragements would be useless. She reacted in a way that Mon Mothma had taught her to respond, thinking of the New Republic first.

"What about the government?" she said. "Won't the Council bicker with each other and accomplish nothing because they can't reach a consensus? Who will they look to for leadership?"

She looked down at Mon Mothma, and the haggard woman blinked at her with shining, hopeful eyes. "*You* will be our leader, Leia," Mon Mothma said.

Leia blinked in shock and opened her mouth. Mon Mothma found the strength to nod slightly. "Yes, Leia.

While you were away, the Council met to discuss our future. My resignation is no surprise to anyone, and we voted unanimously that you should be my replacement."

"But—" Leia said. Her heart pounded; her mind whirled. She had not expected this, at least not now. Perhaps after another decade or two of dedicated service, then . . .

"You, Leia, will be the Chief of State for the New Republic. If I had any strength left to give, I would give it all to you. You'll need it to hold this newborn Republic of ours together."

Mon Mothma closed her eyes and squeezed Leia's hand with a surprisingly firm grip. "Even when I'm gone, I will be watching over you."

Speechless, Leia knelt at Mon Mothma's bedside for a long time, far into Coruscant's night.

30

Inside Maw Installation one of the members of Wedge's Special Forces Team had deciphered enough of the primary controls to sound the facility-wide alarm. Through the intercom system an unfamiliar voice barked, "Red alert, an Imperial Star Destroyer has entered the vicinity. Red alert! Prepare for attack."

Wedge stood next to Qwi inside her empty old laboratory as they gaped at the scarred and blackened hulk of the *Gorgon*. The mammoth ship maneuvered into position over the cluster of lashed-together rocks.

"Oh, my!" Threepio said. "I thought we were supposed to be safe in here."

Wedge grabbed Qwi's pale hand. "Come on, we have to get to the operations room."

They ran through the corridors. Qwi did her best to lead him, though frequently she couldn't remember which direction to go. Threepio, his servomotors whirring, tottered after them as fast as he could go. "Wait for me! Oh, why does this always happen?"

Inside the operations room Wedge was relieved to see that a dozen of his troops had gotten there ahead of him and were already scrambling to operate the controls. A few of the computer banks had malfunctioned, but the rest had been jump-started. Sensor arrays spilled data across their screens.

Wedge put his hands on Qwi's shoulders, pressing his face close to hers and looking into her big eyes. "Qwi, try to remember! Does Maw Installation have any of its own defenses?"

She looked up through the latticed skylight, seeing the looming arrowhead shape of the Star Destroyer. Qwi pointed up. "*Those* were our defenses. Maw Installation depended entirely upon Admiral Daala's fleet."

She hurried over to one of the deadened computer consoles and used her musical keypad to whistle her password into the system, hoping to bypass the damaged circuits with her own files and select some of the higher-order functioning routines. "We do have shields," Qwi said, "if only we could increase them."

Five harried technicians came over to help her, using their own expertise to access the generators and reinforce the protective force field around the primary planetoids.

"That'll hold for now against an assault," a tech said, "but this makes me very uncomfortable, General Antilles. The power reactor is already unstable, and we're placing a tremendous drain on it. We could be sealing our own fate."

Wedge's gaze flicked to Qwi and then back to the soldiers. "Well, it's certain death if we don't do something to protect ourselves now. We've taken what we need. I think it's time to leave Maw Installation. Have the ships prepare for departure."

"If Daala will let us," Qwi said. "I doubt she'll allow us to walk off now that we've uncovered its secrets."

Wedge's eyes suddenly blinked in realization. "We took one of the corvette engines off-line for spare parts for the power reactor! One of my ships is crippled and can't move." He ran to the communications station and switched on a narrow-beam to the disabled corvette.

"Captain Ortola, launch all starfighter squadrons from your bay—now. Take all personnel and shuttle over to the *Yavaris* or one of the other two corvettes. Without maneuverability, your ship is a prime target."

"Yes, sir," Captain Ortola's voice acknowledged.

The broad trapezoidal viewscreen at the far end of the operations room surged with static, and then an image of fiery-haired Admiral Daala filled the screen. She leaned forward into the viewing area. Her eyes seemed to throw pointed javelins right into Wedge's heart.

"Rebel scum, you'll not leave Maw Installation alive. The information contained in this facility is now forfeit, tainted by your sabotage. I'm not interested in your surrender or your flight. Only your destruction."

Daala ended the transmission herself before Wedge could formulate a reply. He shook his head at the flickering static that faded into a dull gray. He turned back to Qwi and felt his heart pounding. "Qwi, are you sure there's nothing else here we can use? Any other weapon?"

"Wait," Qwi said. "Chewbacca took a team down into the maintenance bay to rescue the Wookiee slaves. There were always several assault shuttles or fighter ships being worked on. Maybe those?"

One of the New Republic commandos snapped his head up. "Assault shuttles? Probably gamma class. They're nothing spectacular, but they are heavily armored and well outfitted with weapons, worth ten of our starfighters. It could be a welcome addition in the battle. Daala's got only one Star Destroyer against us, but she still outguns the combined force of the corvettes and the *Yavaris*."

The squad leader looked down at a scrolling list of equipment on a data screen. "Just as I feared, sir. These are old models. They require a piloting droid to fly complicated maneuvers, especially in this gravitational environment. We could probably do it with only one droid and cross-link to the separate navigational systems."

At that moment, with heavy footfalls and buzzing servomotors, Threepio hurried into the operations room, emitting a loud sigh of relief. "Ah, there you are! I've finally found you."

Wedge, Qwi, and everyone else turned to look at the golden droid.

Threepio moved forward, his arms waving in dismay as he negotiated a steep ramp into the rock-lined maintenance bay. "I don't know why everyone keeps treating me as if I were some sort of . . . property," he said.

Chewbacca grunted a sharp retort, and Threepio snapped at him. "That's quite beside the point. In actual fact, I—"

Chewbacca lifted up the golden droid and set him bodily on the entrance ramp of a gamma-class assault shuttle. The recently freed Wookiee slaves, along with a group of New Republic commandos, scrambled into the five armored shuttles that remained in the bay. Each ship had been maintained in perfect working order by Wookiee crews.

From above sudden hollow thumps echoed through the asteroid as the *Gorgon* pummeled them with turbolaser blasts. Chewbacca and the other Wookiees howled at the ceiling, their bestial noises echoing louder than the thunder of attack. Faint dust trickled down, split from the sealed rock walls.

"I still think I'm going to regret this," Threepio said. "I wasn't designed for this kind of work. I can communicate with other tactical computers and coordinate your flight paths, but putting me in charge of strategy—"

Chewbacca ignored him and climbed into the vehicle. Seeing that his arguments were useless, the golden droid shuffled up the ramp into the confines of the assault shuttle. "But, then again, I am always happy to help, where needed."

The other Wookiees, including stunted old Nawruun, took their places in the gunnery seats, ready to blast TIE fighters.

Chewbacca slumped into the assault shuttle's too-small pilot seat and made Threepio sit beside him in the copilot's chair. "Oh, very well," Threepio said, and inspected the computer, deciding how best to communicate with it.

More explosions from the *Gorgon*'s attack pounded through the thick walls, but those noises were soon drowned out by the growling purr of the shuttles' repulsorlift engines.

Chewbacca raised the heavily armed ship off the floor and guided it down the launching corridor. Atmosphere-containment fields sealed behind them just before the heavy launch doors opened into space like a huge vertical mouth.

Threepio linked up to the guidance computers and the directional programming of all five assault shuttles. Behind them identical vehicles flew in a tight formation, picking up speed. "This is rather exhilarating," Threepio said.

Chewbacca punched at the controls until the shuttle rocketed like a projectile through the launch doors and away from the Installation's protective shield.

Above, swarms of starfighters streamed from the Corellian corvettes. The frigate *Yavaris* began to fire on the Star Destroyer as Daala continued to rain turbolaser bolts upon the Installation. From the lower bay doors of the *Gorgon*, squads of TIE fighters streaked out like spooked mynocks from a cave.

234 Kevin J. Anderson

Chewbacca powered up his weapons systems, and Threepio linked into their preprogrammed attack patterns. The five assault shuttles from Maw Installation plunged into the heart of the burgeoning space battle.

"Oh, my!" Threepio said.

31

When Leia answered the summons at the door to her quarters in the rebuilt Imperial Palace, she saw it was the deepest hour of the bustling night. For a moment she had a thrilled thought, that Han might have come back from Kessel already. But when she rubbed sleep from her eyes and opened the door, she found her brother Luke standing there. She paused a moment, utterly astonished, and then rushed forward to embrace him.

"Luke! When did you come to Coruscant?" Out of the corner of her eye she caught sight of another young man standing off to the side in the dim corridor. She recognized the tousled dark hair of Kyp Durron; his eyes were deep-set and averted, no longer the brash teenager that Han had rescued from the spice mines of Kessel.

"Oh, Kyp," she said in a flat, unemotional voice. Seeing the young man unnerved her. He had been Han's dear friend, a companion through enjoyable adventures—but Kyp had also gone over to the dark side, paralyzed Luke, killed millions of people, turned on Han. . . .

Kyp's face and eyes looked old now, exhausted from

the traumas he had endured—and caused. Leia had seen eyes like those only once before: on her brother after he had faced the knowledge that Darth Vader was his own father. But Kyp had been through a hell as deep as Luke's had been.

A small courier droid shot down the hall, blinking red lights to warn others to clear the way as it propelled itself along on urgent business, even this late at night.

With a flush of embarrassment Leia remembered her manners. "Please, come in."

From the back room Winter emerged, gliding forward on silent bare feet, wearing only a loose sleeping garment. Winter appeared ready for action lest some other danger throw itself upon the children. She bowed her head formally when she saw Luke. "Greetings, Master Skywalker," she said.

Luke smiled and nodded to her. "Hello, Winter."

Winter backed into her chambers. "I'll just check on the children," she said. She vanished, giving them no chance to say anything else.

Leia looked from Kyp to Luke again, feeling deep weariness behind her eyes, behind her head. She had been relying on too many stimulant drinks, spending too much time negotiating with other Council members, sleeping too little.

Luke closed the door behind him as he and Kyp entered the common room. Leia remembered when her brother had trained her in this room, trying to unlock her Jedi potential. Now, though, she sensed that Luke had a much more ominous agenda.

"Is Han here?" Kyp blurted, looking around the quarters.

Leia noticed that he still wore the black cape Han had given him as a gift; but now Kyp seemed to carry it as a symbol over a light jumpsuit, a reminder to himself of what he could become.

"He's gone off to Kessel with Lando," Leia said, a tired smile tugging at the corners of her mouth. "Lando wants to try running the spice mines."

Kyp frowned uncertainly. Luke sat down on one of the self-conforming cushions and leaned forward, weaving his fingers together. He directed his intense gaze at Leia. "Leia, we need your help," he said.

"Yeah, I figured that out," Leia answered with a touch of irony. "I'll do everything I can, of course. What do you need?"

"Kyp and I have . . . made our peace. He has the potential to be the greatest of the Jedi I am training, but there's one thing he must do before I can consider him completely absolved."

Leia swallowed, already afraid of what he might say. "And what is this 'one thing'?"

Luke did not flinch. "The Sun Crusher must be destroyed. Everyone in the New Republic knows that. But Kyp must do it himself."

Leia simply blinked, unable to say anything. "But . . . how can he destroy it?" she finally said. "As far as we know, it's indestructible. We already dropped it into a gas planet's core, but Kyp"—she turned her exaggerated gaze on the young man—"managed to retrieve it. I don't suppose even dropping it into a sun would have made much difference."

Kyp shook his head. "No, I could have recovered it just as easily."

Leia looked helplessly at Luke, spreading her hands. "So what else—?"

"Kyp and I will fly the Sun Crusher back to the Maw. He will set the autopilot and drop it down one of the black holes. Quantum armor or no quantum armor, it will be obliterated. There's no more definite way of erasing something from this universe."

Kyp piped up. "I know the Sun Crusher must be taken

away from both the Empire and the New Republic. I . . . Dr. Xux no longer has any memory of how to reconstruct it. The galaxy will never need to fear such a threat again." His posture stiffened, his chin rose, his eyes grew alive again. The guilt and pain were replaced with a look of pride and determination.

Luke placed a hand on the young man's forearm, and Kyp fell silent, content to let Luke continue.

"Leia, I know you've been appointed the new Chief of State. You can make this happen." He leaned forward, speaking to her with the idealistic, boyish energy she remembered from years before. "You know I'm right."

Leia shook her head, already afraid of the enormous diplomatic battle she would have to face at the mere mention of Luke's preposterous request.

"There'll be a lot of heated discussion. Most of the Council members are going to refuse to let Kyp get within sight of the Sun Crusher again. What's to stop him from rampaging around the galaxy and blowing up more star systems? Can they take that risk? Can *we*?"

"They have to take that risk," Luke said. "It must be done. And I'll be there with him."

Leia bit her lip. Her brother could be so forceful. She knew him well enough that she wasn't simply awed by what the Jedi could do . . . but she was confident that Luke could follow through on his claim.

"Do you know what you're asking?" she said in a soft, pleading voice.

"Leia, just as I had to face our father, this is a test Kyp must complete. Tell the Council that if he passes this test successfully, Kyp Durron could become the most powerful Jedi Knight of this generation."

Leia sighed and stood up. "All right. I'll try—"

Kyp interrupted her and said, "There is no try: do or do not." Then he allowed himself a wry smile, gesturing toward Luke. "At least that's what he always says."

Han Solo gritted his teeth as he
yanked on the *Falcon*'s controls. The modified light freighter flew up and around in a tight backward loop. The
blinding flash of the Death Star's superlaser faded to a
glowing streak as the rubble of Kessel's moon mushroomed
in a rapidly expanding cloud.

"That was gonna be my garrison!" Lando cried. His
voice cracked. "First Moruth Doole, now a Death Star—
this deal is getting worse all the time."

Mara Jade, her face hard as chiseled stone, quickly
leaned between Han and Lando in the two cockpit seats
and shouted into the comm unit. "This is Mara Jade. All
ships report. How many did we lose? Did the evacuation
order go out on time?"

One of the cool-voiced Mistryl guards responded. "Yes,
Commander Jade," the warrior woman said. "We scrambled at first sign of the intruder. All but two ships made
it away from the base. One more was struck and destroyed
by the flying debris."

Mara nodded grimly. "Then we still have enough of a fighting force," she said.

"Fighting force!" Han said. "Against that thing? To do what? It's a Death Star, not a cargo freighter." He looked through the overhead viewport and saw the skeletal proto-type over Kessel. The superweapon seemed to be brooding over the destruction it had just caused.

"But, Han," Lando pleaded, "we've got to do something before it blows up the planet, too. Think of all the *spice* down there."

Mara grabbed the comm again. "Attack formation gamma," she said. "We're going to head out and pound that Death Star." She turned to Han and lowered her voice. "If it's just a prototype, my guess is they won't have the defenses the real Death Star had, no squadrons of TIE fighters, no turbolaser fortifications across the surface. That's what did the most damage to your Rebel fleets, wasn't it?"

"Not entirely," Lando said. "The second Death Star used its superlaser against a few of our capital ships."

Mara pursed her lips as she thought. "Then we'll just have to keep them busy. I don't think that superlaser can be very effective at targeting small moving objects."

"I don't like the odds on that," Lando said.

"Never quote me the odds," Han said, hunching over the panel and guiding the ship into position.

"Who, me?" Lando said, raising his eyebrows. "I'm a sucker for lost causes."

The *Millennium Falcon* soared into the vanguard of the smugglers' attack formation. Han was impressed to see the assortment of large and small ships fall into a perfect pattern, as if they were trained and regimented. The motley bunch must have a great deal of respect for Mara Jade, he realized; as a rule, smugglers were noto-riously independent and took orders from no one.

One of the other ships, an insectile Z-95 Headhunter—

the type of ship Mara herself often flew—streaked in beside the *Falcon*. Its pilot spoke over the open channel. "This is Kithra. I'll take the right-hand prong, Shana will take the left. You fly center, *Falcon*, and we'll hit the Death Star in all three places at once."

Han recognized the no-nonsense voice of another Mistryl guard. How many had she brought along with her?

"Agreed, Kithra," Mara said. She turned to look at Han. "Well, Solo, ready to lead the attack?"

"I never intended to take the *Falcon* against a Death Star," he groaned, even as he prepared for battle. "I was just giving Lando a lift to Kessel."

"Think of it as an added bonus," Mara said.

"Come *on*, Han," Lando urged, "before that Death Star fires again."

"Good thing Leia's not here," he muttered. "She'd probably succeed in talking me out of this."

As the ships converged on the skeletal behemoth, the superlaser struck once more, scorching the fabric of space with emerald fire—but the beam passed through the scattered ships descending upon it, causing no damage.

"Shields up," Han said, "for whatever good it'll do against *that*."

On either side of the *Falcon* two segments of the smuggler fleet peeled off like the skin from a rustle snake: one prong led by Kithra in her Headhunter, the other headed by Shana in an angular blockade runner, a clunkier forerunner of the *Falcon*'s light-freighter design.

The smuggler ships drove in, energy cannons blazing, drawing a deadly tracery of fire across the superstructures and girders of the enormous sphere.

Han launched three proton torpedoes into the labyrinth of cross beams and supports as they charged toward the enormous construction. A few reinforced girders glowed molten as projectiles and energy beams hit.

"It's going to take us a year to chop away at this thing," Han said, firing from the *Falcon*'s forward weaponry.

"I never claimed this was going to be easy," Mara said.

Tol Sivron's head-tails twitched. He squinted his black beady eyes at the oncoming small ships. They appeared so trivial, their weapons systems so minor. "I can't believe they're attacking *us*," he said. "What do they think they're going to accomplish?"

At the tactical station the stormtrooper captain spoke through his white helmet. "If I might point out, Director, this battle station is for proof-of-concept only. It was never designed to defend itself against multiple small threats. In fact, the Death Star was meant to house over seven thousand TIE fighters, not to mention thousands of surface turbolasers and ion cannons and an escort of several Imperial-class Star Destroyers. We have none of these.

"Individually, those Rebel ships may be only a minor threat, but together they can harry us for an extended period and, if we are unlucky, cause significant structural damage."

"You mean we don't have any fighters of our own?" Tol Sivron said with stern disapproval. "That was poor planning. Who wrote that section of the procedure? I want to know right now."

"Director," the stormtrooper said with a tinge of exasperation in his filtered voice, "that doesn't matter at the moment."

"It matters to me!" Tol Sivron said. He turned toward demon-faced Yemm, who was already scouring the records.

"It appears that Dr. Qwi Xux was responsible for that section, Director," Yemm said. "She devoted much of her time to the operation and performance of the superlaser, giving short shrift to tactical considerations."

Sivron sighed. "I see we've found a flaw in our approval

system. Such weak spots should never have been allowed to pass through the progress reports and review meetings."

"Director," Doxin said, "let us not allow this to overshadow the marvelous performance of the Death Star superlaser itself."

"Agreed, agreed," Sivron said. "We should have a meeting immediately to discuss the implications of—"

The stormtrooper captain stood up from his station. "Director, we *must* establish certain priorities right now! We are under attack."

An outside explosion made the Death Star framework around the control chamber vibrate.

"That's three direct hits with proton torpedoes," the stormtrooper said. "So far."

As Sivron watched, four Z-95 Headhunters swooped out of the superstructure, their rear engines blazing.

"Well, then fire again with our laser," Tol Sivron said. "Maybe we can hit one of them this time."

"The power core is only half-charged," Doxin pointed out.

Sivron whirled and parted his lips to show pointed teeth. "Isn't that good enough to knock out a few little ships?"

Doxin blinked his piggish eyes as if he hadn't considered the possibility. "Why, yes, sir—yes, it is. Ready to fire."

"At your convenience, Division Leader," Sivron said.

Eagerly, Doxin spoke into the intercom, commanding the gunners to fire. After a few seconds the incredible beam of light seared out; side lasers converged at a focal point and coalesced into a laser battering ram that plowed through the fringe of the oncoming cluster of fighters, vaporizing one old blockade runner in the vanguard of the left prong. Another ship was damaged by the backwash of the blast, but the attacking forces spread out and disappeared into the superstructure like parasites, firing again.

"Did you see that?" Doxin said with obvious pleasure. "We hit one!"

"Hooray," Golanda said sourly from her seat. Her voice carried absolutely no enthusiasm. "Only about forty more to go, and you can't even fire the superlaser again for fifteen minutes."

"Director, if I may make a suggestion," the stormtrooper captain said. "We have successfully tested the prototype laser, but to stay here any longer would serve no purpose. To endure unnecessary damage to this fine weapon is folly. We should protect the Death Star so we may present it intact to the Imperial authorities."

"And what do you suggest doing, Captain?" Tol Sivron said. He dug his long claws into the armrests.

"We should withdraw to the Maw cluster. I doubt these small ships will follow. We are not highly maneuverable, but we can build up considerable speed. Note that we don't need to go all the way back to the Installation, just to the opposite side of the cluster where we can hide." The captain paused, then said slowly, "Once there, you will have time to hold a lengthy meeting, to decide what to do. You can . . . discuss the whole situation by committee if you like."

Tol Sivron brightened. "Good idea, Captain. See to it. Let's head out of here as fast as we can."

The stormtrooper captain fed in a new course for the prototype. The huge open-framework sphere wheeled about on its axis and accelerated away from Kessel, cumbersome but picking up speed as it left the flurry of other ships behind.

After the blaze from the Death Star's third blast faded, Han Solo rubbed sparkles out of his eyes, seeing distorted colors. "That was too close," he said. "The fringe of the beam fried our forward shields."

Shana's old blockade runner had been destroyed, and

some ships now flew off in retreat. "We have to regroup," Kithra's voice came over the comm system.

"I think we should just get out of here," Han said.

"Look!" Lando interrupted as the arching framework of the Death Star spun about and began to accelerate away from Kessel. "We've got it on the run."

"For now," Mara said, "but it may just be retreating long enough to recharge its power core so it can strike again."

"Kessel won't be safe while that thing is out there," Lando said. "Han, we've got to go in. Let's take the *Falcon* all the way to the power core."

"Are you crazy, Lando?" Han asked, his voice rising. "This is my ship, remember."

"I'm not contesting that," Lando said, holding his hands up, "but I've flown her into a Death Star before. Remember?"

"I've got a bad feeling about this," Han mumbled, and he shot a sidelong glance at Mara Jade. "But you're right. We can't just run away. If the prototype falls into the hands of the Imperial navy, it could cause a lot more misery than I want to be responsible for. Let's go in."

He punched his accelerators. Mara sent orders to her fleet. "All ships back off. We're going in. Alone."

The *Falcon* cruised through the nightmarish maze of overhanging girders, coolant and ventilation systems, power conduits and substations that formed the inner structure of the Death Star prototype. Catwalks laced the open spaces like so many spiderwebs.

The *Falcon* shot inward, tunneling deeper and deeper into the construction as the framework grew denser, more complex. Han spun the ship left and right to squeeze through narrow passages.

Just ahead, in the middle of a huge open corridor, a mammoth-sized construction crane toppled from its moorings, dislodged by the smuggler attack and the sudden lurching movement of the prototype. The crane fell, tumbling in silence through the vacuum of space, directly into the path of the *Falcon*.

"Look out!" Lando cried.

Han punched the firing buttons and sent out a converging blast from his laser cannons, disintegrating the falling machine into an expanding plume of incandescent gas and metal steam. Lando leaned back and closed his eyes with a shuddering sigh.

As the *Falcon* careened through, the passengers were bumped and jostled. Large debris struck the deflector shields. Sparks flew out of the control panels, and smoke poured from the engine panels beneath the floor plates.

"We've got damage!" Lando yelled.

Han fought for control. "She'll hold together," he said, as if praying.

Suddenly the Death Star jerked and slammed forward as its heavy-duty sublight engines fired up. Han tried to match the speed, spiraling closer to the power core. The *Falcon* lurched, barely responding to Han's attempts to maneuver.

They passed gargantuan girders ringing the outer core, tumbling into a vast enclosed space, a spherical chamber that contained the two gleaming conical sections of the power core. Green-and-blue fire crackled between the contacts as reactors pumped up the energy level, recharging the weapon to fire again.

"Talk about recurring nightmares," Lando said. "I never wanted to see anything like this again in my life."

"I guess we're just lucky," Han said, scanning his damage reports. "We need repairs bad," he said through gritted teeth. "Lousy time for the engines to act up."

The Death Star rotated again, changing course and accelerating once more with equatorial propulsion units. Han narrowly avoided an arc-shaped girder that swung across to slam at them; he maneuvered the *Falcon* around it in a tight loop and limped toward the superstructure that held the reactor core in place.

"I need to check on those engines," Han said, "but I can't do anything while the Death Star is moving and rocking like this. We're going to have to settle in for the ride."

"Settle in?" Mara asked in astonishment.

"Don't get all bent out of shape. I did this once before to elude Imperial pursuit," he said, flashing a lopsided grin. "A nice little trick built into the *Falcon*. Added it myself." Han brought the ship up parallel to one of the thick girders. "It's my landing claw. I used it to hang on to the back of a Star Destroyer, then drifted off with the garbage as the fleet entered hyperspace."

The *Falcon* attached itself with a *clang*. Directly below them the towering cylinder of the power core blazed into the emptiness, shining its deadly light.

"We're secure here for now," Han said. "But if they plan to go back inside the black hole cluster, we could be in for one wild ride."

33

Riding together in the close confines of the Sun Crusher, Luke felt young Kyp Durron draw mentally closer to him as they journeyed toward the black hole cluster.

Kyp was gradually overcoming his fear and preoccupation with Jedi powers and the potential for abusing them. After his epiphany inside the temple of Exar Kun, Kyp had emerged stronger, able to accept the challenge. If he could face this final test, Luke would know that Kyp had passed through the fire of his testing—tempered by forces as dire and powerful as those Luke himself had endured. . . .

Luke smiled as he recalled how Leia had argued for Kyp in the Council meeting, fighting for the chance that Luke offered. During her very first session as leader of the New Republic, Leia had presented her brother's demand; in the uproar that followed she had reasoned, cajoled, or shamed every one of them into giving Luke a chance.

She had emerged from the hours-long meeting in the middle of a bright Coruscant day. Kyp and Luke, waiting for her in one of the high mezzanine cafés within the enormous Imperial Palace, had sipped warm drinks and sampled delicacies from a hundred planets that had sworn allegiance to the New Republic. Leia had brushed aside her two bodyguards and hurried forward to meet them as other bureaucrats and minor functionaries stood up from their tables in recognition of their new Chief of State. Leia ignored the attention.

Her face was haggard and exhausted, but she could not hide her satisfied smile and the twinkle in her large eyes. "The Sun Crusher is yours to dispose of," she had said. "You'd better take it before someone on the Council decides my victory was too easy and moves to reopen the discussion."

Then Leia had turned a stern face toward Kyp. "I'm gambling my entire future administration on you, Kyp."

"I won't let you down," Kyp had promised, holding his head high. Luke did not need Jedi powers to sense the determination in the young man.

They had flown away from Coruscant into hyperspace on a direct course for the Maw cluster near Kessel.

The two of them ate rations and shared a warm silence. When they finished, Kyp fell into a deep rejuvenation trance, a form of deathlike hibernation that Luke taught all his students; the young Jedi awoke after only an hour, looking greatly refreshed.

En route Kyp had shared fond memories of his home planet, Deyer. He spoke in a halting, wistful voice about his brother Zeth. As Luke listened with quiet understanding, Kyp let loose his sorrow and wept cleansing tears, finally allowing himself the freedom granted by the vision of his brother's spirit in the obsidian temple.

"Yoda made me take a test of my own," Luke told him. "I had to go into a cave in the swamps of Dagobah, where I confronted a vision of Darth Vader. I attacked and defeated him, only to find that I was fighting myself. I failed my test, but you succeeded."

Luke looked into Kyp's dark eyes. "I don't promise it will be easy, Kyp, but the rewards of your efforts will be great, and the entire galaxy will benefit from them."

Kyp looked away as if embarrassed and studied the piloting controls of the Sun Crusher. "Ready to come out of hyperspace," he said. "You strapped in?"

Luke nodded with a slight smile. Around them hyperspace looked bruised and distorted from their proximity to all the black holes.

Kyp stared at the chronometer and concentrated as the numbers spun by. "Three, two, one." He released the levers, and suddenly the blur sprang away from their viewport, and real space snapped into crystal focus around them.

Luke saw the distant gaseous knot of the Maw, but he instantly felt a wrenching inside as if something was terribly wrong.

"What happened to Kessel?" Kyp said.

Luke found the much closer, distorted shape of Kessel masked by an expanding debris cloud.

"The garrison moon," Kyp said. "It's gone."

"We've been detected," Luke said. "Ships coming in." He sensed the anger and dismay from the pilots in the attack ships now gathering speed and converging on the Sun Crusher.

The speaker buzzed with a forceful female voice. "This is Kithra of the Mistryl guard, representing the Smugglers' Alliance. Identify yourself and state your business in the Kessel system."

"This is Luke Skywalker," he said, restraining a confident smile. "We're here on business for the New Republic. Our mission is to destroy the Sun Crusher, and we had hoped to hitch a ride back to Coruscant with one of your ships. Mara Jade cleared us by subspace transmission only yesterday."

"Commander Jade is not here now," Kithra said. "But

she did notify me you would be coming. As you can see, though, we have recently been under attack."

"Tell me your situation," Luke said. "Where's Mara? Is she okay? What about Han Solo?"

Kyp let his eyes fall half-closed, reaching out with the Force, searching. He jerked his head to the left, toward the swirling mass of the Maw. "Han's there—he's over there."

Kithra's voice came over the speaker again. "A Death Star prototype attacked us," she explained as the smuggler ships swarmed around them in a protective contingent. "We suspect it was fleeing the New Republic occupation force that recently entered the cluster."

"Wedge and Chewie are inside the Maw, too," Luke said to Kyp.

"What happened to Han?" Kyp said into the comm with rising urgency.

"Our ships struck at the prototype and caused some minor external damage, but Han Solo flew the *Millennium Falcon* into the superstructure. Commander Jade ordered us to fall back. The *Falcon* was carried along as the Death Star retreated toward the Maw. They were going to attempt to sabotage its power core, but we've heard no word from them since."

"How long has it been?"

"Only a couple of hours," Kithra answered. "We've been considering our options."

Luke looked to Kyp, and their eyes met in shared concern. "We don't have any options," Luke said.

Kyp nodded. "We've got to help Han."

"Yes," Luke said, swallowing hard. "Into the Maw."

For two Jedi, finding a safe path through the labyrinth of gravity wells proved simple enough. Working together, Luke and Kyp reinforced each other's perceptions, flying the Sun Crusher in tandem, like linked navicomputers.

The Sun Crusher rattled and vibrated with the strain. Luke experienced a stretching of his mind as he let his senses extend outward, as if dragged downward into the bottomless black holes.

Kyp flew with his eyes closed, his jaws clenched, his lips drawn back in a grimace. "Almost through the wall," he said through his teeth.

After passing through an eternity of superhot colors, they fell into the quiet bubble within the center of the cluster.

Clearing his vision, Luke searched for the Death Star prototype, expecting to see it firing at Wedge's assault fleet. But instead he saw quite a different space battle in progress: New Republic forces blasting, starfighters launched in frantic dogfights—arrayed not against the Death Star, but against the deadly spear-point shape of a battered and blaster-scarred Star Destroyer.

"It's Admiral Daala!" Kyp said, his voice thick with hatred.

34

The **wire-frame prototype hid,** powered down, on the far side of the Maw cluster as Tol Sivron, Golanda, Doxin, Yemm, and the stormtrooper captain held a meeting to discuss the implications of their changed situation.

It had taken some time to find an empty storeroom that could be converted into an appropriate conference chamber, and they had to forgo their hot beverages and morning pastries. But these were emergency times, Sivron admitted, and they had to make sacrifices in the name of the Empire.

"Thank you, Captain, for pointing out that loophole in our procedures," he said, flashing a pointy-toothed smile.

The stormtrooper had shown them in an appendix to the emergency procedures, under the subheading "Dissemination of Information," a clause pertaining to the total secrecy of Maw Installation inventions—"Rebel access to Maw Installation research and development data must be denied at all costs." This clause, he argued, could be interpreted as mandating the destruction of the facility, now that it had been overrun.

"*At all costs*," the captain repeated, "clearly means we should forfeit the Installation itself rather than let the Rebels have access to our work."

"Well," Doxin said, "it would give us another opportunity to fire the superlaser for the good of the Empire." He raised his wire-thin eyebrows so that his scalp furrowed like treadmarks across a sand dune.

Yemm, the Devaronian, continued to flip through paragraph after paragraph of the procedures on his datapad, studying the terminology. "I see nothing to contradict the captain's assessment, Director Sivron," he said.

"All right, the resolution has passed," Sivron said. "We shall direct the prototype back into the Maw, using our previous flight path. Captain, take care of the details."

"Yes, sir," the stormtrooper captain said.

"So that's all settled, then," Tol Sivron said, clacking his long claws on the tabletop. "If we have no new business, the meeting is adjourned."

Everyone stood to leave, brushing their uniforms and stepping away from the table.

Tol Sivron looked at the small chronometer; barely two hours had passed. He blinked his beady eyes in surprise. This had been one of his shortest meetings ever.

35

Threepio's dizzying preoccupation with battle configurations and tactics and ships swarming around the five gamma assault shuttles absorbed all his concentration. He forgot entirely about his dread.

The *Gorgon* cruised ominously overhead, firing down on the Installation or shooting across at the New Republic ships.

Chewbacca growled, squinting his fur-rimmed eyes to study the Star Destroyer's firing pattern. He chuffed and grunted an idea to Threepio and, without waiting for a response, opened the tight-beam ship-to-ship communications systems.

Chewbacca spoke rapidly in the Wookiee language, which Threepio decided was a tactically wise thing to do. Although he himself was a protocol droid and understood more than six million forms of communication, he doubted that anyone on the *Gorgon* would know what Chewbacca was saying.

Even as acknowledgment came from the Wookiee pilots in the other assault shuttles, Threepio broke away from his full concentration to speak to the Wookiee. "I simply don't see how we can possibly take out all of the starboard turbolaser banks on the Star Destroyer. It's suicide. Why don't we wait for more fighters from the New Republic ships? I think that would be by far the safest strategy."

Chewbacca snarled, and Threepio decided it was unwise to press the point any further.

A combat wing of TIE fighters soared past them, firing bursts from their laser cannons. One of the assault shuttles passed into the crossfire, and as Threepio reconstructed the images an instant later, he determined that it received eight direct hits within two seconds. Its shields failed. Hull plates buckled, and the shuttle exploded as the TIE fighters roared past to face the X-wings and Y-wings pouring from the New Republic battleships.

Chewbacca let out a grief-stricken roar at seeing some of his newly rescued friends die. The cry was echoed across the comm system by the other Wookiees.

With the explosion Threepio experienced a sudden disorientation; he had been partially linked to the destroyed ship. It felt as if a part of him had been disconnected.

"Oh, dear!" he said, then shifted his concentration to managing the other shuttles. "Chewbacca, you have my complete support. We simply cannot allow them to do this sort of thing."

Chewbacca roared agreement and gave Threepio a comradely slap on the back that practically sent the droid through the control panels.

A tiny streak of light shot past them, and Threepio was able to freeze the image in his optical sensors: it was the angular crystalline shape of a tiny two-man ship. He recognized it instantly.

"Oh, my, isn't that the Sun Crusher?" Threepio asked.

Preoccupied, Chewbacca roared a challenge as the four remaining assault shuttles cruised low over the *Gorgon*'s starboard side. They soared above the complex topography of the hull, a blur of indecipherable outcroppings, piping, fuel shafts, portholes, and life-support equipment. Daala's heavy turbolasers shot alternately at the Maw Installation and at the New Republic starfighters.

Seven TIE fighters broke away from the main attack and circled back to head off Chewbacca's squadron. But the Wookiees unleashed a smoking volley from the assault shuttle's heavy blaster cannons. Stunted old Nawruun and several other Wookiees sat in the gunner seats and fired relentlessly.

A web of blaster bolts spewed from the shuttles, clipping four of the attacking TIE fighters. Two others veered wildly away from the sudden firepower and careened into the side of the *Gorgon*. The lone survivor of the attack group peeled off and fled to get reinforcements.

Chewbacca grunted in satisfaction.

The assault shuttles hammered the Star Destroyer's turbolaser batteries as they streaked back and forth, launching their store of concussion missiles. With the smoldering eruptions of hull plates and exploding weapons systems, the *Gorgon* was defenseless on one side.

"Oh, well done, Chewbacca!" Threepio cried. "You did it."

Chewbacca purred in satisfaction. Loud, triumphant roars came from the back of the assault shuttle and the gunner bay. But as TIE reinforcements arrowed toward them, Threepio decided it was time to cease the frivolity.

"Excuse me, sir," he said, "but hadn't we better retreat now?"

Like a master pilot Kyp Durron brought the Sun Crusher into a berth on one of the planetoids. He maneuvered the thorn-shaped ship through the blast doors and into the bay.

Luke let the young man pilot as he himself worked the communications systems, transmitting to the escort frigate and then to the Installation operations center.

"Wedge, are you there? Are you all right? Tell me what's going on. This is Luke."

A response came over the comm, accompanied by a cacophony of alarms and shouted orders, status reports, and the background rumble of direct hits from the Star Destroyer.

"Luke, you're alive! What are you doing here?"

He realized that Wedge had been inside the Maw cluster since before the defeat of Exar Kun. "We brought the Sun Crusher here to destroy it. But it looks like you're having problems of your own."

"I'd need a few hours to tell you everything that's happened since this operation started," Wedge said. His voice was harried. "Are you safe?"

"We're fine for now, Wedge. We're landing in one of your maintenance bays."

"Good. I can sure use whatever help you can offer."

After Kyp secured the Sun Crusher, he popped open the hatch, and the two of them clambered down the metal ladder. They set off at a brisk jog through the curving corridors that tunneled through the dead rock. The rhythmic pounding of Daala's repeated blasts echoed through the tunnels.

The two of them spilled into the operations center, trying to make sense of the frenzy of preparations Wedge had underway.

Wedge Antilles ran forward to embrace his friend. Both men clapped each other on the back. "I'm so glad you're back with us," Wedge said in a voice filled with unasked questions. Then he flashed a distrustful glance at Kyp Durron, who stood contritely on the threshold. "What's *he* doing here?"

Beside him Qwi Xux also saw him and gasped, taking a step backward.

"I'm sorry," Kyp said quietly.

Luke looked sternly at Wedge. "Kyp is here to help us, Wedge. He has returned from the dark side, and I've made my peace with him. If you still hold a grudge, then take it up with him once this is all over."

Wedge looked to Qwi, and her gentle narrow face tightened before she nodded briefly.

"Kyp came here to destroy the Sun Crusher as a form of penance, but now—" Luke gripped his apprentice's shoulder. "Now we are two Jedi offering our services in this fight."

Wedge called to one of the other commandos. "Give me a status update now," he said.

The tactical crew rattled off a list of starfighters deployed, shots fired, a tally of enemy and ally losses. "Chewbacca's team appears to have knocked out the *Gorgon*'s starboard turbolaser batteries."

Wedge looked relieved. "If only we can keep damaging Daala faster than she can damage us." He shook his head.

"Where's Han?" Luke asked. Kyp perked up, eagerly awaiting the answer.

Wedge frowned. "What do you mean?" Luke explained about the prototype and how Han, Lando, and Mara Jade had last been seen inside its superstructure.

Wedge shook his head. "The Sun Crusher and the *Gorgon* are already here—now you're telling me the Death Star is coming back?" He blinked in disbelief before starting to snap out orders to the tactical team. "You heard what Luke said! Looks like we've got another surprise coming our way."

It didn't seem possible, but everyone managed to bustle a little faster. Luke stared through the broad skylights of the operations center. He sensed it before he saw it.

Through the flaring lights of battle overhead and the muffled din of repeated explosions, the armillary sphere of the Death Star prototype emerged through the pastel glow of the Maw and entered the fray.

36

The *Millennium Falcon*'s landing claw clung to the Death Star's superstructure as the skeletal sphere lurched into motion again and careened through the black hole cluster.

Han, Mara, and Lando sat strapped into their swiveling seats, gritting their teeth from gravity's onslaught. The *Falcon* held on, but the prototype bucked from the enormous tidal pulls.

Once the rough passage was over, Han scanned the diagnostics. "Got to do something about these hyperdrives," he said. "If we fly fast enough, we could just blow the reactor core and run. But the way the *Falcon*'s limping along, we'd never get away in time."

Han turned his seat to look at Lando and Mara. He wiped dark hair away from his eyes. "And even if we did get away in time, we'd never make it back through the Maw cluster without top-notch maneuverability."

"Not to mention we don't know the *way* out," Mara said. "My Jedi instincts aren't strong enough for a job like that."

"Uh, now, that's another good point . . . ," Han admitted.

"But Han," Lando said, "we've got to do something. If the Death Star's come back to Maw Installation, it's bound to be up to no good."

"Yeah," Han said, nodding grimly. "Chewie is in here with the rest of the occupation force. I won't just leave him if he's in trouble."

Mara pulled herself to her feet. "So it's obvious," she said. "We've got to deactivate that superlaser." She shrugged. "As long as we're here."

"But the hyperdrive engines—" Han began.

"You've got environment suits, don't you?" she said. "A light freighter like the *Falcon* ought to have at least a couple for emergency repairs."

"Yesss," Han said, drawing out the word, still unable to guess what Mara had in mind. "I've got two suits: one for me and one for Chewie."

"Good," Mara said, cracking her knuckles. "Calrissian and I will go out and plant timed detonators on the reactor core. You work on the hyperdrive engines. The timers will let us get out of the superstructure before they blow."

Lando's mouth dropped open. "You want *me*—?"

Her eyes challenged him. "Got any better ideas?"

He shrugged and grinned. "Why, no. I'd be honored to escort you, Mara."

Lando sneezed as he tugged on the huge padded suit. "This whole thing smells like Wookiee hair," he said. "Did Chewbacca exercise in this thing and put it away wet?"

The sleeves were enormous, and his feet swam in the Wookiee-sized boots. He tugged the bulky fabric around his waist, fold upon fold, and then used the adjustment straps to cinch it tighter around him. He felt as if he were walking inside a giant inflated mattress.

"We've got a job to do, Calrissian," Mara said. "Quit complaining or I'll do it myself."

"No," Lando said. "I want to help you. Really."

"Here." Mara held out a case of the timed detonators. "Carry these."

Lando looked down at them and swallowed. "Thanks."

Han gave a hollow grunt of pain as he bumped his head on something down in the repair crawl space. Lando heard his friend mutter something about wishing for a decent droid to do the dirty work.

"A couple of the components are fried," Han called up to them. His voice sounded tinny through the compartment. "But I've got spares—or at least close enough that I can get the ship running again. We've got three fused circuits. One we can get by without; two I can bypass."

"We'll give you half an hour," Mara said, pulling the helmet on and sealing it over her neck.

Han repositioned himself in the coffin-sized maintenance bay to stick his head above the deck plates. Grease and leaked coolant stained his cheeks. "I'll be ready."

"You better be, if we trigger those timers," Lando said, and secured his own helmet. It seemed as large as a shuttlecraft on his head.

"Come on, Calrissian," Mara said. "We've got some wrecking to do."

From his comfortable chair Tol Sivron squinted out at the panorama of the Maw's center, assessing the situation but making no decisions—like a good manager.

"It's the Star Destroyer *Gorgon*, sir," the stormtrooper captain said. "Shall I hail it?"

Sivron scowled. "About time Admiral Daala came back to do her duty," he said. It still rankled him that she had abandoned her primary mission of protecting the Maw scientists. Now that the Rebels had already taken over the Installation, it was too late for her to make amends.

"Why did she come back with only one Star Destroyer?" Sivron said. "She had four. No, wait—one was destroyed, wasn't it? Well, three, anyway. Does she simply want to flaunt her weaponry?" He sniffed. "Well, this time we've got our own Death Star, and we're not afraid to use it."

"Excuse me, Director," the captain said, "but the *Gorgon* appears to be severely damaged. The Rebel forces are attacking her. I believe it's our duty to come to her aid."

Tol Sivron looked at the captain incredulously. "You want us to rescue Admiral Daala after she deserted us? You have an odd sense of obligation, Captain."

"But," the stormtrooper said, "aren't we all fighting the same battle?"

Sivron frowned. "In a sense, perhaps. But we must have different priorities—as Daala herself evidenced by leaving us behind."

He saw the Rebel ships opening fire on the lone Star Destroyer, saw the attack increasing as starfighters met TIE fighters in a flurry of pinpoint laser strikes. The colorful battle had a hypnotic effect—and he thought of the blazing heat storms on the Twi'lek homeworld of Ryloth.

He felt a lump of comet ice form in his stomachs. His career had been long and successful, but he was about to end it by destroying the facility he had so successfully administered for years and years.

In the pilot chair of the Death Star prototype, Sivron said in a cold voice, "All right, let us show Admiral Daala we scientists can hold our own."

Suddenly an alarm ratcheted through the chamber. Sivron sighed. "Now what?"

Yemm and Doxin both flipped through their manuals, searching for an explanation.

"We've detected intruders," the stormtrooper captain

answered. "On the power core itself. It seems we picked up one of those smuggler ships near Kessel."

"Well, what do they think they're doing?" Sivron asked.

"According to our sensor cameras, two people have emerged from their ship and—as far as we can tell—are attempting some sort of sabotage."

Sivron sat up in alarm. "Well, stop them!" He snatched the manual out of Doxin's hands and flipped through the pages. "Use emergency procedure number—" He continued to skim over the pages, squinting down at the bulleted lists, flipped a few more pages before tossing the book aside in disgust. "Well, just use the correct procedure, Captain. Do something!"

"We have only a few men and not much time," the captain said. "I'll order two spacetroopers to suit up and take care of the intruders personally."

"Yes, yes," Sivron said, waving his clawed hand, "don't bother me with details. Just get the job done."

Lando tilted the face shield of his enormous helmet back and forth, the better to see with, but the Wookiee-sized suit folded around him in strange and uncomfortable ways. He had to work twice as hard just to figure out where he was going.

His magnetic boots clomped on the metal plating of the gigantic cylindrical power core. Tapered at one end like a spindle with a diamond-hard point, the core pressed against another contact point that rose from the south pole of the Death Star. Between the two points starfire crackled as the charge built up.

The skeleton of girders and access tubes, walled-off compartments, temporary quarters, and storerooms, formed a giant cage around them. Linked catwalks spanned open spaces like a tangled net. Though the prototype was the size of a small moon, it held very little gravity. Lando had to work hard to keep his balance, letting his magnetic boots determine the direction "down."

"We have to go closer to the energy pods," Mara said, her voice buzzing through the tiny earphone.

Lando looked for a way to respond and finally figured out how to activate his own helmet microphone. "Whatever you say. The sooner I get rid of these detonators, the happier I'll be." He sighed partly to himself but also for Mara's benefit. "You'd think destroying one Death Star in a man's lifetime would be enough."

"I prefer men who never settle for *enough*," Mara answered.

Lando blinked, not sure how to take her comment. He allowed himself a broad grin.

Holding out his gloved hand to steady Mara, Lando worked his way down the immense cylindrical core. He tilted his visor to shield himself from the glare pouring from the discharge at the contact points. Above them the pronged disk of the *Falcon* clung to a thick girder.

"Should be good enough here," Mara said, reaching out. "Give me the first detonator."

Lando rummaged in the shielded container and withdrew one of the thick disks. Mara cradled it in her padded glove and bent down to fasten it to the metal hull.

"We'll work our way around and place them on the perimeter," she said, pushing her thumb down on the synchronization button. The detonator lit up with seven lights blinking slowly, like a heartbeat, waiting for final activation.

"When they're all emplaced," Mara's voice said, "we'll give ourselves twenty standard minutes. That should be ample time to get back to the *Falcon* and get away."

Without waiting for him to agree, Mara worked her way around the curving reactor core and turned to take a second detonator from him, planting it squarely against the plating.

Lando felt the faint vibrations of the core throbbing against his magnetic boots. The stored power seemed to be restless, building, waiting to be unleashed.

It seemed to take forever to traverse the circumference of the vast power core, planting the seven detonators. When they returned to their starting point, Mara leaned closer so Lando could see her face through the curved faceplate.

"Ready, Calrissian?"

"Sure thing," Lando answered.

She punched the activator button on the first device. All around the perimeter the detonators winked blue as they began their countdown.

"Back to the *Falcon*. Hurry," Mara said. Lando clomped after her.

A movement caught his eye from the side of the bucket-sized helmet, and he turned his head just in time to see the blocky armored suit of an Imperial spacetrooper. The enemy looked like a man-shaped AT-AT walker with reinforced joints on elbows and knees, heavy boots—and vibroblades like claws in his gloves. One slash and the spacetrooper could rip open Lando's suit, killing him with explosive decompression.

The spacetrooper emerged from an access hatch in the framework above. He let the low gravity cushion his fall as his bulk dropped onto the power core. His heavy boots clanged on the metal as he landed next to Lando and Mara.

"Where did *he* come from?" Lando said, ducking as the spacetrooper lunged with the vibroblades in his gloves. Lando bent backward like a mucus tree in a gale. His magnetic boots held his feet in place, but he threw himself in the opposite direction. Vibroblades slashed past his chest.

Mara reacted more swiftly, swinging the empty padded container that had held the detonators, putting all her momentum behind it. The sharp-edged metal banged against the spacetrooper's thick helmet.

The trooper reached up, stabbing through the plated case with vibroblade claws. Mara used his temporary disorientation to grab Lando and add his mass to her own as she shoved the spacetrooper. With her foot Mara pried free one of the spacetrooper's boots as he fought to regain his balance. She slammed against him, breaking the magnetic grip of his other boot. In an instant the trooper snapped free.

Suddenly unattached to the core, he dropped with the momentum imparted by the force of Mara's attack. The spacetrooper scrabbled to find purchase against the smooth cylindrical hull as he slid down toward the fiery contact points. The vibroblades in his glove made long, silvery score marks on the metal, but did no good.

Sucked inexorably down, the trooper plunged into the flaming discharge between the contact points and vaporized in a bolt of green-and-blue static.

The detonators continued their countdown.

Lando signaled. "We're on our way, Han, old buddy. Make sure you're ready to go."

When he felt a vibration through his boots, Lando looked up to see another spacetrooper drop down from the catwalks. This one carried a blaster rifle, but Lando guessed that the trooper dared not use it in the vicinity of the power core.

The second trooper brought his blaster rifle to bear, motioning for them to surrender, but no voice came over their helmet radios. Lando wondered if the trooper had tuned to a different frequency, or if he merely expected the blaster rifle to be a universal language.

"Can he hear us?" Lando said.

"Who knows? Distract him. Our time is running out." Lando waved his gloved hands and pointed down the expanse of metal to the blinking detonators. He flapped his palms frantically and threw his arms wide to mime an explosion.

As the spacetrooper glanced in the other direction, Mara launched herself forward and grabbed the barrel of his blaster rifle, using it like a lever. In free fall her own momentum knocked him free, sending the trooper tumbling back up toward the catwalks.

"Let's go! Don't worry about him," Mara said, returning to Lando's side. "Get to the *Falcon* before those detonators blow."

Mara and Lando toiled back to the ship still clinging to the support girders. Behind them the second spacetrooper managed to reach out and grab one of the tangled coolant pipes, stopping his reckless tumble. He descended toward the power core again, ignoring Lando and Mara as he hurried to the detonators.

Lando felt Chewbacca's enormous baggy suit folding around him, making it difficult to walk. He looked back and saw the spacetrooper working with the detonators, but he knew Mara had cyberlocked them together. With only a few minutes left, the spacetrooper would be able to do nothing.

Less than a minute before the timed detonation, Lando and Mara sealed themselves inside the *Falcon* just as Han disengaged the landing claw.

"Glad you could join me!" Han said, immediately punching the accelerators.

The *Falcon* raced back out along the Death Star's equator. Its sublight engines flared white-hot behind it.

The surviving spacetrooper managed to reach the ring of detonators. He worked meticulously but rapidly, disconnecting each one, using the built-in laser welder in his suit to remove the explosives. He tossed each one, still blinking, into the open space.

He succeeded in disarming six of the seven detonators. He was standing right above the last one, prying it up, when it exploded beneath him.

Outside, in the midst of the space battle, Admiral Daala gritted her teeth. Her face wore a perpetual look of disdain as she stared at the dizzying firefight.

The attack was not going well. Her forces were being gradually worn away. She hadn't had many TIE fighters to start with; most of them had been left behind in the Cauldron Nebula when she had wheeled the *Gorgon* about to escape the exploding stars. She had only her reserves, and most of those squadrons had been wiped out by Rebel starfighters.

When the Death Star prototype reappeared among the gases overhead, Daala felt a thrill of awe. She rejoiced at the enormous destructive potential suddenly available to her. The tide of the battle had turned—now they could wipe out the Rebel infestation.

But when she determined that the prototype was piloted by the incompetent fool Tol Sivron, her hopes dwindled. "Why doesn't he fire?" she said. "One blast and he could take out all three corvettes and the frigate. *Why* doesn't he fire?"

Commander Kratas stood by her side. "I can't say, Admiral."

She glared to make it clear she hadn't expected an answer. "Tol Sivron has never had any initiative in his entire life," she said. "I should have known I couldn't expect him to do his duty now. Redouble our efforts against the Installation. Let us show Tol Sivron how it must be done."

She narrowed her brilliant eyes to look around the bridge. "Enough practice," she said. "It's time to destroy Maw Installation once and for all. Open fire!"

37

In the Maw Installation operations room, one of the technicians pounded her fist on a control deck. "Shields are failing, General Antilles!" she announced.

Another engineer ran in from the outside corridor, florid-faced and puffing. Sweat plastered his hair to his forehead, and his blue eyes were glassy with panic. "All this pounding has knocked out the temporary cooling systems we installed on the reactor asteroid! It was never meant to withstand such punishment. The reactor's going to explode—no chance of patching it this time."

Wedge gritted his teeth and looked to Qwi. He squeezed her hand. "Looks like we're about to save Daala the trouble," he said. "Time to evacuate."

Beside him Luke whirled around. "Hey! Where's Kyp?"

But the young man was gone.

"I don't know," Wedge answered, "but we don't have time to look for him now."

●   ●   ●

Kyp Durron's heart hammered, but he used a Jedi calming routine, forcing himself to relax. He required his bodily systems to operate efficiently, providing strength where he needed it, allowing neither fear nor exhaustion to hinder him.

The tumult of alarms and the external attack rattled the Installation. New Republic soldiers ran across corridors, grabbing equipment and rushing back to their transports.

No one stopped to look at Kyp; if anyone had bothered to question him, he would have used a simple Jedi trick to distract them, blur their memories, making them believe they had never seen him.

Kyp was pleased that Master Skywalker had not noticed his departure. With the sudden appearance of the Death Star prototype and the continued pounding from the *Gorgon*, Kyp had known what he must do.

He also knew Master Skywalker would try to stop him, and Kyp had no time for that.

He had used his own powers—light-side powers, he fervently hoped—to distract everyone while he slipped out into the corridor. He had blanked his thoughts, his keyed-up emotions; unless Master Skywalker made a directed effort to pinpoint him, Kyp would go unnoticed in the chaos.

As he ran, the tempo of the battle outside increased, and he knew that the Installation would not last much longer. If the Death Star prototype managed even one shot, they would be annihilated in an instant. That was the primary threat at the moment.

As he sprinted down the rocky tunnels to the maintenance bay where he had landed the Sun Crusher, he recalled when he and Han had fled through the spice mines of Kessel. The memory of Han brought a deep pang.

The Death Star had reappeared in the center of the Maw, but Kyp had seen no sign of the *Millennium Falcon*.

Did that mean Han was dead, destroyed in his sabotage attempt?

Kyp had been cursed with impulsiveness, making his decisions and acting on them without thinking of the consequences. Right now, though, that was a strength. He had to fight against the New Republic's mortal enemies, and he could not ponder and debate the ultimate results of his actions.

Kyp knew he had a great deal to atone for. He had listened to the dark teachings of Exar Kun. He had struck down his teacher and Jedi Master. He had wiped clean the memories of Qwi Xux. He had stolen the Sun Crusher and obliterated entire star systems . . . he had caused the death of his brother Zeth.

Now he would do all he could to rescue his friends—not only to salve his conscience, but because they deserved to live and continue the fight for freedom in the galaxy.

Kyp stared at the oily metallic texture of the Sun Crusher's faceted sides. The quantum armor reflected light in strange directions, distorting it, making the superweapon appear to have been polished with slow light.

With trembling hands he gripped the rungs of the ladder and ascended. Han Solo and Chewbacca had climbed these same rungs to get into the Sun Crusher during their escape from the Installation. Kyp's brother had attempted to pull himself aboard before Carida's star exploded—but Zeth had not succeeded.

Kyp swung shut the hatch as if he were sealing himself off from the rest of the galaxy for all time. He didn't know if he would ever see the outside again, if he would ever return to Coruscant, or if he would ever speak to Han Solo or Master Skywalker again.

He slumped into the pilot's seat and stilled those thoughts with a Jedi technique. Only a few hours earlier he and Luke had been riding in the Sun Crusher, peaceful companions talking about their lives and their hopes. Now

Kyp could not think beyond working the simple controls of the Sun Crusher.

He raised the spike-shaped craft on its repulsorlifts and guided himself through the long launching tunnel into open space where the battle raged.

He approached the giant framework sphere of the Death Star. Kyp had seen the effectiveness of the Sun Crusher's ultrastrong armor when Han Solo had flown at full speed through the bridge tower of the *Hydra*—but even the quantum armor could not possibly withstand a blast from the Death Star's superlaser.

Kyp had two remaining resonance torpedoes that could trigger a supernova. He doubted he could get a critical mass in the prototype's skeletal structure, but a direct hit would still cause a substantial chain reaction.

He accelerated forward, a mere pinprick on the vast canvas of garish-colored gases around the Maw's black holes.

Then, without warning, a bright flower of orange and white erupted from the power core at the center of the Death Star, a small explosion. An instant later, flying in the opposite direction, the *Millennium Falcon* blasted out of the superstructure, gaining speed.

With a warm melting sensation of relief and triumph, he knew that Han Solo had survived! Now Kyp could strike the crippled Death Star with no second thoughts. And then he would go after Daala.

He powered up his targeting and weapons systems. With Jedi senses Kyp could feel the power surging beneath him in the toroidal torpedo generator—energy sufficient to crack open stars.

For one last time, he had to use it.

The explosion in the power core sent the entire Death Star reeling off its axis. The lone spacetrooper attempting to disarm the detonators was hurled backward, already torn to shreds of plasteel armor and incinerated bone.

The detonator had ripped open a gash in the cylindrical core, splitting the armored plating wide and spraying a jet of radioactive fire.

Tol Sivron's head-tails stretched out straight with outrage. "I ordered those two spacetroopers to stop the sabotage!" He whirled to the Devaronian Division Leader. "Yemm, record their service numbers and make a special disciplinary notation in their files!"

He tapped his claws on the chair arm and finally remembered to say, "Oh, and give me a damage assessment."

Doxin ran to the status console and pulled up a visual. "From what I know of the blueprints, Director, there appears to be a relatively insignificant breach in the power core. We can repair it before radiation levels get too high. It's a good thing no more than one of those detonators blew, though. Otherwise we wouldn't be able to contain it."

The stormtrooper captain was on his feet, chattering orders into his radio helmet. "I've already sent a full squadron of troopers down to suit up, sir. I have instructed them that their personal safety is forfeit."

"Good, good," Tol Sivron said absently. "How soon will I be able to shoot again?"

The stormtrooper studied his panels. The white plasteel helmet masked any hint of expression. "The spacetroopers are suited up and on their way. They are descending the catwalks now." He pointed his featureless black goggles at Sivron. "If the repair work goes as planned, you could fire within twenty minutes."

"Well, tell them to hurry," Sivron said. "If Daala destroys Maw Installation before I do, I'll be very annoyed."

"Yes, Director," the captain said.

Tol Sivron watched with simmering frustration as the *Millennium Falcon* disappeared toward the other fighting ships inside the Maw. He noticed the New Republic battleships that had overrun his facility; he noticed the large conglomeration of planetoids where he had spent so many years of his career. And then he looked at Admiral Daala's Star Destroyer. Daala, whom he loathed, who had deserted him and her duty at the time of greatest need.

Tol Sivron muttered to himself as he fidgeted in the command chair. "So many targets," he said, "and so little time."

38

The battle-scarred Star Destroy-
er cruised so low over the Maw Installation's weakening
defensive shields that Luke's instinct was to duck. The
complex clutter of the *Gorgon*'s hull flowed like an unend-
ing river past the skylights, showing just how immense the
battleship was.

"Shields just failed completely," one of the technicians
said. "We won't survive another pass, and the reactor
asteroid is going critical!"

Wedge punched the facilitywide intercom and shouted
orders. His voice echoed through the labyrinth of tunnels
in the clustered asteroids of the Installation. "Last call for
evacuation. Everyone to the transport ships. Now! We've
only got a few minutes to get out of here."

The alarms somehow grew even louder. Luke turned
to follow the troops running toward the doors. Wedge
grabbed the thin blue arm of Qwi Xux, but she resisted,
staring in horror at the computer screens. "Look!" she
said. "What is she doing? She can't!"

Wedge stopped to glance at the streams of data flying across the screens at high speed. He blinked and saw rapid-fire images of blueprints, weapons designs, test data.

"Admiral Daala must have known Director Sivron's password," Qwi cried. "She's dumping the data backups we couldn't crack. She's downloading all the weapons information!"

Wedge grabbed Qwi by the waist and yanked her away from the terminal, rushing her toward the door. "We can't do anything about that now. We've got to get out of here."

They ran down the corridors with the assault troops in the lead. Qwi's feathery hair streamed behind her, glinting in the harsh white light from the glowpanels.

Wedge felt overwhelmed, his tension rising, as if his internal chronometer were ticking down the seconds until the explosion of the fragile reactor asteroid, until Admiral Daala's next attack, until the whole Installation bloomed into a white-hot cloud of rubble.

Wedge had never wanted to be a general anyway. He was a good wing man, a fighter pilot. He had flown beside Luke down the trench of the first Death Star, and next to Lando Calrissian to destroy the second one.

By far the best assignment had been to escort the lovely Qwi Xux. Even frightened and dismayed, Qwi looked exotic and beautiful. He wanted to hold her and comfort her—but he could do that on the transport back to the *Yavaris*. If they didn't get out of here immediately, they would all die.

As the refugees scrambled across the takeoff area, one of the transports declared itself fully loaded. Wedge grabbed his comm link. "Go, go! Don't wait for us!"

They charged up the ramp of another waiting shuttle. The remaining troops scattered to their seats. Wedge took a second to make sure Qwi had a safe place to strap herself in. Luke bolted for the cockpit and threw himself into the copilot's chair, powering up the sublight engines.

Wedge took one last glance back at the personnel compartment to verify that everyone was at least close to being seated. "Secure the door!" he cried.

One of the lieutenants slammed a palm against the hatch controls. With an impatient hiss the ramp drew in like a retracting serpent's tongue. The doors clamped shut.

Wedge wasted no time securing himself into his seat before raising the transport off the landing pad. With a scream of acceleration the troop ship launched itself away from the dying Maw Installation.

The bootsteps of Commander Kratas sounded like hammers on sheet metal as he ran up to the bridge observation platform. Admiral Daala turned, anxiously awaiting a favorable report.

Kratas tried to regain his composure but did not succeed in wiping the idiotic grin from his lips. "Transfer successful, Admiral. Complete core dump of all the Maw's backup computer files." He lowered his voice. "You were correct. Director Sivron never bothered to change his password. He was still using the same one you obtained ten years ago."

Daala snorted. "Sivron has been incompetent in everything else. Why should he change now?"

Most of her TIE fighters had been wiped out. None of her starboard turbolasers were functional. Engines operated at only 40 percent efficiency, and many systems were severely overheating.

She had never anticipated the battle would take this long. She had meant to obliterate the Rebel forces and then finish mop-up operations at her leisure. She didn't understand why Sivron and his Death Star didn't do anything. But finally something had gone right; she had retrieved the precious data from the Maw Installation computers.

Daala watched as troop transports fled the cluster of rocks below, but she deemed them insignificant targets.

"Installation shields are completely down," the tactical lieutenant said.

"Good," she snapped. "Wheel about. We'll make a final attack run."

"Excuse me, Admiral," Kratas interrupted. "We're getting anomalous readings from the reactor asteroid. It appears to have suffered severe damage and is highly unstable."

Daala brightened. "Ah, excellent. We'll target that. Perhaps the reactor can do most of the destructive work for us."

She looked out the bridge tower and saw the ocean of screaming gases around the infinitely black pinpoints. The *Gorgon* turned about and headed toward Maw Installation.

"Full ahead," Daala said, standing rigid at her station, gloved hands clasped behind her back. Her coppery hair flowed behind her like spraying lava. "Fire repeatedly, until the Installation is destroyed—or until our turbolaser banks are drained dry."

The lumbering ship picked up momentum as the *Gorgon* accelerated forward on its final run.

Wedge flicked on the open communications unit to contact the New Republic fleet. He didn't care about encryption at the moment—if the Imperial forces could decode his transmissions, they wouldn't have time to take action anyway.

"All fighters, regroup and return to the *Yavaris*. Prepare to retreat. We are leaving the Maw. We have everything we came for."

The huge frigate hung like a jagged weapon waiting to receive the fighter squadrons. X-wings and Y-wings looped around, disengaging from space dogfights and heading back to their primary ships. Wedge accelerated toward the *Yavaris*. The squarish opening of the frigate's lower bays glowed with an atmosphere-containment field, like a welcoming open door.

Without warning four square-winged TIE fighters shot up from Wedge's blind spot, mercilessly battering the front of the transport shuttle with laser bolts.

Before Wedge could react, an assault shuttle bearing Imperial markings flew in from the left, firing multiple beams from its forward heavy blaster cannons. The attack took the TIE pilots by surprise. They scrambled and scattered. Two careened into each other to get out of the way. Two others succumbed to the focused blasts, exploding into molten debris.

Wedge heard a loud Wookiee roar of triumph over the open comm channel, echoed by growls and shouts from the assault shuttle's passenger compartment. The clipped metallic voice of See-Threepio interrupted, "Chewbacca, please do stop showing off! We need to get back to the *Yavaris*."

Luke toggled the communications panel. "Thanks, guys."

"Master Luke!" Threepio cried. "What are you doing here? We need to get away!"

"It's a long story, Threepio. We're doing our best to do just that."

On the opposite side of the Maw, the *Gorgon* spun about and accelerated toward the unprotected Installation like a wild bantha, its rear engines blazing with star fire. A flurry of green turbolaser bolts blurred out from the Star Destroyer's fore section, angling down to strike the Installation's clustered asteroids. With the facility's shields down, ionized rock dust sprayed into space.

Daala fired and fired again, picking up speed in what appeared to be a suicide run. Her strafing beams pum-

meled the Installation, striking asteroid after asteroid.
Metal bridges vaporized, transparisteel shattered and blew
outward.

The *Gorgon* came on, unstoppable until—just as she
soared over at closest approach—the attack breached the
containment housing the unstable power reactor.

Sitting in the cockpit of the personnel transport, Wedge
and Luke both flinched as the entire Maw Installation suddenly became a blaze of light, like a miniature exploding
star. The center of the Maw was filled with an incandescent purifying fire.

The glare flooded outward, automatically causing the
viewscreens to darken. Wedge flew blind, trusting the navigation computer's controls and aiming toward the waiting
New Republic flagships.

When his vision finally cleared, he looked back to the
stable point that had held the Empire's most sophisticated weapons-research laboratory. He saw only a far-flung
swarm of broken rocks and smoldering gases in an expanding backwash of energy. Eventually, the debris would drift
far enough to be siphoned down to infinity through one of
the black holes.

As the glare faded and the fiery gases cleared, he saw
no sign whatsoever of Admiral Daala or her last Star
Destroyer.

39

Working like automatons, the team of doomed spacetroopers attached themselves to the breached wall of the Death Star's power core. Intense radiation spewed out, darkening their faceplates so they could barely see, slowly frying their life-support systems.

Moving sluggishly as they weakened under the invisible onslaught, they wrestled thick sheets of plating in the low gravity. They used rapid laser welders to slap patches over the breach, reinforcing it to withstand an energy buildup.

One of the spacetroopers, his control pack sparking with blue lightning as the suit's circuits all broke down, thrashed about in eerie silence; his arm movements gradually slowed until he drifted free. One of the others took his place, ignoring the lost companion. Every one of them had already received a lethal dose of radiation. They knew it, but their training had been thorough: they lived to serve the Empire.

One of the troopers completed a last weld at the hottest point of the breach. His skin blistered. His nerves were deadened. His eyes and lungs hemorrhaged blood. But he forced himself to finish his task.

The cold vacuum of space solidified the welds instantly. With a gurgling voice filled with fluid, the spacetrooper gasped into his helmet radio, "Mission accomplished."

Then the remaining troopers, with failing life-support systems and bodies already savaged by the fatal radiation, released their hold on the power core in unison. They drifted free, dropping toward the brilliant energy discharge like shooting stars.

At the total destruction of Maw Installation and the loss of Admiral Daala's *Gorgon*, Tol Sivron's initial reaction was one of annoyance and disappointment.

"The Installation was supposed to be *my* target," he said. He glared at his other Division Leaders. "How could Daala do such a thing? I have the Death Star; she doesn't."

As the shock waves and light echoes from the huge explosion drifted and faded, Sivron could see the Rebel fleet gathering itself to flee the cluster.

Sivron sighed. "Perhaps we should hold another meeting to discuss options."

"Sir!" The stormtrooper captain got to his feet. "Our power reactor is now temporarily repaired. I lost nine good spacetroopers to bring the weapon back online. I think we should use it. The Rebel fleet is in retreat. We'll lose them if we don't act soon. I know this is nonstandard procedure, Director, but we have no time for a meeting."

Sivron looked from side to side, suddenly insecure. He didn't like to be pushed into snap decisions. Too many things could go wrong if one did not consider the full consequences. But the captain had a good point.

"All right, then, temporary emergency actions. Ad hoc committee decision—shall we use the superlaser to strike out at the Rebel forces? Doxin, your vote."

"I agree," the squat Division Leader said.

Tol Sivron turned to the hatchet-faced woman. "Golanda?"

"Let's cause some damage."

"Yemm?"

The Devaronian nodded, his horns bobbing up and down. "It will look much better in the report if we have a unanimous vote."

Sivron considered. "Since Wermyn is no longer with us, I will act as his proxy and cast my vote along with his. Therefore, the vote is unanimous. We will strike the Rebel forces." He nodded to Yemm. "Please note that in the minutes."

"Director," the stormtrooper captain interrupted, "the Rebel fleet is pulling out. One of the corvettes has already gone into the Maw."

"Captain, you are so impatient!" Sivron snapped. "Can't you see we've already made the resolution? Now it's time to implement it. Go ahead and establish your first target."

He blinked his tiny eyes and spotted one of the Corellian corvettes hanging dead in space. "What about that one?" Sivron said. "It appears to be either crippled or boobytrapped. I don't like it—and besides, it's a stationary target. We can use it to calibrate our aiming mechanisms . . . since you missed a whole planet last time."

"As you wish, Director." The stormtrooper relayed the instructions to the team of gunners in the firing bay.

"I suggest we fire at only half strength, Director," Doxin said, scanning the technical readouts. His bald scalp furrowed again. "Even at reduced power the Death Star superlaser will be more than adequate to destroy a simple battleship. In that way we can manage multiple firings without depleting our reservoir so quickly. We won't have to wait so long between shots."

"Good suggestion, Division Leader," Sivron said with a

smile of anticipation. "I'd very much like to shoot more than once."

Down in the firing bay the gunners hunched over sprawling control banks, fingers moving deftly over the arrays of brightly lit squares to call up the targeting cross and lock in on the doomed corvette.

"Hurry up and fire," Tol Sivron's voice echoed through the speakers. "We want to get a second shot at those ships before they all leave."

Together the gunners focused the secondary laser beams and yanked back on the levers to release the pent-up energy within the power core.

Along the focusing tubes a wide beam of incinerating power shot out. It funneled through the focusing eye and blazed into a deadly spear, striking precisely on target.

The crippled Corellian corvette was so insignificant that it absorbed little of the destructive power. The beam went through the vaporized wreckage and continued into the curtains of the Maw.

"Outstanding!" Sivron said. "See what happens when you follow the correct procedures? Now target the frigate. The big ship. I want to see that one explode."

"We have enough energy reserves for several more blasts," the stormtrooper captain said.

Then a tiny, angular blip of light streaked across their targeting viewport—as seemingly insignificant as a gnat— yet it kept coming. Its hull glistened brightly in reflected light. The small ship fired its ridiculously ineffective defensive lasers at the Death Star.

"What's that?" Sivron said. "Give me a close-up."

Golanda magnified the image on the screen and scowled. Her face looked unpleasant enough to shatter planets. "I believe it's one of our own concepts, Director Sivron. You may recognize it yourself."

As he looked at the shard-shaped vessel, his head-tails twitched. Of course he remembered it—not only from the working model he had seen once, but from all the progress reports and computer simulations its creator, Qwi Xux, had delivered during her years of development.

"The Sun Crusher," he said. "But that's ours!"

The torus-shaped resonance field generator glowed with plasma fire at the bottom of its long spike.

"Open a channel," Tol Sivron said. "I want to talk to whoever is there. Hello, hello? You have appropriated property that belongs to Maw Installation. I demand that you return it to the proper Imperial authorities immediately." He crossed his arms over his chest and waited for a reply.

The pilot of the Sun Crusher answered by launching one of the supernova torpedoes into the Death Star.

Kyp felt a rush of satisfaction as he pressed the firing button, ignoring the Twi'lek administrator's pompous posturing. He watched the high-energy projectile shoot from the bottom of the Sun Crusher and burrow deep within the complicated framework of metal girders inside the prototype.

The resonance torpedo vaporized girders as it tunneled deeper and deeper, until it finally struck heavier primary struts that foamed as they disintegrated.

The torpedo dumped its energy in a shower that triggered a small chain reaction within the solid superstructure, splitting atomic nuclei and causing an arc of spreading dissolution. Girders vaporized in a widening hole that ate its way farther and farther through the heavy framework.

But Kyp's elation faded as the chain reaction slowed, and then stopped. The skeletal Death Star had insufficient mass to continue its own disintegration.

He had ruined a good portion of the support framework in one sector of the prototype, but not enough.

Kyp powered up the weapons panel again and prepared to fire. He could annihilate the Death Star piece by piece if necessary. But looking down at his panel, he noted with dismay that only one of his supernova torpedoes remained.

Grim-faced, Kyp zoomed in closer to the prototype. He would have to make this last shot count.

Wheeling the *Millennium Falcon* in a backward arc, Han Solo tried to check how much damage the detonators had done to the Death Star's power core.

He was disappointed. He had expected to see the skeletal prototype bloom into a fantastic flower of fire, but instead the detonators seemed to have fizzled, leaving only a dimming blaze at the center.

The ship drifted in space for a few moments as Mara and Lando shucked their environment suits. Lando rubbed sweat from his forehead and wiped his hands as if disgusted with the griminess of the suit.

"Now what are we going to do?" Han asked when they had finally joined him back in the cockpit.

Lando looked at the Death Star shrinking in the black distance behind them. "Maybe we'd better go see if Wedge—"

Suddenly the Maw Installation and the *Gorgon* were swallowed in a brilliant flare as everything detonated at once.

"Too late," Mara said.

"Now why couldn't the Death Star have exploded like that?" Lando said miserably.

"Maybe we at least caused some permanent harm," Han said hopefully. But moments later they all groaned as a green beam lanced out from the Death Star to destroy one of the corvettes in the retreating New Republic fleet.

"So much for permanent harm," Mara Jade said.

"That Death Star's causing some harm, big time!" Lando said.

"Wait," Han said as he glanced back at the Death Star, squinting. "Move in closer."

"Closer?" Lando said. "You out of your mind?"

"That's Kyp," Han said as the Sun Crusher streaked across the face of the Death Star and launched one of its static-filled torpedoes into the superstructure.

"If he's taking on the Death Star, we've got to go help." Han said.

The Sun Crusher fled toward the gravitational walls of the Maw cluster, and Tol Sivron ordered the Death Star to track the small but deadly ship.

"Get a lock on it," he said. "We'll blast it out of space the same way we did with that Rebel ship."

"Sir," the stormtrooper captain said, "to lock on to a target so tiny and moving so quickly—"

"Then get close enough so you can't miss," Sivron snapped. "One of his torpedoes ate up eleven percent of our superstructure! We can't afford more losses like that. How are we going to explain it when we get back to the Empire?"

"Perhaps that would be a good reason to stay away from the Sun Crusher, sir," the stormtrooper pointed out.

"Nonsense! How would that look on the report?" Sivron said, leaning forward. "You have your orders, Captain."

The equatorial propulsion units powered up and nudged the massive skeletal craft to greater speed as it pursued the flitting superweapon.

"Fire whenever you have a target," Sivron said.

The Death Star picked up speed, and the tiny Sun Crusher slowed down, as if taunting them.

The gases grew hot in the outer shell of the Maw as they approached one of the bottomless singularities. The

Sun Crusher danced back and forth, shooting its tiny lasers, destroying minor struts here and there, causing insignificant damage. The Death Star had to fight against the gravity of the nearby black hole.

"What's the matter?" Tol Sivron said to the gunners over the intercom. "Are you waiting to read the serial numbers on his engine parts?"

The Death Star shot again. Its green beam tore through the outer wisps of the cluster, firing point-blank at the Sun Crusher—but the laser curved to the left, tugged by the mighty force of the black hole. The green beam spiraled like a ball bearing falling into a drain.

"You missed! How could you miss?" Tol Sivron ranted. "Captain, give me those flight controls. I'm going to pilot the Death Star myself. I'm tired of your incompetence."

All of the Division Leaders suddenly looked at Tol Sivron, aghast. The stormtrooper captain turned slowly in his chair. "Are you sure that's wise, Director? You don't have the experience—"

Sivron crossed his arms over his chest. "I have read the procedure and I've watched what you're doing. I know everything I need to know. Give me the controls right now. That's a managerial directive!"

Sivron grinned with anticipation as he began to issue commands directing the Death Star. "Now we'll finish this properly," he said.

Just like a pet floozam on a leash, thought Kyp as he flew toward the black hole. The Death Star followed his every move.

He reversed course and arrowed back toward the prototype, increasing speed and calling up his weapons controls. The maze of metal girders and cross braces spun below him—and he launched his last resonance torpedo. The blazing cloud of plasma chewed through the outer layers of the prototype as it plowed ever-widening circles of destruction.

The last shot would make them panic. It wouldn't cripple the Death Star entirely, but merely crippling the prototype would never be enough. He had to go for the full victory.

As the chain reaction initiated by his last torpedo petered out, Kyp sped over the metallic horizon of the Death Star and raced for the Maw's nearest black hole.

Kyp used his onboard tactical systems to estimate the exact position of the event horizon, the point from which no ship, however powerful, could ever escape. He came closer and closer—and the Death Star howled after him.

Han shouted into the comm systems, "Kyp, Kyp Durron! Answer me. Don't go so close. Watch out!"

But he received no reply.

Death Star and Sun Crusher were locked in mortal combat, paying no heed to outside distractions. The Death Star prototype orbited close to the black hole. The Sun Crusher danced from side to side, hammering with tiny laser blasts.

"I think I know what he's doing," Han said with deep uneasiness. "The prototype has greater mass and a much larger volume. If Kyp can lure it near the point of no return . . ."

"Without getting sucked down himself," Lando said.

"That's the catch, isn't it?" Han answered.

The Death Star fired again, and the superlaser beam curved around, bent even more severely in the deep gravity well; but this time the gunner had compensated. The blurred fringes of the beam actually struck the Sun Crusher and knocked it spinning out of control.

Any other ship would have been vaporized instantly, but the quantum armor plating protected the superweapon— just barely.

Kyp's propulsion systems were obviously damaged. The Sun Crusher struggled along on a tangential course, attempting to pull away from the event horizon. But it was too close, and gravity was too strong. It spiraled in a tight orbit, sinking deeper and deeper.

The Death Star pilot couldn't resist making the final kill, and the prototype loomed closer. The Sun Crusher and the giant skeletal sphere orbited the black hole like the ends of a baton, speeding up.

Only then did the Death Star pilot seem to realize his peril, and all equatorial thrusters kicked on at once, attempting to pull the prototype away. But the giant vessel had already crossed the edge of the black hole.

The Sun Crusher could not achieve sufficient velocity to escape its tightening orbit either. It spiraled in the wake of the Death Star, with no hope of getting away.

Han felt as if his chest were being torn apart by the tidal forces. "Kyp!" he cried.

A final streak of light shot away from the Sun Crusher, and then it was too late for the tiny superweapon.

The Death Star prototype plunged into the thickening cascades of superhot gases that shrieked down into nothingness. The spherical prototype elongated like a great egg under the uneven gravitational stresses. The curved girders ripped apart, then were crushed into a cone that stretched into the black hole's funnel.

With a wink of brilliance the tiny Sun Crusher followed its nemesis down into the black hole.

Lando and Mara remained utterly silent. Han hung his head and squeezed his eyes shut. "Goodbye, Kyp."

"It's a message cylinder," Mara said, identifying the small streak shot out by the Sun Crusher. "We'd better get it quick, because it's falling toward the black hole, too."

"Message cylinder?" Han sat up, trying to find his enthusiasm. "Okay, let's snag it before it's too late."

The *Falcon* raced toward the event horizon. Lando and

Mara worked together, wrestling to navigate the ship in the buckling jaws of gravity. They detected the metallic container, and Lando swooped in, latching on to it with the tractor beam moments before the small message pod could fall over the brink of the gravitational pit.

"Got it," Lando said.

"All right, pull it inside, and let's get out of here," Han said in a bleak voice. "At least I can hear the last words Kyp had to say."

40

Han and Lando both pulled on stiff gloves before they wrestled the Sun Crusher's message canister into the *Falcon*'s common area. Deep cold had penetrated the canister, and as they brought it into the enclosed atmosphere, tendrils of frost grew like lacy ferns across its surface.

The thin metal hull gleamed bright, splotched in places by electrostatic discharges from when the cylinder had been launched at high speed from the Sun Crusher.

"That's one heavy message," Lando said as they lugged the canister to a flat spot on the floor and set it down with a metallic *thump* on the deck plates.

Little more than a meter long and less than half a meter wide, the message pod was used by the captain of a doomed ship to launch his last log entries and to dump his computer cores and navigation records for later investigations.

Han remembered Kyp telling him that when the Coruscant scientists had stumbled upon the message canisters inside the Sun Crusher, they had panicked, thinking they had uncovered the dangerous supernova torpedoes—even though the cylinder was standard Imperial issue, and any smuggler or starfighter pilot should have recognized it immediately.

On his rampages in the Cauldron Nebula and the Carida system, Kyp had left message cylinders to explain what he had done and why, so that no one would construe his actions as simple astronomical accidents.

Han felt stunned and lethargic with sadness. His friend had been right, but only to a point. Kyp Durron's agenda to destroy the Empire had used tactics as vicious as those of the Emperor's.

Luke Skywalker had claimed the young man would redeem himself fully, but now Kyp's potential as a great Jedi had been extinguished.

Han could not question Kyp's sacrifice, though. Kyp had eliminated both the Death Star prototype and the Sun Crusher. He had bought the galaxy's freedom from terror at the cost of his life . . . one life for potentially billions.

That made sense, didn't it?

Didn't it?

Mara Jade knelt beside the message cylinder, running her slender hands over its hull. She popped open the access plate. "Well, it's not encrypted," she said. "Either Kyp didn't have time, or he knew we'd be the ones to pick it up. He left the homing beacon off."

"Just open it," Han said roughly. He'd had enough of this grim waiting. What had Kyp thought to say in his last moments?

Mara punched in the standard sequence. The lights blinked red, then amber, then flashed green. With a hiss of escaping air, a formerly invisible seam appeared down the center of the pod. The long black line widened as the two halves split, opening up.

Inside, looking waxen and emotionless as a statue, lay Kyp Durron. His eyes were closed, his face drawn into an expression of intense—yet surprisingly peaceful—concentration.

"Kyp," Han shouted. His voice cracked with astonished joy, yet he tried to hold back his hope. "Kyp!"

Somehow Kyp had crammed himself inside the small volume of the message cylinder, a vessel barely large enough to hold a child. But Kyp had managed to crush his legs, fold his arms until the bones snapped, pressed down on his rib cage until ribs cracked, compacting himself.

Han leaned closer to the ashen face. "Is he alive? He's in some kind of Jedi trance." In his final desperation Kyp had somehow found the strength to use his Jedi pain-blocking techniques, his determination, and all the knowledge Luke had taught him . . . to do this to himself, as his only chance for survival.

"He's slowed his functions almost to the point of suspended animation," Mara said. "He's in so deep that he might as well be dead."

The message canister was airtight but had no life-support systems, no air other than the small amount that had fit around his own broken body.

"That's impossible," Lando said.

"Let's get him out," Han said. "Careful."

Han gently, meticulously pried the young man free of the tiny cylinder. As Lando and Mara helped him carry Kyp to one of the narrow bunks, the young man's body sagged and flopped from grievously smashed bones, as if someone had crumpled him into a ball and then tossed him aside.

"Oh, Kyp," Han said. As he set Kyp on the bunk and straightened his arms, Han could feel the shattered wrists like jelly under his skin. "We have to get him to a medical center," he said. "I've got first aid here, but not nearly enough for something like this."

Kyp's black eyes fluttered open, glazed and unfocused with incredible pain; but he drove it back. "Han," he said in a voice as faint as beating wings. "You came to get me."

"Of course, kid," Han said, bending down. "What did you expect?"

"The Death Star?" Kyp asked.

"Sucked down into the black hole . . . along with the Sun Crusher. They're both gone."

Kyp's entire body shuddered with relief. "Good."

He looked as if he were about to collapse back into unconsciousness, but then his eyes blinked again, brightening with a new confidence. "I'll be all right, you know."

"I know you will be," Han answered.

Only then did Kyp succumb to the pain and allow himself to sink back into his Jedi trance.

"Good to have you back, kid," Han whispered, then looked up to Mara and Lando. "Let's get him back to Coruscant."

A Wookiee bellow split from the intercom system, and Han stood up straight, rushing back to the cockpit to see a battered Imperial gamma assault shuttle hanging in space in front of the *Falcon*, its engines white-hot and ready to go.

"Chewie!" Han shouted into the voice pickups, and the Wookiee responded with a roar.

"What Chewbacca is saying," Threepio's voice translated unnecessarily, "is that if you would like to follow us out of the Maw, we have the appropriate course programmed into our navicomputer. I believe we are all anxious to go home."

Han looked at Lando and Mara and smiled. "You're sure right about that, Threepio."

41

Inside the dining hall of the Great Temple, Cilghal stood silent and firm, studiously showing no reaction to Ackbar's insistence.

Clad once again in his white admiral's uniform, Ackbar leaned closer to Cilghal. He placed his splayed hands firmly on the shoulders of her watery-blue robe. She could feel the heavy musculature in his hands as he pressed down. She flinched, afraid of what he would demand of her.

"You cannot surrender so easily, Ambassador," Ackbar said. "I will not accept that this task is impossible until you prove to me it is impossible."

Cilghal felt small under the probing gaze of his large eyes. No human would recognize it, but she could see the effects of long-fought stress on his face, in the mottling of his dark-orange color. Ackbar's skin looked dry, and his lobes had sunk deeply into the sides of his head. The small tendrils around his mouth looked frayed and cracked.

Since the terrible crash on the planet Vortex and his resulting disgrace, Ackbar had lived with an enormous weight on his conscience. But now he had come back to himself, returning to serve his people and the New Republic with greater determination—and coming to speak with her on Yavin 4.

"There have been no Jedi healers since the great purges," Cilghal said. "Master Skywalker believes I possess some aptitude in this area, but I have had no appropriate training. I would be swimming in murky waters, uncertain of my course. I don't dare—"

"Nevertheless," Ackbar interrupted sharply. He released her shoulders and stepped back so that his clean white uniform dazzled her eyes in the dimness of the Massassi temple's dining hall.

Dorsk 81 stepped into the chamber, looking surreptitiously at Ackbar. His eyes widened as he recognized the commander of the New Republic Fleet. The cloned alien muttered his apologies and backed out, flustered.

But Ackbar's gaze did not waver from Cilghal. She raised her head to meet his stare but waited for him to speak.

"Please," Ackbar said. "I beg you. Mon Mothma will die within days if you do nothing."

"I made oaths to myself, both when I became an ambassador and when I arrived here to train as a Jedi," Cilghal said, bowing her head with a sigh, "that I would do everything in my power to serve and to strengthen the New Republic."

She looked down at her spatulate hands. "If Master Skywalker has faith in me, who am I to question his judgment?" she said. "Take me to your ship, Admiral. Let us go to Coruscant."

In the former Imperial Palace, Cilghal reviewed the situation with growing dread.

Mon Mothma no longer remained conscious. The infestation of nano-destroyers filled her body, tearing her cells apart one by one. Without the life-support systems that kept her lungs filling, her heart beating, her blood filtered—the human woman would have died days earlier.

Some Council members had begun advising that she be allowed to die, that forcibly keeping Mon Mothma alive in such a state was a lingering torture. But upon hearing that one of Master Skywalker's new Jedi would come from Yavin 4 to attempt healing her, Chief of State Leia Organa Solo had insisted that they wait for this last chance, this slim hope.

Arriving in Imperial City, Cilghal was flanked by Ackbar and Leia as they ushered her down corridors to the medical chambers where Mon Mothma lay surrounded by the growing stench of death.

Leia's dark gaze flicked from Mon Mothma to Cilghal. Her human eyes glittered with gathering tears, and Cilghal could sense her hope like a palpable substance.

The smells of medicines, sterilization chemicals, and throbbing machines made her amphibious skin feel irritated and rubbery. She wanted to swim in the soothing waters of Calamari, to wash the disturbing thoughts and poisons from her body—but Mon Mothma needed that purging even more than Cilghal did.

She stepped to Mon Mothma's bedside, leaving Leia and Ackbar behind her. "You must realize that I know nothing specific about the healing powers of the Jedi," she said, as if offering an excuse. "I know even less about this living poison that is destroying her."

She drew a deep breath of the tainted air. "Leave me alone with her. Mon Mothma and I will fight this together." She swallowed. "If we can."

Murmuring warm wishes and reassurances, Ackbar and Leia faded into the background. Cilghal paid little attention to them as they departed.

Her shimmering blue ambassadorial robes flowed around

her like ethereal waves. She knelt to stare at Mon Mothma's motionless form. Reaching out with the Force, but at a loss for what exactly she was supposed to do, she tried to assess the scope of damage inside Mon Mothma's body.

As she began to see deeper, the extent of the poison's ravages astounded her. She could not comprehend how Mon Mothma had managed to stay alive for so long. Uncertainty fluttered in Cilghal's mind like gathering shadows.

How could she possibly combat such a disease? She did not understand how working with the Force could heal living things, how it could strengthen the life of someone as devastated as Mon Mothma. The best available medical droids had not been able to remove the malicious poison. No medicines had been able to cure her.

Cilghal knew only what Master Skywalker had taught her—how to sense with the Force, how to feel living things, how to move objects. She touched Mon Mothma with glowing currents of the Force, searching for some kind of answer, or at least an idea.

Could she use her Jedi skills but in a different manner that might strengthen Mon Mothma? Help her body to heal? Find some method to remove the poison?

Cilghal hesitated as a possibility struck like a meteor. The magnitude of the effort stunned her, and she wanted to dismiss the thought automatically—but she forced herself to study the idea.

Master Skywalker had explained Yoda's teachings, his insistence that "size matters not." Yoda had claimed that lifting Luke's entire X-wing fighter was no different from lifting a pebble.

But could Cilghal turn it the other way around? Could she use her precise control of the Force to move something *so small*?

She blinked her round Calamarian eyes. Millions of the tiny nano-destroyers saturated Mon Mothma's body.

Size matters not.

But if Cilghal could remove the destructive poison molecules, if she could somehow keep Mon Mothma from toppling over the abyss into death—then her body could restore itself, in time.

Cilghal refused to let her thoughts overwhelm her with visions of the sheer number of poison molecules. She would have to move them one by one, tugging each nanodestroyer through cell walls and out of the dying leader's body.

Cilghal placed her broad fins on Mon Mothma's bare skin. She picked up the leader's left hand and raised it over the side of the bed frame, letting the woman's fingertips rest in a small crystal dish that had once been used to dispense medications. Even this gentle touch was enough to cause red bruises to bloom on the woman's fragile skin.

Cilghal opened her mental doors, freeing her thoughts, allowing currents of the Force to flow into Mon Mothma's form. She let the nictitating membranes slide over her Calamarian eyes as she began to see with an inner vision, traveling through the cellular pathways of Mon Mothma's body.

She found herself in a strange universe of rushing blood cells, electrically firing neurons, contracting muscle fibers, laboring organs that could no longer perform their functions. Cilghal couldn't exactly comprehend what she saw, but somehow she understood instinctively which parts were healthy, which molecules were sustaining Mon Mothma, and which were the black scourge.

With the Force, Cilghal could touch with fingers infinitely small, infinitely precise, to grasp one of the nanodestroyers and send it careening out of the dying body.

Cilghal found other microscopic destroyers and nudged them, pushed them, herding the poison away from healthy cells, preventing further damage.

The task was incomprehensibly large. The poison had

spread and replicated, scattering itself through the billions and billions of cells in Mon Mothma's body. Cilghal would have to search and remove every one of them.

After succeeding with the first one, Cilghal sought out another.

And another.

And another.

And another.

"Has there been any change?" Leia whispered at the doorway. She had just returned from a meeting where General Wedge Antilles, Doctor Qwi Xux, and Han Solo had given a detailed debriefing on the entire Maw assault.

Leia had listened with fascination, making eyes at her husband Han—whom she had seen too little of in the past several days. But always in the back of her mind was a pressing concern for Mon Mothma.

"No change," Ackbar said in a tired voice. "I wish we understood what Cilghal is attempting to do."

The female Calamarian had not moved in nine hours, kneeling beside Mon Mothma's bedside, flippered hands resting on the dying woman's skin, deep in a trance. The medical droids had not expected Mon Mothma to live for this long, so the mere fact that she still had not succumbed to death meant something.

From outside the door Leia peeked in to see that nothing had changed. The leader's hand lay in a crystal dish as droplets of an oily grayish liquid emerged from the tip of her index finger. The process was too slow to watch, but over the course of half an hour a small droplet would gather at the tip of her finger, dangling, until gradually gravity pulled it off into the dish.

Terpfen walked slowly down the tiled corridors dressed in a dark-green close-fitting uniform that bore no insignia. Even after his full pardon Terpfen had refused to accept his rank again. He had sequestered himself in his rooms for much of the time since returning from Anoth.

The scarred Calamarian stopped several meters away from them, reluctant to go closer to the room that held Mon Mothma. Leia knew that Terpfen still blamed himself for the dying woman's condition, and he refused to let the guilt be assuaged. Though she understood his misery, she was getting impatient with his withdrawal and hoped he climbed back to his feet soon.

Terpfen bowed ponderously, displaying the network of scars on his disfigured head. "Admiral, I have reached a decision." He drew a deep breath. "I wish to return to Calamari and continue your work—if our people will have me. I wish to assist in rebuilding Reef Home. I fear . . ." He looked up to stare at the intricate mosaics on the walls of the Imperial Palace. "I fear that I will never be comfortable on Coruscant again."

"Believe me, Terpfen," Ackbar answered, "I know exactly how you feel. I would not try to talk you out of your decision. It is a fair compromise between your need for healing and your desire to make amends."

Terpfen straightened, as if some measure of self-esteem had been returned to him. "I would like to depart as soon as possible," he said.

"I will arrange a ship," Ackbar replied.

Terpfen bowed again. "If I have your leave, Chief of State?"

"Yes, Terpfen," Leia answered. She turned once again to watch the motionless tableau inside the medical chamber.

At a forgotten hour in the depths of Coruscant's night, Cilghal emerged from the medical chambers. She staggered, cradling in her right hand a shallow crystal bowl half-filled with the deadly poison from the drink that Ambassador Furgan had thrown in Mon Mothma's face.

The two New Republic guards stationed at the door snapped to attention and rushed to help Cilghal. She was so exhausted she could hardly place one foot in front of another. She leaned against the stone doorway, drawing strength from the solidity of the rock.

Her arm trembled as she extended the crystal dish to one of the guards. Cilghal barely had enough strength remaining to lift the small poison-filled container, but she did not dare drop it. She felt a deep, bone-melting relief when the guard took it from her.

"Be careful," she said in a husky, utterly exhausted voice. "Take this . . . and incinerate it."

The second guard scrambled to the intercom system and signaled for all Council members to come immediately.

"Do you have news of Mon Mothma?" the first guard asked her.

"She has been cleansed and she will heal." The lids dropped over Cilghal's glassy eyes. "But for now she must rest." Her flowing robes whispered against the tiled walls as she slid down to collapse on the floor.

"As must I," she said, falling immediately into a Jedi recovery trance.

42

The Star Destroyer *Gorgon* limped through open space like a wounded dragon, leaking radiation from a thousand damage points.

Only one of the *Gorgon*'s primary sublight engines still functioned. Admiral Daala's engineers assured her it would be many days before they could attempt to enter hyperspace.

Life-support systems were down for the lower twelve decks. But Admiral Daala's soldiers were accustomed to harsh and difficult conditions. Cramped living quarters might encourage them to make repairs faster. Heating systems were low, giving the air a frigid edge, making spoken words emerge from her lips accompanied by a plume of steam.

Her precious flagship had been grievously wounded, Daala knew; but she realized she did not need to make the *Gorgon* into a top-flight fighting machine again. Not anymore. This time she merely needed to complete sufficient repairs to crawl back to Imperial-controlled territory, where she could start from scratch.

Daala's best advantage was that the Rebel forces must have assumed her ship had been destroyed in the explosion. Their sensors would have been blinded in the eruption of the reactor asteroid.

Watching Maw Installation vaporize, Daala had ordered full shields and full speed, throwing caution aside as she drove the *Gorgon* straight to the walls of the Maw, seeking her own way out. Now, crawling away from the energetic outbursts of the black hole cluster, the battered Imperial battle cruiser would not be noticed on any Rebel scopes.

Half the consoles on her bridge remained dim, unable to function after sustaining so many overloads. Technicians tore open access plates, bundled in heavy uniforms to keep warm, rubbing their numb hands together as they tinkered with electronics. But they did not complain, at least not while Daala was watching.

A significant percentage of her stormtroopers had been killed in sudden hull breaches or explosions belowdecks. The sick bays were filled with injured personnel. Many of the computer systems were off-line. But they had survived.

Commander Kratas stepped up to Daala and saluted. His face looked devastated, smudged with grease and smoke from his attempts at hands-on repair work.

"The news is not good, Admiral," he said.

"I want to know our true status," Daala said, forcing her concern back inside, where it could increase the pressure in her heart, crystallizing a diamond of her own resolve. "Tell me, no matter how bad it is."

Kratas nodded, swallowing. "We have only seven functional TIE fighters remaining in the hangar bays. All others were lost."

"Seven!" she cried. "Out of—" She gritted her teeth and shook her head so that her hair whirled like an inferno around her face. She drew a short, controlled breath and nodded. "Yes. Continue."

"We don't have sufficient spare parts to repair the damaged external weapons systems," he said. "Our starboard turbolaser batteries have been wrecked, but we may be able to get two guns functional again."

Daala tried to be optimistic. "That might be enough to defend ourselves if we are attacked. But we must hope not to encounter such a situation. We will not initiate any aggressive action at this point. Is that understood?"

Kratas looked relieved. "Understood, Admiral. We can repair most of the hull breaches and repressurize some of the decks, although . . ." He hesitated, and his thick eyebrows knitted together like a giant furworm. "But I don't really see the point in that, Admiral," he finished. "We don't need those quarters, and it would only tax our resources at this point. Our repair crews are working around the clock, and I suggest we devote our efforts to completing only the systems critical to life support and those necessary for us to be on our way."

Daala nodded slowly. "Again I agree, Commander. It is a difficult decision, but we must be realistic. We have lost this battle—but the war continues. We will make no excuses for ourselves but continue to give our best effort for the good of the Empire."

She drew another controlled breath of the frosty air, staring through the bridge viewport at the lush starfield that waited ahead, crossed by a wide swath like a milky river. Looking through the disk of the galaxy toward the dense core, she saw the stars appear to stream like a wide river. The *Gorgon* headed toward the luminous bulge of the galactic center.

"Commander"—she lowered her voice—"what is your opinion of the overall morale on the ship?"

Kratas took a step closer so he could answer in a soft voice. "We have good people, Admiral, as you know. Well trained and well drilled. But they have repeatedly suffered grievous defeats. . . ."

"Have they lost faith in me?" Daala asked. Her face was chiseled in stone. She made herself strong and tried not to show that Kratas's answer could devastate her. She averted her emerald eyes, afraid that he might see something in them.

"Absolutely not, Admiral!" Kratas answered with a tinge of surprise. "They have the utmost confidence in you."

She nodded to cover her long sigh of relief, then raised her voice, turning to the communications lieutenant. "Give me an open-ship channel," she said. "I want to address all of our troops."

Daala gathered her thoughts until the lieutenant nodded to her. She spoke in a loud, firm voice that reverberated through the damaged ship.

"Attention, all crew members of the *Gorgon*. I wish to commend you for your efforts against overwhelming odds, against a foe that continues to gain the upper hand through treachery and uncanny luck. We must now prepare for the next phase in this battle, however. We are making our way to the Core Systems, to the last strongholds that still swear loyalty to the Empire.

"It was not originally my intention to join with one of the Imperial warlords struggling for dominance, but it now appears that we must fight the larger fight. We need to convince them of their real enemy and show those still faithful to the Emperor that we must be united to be strong."

She paused before raising her voice. "Yes, the *Gorgon* has been damaged. Yes, we have suffered severe losses. We have been wounded—but we will never be defeated!

"Trials such as these only strengthen us. Continue your efforts to make the *Gorgon* powerful again. Thank you for your service." She signaled for the communications lieutenant to stop the transmission. She looked out again at the moving stream of stars.

The *Gorgon*'s computer banks held all the information Daala had pulled from Maw Installation's classified computer banks. The weapons designs and new concepts alone would help the Empire win the next phase of the war.

As she stood on the cold bridge with gloved hands clasped behind her back, she watched the universe unfold in front of her.

The Star Destroyer *Gorgon* sailed on toward the Core Systems. Through persistence she could become victorious. One day.

43

The *Lady Luck* cruised low over the jagged surface of Kessel. Bleached sunlight washed across the alkali flats. The sky scintillated with intermittent streaks of light, flaming trails of meteorites—chunks of Kessel's destroyed moon burning down through the thin atmosphere.

"You know, this is all kind of beautiful," Lando said, "in its own way."

Beside him in the space yacht's overly padded passenger seat, Mara Jade frowned skeptically. She looked at him as if she thought he was crazy—not a new thought. "If you say so," she said.

"Of course, it'll take a lot of work," Lando admitted, lifting one hand off the controls so he could rest it on the arm of her chair. She flinched at his move . . . but not too much.

"First order of business will be to get the atmosphere factories up to full capacity again. I'll have to bring in specially modified droids. I've already talked to Nien Nunb, my Sullustan friend, who says he'd love to make his home down in those tunnels. I think he'll make a great crew boss."

Lando raised his eyebrows and flashed her his most dazzling smile. "Defense will be difficult without the moonbase, but I'm sure with the help of the Smugglers' Alliance we can put together a great system. You and I will make quite a team, Mara. I'm really going to enjoy working closely with you."

Mara sighed, but it was more of a resigned, tolerant noise than actual annoyance. "You just don't give up, do you, Calrissian?"

He shook his head, still grinning. "Nope. Giving up is not my style. Not ever."

Mara slumped back in her passenger chair and stared out the *Lady Luck*'s front viewport. "I was afraid of that."

Overhead in the white skies of Kessel, shooting stars continued to rain down.

Two medical droids supported a recovering Mon Mothma. She stood dripping as she emerged from the bacta tank. She wavered a little and held on to the smooth shoulder plates of the droids. Finally she stood on her own again, took a deep breath, and lifted her head to smile.

Leia stood watching, impressed at the rapid improvement. "I never thought I'd see you stand again, Mon Mothma."

"Neither did I," the former Chief of State admitted with a rueful shrug. "But my body is healing itself with a vengeance. The bacta tanks are working overtime, effective again now that Cilghal removed the nano-destroyers. I'm anxious to move about, to see all the things that happened while I was sick. I have a lot to catch up on. But the medical droids say I have to stay here and rest."

Leia laughed. "You have plenty of time, don't worry. Do you—" She hesitated, not wanting to push Mon Mothma, but anxious to know. "Do you have any idea when you'll be ready to take back your duties as Chief of State?"

Assisted again by the droids, Mon Mothma toiled over to one of the padded seats near the bacta tank. She slowly sank into the cushions. Still-damp garments clung to her wasted body. She did not answer for a long time. When Mon Mothma looked up, her expression made Leia's heart skip a beat.

"Leia, I am no longer Chief of State. You are," she said. "I served well for many years, but this wasting illness has made me weak—not only physically, but also in the eyes of the New Republic. The New Republic must not waver in these trying times. Our leadership must be strong and dynamic. We need someone like you, Leia, daughter of the legendary Senator Bail Organa.

"My decision is firm. I won't attempt to regain my title. It's time for me to rest and recover with a great deal of thought on how best to serve the New Republic. Until such time as that changes, our future is in your hands."

Leia swallowed and forced a comically stoic expression on her face. "I was afraid you were going to say that," she said. "But if I can handle a few Imperial renegades, I suppose I can keep the Council members in line. After all, they're on *our* side."

"You may find that the Imperials surrender a bit more readily than Council members, Leia."

Leia groaned. "You're probably right."

The winds sang on the planet Vortex. Leia stared up at the newly rebuilt Cathedral of Winds, which rose like a gesture of defiance against the terrible storms. Beside her Han kept blinking as the breezes stung his eyes, but he seemed awed by the tall structure.

The new Cathedral was different from what had been destroyed by Ackbar's crash, more streamlined. The winged

Vors had shown no interest in recreating their previous design, following a plan that seemed to flow from their collective alien minds.

Crystal cylinders glittered in the sunlight, large and small tubes like a towering pipe organ. Notches and windows had been cut into the curved surfaces. The leathery-winged Vors flew about, opening and closing the orifices to shape patterns of music as the winds whistled through. Everything else hunched low to the ground, but the Cathedral of Winds soared, like the spirit of the New Republic.

The impending storm rippled the thick carpet of purple, vermilion, and tan grasses that covered the plains. Low hummocks, underground Vor dwellings for the vicious storm season, lay in concentric rings around the pinnacles of the new cathedral.

Leia and Han stood surrounded by a New Republic formal escort on a patch of grass packed down with polished squares of synthetic marble, laid out to form a low viewing stage. The Vors wheeled about in the air, flapping their wings and circling over the audience.

The winged aliens had allowed no off-worlders to hear the concert of winds since the Emperor Palpatine had established his New Order; but with the success of the Rebellion, the Vors had finally permitted spectators again, not only representatives from the New Republic but also dignitaries from a host of populated worlds. Leia's first attempt to come here with Ackbar had ended in disaster, but she was certain that this time everything would turn out well.

Han stood beside her, dressed in the diplomatic finery that he obviously found uncomfortable, but she thought it made him look dashing. That seemed no consolation to her husband as he chafed under the rough and stiff formal dress.

He must have sensed Leia looking at him, because he glanced down to give her a roguish smile. He snuggled closer, slipping an arm around her waist and pulling her tightly against him. The wind whipped around them.

"Feels good to relax," he said. "And it's good to be with you, Your Highness."

"I'm Chief of State now, General Solo," she said with a twinkle in her eyes. "Maybe I should *order* you to stay home more often."

He laughed. "Think it would make any difference? You know how good I am at following rules."

Leia smiled as the wind stirred her hair. "I suppose the two of us will just have to work out a compromise," she said. "Why does it seem as if the whole galaxy conspires to keep us away from each other all the time? We *used* to have adventures together!"

"Maybe it's payback for all the lucky breaks I've had," he said.

"I hope your luck comes back soon, then." She snuggled against him.

"Never quote me the odds." Han ran his fingers up and down her back, making her skin tingle. "I feel lucky enough right now."

The wind picked up and the hollow music lifted higher.

Chewbacca's matted fur blew in all directions, making him look as if he had toweled off after a steam bath and forgotten to comb his body hair. He bellowed over the winds and the music of the cathedral.

Threepio's tinny voice rang out. "Anakin. Jacen and Jaina! Children, where are you? Oh, please do come back here. We're growing very worried."

Chewbacca and Threepio waded through the thick grasses in search of the twins and their little brother. Anakin had crawled off to hide during the cathedral's opening ceremony. Distracted by the ethereal harmonies, none of the spectators had noticed the baby disappearing into the grasses, including Chewbacca and Threepio.

Upon seeing their little brother missing, Jacen and Jaina had both dashed out into the expansive fields, claiming they would help find baby Anakin—and of course now all three children were lost. Chewbacca and Threepio tried not to cause too much of a distraction as they searched.

"Jacen and Jaina!" Threepio said. "Oh, dear, what are we to do, Chewbacca? This is most embarrassing."

They stumbled through thick rustling grass that rose to Chewbacca's chest. Threepio spread his golden arms to clear a path for himself. "This is scratching up my plating," he said. "I was never meant for duty like this."

Chewbacca cocked his head to listen, ignoring Threepio's complaints. He heard children giggling somewhere among the whispering grass blades. The Wookiee plunged through the thickets, swiping with his hairy paws to knock the blades out of his way. He found no one—only a trampled path from where he had heard the sounds. He would find them sooner or later.

From behind him, swallowed up in the dense grass, he heard another thin voice. "Oh, Chewbacca! Where have you gone? Now *I'm* lost!"

Standing on the polished mosaic platform of synthetic marble squares, Admiral Ackbar held himself rigidly at attention beside white-robed Winter as the cathedral played its music. They sat among other off-world dignitaries and lavishly clad representatives from various planets.

He had been reluctant to come for the christening ceremony, since he had accidentally destroyed the old Cathedral of Winds. He had feared the Vors might hold a grudge against him—but the Vors were a flat, emotionless race who seemed unaffected by individual events. They simply pushed on, recovering and striving to complete their plans. They had not censured the New Republic, had demanded no retribution; they had simply fallen to work reconstructing the Cathedral of Winds.

The wind whistled cold around his exposed skin. The music sounded beautiful.

Nearby, a lovely woman decked in jewels and bright primary colors clung to a haggard, weary-looking young man, who slumped in his chair. Ackbar glanced at them, then bent close to Winter, lowering his voice. "Could you tell me who those people are? I do not recognize them."

Winter studied the pair, and her face took on a distant look as if she were sifting through various files in her mind. "I believe that is the Duchess Mistal from Dargul and her consort."

"I wonder why he appears to be so miserable," Ackbar said.

"Perhaps he is not a music lover," Winter suggested, then settled into an awkward silence. Finally she spoke again. "I am glad you decided to return to the service of the New Republic, Ackbar. You have much to give to the future of our government."

Ackbar nodded solemnly, looking at the human woman who had served so many years as Leia's close personal aid.

"I am pleased that you yourself have been freed from exile on Anoth," he said. "I was concerned for you. Your personal talents and perceptiveness are greatly needed, and I have always valued your input."

Ackbar could see that Winter masked her expression carefully, allowing just a glimmer of a smile to show that she was holding back as much as he was.

"Good, then," Winter said. "We shall be seeing a great deal more of each other in times to come."

Ackbar nodded to her. "I would enjoy that."

• • •

Qwi Xux listened longingly to the music of the winds. The notes rose higher, dipped lower, wove around themselves to form a complex, never-to-be-repeated melody, since the Vors forbade any recording of their storm concerts, and no two were ever alike.

The flying creatures flitted up and down the shafts of crystal, opening hatchways, covering small holes with their hands or bodies as they shaped the symphony, building it as the storm grew closer.

The music seemed to tell Qwi's own life story. It struck her emotional chords, blowing through the hollows and crevices of her heart so that she heard the feelings she had experienced through her life: her childhood loss, her agonized training, her brainwashed imprisonment for years in Maw Installation . . . and her sudden thrill of freedom as she met members of the New Republic who helped her escape . . . then Wedge Antilles, who had opened up more new worlds for her, bright dawns she had never before imagined.

Now, after her time of healing, after she had returned to Maw Installation and walked along the old corridors, set foot in her former laboratory—Qwi no longer chose to mourn those lost memories.

When the misguided Kyp Durron had erased her thoughts, it had been a violent act. But, in hindsight, she thought he might have inadvertently done her a great favor. She did not wish to remember her devastating weapons work. She felt as if she had been reborn, given a new chance to start a life with Wedge, unencumbered by dark thoughts of the deadly inventions she had helped to create.

The music continued: hollow and mournful, then joyous and uplifting, in an eerie counterpoint like nothing she had ever experienced before.

"Would you like to go back to Ithor with me?" Wedge

bent close and whispered in her ear. "We can do our vacation right this time."

Qwi smiled back at him. The idea of returning to the lush jungle world sounded wonderful to her: the self-contained cities drifting over the treetops, and the peaceful alien people. The experience would do much to ease the pain from the memories she had lost there.

"You mean we'd no longer have to hide from Imperial spies? From Admiral Daala?"

"We wouldn't have to worry about any of that," Wedge said. "We could concentrate entirely on enjoying ourselves."

The Vors opened up all of the hatchways and windows in the Cathedral of Winds. As the storm center hurled its greatest gales at the structure, the music built to a spiraling crescendo, a triumphant finale that seemed to echo throughout the galaxy.

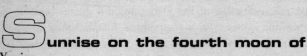

44

Sunrise on the fourth moon of Yavin.

Artoo-Detoo trundled ahead up the flagstoned ramp, chittering and bleeping as the new Jedi Knights followed him. In silence they gathered atop the Great Temple to look across the mist-covered treetops. The orange gas giant glowed from behind as the system's sun came closer to the limb, suffusing the upper atmosphere with light.

As the jungle moon continued in its headlong orbit, Luke Skywalker took his position in front of the procession to greet the coming dawn. Beside him walked young Kyp Durron, still limping slightly from his newly healed injuries, but moving with an enormous inner strength. His entire attitude had changed in such a short time.

But while Kyp had been through the greatest ordeal of the new Jedi, Luke's other students had also proved themselves to be greater than he had foreseen, greater than he had hoped.

Together they had overthrown Exar Kun, the Dark Lord of the Sith. Cilghal had saved Mon Mothma's life with new techniques in Jedi healing. Streen had recovered his confidence and had shown remarkable adeptness at feeling and touching the weather.

Tionne continued her quest to resurrect Jedi history, a job made more difficult now that the Jedi Holocron had been destroyed—but Luke knew there were other Holocrons to be found, though they might have been lost over the millennia. Many of the ancient Jedi Masters had recorded their lives and their wisdom in such devices.

Others, such as Dorsk 81, Kam Solusar, and Kirana Ti had not exhibited their particular aptitudes yet, though their powers were broad and strong. Some of the new Jedi would stay on Yavin 4 and continue to train and grow; others would take their skills out to the galaxy, as knights to defend the New Republic.

Artoo warbled an announcement, his prediction of when the first sunlight would strike the apex of the temple. The little droid seemed immensely pleased to be at Luke's side.

Luke gathered his Jedi Knights around him, sensed their growing power intertwined. They were a *team*, not just wild cards with powers and abilities they did not understand.

The others stood on the chipped flagstones of the observation platform, looking out toward the hidden sun. Luke tried to find words to express his glowing pride and his high expectations.

"You are the first of the new Jedi Knights," he said, raising his hands as if in a benediction. "You are the core of what will become a great order to protect the New Republic. You are champions of the Force."

Though his students did not speak or respond, he felt the upsurge of their emotions, their swelling pride.

There would be other students, new trainees who would come to his Jedi academy. Luke had to face the fact that he might lose a few to the dark side—but the more defenders of the Force he could train, the stronger would be the legions of the light side.

With a collective gasp the gathered Jedi on the rooftop watched as the sun burst from the fringe of Yavin. Brilliant white rays gleaming like firefacet gems sprayed across the jungle moon, reflecting and refracting from the swirling atmosphere.

Artoo whistled; Luke and the other Jedi simply watched in awed silence.

The rainbow storm cast its glow over all of them as the dawn continued to brighten.

About the Author

After working for ten years as a technical writer for one of the largest government research laboratories in the country, KEVIN J. ANDERSON can honestly say he has never, ever met a brilliant but naive weapons scientist who even remotely resembles Qwi Xux. Never in his career has he attended meetings as pointless or time wasting as those described in this book. He has never worked for an incompetent manager as wrapped up in procedures and irrelevancies as Maw administrator Tol Sivron.

And he has never told a lie in his entire life.

On the other hand, he *has* written more than 150 short stories and over a dozen novels, including LIFELINE, THE TRINITY PARADOX, and ASSEMBLERS OF INFINITY (all with Doug Beason), and his latest, CLIMBING OLYMPUS, a novel about people adapting to the harsh environment of Mars. He has been nominated for both the Nebula and the Bram Stoker awards.

He has been to the top of Mount Lassen and the bottom of the Grand Canyon. He has been inside a Minuteman III missile silo and its underground control bunker; inside a plutonium plant at Los Alamos, New Mexico; on the floor of the Pacific Stock Exchange; out on an Atlas-E rocket launch pad.

His next *Star Wars* projects will be to edit three anthologies, *Tales from the Mos Eisley Cantina, Tales from Jabba's palace,* and *Bounty Hunters.*

A special preview of

Star Wars®: The Crystal Star

by Vonda N. McIntyre

From the author of four *New York Times* bestselling *Star Trek* novels, and the winner of both the prestigious Hugo and Nebula Awards, comes an exciting new *Star Wars* adventure set ten years after the resounding victory at Endor.

It is a time of peace for the New Republic: a time when Leia Organa, Head of State, can tour the solar systems with her children, the twins Jaina and Jacen and their little brother Anakin; a time when Han Solo and Luke Skywalker can take some time off from their duties as protectors of the state . . . and when a new evil is brewing on the edge of known space. One quiet spring day on the world of Munto Codru, a page stumbles into a reception for Princess Leia with devastating news. . . .

The children had been kidnapped.

Leia ran headlong toward the glade, leaving behind the courtiers and the chamberlain of Munto Codru, leaving her attendants, leaving the young page who—completely against protocol—had stumbled into Leia's receiving room, bleeding from nose and ears, incoherent.

But Leia understood her: Jaina and Jacen and Anakin had been stolen.

Leia ran, now, through the trees and down a soft mossy path that led into her children's playground. Jaina imagined the path was a starship course, set to hyperspace. Jacen pretended it was a great mysterious road, a river. Anakin, going through a literal phase, insisted that it was only a path through the forest to the meadow.

The children loved the forest and the meadow, and Leia loved exclaiming in wonder at the treasures they brought her: a squirmy bug, a stone with shiny bits trapped in its matrix— rare jewels perhaps!—or the fragments of an eggshell.

Her vision blurred with tears. Her soft slipper snared in

the tangled moss. She stumbled, caught herself, and plunged onward, holding the skirts of her court robe high.

In the old days, she thought, *in the old days, I'd be wearing boots and trousers. I wouldn't be hampered and tripped by my own clothing!*

Her breath burned in her throat.

And I'd be able to run from my receiving room to the forest glade without losing my breath!

The green afternoon light shifted and fluttered around her. Before her, the light brightened where the forest opened into a water-meadow, the meadow where her children had been playing.

Leia ran toward it, gasping, her legs heavy.

She was running toward an absence, not a presence, toward a terrible void.

She cried out to herself, *How could this happen? How is this possible?*

The answer—the only way it *could* be possible—terrified her. For a short time, her ability to sense the presence of her children had been neutralized. Only a manipulation of the Force could have such an effect.

Leia reached the meadow. She ran toward the creek where Jaina and Jacen had splashed and played and taught little Anakin to swim.

A crater ripped into the soft grass. The leafy blades had been flattened into a circle around the raw patch of empty dirt.

A pressure bomb! Leia thought in horror.

A pressure bomb had gone off, near her children.

They aren't dead! she told herself. *They can't be, I'd know if they were dead!*

At the edge of the blast area, Chewbacca lay sprawled in a heap. Blood flowed bright against his chestnut coat.

Leia fell to her knees beside him, oblivious to the mud. She feared he was dead—but he was still bleeding, still breathing. She pressed her hand against the deep gash in his leg, desperate to stop the flow of blood and save his life. His powerful pulse drove the blood from his body. Like the page, he also bled from ears and nostrils.

A dreadful, grieving, keening sound escaped him, not a groan of pain but a cry of rage and remorse.

"Lie still!" Leia said. "Chewbacca, lie still! The doctor is coming, you'll be all right, what happened, oh, what *happened*?"

He cried out again, and Leia understood that he felt such despair that he wanted to die. He had adopted her family as his own, his honor family, and he had failed to protect the children.

"You can't die!" *He must live*, she thought. *He* must. *Only he can tell me who stole my children.* "Come back! Come back to me!"

Her aides and the chamberlain hurried out of the forest, tramping the delicate high grass, exclaiming in outrage when the slender blades cut them. Leia's children had wandered the meadow at liberty, neither leaving footprints nor receiving any harm. The grass parted before them like magic.

Magic, for my magic children, Leia thought. *I thought I had protected them, I thought they could never come to any harm.*

Hot tears ran down her cheeks.

The courtiers and advisers and guards gathered around her.

"Madam, Madam," said the chamberlain of Munto Codru. Out here in the wild sun and the wind, Mr. Iyon's face was flushed and he looked uncomfortable.

"Did you bring the doctor?" Leia cried. "Get the doctor!"

"I sent for her, Madam."

Mr. Iyon tried to make her get up, tried to take over stanching the flow of blood from Chewbacca's wound, but she pushed him away with a sharp word. Chewbacca's pulse faltered. Leia feared he was failing.

You will not die, she thought. *You must not die. I won't let you die!*

She drew on her inadequate knowledge to strengthen him. She bitterly regretted the responsibilities of statecraft that had prevented her from being properly trained in the ways of the Force.

Leia knew that if she allowed Chewbacca's hot blood to

gush past her hands, his life, too, would stream away.

The doctor ran across the field. Her wyrwulf loped behind her, carrying her equipment and supplies.

Dr. Hyos knelt beside Leia. She observed Chewbacca's wound and Leia's first aid with a glance. "Ah," she said briskly. "Good work."

"Come away, now, princess," the chamberlain said.

"Not yet!" Dr. Hyos exclaimed. "I have only four hands, after all. The princess is quite all right where she is."

The wyrwulf sat on its haunches between Leia and Dr. Hyos. Leia shuddered. The wyrwulf turned its massive head, slowly, gently, staring at her with great limpid liquid blue eyes. Its coat was thick and brown, with long coarse black guard-hairs.

Dr. Hyos's four hands, so languid at rest, moved quickly over the panniers strapped to the wyrwulf's sides.

"Do you see what I am doing, my dear?" she said softly. "The bleeding is most important. Our princess has stopped it."

The doctor spoke to the wyrwulf, explaining everything she did.

Dr. Hyos drew pressure bandages from one compartment as she chose the proper medicine from another. Her long gold fingers were deft and sure.

Leia allowed herself a moment of hope, even with her hands covered by Chewbacca's hot blood. He had closed his eyes; he had stopped moving.

"As the bandage seals itself, my princess," Dr. Hyos said, "move your hand from the wound."

Leia obeyed. Dr. Hyos pressed the bandage to Chewbacca's flank. The bandage pressed itself against Leia's hand, clasped itself to Chewbacca, and wound its connecters through his fur.

Leia sat back on her heels. Her hands were sticky and her robes were smeared and she viewed everything in the clarity of horrified belief.

Dr. Hyos examined Chewbacca, frowning over the drying streaks of blood that had trickled from his nose and ears.

"Pressure bomb . . ." she said.

Leia remembered, as if from a distant dream, the sound of a single clap of thunder. She had thought—her thoughts had been so slow—that the morning must have turned from fair to rain; she had thought, fondly, that Chewbacca would soon bring the twins and Anakin in from the meadow. She could take a moment from her duties to cuddle them, to admire their newest treasures, to see that they had their lunch.

Now it was mid-afternoon. How could it be so late in the day, when such a short time ago it had not yet been lunchtime?

"Madam—" Chamberlain Iyon said. But he did not try again to make Leia come away.

"Close the port," Leia said. "Block the roads. Can the page be questioned? Check the port controller—is there any chance the kidnappers have left the planet?"

As she spoke, she feared any measures she might take would be useless, and if not useless, too late.

But if they've fled, she thought, *I could chase them in* Alderaan. *I could catch them, my little ship can catch anything—*

"Madam, closing the port would not be wise."

She glared at him, instantly suspicious of a man she had trusted only a moment before.

"I understand our traditions, which you—I beg your pardon—do not. Closing the spaceport is unnecessary."

"The kidnappers will try to escape Munto Codru,' she said.

Mr. Iyon spread his four hands.

"They will not. There are traditions," he said. "If we follow them, nothing will happen to the children—that too is the tradition."

Leia knew of Munto Codru's traditions of abduction and ransom. That was why Chewbacca had been staying so close to the children. That was why extra security surrounded and guarded the ancient castle. For the people of Munto Codru, coup abduction was an important and traditional political sport.

It was a sport in which Leia did not care to participate.

"It's a most audacious abduction," the chamberlain said.

"And a cruel one!" Leia said. "Chewbacca is wounded! And the pressure bomb—my children—" She fought for control of her voice and of her fear.

"The coup-counters detonated a pressure bomb only to prove that they could, Madam," Mr. Iyon said.

"But no one is supposed to be injured, during your coup abductions!"

"No one of noble birth, Princess Leia," he said.

"They must know they haven't a hope," Leia said. "Of receiving a ransom, of escape. And if they should . . ." She could not bring herself to say the word "harm."

"Please allow me to advise you in this matter," the chamberlain said. He leaned toward her, intense. "If you apply the rules of the Republic, disaster—tragedy—will be the result."

"The ransomers," Dr. Hyos said, with every evidence of approval. "Must be very brave. But young and inexperienced as well. The family . . . which would it be?" She glanced at Mr. Iyon. "The Sibiu, perhaps?"

"They have insufficient resources," the chamberlain said.

Whoever it was, Leia thought, *needed only the resources of the Force. The dark side of the Force.*

Mr. Iyon gestured to the broken ground, to Chewbacca. "This required a skiff, a tractor beam. Connections with arms smugglers, to obtain the pressure bomb."

"Ah. The Temebiu, then."

"It could be," the chamberlain said. "They are ambitious."

"I'll show them ambition," Leia muttered.

"Madam, please. Your children will not be harmed—*cannot* be harmed, for the ransomers to achieve their goals. They may look upon the event as a great adventure—"

"Our friend Chewbacca has been wounded nearly to death!" Leia cried. "My children will *not* find that amusing. Nor do I!"

"It is a shame," the chamberlain said. "Perhaps he did not comprehend the information on our traditions? He was meant to surrender."

"Close the port," Leia said again, her voice tight. She was

too angry to respond to the chamberlain's comment. "I won't take any chance that they'll leave Munto Codru."

"Very well," Mr. Iyon said. "It is possible . . . but we must do it carefully. We must do it . . . in a way to amuse rather than offend. . . ." His voice trailed off thoughtfully.

Dr. Hyos checked Chewbacca's pulse at the large vein the wound had come so close to piercing. "Stable. There. Good. To the surgery with you."

Chewbacca, barely conscious, gazed at Leia with uncomprehending eyes.

"Battlefield medicine," Dr. Hyos said. "Haven't done any in a long time. Didn't think I'd ever have to see a battlefield again."

"Neither did I," Leia said.

"Just like old times, hey, kid?" Han Solo said to Luke Skywalker.

Sitting in the copilot's seat of the *Millennium Falcon,* Luke grinned.

"Just like old times except the Empire isn't trying to shoot us out of the sky—"

"You got that right."

"And Jabba the Hutt isn't after your hide for dumping that cargo—"

"Yeah."

"And nobody is trying to collect old gambling debts from you."

"Also true," Han said, thinking, *but I might get around to running up some new gambling debts. After all, what's a vacation for?*

"Finally, you can't ogle every beautiful woman who comes by."

"Sure I can," Han said, then hurried to defend himself as Luke chuckled. "Nothing wrong with looking. Leia and I know where we stand with each other, we trust each other, she's not jealous."

Luke burst into outright laughter.

"And you wouldn't mind," he said, "if she flirted with the

Kirlian ambassador. Good-looking guy, that Kirlian ambassador."

"Nothing wrong with looking," Han said stubbornly. "Or a little innocent flirtation. But the Kirlian ambassador better watch his hands. All four of them. Hey, kid, listen, flirting is one of the best inventions of civilization." Han grinned. Luke hated it when Han called him "kid." That was why he did it.

Luke stared out into hyperspace.

"You ought to do more flirting yourself," Han said.

"If I might be of service, Master Luke," See-Threepio said, leaning forward from the passenger seat. "I have an extensive library of love poetry at your disposal, in several languages suitable for the human tongue, as well as etiquette, medical information, and—"

"I don't have time for flirtations," Luke said, "or love poetry. Not right now . . ."

Threepio sat back in the passenger seat. In the corner of Han's vision, the droid looked like a shadow. To disguise himself, See-Threepio had covered his glossy gold finish with a coat of purple lacquer. Han had not yet gotten used to the change.

"Don't be so damned dedicated," Han said to Luke. "Don't Jedi Knights get to have any fun? Little Jedi Knights have to come from *somewhere*. I'll bet old Obi-Wan—"

"I don't know what Ben would have done!"

Luke spoke in a tone of distress, not anger. The fundamental loneliness of the young Jedi struck Han deeply.

"I don't know what other Jedi Knights did," Luke said softly. "I didn't know Ben long enough, and the Empire destroyed so many records, and . . . *I just don't know.*"

Han wished Luke could fine someone to share his life and his work. Han's marriage to Leia grew and strengthened with each year, with each day. As his own years of happiness continued, Han was increasingly troubled by his brother-in-law's solitude.

"Take it easy, Luke," Han said. "Take it easy. You're doing great—"

"But the traditions—"

"So if you have to make them up as you go along, that's not so bad, is it?" Han asked. "We always were pretty good at bluffing. In the old days."

"In the old days." Luke sounded glum.

"And who knows what we'll find when we get where we're going? Maybe some more Jedi Knights to help with the school."

"Maybe," Luke said. "I hope so."

Anakin wriggled furiously in Jaina's arms, trying to get down.

"Bad mens, Jaya!" he said. "Bad mens!"

"Stop wiggling, Anakin," Jaina said. She hugged her little brother, but that just made him struggle even more. His face was streaked with furious tears. He had stopped crying, but he was still so angry and scared that his whole body trembled.

"Papa!" he shouted. "Papa! I want Papa!" He started to cry again.

Jaina was sacred, too, and confused. She pretended not to be.

They were on a perfectly circular patch of Munto Codru feather grass. Jacen slept on the grass beside Jaina. Jaina wanted to wake Jacen up. But she had just woken up. Waking up had hurt. It never hurt to wake up before. Never before in her whole life.

The patch of grass was not part of the meadow any more. It was in a big metal room. It sat in the middle of the metal floor, as if someone had cut it out with a big round cookie-cutter. Metal walls rose very high above, all around. Jaina could not see any doors. She could not see any windows. Big lights glared down at her from the ceiling.

"Don't cry, Anakin," Jaina said. "Don't cry. I'll take care of you. I'm five, so I'll take care of you, because you're only three."

"Three and a half!" he said.

"Three and a half," she said.

He sniffled and rubbed his sticky face. "Want Papa," he said.

Jaina wished Papa was here, too. And Mama. And Winter. And Chewie. But she did not say so. She had to be the adult. She was oldest. She was almost already getting her grown-up teeth. Her right front tooth was really loose. She wiggled it with her tongue while she thought what to do.

She was two years older than Anakin. Okay, one and a half years older. She was only five minutes older than Jacen. They were twins, even though they did not look exactly alike. Her hair was light brown and very straight. Jacen's was dark and curly. But she was still oldest.

"Down!" Anakin demanded. "Jaya, down!"

"I'll let you down," Jaina said, "if you promise to stay on the grass."

Anakin stuck out his lower lip. His dark eyes sparkled with tears of frustration and anger. He was always stubborn when anyone said no to him. About anything.

"Promise?" Jaina said.

"Stay on the grass," he said.

She let him down. He dashed across the grass. He peered over the edge. Jaina took her gaze off him for a second. She crouched down next to Jacen, wishing he would wake up.

Jaina looked around for Anakin. He was sticking his foot over the edge of the grass. Jaina ran after him and pulled him back.

"I said stay on the grass!"

"*Am* on the grass," he insisted. He pointed toward the floor. "Just a floor, Jaya. No krakana!"

The last place they had been, on Mama's tour, they had not been allowed to swim in the ocean. Mon Calamari was mostly ocean, and its ocean was full of krakana. Krakana would eat anything, even children. *Especially* children.

Now, every time anybody told Anakin "no," he would argue by saying, "No krakana!"

Jaina did not want to scare him. She did not know if there was anything to be scared of yet. She wished she knew how they had gotten here. Something bad must have happened, but maybe getting taken away like this was how they got rescued.

Jacen whimpered. Jaina grabbed Anakin's hand and pulled him across the little patch of grass to her twin's side.

"Hold Jasa's hand," Jaina said. Anakin grabbed Jacen's hand in both his little fists. Jaina took Jacen's other hand.

"Jasa, Jasa, wake up," Anakin said. "Sleepybones!"

Jacen opened his eyes. "Ouch!" he said, just as Jaina said, "Ouch!" She could feel what he felt. He could feel what she felt. Jaina's head hurt, like somebody was screaming in her ear.

Both their eyes were filled with tears. Jaina's lower lip trembled. She pressed her lips together to keep from crying. Her front tooth wiggled.

She *made* the scream and the hurt go away. From her and from Jacen, before he was all awake.

She was not supposed to use her Jedi abilities unless Uncle Luke was with them. Jacen was not supposed to. Anakin especially was not supposed to. Uncle Luke was teaching them what to do. How to do it right.

But sometimes it was hard not to do something. Like now.

Jacen sat up. Bits of grass stuck to his homespun shirt. Some was stuck in his curly dark brown hair. Jaina brushed her hands against her own hair, but she did not find any grass blades. Her light brown hair was very straight, so hardly anything ever got tangled in it. Jacen roughed his fingers through his hair, leaving it rumpled as usual. The grass fell out.

"Okay now?" she said.

"Okay now," Jacen said. He looked around. "Where are we?"

"Remember what happened?"

"We were playing with Chewie—"

"—and he jumped up—"

"—and then he fell down—"

"—and then I went to sleep."

"Me too."

"Skiff!" Anakin said. "Jaya forgot the skiff!"

"What skiff?"

"I *saw* it!" Anakin insisted.

"*This* isn't a skiff!" Jacen said.

He was right. The room they were in could hold a whole skiff.

"Maybe the skiff brought us here."

"Where?" Jacen said.

Jaina shrugged. They might be on a spaceship. They might be in a great big building. They might even still be on Munto Codru, underground. Jaina and Jacen had explored under the castle. They had found halls and caves and tunnels. But they had never found any place that looked like this.

Jacen looked around. "Maybe Chewie is here someplace, maybe he's still asleep too." He jumped to his feet and walked right off the edge of the grass.

Nothing happened.

"See, Jaya?" Anakin said, pleased with himself. "No krakana!" He ran after Jacen.

Jaina took one step after Jacen and Anakin. She stopped. She was sure that if they stayed on the grass, nothing could hurt them. But she did not want her brothers to go off alone. She was the oldest, after all.

She ran after her brothers.

Her feet clanged on the metal floor. She caught up to Jacen. He was looking at the wall. Anakin did not bother to look. He kicked it.

"Bad wall!"

"Don't do that, you'll hurt yourself," Jacen said.

Anakin glowered and bumped the toe of his shoe against the wall. Not kicking. Not kicking for real.

"There's got to be a door," Jacen said reasonably. "For us to come in."

"Maybe there's a trap door," Jaina said. "A secret door." She rapped her knuckles against the metal. The knock was very solid. She looked up. "Here's the support," she said.

Jacen, too, looked up at the ceiling. Narrow metal beams curved over them. The lights hung from the beams.

"We have to look for a door *between* the beams," Jaina said. She walked around the room, knocking on the wall. She found some hollow spots. She looked at the wall as close as she could. She thought she found a seam. A crack?

A door opened.

Jaina jumped back. She grabbed Anakin's hand and pushed him behind her. She and Jacen stood side-by-side, defending their little brother.

Anakin wailed and tried to burrow his way between Jaina and Jacen, to see what was happening.

A tall and very beautiful man walked out. He had gold and copper and cinnamon-colored striped hair, very pale skin, and very big black eyes. His face was sharp and thin, all corners. He wore a long white robe.

He smiled down at Jaina.

"You poor children," he said.

He knelt in front of them.

"My poor children! I'm so sorry. Come to me, I'll keep you safe from now on."

"I want Papa!" Anakin shouted. "Mama!"

"I'm very sorry, sir," Jaina said with her best court manners. "We can't go to you."

"We aren't allowed," Jacen explained. "We don't know you."

"Ah, children, don't you remember me? No, how could you, you were only just born. I'm your hold-father Hethrir!"

Jaina stared at him, uncertain. She had never heard of any hold-father Hethrir. But she and Jacen had lots of hold-fathers and hold-mothers. Anakin had lots of hold-fathers and hold-mothers.

"Candy?" Anakin asked hopefully.

The beautiful man smiled. "Of course. As soon as we get you cleaned up."

Their hold-parents always brought them toys, and treats that were not often allowed otherwise.

"Do you know the password?" Jaina asked. Mama had told her never to go with anyone who did not know the password.

Hold-father Hethrir sat crosslegged on the floor in front of them.

"Children," Hethrir said, "a terrible thing has happened. I came to visit you, to see my sweet friend Leia and my old comrade Han. To meet your Uncle Luke. But when I came,

I saw a horrible thing! An earthquake!" He cocked his head at Jaina. "Do you know what an earthquake is?"

Uneasily, Jaina nodded.

"I'm sorry, children. The castle—it was so old! It fell down, and . . ."

He stopped, and took a deep breath. Jaina's lower lip started to quiver again. Her eyes got all blurry. She blinked. She did not want to hear what hold-father Hethrir had to say.

"Your mama was in the castle. And your papa, and your Uncle Luke. You were in the meadow—do you remember—and the ground opened up and swallowed friend Chewbacca, and you were about to slide down into the horrible crack in the earth, but I was right there and I swooped down and I saved you. But I couldn't save friend Chewbacca, and . . ." He glanced down, and wiped a tear from his cheek, and looked up again. "I'm so sorry, children, we could not rescue your mama or your papa or your uncle."

Anakin started to wail. "Papa! Mama! Uncle Luke!"

Jaina clutched his hand and pulled him close. "Don't cry," she whispered. Anakin stopped wailing, but he still sniffled and sobbed.

"But Papa and Uncle Luke—" Jacen's voice was trembly, but suspicious.

Jaina *nudged* him. He shut up.

"None of that, now." Hold-father Hethrir smiled.

Somehow, he knew what she had done. And it made him angry, though he was smiling. Scared, Jaina pulled back inside herself. She pretended she had never touched Jacen with her mind.

"If I had landed, if the earthquake had not happened, your mama and papa would have introduced you to me. They would have told me your password. We would have had a party, and we would have been friends!"

He stretched both his hands toward Jaina and Jacen.

"Your dear family is gone, my children. The Republic asked me to take you, to keep you, to protect you and teach you. I am so sorry . . . that your mama and papa are dead."

Jaina huddled together with her brothers. How could it be true? But why would anyone lie about it?

"We—we're supposed to go with Winter," Jaina said. Her voice trembled. "If anything hap . . ."

"Winter? Who is Winter?"

"She's our nanny," Jaina said.

"She went on a trip," Jacen said.

"Are you keeping us till she comes home?"

"Can we call her?" Jacen said hopefully.

"She'd come right back," Jaina said.

"Her services are no longer necessary," Hold-father Hethrir said. "Children, children! You are important! Your abilities are precious! You cannot be raised, you cannot be *taught*, by a servant."

"She isn't! She's our friend!"

"She has her own life to live, she cannot raise you properly with no one to pay for you."

"We wouldn't eat much," Jacen said hopefully.

Jaina wanted to say Hold-father Hethrir was a liar!—and run away. But she had nowhere to run. And maybe Papa and Uncle Luke *had* come home, while she and her brothers were in the meadow, and maybe the earthquake *had* come before Papa came out to greet them, and maybe Hold-father Hethrir really *had* rescued them.

And maybe Winter really wouldn't come back. Not *ever*.

Or maybe Hold-father Hethrir did not know that Papa and Uncle Luke and Mister Threepio had gone on a secret mission. No one was supposed to know about the secret mission, except Chewbacca and Mama—but Jaina did! And she had told Jacen, of course, because he was her twin. Maybe no one could tell Hold-father Hethrir because then Papa and Uncle Luke would be in danger. That meant Papa and Uncle Luke might be all right. But she could not say so, because then *she* would put Papa and Uncle Luke in danger.

Anakin huddled against her, sniffling. He was trying not to cry, but his tears left a cold wet spot on her shirt.

Or maybe, Jaina thought, *Hold-father Hethrir isn't who he says he is. Maybe he's making it all up, about the earthquake.*

Maybe he stole us.

Maybe Mama and Papa and Uncle Luke and Chewbacca are all right.

Jaina looked at Hold-father Hethrir. His huge dark eyes gleamed with tears. He gazed at her, his hands outstretched.

A second set of eyelids swept across his eyes. Jaina could see through the second eyelids. They looked like smoke. They pushed away the tears. Then they disappeared again.

Without meaning to, without wanting to, Jaina started to cry.

Don't cry, she said furiously to herself. Don't cry, if you don't cry it means Mama is alive!

She made herself stop crying.

"Jacen," Jaina said, "*you* have to say whether we believe him. Because *you're* the *oldest*."

"I'm oldest," Jacen said. "*I'm* oldest, Hold-father Hethrir!"

"I remember," Hold-father Hethrir said. "I remember when you both were born, your mama and papa were so happy, they said to me, 'Here is Jacen, our firstborn son, and here is Jaina, our beautiful daughter.'"

He's a liar! Jaina thought. *A liar!*

"We believe you, Hold-father Hethrir," Jacen said.

For just a second, Jaina thought maybe Jacen really meant it. But then she thought, *No, that's stupid*. She was afraid to *touch* him for reassurance, because Hold-father Hethrir would know.

She was crying again.

It's all right to cry now, she thought. *Because I'm just pretending, because I have to, and Mama and Papa and Uncle Luke and Chewbacca are all alive!*

She and Jacen and Anakin huddled together, all of them crying, Anakin wailing, "Papa! Papa!"

Hold-father Hethrir took Jaina's hand. He took Jacen's hand. He squeezed gently. His skin was very cold. He pulled on Jaina's hand. She had to move nearer to him. She wanted to move away from him.

I don't believe he's really my hold-father! Jaina thought. *I'm not going to call him that anymore.*

Hethrir put his arms around her and her brothers. Jaina shivered.

"Poor children," he said. "Poor little children."

The kidnapping of Han Solo and Princess Leia's children is only one sign among many that a dark power hovers on the horizon, waiting for the time to strike. Han and Luke have no idea about the strange goings on they have yet to face at a far-flung space station called Crseih. And Leia and Chewbacca can't anticipate the journey ahead of them, the mad dash across space in search of the children. It will all come together at an old Imperial research station that orbits a peculiar crystal star.

Star Wars®: The Crystal Star
by Vonda N. McIntyre

On sale in hardcover in
November, 1994
wherever Bantam Spectra hardcover books are sold.
Don't miss it!

Turn the page for a special preview of

CONQUERORS' PRIDE

by Timothy Zahn

Timothy Zahn, *New York Times* bestselling author of the blockbuster **STAR WARS** trilogy *Heir to the Empire, Dark Force Rising,* and *The Last Command,* now gives us a spectacular new science fiction novel of action, adventure, mystery and intrigue. CONQUERORS' PRIDE spans the mighty interstellar Commonwealth, which is dealing with a new threat to galactic peace: the alien Conquerors. But there is much more to this conflict than meets the eye, as readers will discover in this brilliant new tale. Here is a special preview, the opening scene of *Conquerors' Pride,* featuring a blazing battle that will change the course of Commonwealth history.

CONQUERORS' PRIDE, **available now in paperback wherever Bantam Books are sold.**

They were there, all right, exactly where the tachyon wake-trail pickup on Dorcas had projected they would be: four ships, glittering faintly in the starlight of deep space, blazing with infrared as they dumped the heat that zero-point energy friction had generated during their trip. They were small ships, probably no bigger than Procyon-class; milky white in color, shaped like thick hexagonal slabs of random sizes attached to each other at random edges.

Alien as hell.

"Scan complete, Commodore," the man at the *Jutland*'s sensor station reported briskly. "No other ships registering."

"Acknowledged," Commodore Trev Dyami said, flexing his shoulders beneath his stiffly starched uniform tunic and permitting himself a slight smile as he gazed at the main display. Alien ships. The first contact with a new self-starfaring race in a quarter of a century.

And it was his. All his. Trev Dyami and the *Jutland* would be the names listed in the Commonwealth's news reports and, eventually, in its history books.

Warrior's luck, indeed.

He turned to the tactics station, fully aware that everything he said and did from this point on would be part of that history-book listing. "What's the threat assessment?" he asked.

"I estimate point one to point four, sir," the tactics officer reported. "I don't find any evidence of fighter ejection tubes or missile ports."

"They've got lasers, though, Commodore," the tactics second put in. "There are clusters of optical-discharge lenses on the leading edges of each ship."

"Big enough to be weapons?" the exec asked from Dyami's side.

"Hard to tell, sir," the other said. "The lenses themselves are pretty small, but that by itself doesn't mean much."

"What about power output?" Dyami asked.

"I don't know, sir," the sensor officer said slowly. "I'm not getting any leakage."

"None?"

"None that I can pick up."

Dyami exchanged glances with the exec. "Superconducting cables," the exec hazarded. "Or else just very well shielded."

"One or the other," Dyami agreed, looking back at the silent shapes floating in the middle of the main display. Not only a self-starfaring race, but one with a technology possibly beyond even humanity's. That history-book listing was getting longer and more impressive by the minute.

The exec cleared his throat. "Are we going to open communications, sir?" he prodded.

"It's that or just sit here staring at each other," Dyami said dryly, throwing a quick look at the tactical board. The rest of the *Jutland*'s eight-ship task force was deployed in his designated combat formation, their crews at full battle stations. The two skitter-sized watchships were also in position, hanging well back where they would be out of danger if this meeting stopped being peaceful. The *Jutland*'s own Dragonfly defense-fighters were primed in their launch tubes, ready to be catapulted into battle at an instant's notice.

Everything was by-the-book ready . . . and it was time to make history. "Lieutenant Adigun, pull up the first-contact comm package," Dyami ordered the comm officer. "Get it ready to run. And alert all ships to stand by."

"Signal from the *Jutland*, Captain," Ensign Hauver reported from the *Kinshasa*'s bridge comm station. "They're getting ready to transmit the first-contact package across to our bogies."

Commander Pheylan Cavanagh nodded, his eyes on the linked-hexagon ships in the bridge display. "How long will it take?"

"Oh, they can run the first chunk through in anywhere from five to twenty minutes," Hauver said. "The whole package can take up to a week to transmit. Not counting breaks for the other side to try to figure out what we're talking about."

Pheylan nodded. "Let's hope they're not too alien to understand it."

"Mathematics is supposed to be universal," Hauver pointed out.

"It's that 'supposed to be' I always wonder about," Pheylan said. "Meyers, you got anything more on the ships themselves?"

"No, sir." The sensor officer shook his head. "And to be honest, sir, I really don't like this. I've run the infrared spectrum six ways from April, and it just won't resolve. Either those hulls are made of something the computer and I have never heard of before, or else they're deliberately skewing the emissions somehow."

"Maybe they're just shy," Rico said. "What about those optical-discharge lenses?"

"I can't get anything on those, either," Meyers said. "They could be half-kilowatt comm lasers, half-gigawatt missile frosters, or anything in between. Without power-flux readings, there's no way to tell."

"That part bothers me more than the hull,' Rico said to Pheylan, his dark face troubled as he stared at the display. "Putting that kind of massive shielding on their power lines tells me that they're trying to hide something."

"Maybe they're just very efficient," Meyers suggested.

"Yeah," Rico growled. "Maybe."

"There it goes," Hauver spoke up. "*Jutland*'s running the pilot-search signal. They've got a resonance—fuzzy, but it's there." He peered at his board. "Odd frequency, too. Must be using some really weird equipment."

"We'll get you a tour of their comm room when this is all over," Pheylan said.

"I hope so. Okay; there goes the first part of the package."

"Lead bogie's moving," Meyers added. "Yawing a few degrees to port—"

And without warning a brilliant double flash of light lanced out from the lead alien ship, cutting across the *Jutland*'s bow. There was a burst of more diffuse secondary light as hull metal vaporized under the assault—

And the *Kinshasa*'s Klaxons blared with an all-force-combat alert. "All ships!" Commodore Dyami's voice snapped over the radio scrambler. "We're under attack. *Kinshasa*, *Badger*, put out to sideline flanking positions. All other ships, hold station. Fire pattern gamma-six."

"Acknowledge, Hauver," Pheylan ordered, staring at the display in disbelief. The aliens had opened fire. Unprovoked, unthreatened, they'd simply opened fire. "Chen Ki, pull us out to sideline position. Ready starboard missile tubes for firing."

"How do we key them?" Rico asked, his fingers skating across his tactical setup board. "Proximity or radar?"

"Heat-seeking," Pheylan told him, acceleration pressing him back into his chair as the *Kinshasa* began to move forward to its prescribed flanking position.

"We're too close to the other ships," Rico objected. "We might hit one of them instead of the bogies."

"We can pull far enough out to avoid that," Pheylan told him, throwing a quick look at the tactical board. "Point is, we know the bogies are hot. With those strange hulls of theirs, the other settings might not even work."

"Missile spread from the *Jutland*," Meyers announced, peering at his displays. "They're going with radar keyed—"

And suddenly all four alien ships opened up with a dazzling display of multiple-laser fire. "All bogies firing," Meyers shouted as the warble of the damage alarm filled the bridge. "We're taking hits—hull damage in all starboard sections—"

"What about the *Jutland*'s missiles?" Rico called.

"No impacts," Meyers shouted back. The image on the main display flared and died, reappearing a second later as the backup sensors took over from the vaporized main cluster. "Bogies must have gotten 'em."

"Or else they just didn't trigger," Pheylan said, fighting down the surge of panic simmering in his throat. "The *Kinshasa* was crackling with heat stress now as those impossible lasers out there systematically bubbled off layers of the hull . . . and from the barely controlled voices shouting from the audio-net speaker it sounded as if the rest of the Peacekeeper ships were equally up to their necks in it. In the wink of an eye the task force had gone from complete control of the situation to a battle for survival. And were losing. "Key missiles for heat-seeking, Rico, and fire the damn things."

"Yes, sir. Salvo one away—"

And an instant later there was a sound like a muffled thunderclap, and the *Kinshasa* lurched beneath Pheylan's chair. "Premature detonation!" Meyers shouted; and even over the crackling of overstressed metal Pheylan could hear the fear in his voice. "Hull integrity gone: forward starboard two, three, and four and aft starboard two."

"Ruptures aren't sealing," Rico called. "Too hot for the sealant to work. Starboard two and four are honeycombing. Starboard three . . . honeycombing has failed."

Pheylan clenched his teeth. There were ten duty stations in that section. Ten people who were now dead. "Chen Ki, give us some motion—any direction," he ordered the helm. If they didn't draw the aliens' lasers away from the ejected honeycombs, those ten casualties were going to have lots of company. "All starboard-deck officers are to pull their crews back to central."

"Yes, sir."

"The ship can't handle much more of this, Captain," Rico said grimly from beside him.

Pheylan nodded silently, his eyes flicking between the tactical and ship-status boards. Rico was, if anything, vastly understating the case. With half the *Kinshasa*'s systems failing or vaporized and nothing but the internal collision bulkheads holding it together, the ship had bare minutes of life left to it. But before it died, there might be enough time to get off one final shot at the enemy who was ripping them apart. "Rico, give me a second missile salvo," he ordered. "Fire into our shadow, then curve them over and under to pincer into the middle of the bogie formation. No fusing— just a straight timed detonation."

"I'll try," Rico said, his forehead shiny with sweat as he worked his board. "No guarantees with the ship like this."

"I'll take whatever I can get," Pheylan said. "Fire when ready."

"Yes, sir." Rico finished his programming and jabbed the firing keys, and through the crackling and jolting of the *Kinshasa* writhing beneath him, Pheylan felt the lurch as the missiles launched. "Salvo away," Rico said. "Sir, I recommend we abandon ship while the honeycombs are still functional."

Pheylan looked again at the status board, his stomach twisting with the death-pain of his ship. The *Kinshasa* was effectively dead; and with its destruction he had only one responsibility left. "Agreed,' he said heavily. "Hauver, signal all hands: we're abandoning. All sections to honeycomb and eject when ready."

The damage alarm changed pitch and cadence to the ship-abandon signal. Across the bridge, board lights flickered and went dark as the bridge crew hurriedly disconnected their stations from the ship and checked their individual life-support systems.

Pheylan himself, however, still had one task left to perform: to ensure that those alien butchers out there would learn nothing about the Commonwealth from the wreckage of his ship. Getting a grip on the underside of his command board, he broke it open and began throwing the row of switches there. Nav computer destruct, backup nav computer destruct, records computer destruct, library computer destruct—

"Bridge crew reports ready, Captain," Rico said, a note of urgency in his voice. "Shall we honeycomb?"

Pheylan threw the last switch. "Go," he said, pulling his hands back inside the arms of his chair and bracing himself.

And with a thudding ripple that jerked Pheylan against his restraints, the sections of memory metal whipped out from the deck and ceiling, wrapping around his chair and sealing him in an airtight cocoon. A heartbeat later he was jammed into his seat cushion as the bridge disintegrated around him, throwing each of the individual honeycomb escape pods away from the dying hulk that had once been the *Kinshasa*.

"Goody-bye," Pheylan murmured to the remains of his ship, fumbling for the viewport shutter-release control. Later, he supposed vaguely, the full emotional impact would hit him. For now, though, survival was upper-most in his mind. Survival for himself, and for his crew.

The shutters retracted, and he pressed his face up to the viewport that looked back on the *Kinshasa*. The other escape pods were dim flickers of light drifting outward from the twisted and blackened hull still being hammered by the aliens' lasers. There was no way to tell how many of the honeycomb pods were intact, but those that were should keep their occupants alive until they could be picked up. Moving carefully in the cramped confines of the pod, he got to the viewport facing the main part of the battle and looked out.

The battle was over. The Peacekeeper task force had lost.

He floated there, his breath leaving patches of fog on the viewport, too stunned to move. The *Piazzi* was blazing brightly, some fluke of leaking oxygen tanks allowing fire even in the vacuum of space. The *Ghana* and *Leekpai* were blackened and silent, as were the *Bombay* and *Seagull*. He couldn't find any trace of the *Badger* at all.

And the *Jutland*—the powerful, Rigel-class defense carrier *Jutland*—was twisting slowly in space. Dead.

And the four alien starships were still there. Showing no damage at all.

"No," Pheylan heard himself murmur. It was impossible. Utterly impossible. For a Rigel-class task force to have been defeated in six minutes—*six minutes*—was unheard of.

There was a flicker of laser fire from one of the aliens; then another, and another. Pheylan frowned, wondering what they were shooting at. Some of the *Jutland*'s Dragonfly fighters, perhaps, that were still flying around? The aliens fired again, and again—

And with a jolt of horror, Pheylan understood. The aliens were firing on the honeycomb pods. Systematically and painstakingly destroying the survivors of the battle.

He swore viciously under his breath. The pods were no threat to the aliens—they weren't armed, armored, or even equipped with drives. To destroy them like this was to turn a military victory into a cold-blooded slaughter.

And there was nothing that he could do about it except sit here and watch it happen. The pod was little more than a minuscule cone with a power supply, a dioxide/oxygen converter, a backup oxygen tank, an emergency radio beacon, a short-range comm laser, two weeks' worth of rations, a waste-reclaimant system—

He was clawing the equipment access panel open almost before the thought had completely formed in his mind. The aliens out there weren't just blasting every chunk of rubble in sight; they were specifically and deliberately hunting down the pods. And suddenly it was blindingly obvious how they were doing that.

The emergency beacon was a deliberately simple gadget, as unbreakable and foolproof as anything in the Peacekeepers' inventory. But foolproof didn't necessarily mean sabotage proof. A minute later, every wire and circuit line to it cut and the blade of his multitool jabbed into its internal power backup, it had finally been silenced.

Pheylan took a deep breath, feeling the coolness of sweat on his forehead as he turned back to the viewport. The flashes of laser fire were still flickering through the battle debris as the aliens went about their grisly business. One of the ships was working its way in his direction, and he wondered tensely whether any of his crew had figured out what was going on and had knocked out their own beacons.

But there was no time to think about that now. That alien ship was coming almost straight toward him, and if they were really determined to be thorough about this, there were other ways besides the beacon to pick him out of the flotsam. Somehow he had to get the pod moving. Preferably in the direction of the watchships that should still be skulking out there somewhere.

He watched the ship's deliberate approach, mentally running through the list of available equipment. But there was really only one possibility, and he knew it. He needed propulsion; ergo, he needed to throw something overboard.

It took longer than he'd expected to get the oxygen tank release valve on the far side of the narrow equipment bay, and the alien ship was looming large in the viewport by the time he was finally ready. Mentally crossing his fingers, he tweaked the valve release open.

The hiss was loud in the enclosed space of the pod— as loud, he thought with a macabre shiver, as the hiss of gas in one of those death cells the Commonwealth was forever lodging strong protests about with the Bhurtist governments. It wasn't an irrelevant comparison, either: with the pod's oxygen reserve spewing into space, his life was now solely dependent on the uninterrupted functioning of his dioxide/oxygen converter. If it flicked out on him—and they did so with depressing regularity—he would have only as long as it took the air in the pod to get stale to get it running again.

But so far the plan was working. He was drifting through the wreckage now, slowly but steadily, moving roughly crosswise to the alien ship's approach vector toward the area where the watchships would be if they hadn't already meshed out. Now if he could just make it outside the cone of whatever focused sensor beams the aliens were using . . .

Concentrating on the first ship, he never even saw the second ship's approach. Not until the blue light abruptly flared around him.

"Keller? You still there?"

With an effort Lieutenant Dana Keller pulled her eyes away from the distant flickering of laser light and keyed her comm laser. "I'm here, Beddini," she said. "What do you think? We seen enough?"

"I'd seen enough five minutes ago," Beddini told her bitterly. "Those lousy, f—"

"We'd better get moving," Keller cut him off. Watching Commodore Dyami's task force get sliced to ribbons like that had sickened her, too, but letting Beddini get started on his extensive repertoire of curses wouldn't accomplish anything. "Unless you want to wait and see if they'll come after us next."

She heard the hiss as Beddini exhaled into his mike. "Not really."

"Fine," she said, keying her nav map. Actually, it was unlikely that the aliens even knew they were here—watchships were about as sensor-stealthed as it was theoretically possible to make them. But she wouldn't have bet a day's pay on that, let alone her life. "The book says we split up. I'll take Dorcas; you want Massif or Kalevala?"

"Kalevala. My static bomb or yours?"

"We'll use mine," Keller told him, keying in the sequence to activate and drop the high-intensity tachyon explosive. "You might need yours on the way off Kalevala. Don't start your engines until I give you the word."

"Right."

Behind her Keller felt a whisper of air as the copilot returned from her abrupt visit to the head. "You okay, Gorzynski?" she asked the other.

"Sure," Gorzynski said, sounding embarrassed and still a little sick. "I'm sorry, Lieutenant."

"Forget it," Keller told her, studying the younger woman's tortured face as she maneuvered carefully in zero-gee to her copilot's seat. Younger woman, hell—Gorzynski wasn't much more than a kid. Fresh out of basic, her first real tour . . . and this was how it had ended. "We're heading back. Get the drive sequence ready to go."

"Right," Gorzynski said, getting shakily to work. "What did I miss?"

"Just more of the same," Keller said. "They're still going around icing the survivors."

Gorzynski made a sound in the back of her throat. "I don't understand," she said. "Why are they doing that?"

"I don't know," Keller told her grimly. "But we're going to pay them back with interest. Bet on it."

The board pinged: the static bomb was ready. Keller touched the primer and the release key, and there was a slight lurch as the bulky cylinder dropped free of the watchship. "Beddini? Static bomb away. Ninety seconds to detonation."

"Acknowledged," Beddini said. "We're out of here. Good luck."

"You, too," Keller said, and keyed off the comm laser. "Let's go, Gorzynski."

They had swung the watchship around and were pulling for deep space when the static bomb blew up behind them, sending out a wide-spectrum saturation burst of tachyons that would blind whatever wake-trail detectors the enemy out there had. Or so went the theory. If it didn't' work, the Peacekeeper garrisons on Dorcas and Kalevala had better hope they were ready for company. "Here we go," she told Gorzynski, and pressed the keys.

The sky shimmered, the stars spinning briefly into an illusion of a tunnel as the space around them twisted. And then the twist became a sphere, the stars winked out, and they were on their way.

Keller looked over at Gorzynski. The kid still looked sick, but there was something else there, too. The kind of quiet, dark determination that Keller had seen so often in hardened combat veterans.

She shook her head. What a way for the kid to have to grow up.

• • •

The door slid open, and Lieutenant Colonel Castor Holloway stepped into the Dorcas colony's Peacekeeper garrison sensor center. Major Fujita Takara was waiting just inside the door, his face looking somber in the dim red light. "What've we got, Fuji?" Holloway asked.

"Trouble, looks like," Takara told him. "Crane just picked up the leading edge of a static-bomb discharge."

Holloway looked across the room at the tachyon pickup display and the young sergeant sitting stiffly in front of it. "The *Jutland* task force?"

"I don't know what else it could be," Takara said. "You can't really pin down a static bomb from anything but point-blank range, but it's from the right direction."

"Strength?"

"If it's from the same spot where we placed the bogies, it's about the size of a watchship's backstop bomb." Takara's lip twitched. "I don't know if you knew, Cass, but it's only been forty minutes since the task force meshed in out there."

The room, Holloway noted, was very quiet. "I suppose we'd better alert Peacekeeper Command," he said. "We have a skitter ready to fly?"

Takara's forehead creased slightly, and Holloway could tell what he was thinking. There were only two stable stardrive speeds, three light-years per hour and twice that, with only small ships like fighters and skitters able to achieve the higher equilibrium. The problem was it cost nearly five times as much per light-year to fly at the higher speed, which on the Dorcas garrison's budget was a nontrivial consideration. "Number Two can be ready in half an hour," the major said. "I assumed we'd be waiting until we had something more concrete to send them."

Holloway shook his head. "We can't afford the wait. Whatever happened out there, the fact that a watchship dropped its static bomb means there's been serious trouble. Our job is to buy the commonwealth every minute of prep time that we can. The details of the trouble can wait until later."

"I suppose so," Takara said heavily. "I'll get the skitter crew moving."

He left, the door sliding shut behind him, and Holloway

stepped over to the tachyon station. "Can you sift anything at all out of that mess, Crane?" he asked.

"No, sir," the young man said. "The tachyon static will blanket everything else in the region for at least another hour. Maybe two."

Which meant that they'd be on Dorcas's doorstep before anyone knew how much of the task force was coming back. Or, perhaps more important, if any uninvited guests were following them in. "Keep an eye on it," he told the other. "I want to know the minute the static starts to clear."

"Yes, sir." Crane hesitated. "Sir, what do you think happened?"

Halloway shrugged. "We'll find out in a couple of hours. Until then, I suggest you try to keep your imagination from running away with you."

"Yes, sir," Crane said, a bit too hastily. "I just meant—well—"

"I understand," Holloway assured him. "It's not much fun sitting blind while you wonder what might be coming your way. Just bear in mind that the Commonwealth has a long history of winning these little encounters. Whatever's out there, we'll handle it."

"Yes, sir," Crane said. "There's always CIRCE, too."

Holloway grimaced. Yes, that was always the option. The option, and the unspoken threat behind it. There were a lot of people—not all of them nonhumans—who resented living beneath the shadow of CIRCE and the Northern Coordinate Union leaders who held sole possession of the weapon's secrets. A lot of people who felt that NorCoord's domination of the Peacekeepers and the political structure of the entire Commonwealth was based on CIRCE and CIRCE alone. But the simple fact was that in the thirty-seven years since that awful demonstration off Celadon, the NorCoord military had never again had to fire the weapon. It had kept the peace without ever having to be used.

He looked at the tachyon display, feeling his throat tighten. Perhaps this time it was going to be different. "Yes," he agreed quietly. "There's always CIRCE."